BLOOD SO BRUTAL

A GOLDEN CITY NOVEL
BOOK TWO

EMILY BLACKWOOD

Cover design by MoonPress www.moonpress.co

Editing by The Fiction Fix

Created with Vellum

For Lauren, who stayed up many nights with me fixing plot holes, and who also forced me to add the "hate-touching" scene.

CHAPTER 1
HUNTYR

The sound of my heart beating became the one thing that reminded me I was still alive. I slipped my bloodied, bruised hand up to my chest and felt it there, thud after thud.

Vampyre.

It was impossible, right? I would have known if I was one of those violent, depraved bloodsuckers. I would have known if I'd spent my entire life killing my own kind. But my twenty-fifth birthday was right around the corner, and vampyres didn't develop cravings until then.

My head fell back onto the metal bars behind me. The damn archangel had no reason to lie to me. If he believed I was the heir to the vampyre kingdom...

Hells. The missing pieces in my life were exactly what he needed to make sense of it all. I never knew my real parents. Lord was the one who raised me, who told me the story of who I really was.

Did he know? Had he known all along? Maybe that's why he shipped me off here. Maybe he knew my twenty-fifth birthday was approaching, and he wanted me to be somewhere far, far away when my cravings for blood developed.

Tears stung my eyes, but I blinked them away. I wouldn't cry down here in these dungeons, not with the enemy watching every move.

Asmodeus and his errand boy, Luseyar, visited every day since they shoved me into this cage. Asmodeus would insist I show him my magic, and I would tell him time and time again that I possessed no magic.

I was starting to believe it myself.

Footsteps in the distance skyrocketed my already-racing heart. I grew accustomed to those footsteps over the last week or so, and I could identify the all-powerful archangel easily. He was always walking too fast, too eager.

But these footsteps were different. They were slow. Lazy. I could picture the way Wolf walked with that annoying swagger of confidence, his massive wings trailing on the ground behind him as if he didn't care enough to pick them up.

My thoughts halted.

Wolf didn't have wings. Not anymore. Not after his own father cut them off for not exposing my magic.

Good. He deserved it.

Wolf's wings being taken from him was one of the hardest things I'd ever watched, but I wasn't going to let him manipulate me. I wasn't going to let *them* manipulate me. I couldn't trust any of them anymore, not after what they did.

Wolf tricked me.

He made me think he truly cared about me, made me think I couldn't get through the Transcendent on my own, and for what? So he could keep tabs on me while delivering me to his father?

He probably never felt anything for me, either. I could picture him laughing at how foolish I was, at how easily I fell into his trap.

Anger swarmed me again, followed by a sharp pang in my chest. Every time he came down to these dungeons, I was reminded of how stupid I was to trust him, how naive I was to think he actually cared about me.

No, he was working for his father, Asmodeus. This was all part of their master plan to find the last living heir to Scarlata Empire.

None of it was real.

For all I knew, his wings getting sliced from his body wasn't real either—just another way to manipulate me, another way to turn me into someone they could control. I turned my head away from the front of the cell as Wolf approached. When his footsteps stopped a few feet away from me, I held my breath.

"Huntress." His voice was a mere whisper. He hadn't been in here since that night, since his bloodied body was dragged from the floor outside my cell. The mark of his blood still stained the floor, alongside a sole black feather to remind me of the atrocity.

I squeezed my eyes shut and pushed my hand deeper into my chest, shoving my fingernails into the skin to distract me from the ache festering there.

"Can you at least look at me?"

I kept my mental shields up, forcing myself to pull as far away as possible from our bond. It was a difficult task, but for a few minutes at a time, I could separate the messy emotions that combined in a raging tornado within me. My anger, his resentment; it all added to that never-ending ache in my chest I could never escape from.

I hated him for what he did to me. After everything, I chose to trust him. Hells, he was a vampyre and he hid that from me our entire time at Moira Seminary. Still, I chose him. I let him *drink* from me, for fuck's sake.

And here I was, trapped in this disgusting cell with nothing but a bucket to piss in.

My thoughts distracted me, and I let my shields slip enough to hear him inhale sharply. Part of me wanted to lower the shields entirely and throw every single thing I felt his way. Part of me wanted him to feel that pain, that anger, that hatred.

But then, he would know how badly I still fucking cared, because anger still meant I cared. Anger was still *something*.

"Here," he said, and I heard rustling through the bars. "At least eat something, please. My father will be down here to speak with you soon, and you need your strength."

I finally turned to face him.

He looked smaller without massive black wings towering over each of his shoulders, but the sight of him still took my breath away. His black shirt hung loose on his lean figure, and his eyes looked much wider than usual. The electric blue of his irises glowed in the dark underground of The Golden City.

My stomach lurched at the sight of the bread he offered through the bars.

"Bread?" I asked. "Really? I recall offering my own veins to you when you were hungry once, Wolf. Nice to see you repaying the sentiment with such a warm meal."

A sliver of relief flooded me from his side of the bond, and I looked away before he could see any of the emotion on my face.

"Take it," he pushed. "Please."

His voice cracked, and I shoved my fingernails into my chest so hard, I drew blood.

He was hurting, I knew he was. Without his wings, he was only a vampyre. He had those glowing eyes, yes, but without the ability to fly? He was just like the rest of them.

He gave that up to protect me, goddess knows why. He already caused enough damage; it was a little too late to start saving me now.

I took a deep breath before crawling over the front of the cell and taking the bread from his outstretched hand.

Wolf said nothing, but he didn't move away as I tore a small piece and ate. I didn't try to hide my matted hair, my bruised, dirty skin. Wolf could damn well see what was happening to me down here in this dungeon.

I was rotting away.

"You could have told him, you know," I whispered without looking at him.

He stiffened. "Told who what?"

"You could have told your father the type of magic I have. It would have saved your wings, and I would still be in this shit position. You already dragged me here to deliver me directly to him. No use in saving me now."

I glanced at him in time to see his jaw clenching. "I've already betrayed you enough. The second he knows anything more, he'll do everything he can to get it out of you."

Guilt gently nudged through his side of the bond, but I threw my mental walls back up. *I would not pity him.* I had enough to deal with.

"Didn't seem to bother you the first time," I sneered. "Not sure why you'd have a problem with it now."

"Huntyr," he hissed, his voice turning into a warning. "You know exactly why I have a problem with it."

5

I eyed him suspiciously, taking in his shockingly pale skin and messy hair. He wasn't himself—or, perhaps, he was. Perhaps this was the real Wolf, and he was showing me the fake, formulated version of himself back in Moira.

I didn't really know him at all, did I?

"I can still feel you, Huntyr." His hands moved to grip the bars of the cell. "I know you're angry with me, but I also know you want to let me help you."

Yeah fucking right.

"Don't push me away. I have a plan to get us both out of this mess."

"Oh, you do?" My laugh sounded foreign, even to me. I pushed myself up to my knees and gripped the bars right below his hands, shaking gently. "Was *this* all part of getting me out of here?"

He glanced over his shoulder before continuing. "There are certain things I can't control. My father has power, and he wants to rule Scarlata, has wanted to for a very, very long time."

"I don't give a damn about what your father wants."

His lips turned up in a scowl. "But you should!"

"Why? Because I'm supposedly the secret heir to the throne?"

He leaned in so close, I could feel his breath as he whispered, "Because you are more powerful than any of them. You are the vampyre queen, Huntyr. Your blood, it—"

I cut him off before he could get the rest of the words out. "Don't you dare start telling me about my blood. I should have never let you drink from me. I should have let you die in that damn forest."

Ice flooded our bond. "Don't say that."

"What about now?" I asked. "Who have you been feeding

from up there in the shambles of The Golden City? More innocents? Are you part of this, Wolf? Did you help your father
take over The Golden City?"

"Keep your voice down," he hissed.

"Why should I? I don't want you here, Wolf!" The dam of
tears I held back for weeks slowly pushed open. "I don't want
to look at you. I don't want you to bring me food. I don't want
you saving me. I just want to be left alone."

My chest heaved as I tried to channel the fighter who Lord
trained, the vampyre assassin, the heartless killer. I wanted
her back. I didn't want to *feel*.

And I sure as hells didn't want to feel Wolf's emotions,
either.

"You can hate me all you want," he whispered, "but this is
fucking real." He moved so quickly, I couldn't pull back before
his hand snuck through the bars and wrapped around my
forearm. He tugged me forward, sending us both tumbling
into metal.

I gasped and tried to free myself, but he held tighter.
Warmth radiated from his skin—his entire body, actually. I
could feel him, his energy, his essence.

It was a feeling I grew accustomed to back in Moira,
but now?

"Feel that?" Wolf whispered. "Because I can. I feel everything, Huntyr, even if you're trying to fight it."

The fierceness in his eyes returned with a vengeance. I
stopped trying to pull away but said nothing. Instead, I
focused on mustering as much hate as I possibly could up to
the surface, throwing it through the bond.

I hated him. I should have hated him all along. I was a
stupid, naive girl to think I could trust anyone.

Lord would be *ashamed*.

"Eat. Rest. My father is insisting on discovering what type of power you possess, but if you want out, you'll act clueless."

"I *am* clueless," I retorted. "I have no idea what power I have. I could barely summon magic in Moira, remember?"

He smirked, his eyes flickering down my face. "I remember everything, but I tasted your blood, too. Trust me, there's something special running through your veins."

This time, when I pulled my arm away, he let me.

I continued picking at the bread in my hands as I waited for him to storm away, but he remained standing in front of my cell.

"I would cut my own wings off for you any day, Huntress. Do not think I'm done doing everything in my power to keep them from touching you."

And then, he was gone, leaving me and my growing pit of despair alone in the dungeon of the enemy.

CHAPTER 2
WOLF

It took all the self-restraint I had left to drag myself away from that dungeon. I couldn't lay eyes on Huntyr again without doing something very, very idiotic.

Like breaking her out of there and burning this whole damn place to the ground.

So, instead of putting both our lives in danger again, I made my way to speak with my father.

I climbed the stairs to his chambers and quietly pushed the door open. I was late to the court meeting, but I didn't give a shit. I didn't give a shit about anything, actually, other than saving Huntyr's life. It took me days to get out of bed after my wings were sliced off, and even longer than that to gain the energy to walk. She was down there all alone with nobody to look out for her. Strengthening myself enough to see her had been my only focus.

Even if she fucking hated me.

"Did you enjoy your visit with our prisoner?" My father's voice cascaded through the room the moment the door shut behind me.

I huffed a breath. "She won't be willing to give us the information we need if you keep treating her like that."

My father sat at the head of the massive table in the center of the room. My older brother, Jessiah, sat to the right of him, across the table from Luseyar, who still couldn't look me in the eye since the day he severed my wings.

Cowardly bastard.

"You're right. *You* could simply tell us what she knows."

I sauntered to the table and pulled out the seat beside my brother. Pain shot through my back as I sat down, my still-healing wounds pressing against the wood. Fighting my own healing magic was more difficult than it sounded. I didn't need my father knowing about my gift, I didn't need to give him another reason to use me as his own personal weapon. Instead, my body healed at a torturous pace, leaving me in agony for the last week. "I already told you—I don't know any more than the rest of you. It won't matter what I say. She no longer trusts me."

"Even after you lost your wings?" My father eyed me with a hand stroking his chin. He didn't seem the least bit guilty, but Luseyar shivered. He had no problem cutting my wings off after Huntyr refused to give him what he wanted.

But how could she? Huntyr was right. She had no idea what ran through her veins. She didn't even know she was a vampyre until recently, when we dropped that new information and left her to deal with the aftermath.

Yet she was down in that cell, being tortured by her own thoughts every single night.

My brother was the one who spoke next. "Did you really believe that was necessary?" he asked our father. "You already turned his wings black, and now you cut them off completely?" His own wings were so white, they almost glistened under the sunlight filtering in through the window.

My wings used to glisten the same way, used to reflect any light on their white feathers. But that was before my father made the sacrifice to Era, Goddess of Vaehatis. That was before she gripped my soul in her wicked hands and turned me into this, this half-undead being of impure power.

But I missed the way my black, wicked wings trailed my every movement. Even as a fallen angel, I still had the company of them. A piece of me was sliced away with them, a piece of my soul now hollowed.

"Do not question my motives, Jessiah," our father answered. "Wolf made a great sacrifice for our plan here in The Golden City. With his wings gone, he has a better chance at regaining her trust."

"Why does it matter, anyway?" I asked. "We have her here; why does she need to trust me at all?"

"You're not seeing the big picture, son." His temper flared, the glowing magic surrounding his archangel form simmering in anger. "She is the heir to Scarlata Empire. She holds more power than any fae or vampyre alive. With her on our side, we can conquer all kingdoms. We would hold *all* power."

"And if she's not on our side?" I asked. "What then? You force her to use her power—power we don't even know she has?"

My father eyed me, and Jessiah shifted uncomfortably in his seat. "Oh, she has power. I can feel it in the air. I know you can, too—we all sense it."

My stomach dropped. I knew Huntyr had power—I felt it, tasted it—but he cut my damn wings off to get that information from us.

And still, he knew nothing.

"She'll be a fully matured vampyre soon," Jessiah interrupted. "Perhaps her power will develop more then."

My father's energy seemed to settle. Jessiah was always good at that, good at ensuring Asmodeus didn't explode and kill us all. He was our father, yes, but I seldom forgot the power the archangels held.

I was nothing compared to him. I stood no chance, which was why I needed to be smart about this. If he knew the power Huntyr held, if he knew we bonded, that I could practically feel it pumping through her veins...

No. He couldn't find out, not when he was planning on using it to conquer.

"That's enough for now," Asmodeus dismissed, pushing himself up from the head of the table. "The hungry ones are attacking the south wall again. Keep your eyes on the girl, both of you. If her power holds true, she could be the one to end this damn madness once and for all."

"Yes, Father," Jessiah dismissed, bowing his head. Hells. I didn't have enough patience to give our father a proper dismissal. I bit the inside of my cheek to keep from pissing him off even further as he stormed out, Luseyar following behind him like a lost animal.

The massive doors slammed shut again, leaving me and Jessiah sitting in his wake.

"Are you a fucking idiot?" Jessiah hissed. "He's going to learn the truth, and soon. You don't have time to keep lying about this."

I pushed myself up from the table too, groaning at the dull pain radiating down my back. "I have no idea what you're talking about."

Two seconds later, Jessiah shoved me into the stone wall,

pressing a hand against my throat. *Fuck, my back.* I struggled against him, but the pain threatened to drag me to my knees. "What the fuck is this?" I seethed. "Get your hands off me!"

"She has the power, Wolf. It would take a damned fool not to see that you're in love with her. Anyone can see it." He let go of my throat, but the turmoil in his eyes remained. "He'll use her against you. You know he will."

I gaped at my brother. "Don't pretend like you know what you're talking about. You weren't the one who went to Moira to find her. You weren't the one cursed into becoming a damn vampyre so we could make Father's wicked dreams come true."

"You act like that's my fault," he replied. "Father chose you, and there was nothing I could do about it." He turned his back to me and slowly paced the large room. "If I could have helped you, trust me, I would have."

"And where is your help now?" I asked. "Because I don't see you with severed wings and a woman you care about in the dungeons."

Jessiah turned to face me, and I saw my own eyes in his, simmering with power. It was our one physical sign of being born from one of the most powerful archangels in existence. "You want my help?" he asked. "Fine. Let's go."

He started toward the door.

"Go where?" I called out.

"We're going to talk to your prisoner."

13

I walked a few feet behind Jessiah. He was barely an inch taller than me, with those glorious wings and broad shoulders. Would Huntyr recognize that he was related to me? Would she hate him just as much?

The smell of her hit me as we turned down the hall to her cell. I bit my tongue to keep from reacting in front of Jessiah, to keep from showing any sign of my emotions. It would expose how much I really cared, as if everyone didn't already fucking know.

"You must be Huntyr," Jessiah announced as he stopped in front of her cell. I sidled up to him, only to see her hunched in the very back corner.

"Fuck off," she groaned. Her voice didn't have the fire it usually had, though. She sounded tired. Broken.

My chest tightened.

Jessiah laughed. "I heard you were a pain in the ass. I can respect that, honestly, but if you want to stay alive, you need to start talking."

Huntyr lifted her head from where it rested on her bent knees, strands of her black curls plastered across her sweaty forehead. It killed me to see her like this. This was so, so wrong.

"How convincing, asshole, but I'm good. Thanks."

Jessiah glanced at me once before stepping forward, closer to those bars. "Asmodeus will kill you for your power. You're a smart girl; you survived Moira. You have to know that's coming."

"I only survived Moira because he practically dragged me through with him. But that was all part of your plan, wasn't it?" She scoffed, dropping her head back to her knees and wrapping her arms around them. "Well, you should have left me to die out there, because I won't help you."

I clenched my jaw. "Huntyr, please, listen to us."

I tried to push through our bond, tried to nudge her walls with the subtle urgency I was feeling. *Listen to us. Let us help you.*

For a single second, I thought she might let me in, but I was quickly corrected with her sharp walls forcing me back out. I physically flinched at the feeling.

Jessiah turned his attention to me, and for a second, I thought he would realize what just happened. The fact that we bonded was something only Huntyr and I knew, and I would do whatever it took to keep it that way.

"I told you to leave me alone," she muttered. "After everything, can you please allow me that much?"

"This is my brother, Jessiah," I said before she could keep pushing. "He wants to help us."

She lifted her head again and her eyes landed on my brother. Jealousy tugged at my chest as I watched her gaze rise and fall across his body, taking in his wings. "Your brother gets an angelic name and you're stuck with Wolf? Seems fitting."

I clenched my jaw to keep my reaction at bay. That was just the beginning of how deep my father's hatred for me ran. If Huntyr stayed here long enough, she would see how fitting those names were.

Huntyr rolled her eyes before adding, "If he's anything like you, I'm not interested. Are you here to betray me too?"

Jessiah smiled as my fists clenched. "No, I'm not. My brother seems to care about you, however little of that you believe. You'd be right to listen to him. He wants to help you, Huntyr."

Her eyes landed on me for the first time since our conversation began. "Wolf betrayed me. He let me think he was good, made me turn my back on everything I knew. That was all before he delivered me into the hands of your father in this grand, fucked-up scheme that everyone calls The Golden City. Now you want me to believe you'll help me?"

"My father would have come for you, Huntyr," I pushed. Hells, how did she still not see it? "I did what was necessary to keep you *alive*."

"You did a lot more than that, didn't you? Should I offer you my vein once more, or are you waiting to chain me up and take it by force?"

I stepped back. "I would *never* harm you. I—"

"I don't believe you!" Her emotions cracked, and for a second, the walls blocking our bond fell as a rush of anguish, grief, and misery flooded me. But there was something else there too, like a dark moon, a dull tide. It wasn't quite pain—it was worse. It was *empty*.

And that broke my heart more than fucking anything.

She realized her mistake quickly, regaining her composure in the back of the cell. "I don't want to help you. I am a prisoner here already. There's nothing you can say to change that."

"Well," my father's voice sounded from the back of the dungeons. Jessiah and I both spun around to find him standing with his back shrouded in shadows. "It seems we should change our approach, then, shouldn't we?"

Jessiah cursed under his breath and backed away.

"We are only trying to help," I said to him.

Asmodeus stepped forward. "Huntyr here has been in this cell for long enough, wouldn't you agree, boys?"

Jessiah and I stood still, frozen.

"Take her out. Let her see what we're really doing here. She may hate us now for what we've done, but no one can deny the power of The Golden City. Isn't that right, Wolf?"

My breath hitched.

"You're letting me out?" Huntyr asked from the back. I fought the urge to step between her and my father's view.

He smiled as he looked down at her. "You may not be willing to help me now, Huntyraina, but you will. If getting out of this dungeon is what will change your mind, then so be it."

He turned on his heel, and I let out a breath.

"I'll never give you my power," Huntyr mumbled.

Asmodeus stopped on his heel. "What did you say?"

Shit. I forced myself not to step between them.

"Whatever power I have, whatever is running through my veins, you'll never have it."

He laughed quietly, his shoulders shaking as he stood with his back to us. "Yet you had no problem sharing with my son."

Huntyr's chest heaved. I said nothing. *There was no way he knew.*

"You bonded with him, did you not? Which means Wolf here has access to your power."

"How do you know that?" I asked, dumbfounded.

Asmodeus glanced over his shoulder at me, dropping his voice to a dangerously low level as he said, "Do not forget who I am and where I come from, son. I am no mortal being in this realm. I am an archangel; I know *all*. Now, take her from this dungeon before I change my mind."

And then, he was gone, leaving Huntyr, Jessiah, and I alone with our echoing breaths.

I didn't have to use the bond to know what Huntyr was

thinking. The sound of her heart radiated around me, filling the room. *Fear.* We bonded, yes, but I hadn't used her power since that day during the Transcendent. I hadn't even considered tapping into that bond; it was so foreign and violating and wrong, and I had already taken too much from her.

I wouldn't take that. I would *never*.

But she didn't know that. She didn't trust me, didn't believe a thing I said.

"Come on," Jessiah finally said, breaking the silence. "Let's go before he comes back."

"I'm not going anywhere with you two," she argued.

"Now is not the time to be stubborn, Huntyr. Let's go." Jessiah fumbled, pulling the keys from his pocket before unlocking her cell. The bars creaked open loudly before clanging against the rest of the metal cage.

Huntyr slowly pushed herself to her feet, using the bars beside her as support. Her legs shook, quivering beneath the weight of her. Fuck, she looked so thin, so pale. I should have never let this happen, should have never left her down here.

Jessiah entered the cage first, cautiously. "You need to bathe and get some clean clothes. Wolf can take you to—"

"No," she argued. "I won't go anywhere with him."

Jessiah cocked his head to the side. "You'll die out there alone. Do you know how many hungry ones are crawling the streets as we speak?"

"I'm not going with Wolf," she pushed. "I'll go with you instead."

"Absolutely not," I interrupted before Jessiah could say anything further. "Not an option. You'll come with me willingly, or I'll throw you over my damn shoulder and carry you out."

Even with her legs shaking, even with her body so weak

that she could barely stand, she glared at me, jaw set. I knew her well enough to know she wasn't going with me easily. She was serious about leaving with my brother, but there was no way I was letting that happen.

"Let's go, Huntress." I waved my arm out in front of me, toward the hall that led to our rooms.

A few painful seconds passed before she finally stepped toward me, and Jessiah sighed in relief. He would have kept her safe, but that wasn't what I worried about. She needed to shower. She needed clothes. She needed to eat and decompress and breathe. I wouldn't allow that to happen around anyone else but me.

"I still hate you both," she muttered as she passed me.

Jessiah looked at me and raised an eyebrow as I smirked. "I would expect nothing less."

CHAPTER 3
HUNTYR

"Your rooms are seriously this close to each other?" I asked, not bothering to keep the venom from my voice. Wolf led me down the hall with a hand hovering at my back, barely touching me. Still, it was enough to light up every one of my senses. If I had a single ounce of energy left, I would swat him away.

Lucky for him, I was exhausted.

"Yes, they are. Not like we had a choice in the matter, but it comes in handy when hungry ones get too close," Jessiah answered from ahead.

We walked through the dark shadows. A small window, barely large enough to look out of, lit the hallway every few feet, but aside from that, nothing. You would have thought we were deep underground in a cave somewhere with the lack of, well, anything. No furniture, no carpeting on the floors. Just empty space.

It made me uneasy. Everything about this place did.

"This is my room," Wolf said. "Jessiah stays across the hall. He'll be there if you need him, but I'm sure you won't."

I rolled my eyes at the arrogance in his voice and pushed open the door to Wolf's bedroom. It was smaller than I expected. Cozier, too. There was minimal furniture, with one bed pressed against the back wall and a singular wardrobe beside it.

"Not much for personal effects?" I asked.

"There are no personal effects around here," he answered. "It's best to keep things as simple as possible."

A pile of fabric caught my attention in the corner of the room, and I realized quickly what I stared at—bloodied cloths and gauze from his severed wings. I blinked my attention away before he caught me staring.

Wolf brushed past me, toward a door on the far side of the room. "You can wash up in here," he said. He opened his wardrobe and pulled out a pair of black men's trousers and a matching top. "Take these."

"You expect me to wear your clothes?" I asked.

His eyes raked down my body, and I fought the urge to cover my arms over my chest. I looked like an absolute disaster, I knew that. I wore the same clothes for days now. Or was it weeks? My hair was one massive knot of sweat, dirt, blood, and tears. Mud from the dungeon caked my skin from the floor I'd slept on.

Still, I stared Wolf in the eye. It was his fault I looked like this, after all. He was the one who dragged me into this mess, who lied to me about why he was helping me and delivered me directly to his father.

I still wasn't sure what he truly wanted from me, but I did know he was awfully interested in my power.

"It's my clothes or nothing," he said before smirking. "Both options are fine with me."

I snarled and yanked the clothes from his grasp before storming into the bathroom and shutting the door.

Thankfully, this place had running water. It seemed to be nicer than the building Wolf and I stayed in that first night in The Golden City. I had no idea where we were directionally, but I guessed that Asmodeus and his crew lived in the center of it all.

I avoided looking in the mirror entirely and started the shower, letting the water grow hot as I peeled my disgusting clothes from my body. I took everything off—including my underwear and chestwrap—and threw everything in the garbage. I sure as hells never wanted to see those clothes again.

Wolf didn't so much as knock on the bathroom door, but I could feel him out there. Since we bonded, I was much too aware of his presence at all times. It was a damn curse. I wanted nothing more than to forget all about him and everything he put me through.

My mind wandered to his wings—or the lack thereof.

Don't even go there, I reminded myself. *He deserved this punishment. He's still working with his father to keep you a damn prisoner here.*

I stepped into the hot water and moaned at the feel of it. There were times in that dungeon when I thought I would never see the light of day again, let alone take another shower.

I accepted my fate. If I really was the heir to the vampyre kingdom, *the blood kingdom,* death would come soon enough.

Wolf cracked the door open but didn't come inside. "Doing okay in there?"

I picked up one of the few soap bars and threw it at the door.

Jessiah would have been a much, much better option. I was surprised at how similar he and Wolf looked, but they were brothers, after all. They both had lightning eyes and fierce brows to frame them, but Jessiah was softer than Wolf. His angel wings were white, certainly not fallen, and he carried himself less rigidly.

I tried not to think about everything Wolf went through in his life. If his brother was here this entire time living with Asmodeus, what did Wolf think? Or had Wolf done something to piss his father off so badly, he was now the one to take all the hits?

The water washed the dirt from my skin after a few minutes. I dunked my head beneath the stream and massaged my curls with the pine-scented soap that made it absolutely impossible not to think of Wolf.

This was great. Really fucking great.

I would have stayed in that shower for ages, but my legs began to shake once more as I stood there. The second I was clean, I braced myself against the wall and turned off the water.

I had never been so exhausted in my entire damn life. Even after days and days of training with Lord and killing vampyres in Midgrave, I hadn't been this sore. I would have taken one of Lord's whippings again over this bone-deep tiredness.

I dried myself off with a clean towel and pulled Wolf's loose trousers over my bare legs. I tugged the tunic over me next, grateful it covered more of my body than any of my own clothes would.

I already felt way too exposed here. Drowning in these clothes would help.

By the time I slicked my curly black hair into a tight braid over my shoulder and pulled Wolf's door open, he was nowhere to be seen. I glanced around the empty bedroom one more time, ensuring no one else lurked in the shadows, before walking to Wolf's perfectly-made bed.

Black linens draped over the large wooden structure. I wasn't surprised; everything about this place was dark, black, and shadowy. Still, as I ran my hand over a pillow, I felt my eyes growing heavy.

I tried to sleep in the dungeons. Trust me, I did. But there was no amount of exhaustion that would have let me fully relax there. I was too unprotected, too vulnerable.

Although, I supposed little had changed about my situation since then.

I was still exposed, still vulnerable to anyone who might enter that door, still unsafe.

The edge of the bed shifted around me as I sat, and I became immediately grateful for the support. I sank into the thick fabric like I belonged there, like I was drawn to this bed for more than just temporary support.

My body screamed in relief as I kicked my feet up next, reclining back onto the pillows.

This. This was fucking nice. I tried to keep my awareness on the door, tried to shut my eyes for one singular moment before Wolf came back, but the darkness of sleep called me home.

T n the span of four days, I saw Wolf once. Strangers brought me food every day, but other than that, I was left alone.

So much for showing me The Golden City.

I didn't mind it, though. It gave me time to think, to plan my fucking escape. Because there was no way in all hells I was going to sit here, cooped up, waiting for Asmodeus to tire of me.

Wolf was no longer someone I could trust to help me. I had to make it out on my own.

Luckily, on the second day, the woman who delivered my food also brought me a few books. She didn't say anything as she set them on the edge of the bed, but I gave her a reassuring nod anyway.

It was the best I could do.

I immediately dove in, looking for anything to fill the mindless hours of imagining the demise of The Golden City. They were older texts, the spines bound in leather and coated with dust. Clearly, the people living here weren't big on reading.

I couldn't say I was either. I learned to read as a child, but there weren't many books that survived the war. Not in Midgrave, anyway.

The first book I picked up was about vampyres. Go fucking figure. I ran my fingers over the delicate cover, taking in the thick texture of the red words. *Blood and War.* The smell of old pages wafted up at me as I cracked the book open, skimming the first few pages. It seemed to be mostly boring history, but I quickly realized there was something else in this text. Along with the history of the species and some well-known facts, there were dozens and dozens of pages filled with half-scribbled notes and stories of lore.

And I hadn't heard of a single one of the stories.

One of them in particular discussed an old tale about a powerful descendent who could stop the hungry ones from attacking others. This was someone who could change the world as we knew it, who could end wars and control others with an all-powerful bloodline.

It was interesting enough to distract me for a few hours, interesting enough to make me wonder how much of this was true...

I read, I slept, and I ate just enough to stop anyone from force-feeding me.

Eventually, I was going to make it out of here.

Eventually, I would make them all pay.

I jolted awake to the sound of a male screaming and snapped my attention to the foreign room around me.

Right. Wolf's room. Wolf's bed.

A blanket covered me now, one I was sure I hadn't put on my own body, but the other side of the bed was still empty aside from the small stack of books I was in the middle of devouring.

The muffled scream rang out again, and I scrambled to the edge of the bed, peering at the floor, only to find Wolf sleeping—shirtless—on his stomach, exposing two massive, angry wounds that spanned his lower back to the top of his shoulder blades.

Goddess above.

"Wolf!" I called out in the night. He was flinching, glistening in sweat, fighting something in his sleep—something I couldn't see, somewhere I couldn't follow.

I shouldn't have cared. I should have enjoyed the sound of his helpless whimpers, but when a scream threatened to crawl from his throat the third time, I jumped out of bed and knelt at his side.

"Wolf, wake up!" I said again as I gripped his bare arm—careful not to get any closer to his wounds—and shook him.

He opened his eyes instantly and scrambled to a kneeling position. His chest rose and fell rapidly, heavily, as if he had just been in combat. Sweat plastered his dark hair to his forehead, beading down the sides of his face and dripping onto his chest.

His eyes scanned the entire room before falling on me. "It's you," he breathed between pants.

"It's me," I answered. "You were having a nightmare."

Wolf tilted his head back and laughed. Loudly. "Yeah, that seems to be happening a lot these days. The problem is, my real life has become equally nightmarish."

My stomach knotted. "Why were you asleep on the floor? How long was I out?"

"A day. I didn't want to wake you."

"So you slept on the floor of your own bedroom?"

He tore his eyes away and ran a hand through his damp locks. "No offense, Huntress, but the last thing I want to do is make you feel even more uncomfortable. I'm perfectly fine on the floor."

Wolf didn't wait for my reply. Instead, he pushed himself up and walked to the bathroom, turning on the sink without closing the door.

I stood and followed him, lingering at the door frame.

"Your scars look horrible," I noted.

He splashed water on his face and hunched over the sink. His long, broad muscles flexed against the movement, the wound of his absent wings on full display.

"You really know how to make a man feel better. Thank you." He splashed more water.

"I'm serious." I stepped forward, reaching out but pulling my hand back before I touched him. "Not that I care, but I think it's infected. Weren't these supposed to heal by now? I figured your angel blood would have taken care of it."

"I'm a *fallen* angel, remember?" His words held more anger than I heard in some time, but I knew it wasn't anger toward me. "Though I'm not even sure I would call myself *that* anymore."

The wounds on his back looked fresh, like they were inflicted just yesterday. They certainly did not look like the wounds of a healing magical creature.

"Do you have healers here?" I asked. "If you can't heal yourself, maybe you should see one."

He spun around to face me, quicker than I was prepared for. His brows were drawn together, and the light in his eyes sparkled with emotion. "Does my father strike you as the type of person to keep healers in his kingdom?" He smiled to himself. "He would love to know I was suffering even more than he originally intended."

"He is that cruel?"

"Have you learned nothing?"

I froze, staring at him. Wolf had told me stories of his father, but now that I knew he was an archangel, everything changed.

Angels were supposed to be good—keepers of the goddesses, protectors of peace.

But this? How he treated his own son?

"Well, all I'm saying is that it looks bad. Why won't your own magic heal it like it healed me at Moira?"

He shook his head like this was all humorous to him. "I don't need anyone else knowing about that little gift of mine. If I heal my own wounds, they'll start to ask questions."

"You'd rather walk around in pain than tell them of your healing magic?" When he healed me, he ensured we were the only two who knew about it. But why would he be keeping his abilities a secret from his own father?

Okay, maybe I could understand why he didn't want his father knowing. But there had to be more to it.

Wolf's eyes searched mine. His face was fierce, no smirk, no smile, no flirty comeback. It was just Wolf, just the male I fought with in Moira, the male who saved my life, the male who—

No. I stopped my thoughts before they could continue any further.

He betrayed me.

But just when I thought Wolf had finally dropped the arrogant asshole persona, he cocked his head to the side. "Caring about me, Huntress? I thought you hated me now."

"I *do* hate you."

He stepped closer, his bare chest almost touching me. "Good. I can live with hate, just as long as you feel *something* for me." He reached out and pulled on a loose piece of hair from my braid. A thick sadness washed over his eyes, threatening our bond. It was hard to keep my shields up when he stood this close, when he touched me. "As long as you still feel something."

My heart raced at the closeness of him. I wanted nothing more than to shove him away, to forget about all this and go back to sleep.

But I was wide awake now and so was he. As much as I wanted to forget everything between us, it was impossible.

"Loving you was the biggest mistake of my life," I said carefully. "I hate you because you made me forget what was at stake. I hate you because, after everything, you betrayed my trust, the trust you practically forced out of me. So, yes, I do hate you. But rest assured, Wolf—the hate may fade as I slowly forget you, but I will *never* love you again."

The muscles in his jaw tightened.

And then he smiled.

"Never say never, Huntress." He turned around, grabbing a shirt from his wardrobe and throwing it on. "Take a walk with me. We both need some air, and I want to show you something."

"I'm not going anywhere with you."

He shrugged. "Suit yourself. You're more than welcome to stay in here and rot until my father decides he's done entertaining you."

Well, shit. I still hated his guts, but I shoved my feet into my shoes and stormed after him anyway.

CHAPTER 4
WOLF

The moon was full tonight. I appreciated the extra light for Huntyr's sake. I could already picture the way she'd refuse to take my hand in the darkness, and she'd likely stumble and hurt herself out of stubbornness.

I liked that about her. Her stubbornness.

But now, it was becoming my biggest weakness.

"This way." I turned and made my way out of the main building.

Everyone else in The Golden City lived outside of the main castle. The city was set up in rings, with the poorest and weakest living on the outside. It wasn't fair—anyone could see that—but when Asmodeus decided something, that was what happened.

I wouldn't be hiding it from Huntyr, though. If she was ever going to accept her position as heir to Scarlata Empire, she would have to see what it had become.

"Where are you taking me?" she asked. A cool breeze caressed my skin, and I heard her shiver behind me.

31

"I want to show you what this place has turned into."

"You mean what you've turned it into? How many people here are really vampyres, anyway? And how did they get into The Golden City?"

The towering buildings shadowed us with the moon's light. A crow cawed in the distance, followed by a grunted cry that I could only assume was one of the hungry ones outside the wall.

"Do you really want to know?" I asked. "Or are you simply trying to insult what I am? Don't forget that *you* are a vampyre too, Huntress."

She scoffed but said nothing. I could have easily pushed her, could have given her a long speech on how important it was to accept her destiny, but I kept my mouth shut.

The right time would come when she was ready—or when she began craving blood. Any day now, her first craving for blood would hit. Any day now, her vampyre fangs would come in, possibly even with a new wave of her magic.

Then, it would be impossible to deny.

"This place is nothing like what they told us," she whispered. I barely heard her over the creaking of a dark building to my right. "How many of them knew The Golden City is... this?"

"None of them know," I answered, "but they have their suspicions. The teachers at Moira are kept in the dark, even Headmistress Katherine. They stepped foot in The Golden City ages ago, but since accepting their positions in Moira, they're no longer granted entrance. For all they know, The Golden City is still as beautiful and magical as they remember."

"And you?" she asked. We turned another corner, heading

down an alley with practically no lights. If I still had my wings, I would have to turn to fit.

"What about me?"

"How can you live with yourself knowing that so many people die for this? All our friends... They didn't deserve that. They didn't deserve to die just when they thought they made it."

"Who said they deserved it?" I questioned. "If I could do anything to stop it, Huntress, I would. Trust me, I have little power against the archangel." I stopped at a slim doorway covered with a tapestry. I pushed the cloth aside, exposing the hidden pub that lay inside.

I watched as Huntyr's mouth fell open. "What is this place?" she asked.

"Go on in and find out."

She turned and shot me a sideways glance, but her eyes were finally lighting up for the first time since Asmodeus found us. I missed that look, that slight twinkle in her eyes.

She stepped forward, her black boots gliding over the gray stone beneath us.

Inside was nothing like the rest of The Golden City. It was warm, with red lanterns illuminating the interior and colorful paintings decorating the four walls. A bar filled the back half of the room, leaving plenty of room for tables to fill the rest. I recognized the usual barmaid, as well as a few of the patrons.

"Look who's finally showing his face around here again?" one of the males at the closest table called out. I walked over to him and clapped his shoulder.

"They still let you in here, Nathan?"

He laughed, and I couldn't help but smile at my old friend. I used to come here every night before I was sent to Moira. This was my hidden escape from the cruelty of The

Golden City, from the evil and darkness that surrounded the place.

"And who's this?" he asked. His eyes slid to Huntyr, eyeing her skeptically. Nobody knew about my mission to attend Moira and find the princess. Nobody knew who she really was, what she could mean for this kingdom.

It was all part of my father's plan to keep this as quiet as possible.

"This is Huntyr," I said, waving my hand in her direction. "She'll be staying with me for a while."

She glared at me once before she held her hand out for him to shake. "Nice to meet you," she said.

Nathan's smile only grew. "Likewise, Huntyr. We don't get many newcomers around here. You ought to tell Wolf here to stop being a stranger. We barely see his face around here anymore!"

Huntyr smiled. "The more time he spends here with you, the less time he has to piss me off. I'll do my best."

They both laughed. My chest twisted.

"Alright, alright. We're here to grab some drinks."

I started to turn toward one of the empty tables when his hand shot out and grabbed my wrist. When I met his gaze, he was already staring at me with wide eyes. "It's not right, Wolf, what they did to you."

He motioned to my missing wings.

I clenched my teeth. "You know me," I smiled. "I probably did something to deserve it."

He let go of my wrist, but his scowl didn't disappear. "I seriously doubt that."

And that was the end of it. I turned and ushered Huntyr to one of the nearby secluded tables where we could talk in private.

I tried to brush off the fresh wave of grief that hit me. Nobody in the castle showed an ounce of empathy over my wings. Jessiah was shocked, yes, but nobody truly cared the same way these people did. These people were my real friends, the ones who actually cared about me, not just about who my father was or where I came from.

No, these people loved me in spite of that.

"Who were they?" Huntyr asked as she sat across from me.

"Just some old friends."

"And you have to meet here in this secret, secluded pub because...?"

"You've met my father," I pushed. "He likes to know everything that goes on around here. He doesn't appreciate people meeting like this, not when he can't control what's being discussed at all times. He prefers people to be hidden, powerless, and alone."

Her eyes scanned the room once more as she leaned forward, putting her elbows on the table. "And all these people—they're angels? Fae? Why wouldn't they obey your father's rule?"

I took a long breath before answering. There was so much she didn't know, years and years of history that would take days to unpack.

"The Golden City used to be everything you've dreamed of," I started. "My father was part of it. Magic ran rampant, elite fae and angels alike lived here, free and powerful." Her eyes widened, and I kept my mouth shut as the barmaid brought over two large ales. I nodded and waited for her to walk away before I continued. "He was the one who changed things around here. Scarlata had been gone for years; it wasn't on anyone's radar that he might want to conquer the vampyres, too. Not when he already had so much power here in The Golden City."

She nodded as my words landed.

"There are vampyres here now, though. Why would he do that? Why would he bring vampyres here when The Golden City was safe from them for so long?"

"Power. Power will make anyone do reckless things, Huntyr. He brought vampyres here to inflict chaos. They were all vampyres like you and I at first, but then, more hungry ones began turning up, and now, The Golden City is the furthest thing from safe."

Her eyes darkened. "And he forced you to turn to a vampyre? He used his magic to change you?"

I fought to keep my breath steady. "In his eyes, having a vampyre son would give him more control. I can't say it's worked out great for me, though."

She picked up the ale and took a long drink, her eyebrows raising as she swallowed. "Wow, this is actually really good."

I smiled. "Better than the ales in Midgrave?"

I watched as the corner of her mouth turned up. She stared into her ale mug and spun the glass absentmindedly as her mind wandered. "The taste is better, yes, but there are plenty of things I miss about home."

"Like what?" I drank my own ale. I wasn't going to push her, but if she was actually willing to talk to me for the first time since we arrived, I wasn't going to stop her.

"Like...like the smell of freshly baked bread wafting from the bakery in the mornings as the sun rose in the distance. Like being able to hear laughter from three streets over. Like my best friend. I miss her the most, I think. Her and Lord." Her breath hitched.

"The man who gave you those scars?"

Her eyes met mine. "It's complicated, Wolf. He cares for me. He just shows it differently."

Anger flooded my veins. I leaned forward, coming inches from her so she could feel my words as I said them. "Someone who loved you—who truly, deeply cared for you—would never do anything to hurt you. He sure as all hells wouldn't leave those scars on your skin. Whoever Lord is, whoever he pretends to be, he isn't your family."

Her eyes darkened as she stared at me, nostrils flaring and chest rising. "He's all I have, Wolf. He's the reason I'm here, the reason—"

"He sent you here knowing how dangerous it would be, knowing how much it would hurt you."

She took another long drink before asking, "And what about you? *You* swore you cared about me. *You* swore you loved me. I guess that was my own fault for believing you, right? Lord told me not to trust a single soul out here. I should have listened."

Goddess above, this woman. "I still love you, Huntyr."

She sucked in a breath. "Don't say that."

"It's true."

"Just *stop*. I don't believe you anymore."

"You can believe whatever you want, but I'll spend every day of my life protecting you from this. If I could take you out of here right now, I—"

"What did I just say, Wolf? You can't start *saying* things like that again and expect me to believe it! Hells, I—" She ran her hands through her curly black hair. "I believed you once and look where that got me. I can't do that to myself again, not after this."

She didn't meet my gaze again as she picked up the mug and finished her ale. I lifted my hand to the barmaid, who was already staring at us, and signaled for two more. "I know you have no reason to believe me, Huntyr, but I never expected to fall in love with you. If I would have known what was going to happen, I—"

"You would have stopped your father from kidnapping me for my blood?"

"Shhh," I cooed as we received two more drinks. "Don't say things like that so loudly."

"Right. I forgot everyone is afraid to stand up to him. We'll all just let this corruption continue. What exactly does he want with me, anyway? What does he think I'll do for him? Rule over the vampyres on his behalf?"

I shrugged. "Pretty much."

"Well, I'll never give him what he wants. He can kill me before I ever step in to rule Scarlata."

I sat back and watched her. She was finally not *entirely* repulsed by the fact that she may be the heir to the blood kingdom. Accepting who she really was would be the first step.

The rest would come later.

Her eyes dropped back down to the mug of ale that she twisted mindlessly between her palms. "Do you really believe I'm the heir?"

"I don't doubt it for a single moment," I answered. "I can sense the vampyre in you too. You'll start turning soon. You'll start craving—"

"Blood?" Her chest heaved. "I can't picture myself doing that. I don't know if I can."

"You can because you have to," I answered. "Trust me, nobody *wants* to drink blood before they're a fully turned vampyre. Even vampyres raised in the blood kingdom were repulsed by blood until they matured."

"What about you?" She met my gaze again. "When was your first time?"

The dark memory haunted me. I tried many, many times to forget the details of my turning. I tried to forget how disgusted I felt as soon as I woke up from the sacrifice, how hurt I was that my own father would stoop to such lows.

But I also remember the pain. The hunger. "It was unlike anything I ever felt. As soon as my father made the sacrifice, I changed. It felt like someone reached into my stomach and curled my insides in their fist."

"Lovely," she sighed.

"You're ready for it, though," I added. "You've felt my hunger through the bond. It's manageable."

"Until it's not."

I shrugged. "I do what I can."

"Can vampyres feed off other vampyres? How is it that you were able to drink my blood when I'm also a vampyre?"

"Half a vampyre," I corrected. "You still have fae blood in you, and I still have angel. Normally, vampyres would need blood from another species. Animals, fae, angels. You and I seem to be exceptions, along with the rest of the half-breeds."

She took a long, deep breath. "I can't believe this is my life."

"Yeah." I glanced around the room. "You and I both."

We sat at the bar for the next few minutes in silence. Drinking. Waiting. Breathing. I let my own thoughts drown me, let them pull apart my mind and fight with my memories.

I didn't want to be the blood-drinking vampyre I was forced into being, but here I was. I never wanted to feed off Huntyr, but I had, and I damn well enjoyed it, too.

I didn't want any of this. Not for me, and especially not for her.

There was nowhere in this entire kingdom that would be safe from him. He would never let us go freely. He would track us down, either himself or with his own army, and he wouldn't stop until he got us back.

Until he got *her*.

He wanted power that badly.

"Huntyr?" a familiar female voice called out from behind me. Huntyr's eyes widened as her gaze landed on the visitor. I spun around to see who it was, only to find—

"Voiler."

CHAPTER 5
HUNTYR

"*Goddess above.*" I was out of my seat before I could stop myself, the tall wooden stool almost tipping over as I ran to her.

Voiler.

"I thought you were dead!" I called out. I pulled her to me, crushing her small body to my chest. She hugged me back just as fiercely, laughing and half-crying in relief.

"I thought you were dead too! What are you doing here? How are you here? I mean, I thought I was the only one who survived!"

I pulled back to look at my friend. She somehow looked even better than she did in Moira, like Moira had been draining the life from her, and now, she was finally free. Her black hair was no longer in braids, hanging past her shoulders in loose waves.

"I'm here with him." I turned and pointed at Wolf, who still sat lazily on his barstool. Voiler's attention turned to him, but I didn't miss the way her gaze wandered over his shoulders.

"His wings, they're—"

"It's a long story," I said. "Tell me about you. How are you here? How did you survive?"

"I thought I died," she started, lowering her voice. "I was supposed to be dead, anyway. After the Transcendent, I shouldn't be here, but I woke up inside The Golden City. Of course, I was confused as all hells when I first woke up. It's nothing like they told us."

"Yeah," I sighed. "It's awful."

"I stumbled through some buildings, fighting off as many hungry ones as I could, until I found them." She turned and looked at a small group of people who funneled toward a table by the door. Some possessed angel wings, some didn't. Their pointed ears told me they were fae, too. "They brought me in, protected me. I've been living with them since.

"I saw Ashlani die. And Lanson. Though I guess everything we saw there was a test. It's hard to believe anything that actually happened. I died too. I mean, *died*." That last word was barely audible, like I still couldn't truly believe it myself.

She reached out and pulled me back into her arms, giving me another quick hug. "You're here now," she whispered into my ear. "For whatever reason, you made it. You survived. That's all that matters."

"Why us, though? Why did we survive when everyone else died?"

She shrugged. "I guess Era's not done with us yet. But at least the others have peace in death. They didn't have to wake up in this mess."

"Look, Voiler." I stepped even closer to her and lowered my voice, ensuring nobody else could hear us. "I need to talk to you. There's obviously something horrible happening here.

I'm trying to figure it all out, but I could really use a friend here, someone I can actually trust."

"Of course," she smiled. "Anything you need, I'm here. Wolf isn't friendly enough for you, I take it?" Her eyes flickered behind me.

I looked back over my shoulder to where Wolf still glared at us, pulling his mug of ale to his lips.

"Has he *ever* been friendly?" I joked. Now was *not* the time or place to tell Voiler about everything. I still wasn't sure who I could trust. Half the people in this tavern could be funneling information directly back to Asmodeus. Wolf's friend seemed nice enough, but I had no idea where his loyalties lied.

"Not everything is as it seems here." She slid her hand into mine and interlocked our fingers. It was a strange show of affection I had never seen from her. She was much more closed off in Moira, very reserved. I was even more surprised when she tugged me forward and wrapped both arms around me, hugging me tightly and nuzzling her face into my black hair.

"I know what they're doing to you," she whispered. I kept my face blank, wrapping my arms around her and showing just as much affection for my old friend. "You aren't alone, Huntyr. You have allies here, and we're not going to let him use you. Just hang on."

I said nothing, just stood and hugged her for a few more seconds before she pulled away slowly.

"It was nice to see you again." She put a polite smile on her face. "Stay safe, Huntyr."

I gave her one more squeeze before she turned away, smiling just as casually. "You too."

My eyes didn't leave her body as she made her way back to her friends. *I'm not alone here.* Who were these people she found? Clearly, she made her way into a very different group of friends. Did she really know I was the blood queen? Did she know Asmodeus's plans to take over Scarlata? She drank her ale, laughing and bumping shoulders with one of the males at the table.

In the months we spent together at Moira, I never saw her like this. So relaxed. So natural.

"You're staring," Wolf said from behind me.

"Fuck off." I snapped out of my gaze and returned to my table, taking Wolf in for the first time since I'd seen Voiler. "Did you know she was here? Did you know she survived?"

He shrugged. "I suspected. There was no way to know for sure. I've been a bit preoccupied here."

"I can't believe this. Voiler survived! I mean, who else survived and is wandering around here in The Golden City?"

Wolf glanced over his shoulder at the people Voiler befriended. He let his eyes linger before answering, "There's no telling, but I can guarantee that surviving the Transcendent was the least of their problems. These streets are crawling with vampyres, Huntyr. Hungry ones, too. Voiler's lucky she found them."

"How is that possible? Nobody can enter The Golden City without going through Moira, yet hungry ones are here?"

His chin dipped. "He lets them in."

I repeated those words in my mind, ensuring I heard him correctly. "He lets the hungry ones into The Golden City? That doesn't make any sense."

"My father doesn't care if the people living here are safe or not. In his mind, you'll survive if you're strong enough. This is a power move for him. Keep the people weak, and nobody will challenge his rule. He thrives on chaos, not to mention his deep infatuation with the vampyres."

My mind spun. The entire point of The Golden City was to keep vampyres out. It was supposed to be a safe space, a luxurious place for the elites to live in comfort.

But this? This was no better than living in Midgrave. It was worse, actually. At least in Midgrave, I had the illusion of freedom.

"Hells," I muttered. "I can't tell if he hates vampyres or loves them."

"He loves the destruction they bring. He loves that Scarlata was once the most powerful kingdom in existence. He loves that if he could control them, if he could use the hungry ones to spread even more chaos; he could take over the entire world."

The entire fucking world. I pulled my mug to my lips and swallowed a mouthful of the golden liquid. How did things get so messed up? How did we get here? Wolf sat in silence beside me. I wanted nothing more than to wring him out for being a part of this, for allowing such a sacred place to crumble entirely.

But a heaviness radiated from him now as we both sat here, reveling in the truth. It felt almost impossible to bring light back here. So much evilness, so much hatred, lingered here, all brought on by his father. The same father who forced him to turn to a vampyre, who cut his wings from his body.

I was talking too much. I knew I was. It had to be the ale softening me, making me forget the heinous things he, too, was guilty of.

I still hated him. I sent him another glare to prove that point. But I couldn't deny the fact that he was comfortable here. He was some piece of my old life I couldn't entirely get rid of.

"Your thoughts are loud," he said. "And so are your emotions."

I looked at him again, only to find him staring at me with a fierceness that made my stomach drop.

"This damn bond is annoying. If I knew you were going to feel my emotions forever, I would have thought twice about—"

"About what? About saving your own life during the Transcendent? We would have died out there, Huntyr. We did what we had to do to survive."

"Don't act like being bonded to me isn't working out in your favor, Wolf." I drank again, starting to feel the effects of the bubbling liquid. "I heard what your father said about me. Do you really intend on using my power against me? On taking it all for yourself? The second he learns I do actually have power, he'll use you to drain me entirely."

"You know I would never do that." He dropped his head, eyes growing serious. "My father wants a lot of things, Huntyr. I don't intend on giving him what he wants."

"But you have so far, haven't you? You delivered me here, directly to him. What did that cost you? Your wings? Me— whatever I am to you? How much more will you let him take?"

His knuckles tightened around his mug. "He has already taken too much. You have no fucking idea."

Minutes passed without us talking. I looked around the room, surveying Wolf's friends as they drank and laughed and told stories. They all looked so trustworthy. So welcoming. Voiler's friends, too. It made me question what I knew about Wolf. If these people trusted him....

No. I couldn't trust him again, not without more information, without him proving he really had my best interests in mind.

I shifted in my seat so we were no longer so close to brushing arms. I didn't want to feel drawn to him, to feel safe with him. I didn't want to lean on him for support here. He wanted me to trust him again, but I couldn't tell what side he was really on. Why drag me all the way here, only to defy his father at the last second? Why hold me as a prisoner, but keep my magic a secret?

When I looked at him again, he was already staring at me. "Dance with me."

I nearly spit out my drink. "Excuse me?"

Music flowed into the room from somewhere outside. It was playing for a few minutes, I realized, but now, some of the other patrons were dancing, swaying, relaxing to the music.

Music. My chest bubbled. Music seemed so normal, and in this foreign, wretched place? I welcomed anything normal.

"Just one dance, Huntress. Have at least a bit of fun with me tonight. It will make going back to the castle slightly more manageable. I owe it to you." He stood from his seat and walked around the table to take both of my hands.

"Absolutely not. I *don't* want to dance with you," I argued. "Just because we are talking here does not mean I've moved past my deep, undying hatred for you." But with him standing so close, I could smell the soft notes of pine that wafted from his skin. I could make out the fresh scent of soap from his clean linen shirt.

"Enough lies, princess," he whispered, close enough that his breath tickled my ear. "Pretend like none of this shit exists between us, only for a minute, and dance with me. Either that, or we'll go back to my room, and you can say goodbye to this small excursion. Who knows when you'll be let out of that castle again? It could be weeks. Months." He clicked his tongue for dramatic effect.

"You're an asshole." I shoved his hands away.

But he was not so easily swayed. "Perhaps I am an asshole, but the moon is high, and the music is contagious. One dance, and then we'll go."

I shouldn't have. I knew that this was a bad idea, that I would be giving him too much, but I wanted so badly to stop fighting, to stop feeling so much hatred and betrayal and pain. I *wanted* to forget about everything he'd done; trust me, I did. The bitterness in my chest was starting to swallow me whole, starting to make me forget I could feel anything other than darkness.

One dance.

And then it would be over, and I could go back to threatening death for even looking in my direction. Before I could think for another second, I slid my hand into his and let him pull me to my feet.

He said nothing, but I felt his satisfaction flicker through our bond. He guided me a few feet away, tugging me closer with a hand on my hip.

I let him lead me, let him pull my hands up to his shoulders and start to move my body.

His breath hit my cheek as he whispered, "This reminds me of Moira, when I had to watch you dance with Lanson while I attempted not to kill him."

The memory washed over me, and I tried my best not to shiver. "You should have. It would've saved both of us some pain."

He shook his head, his muscles flexing beneath my palms.

"No, because the night he hurt you was the night you finally started looking at me as your ally."

Right. "Also not a great decision on my end."

"Come on, Huntress. You trusted me. We were good together."

We *were* good together. That was the part that sucked the most. Our training, our fighting, it was almost as if he became an extension of me. He knew my next move before I did, and he executed it ten times better than I could. He was so similar to me, yet so different in the ways that counted. At least, that's what he made me believe. I was still trying to piece together what was real and what wasn't. What parts did he make up, simply to trick me into falling for him?

"Don't remind me," I sighed. I lifted my chin and stared into his bright blue eyes. "Look where that got us."

"You have to start trusting me again, Huntress." His hands on my waist practically burned. They radiated heat through my entire body, making me painfully aware of every inch of our chests touching. "I know you don't want to, but I am trying to help you. Feel it through our bond. *Feel* that all I want to do is protect you."

I sucked in a sharp breath at the emotion he sent flooding toward me. It was warm, predatory, sharp, like he would truly end anyone who dared hurt me. I threw up my shields, blocking out that emotion before I could let myself be tricked again. "It doesn't matter what you feel, Wolf. It matters what you *do.*"

Both of us had been drinking. Neither of us were taking logic into account here, not when we were this close, our bodies swaying to the music together.

"Then tell me what to do," he whispered. He leaned

down, brushing his lips across my ear and making me shiver. "Tell me what to do to make you trust me again."

"There isn't—"

"Don't say that, Huntress. Don't tell me there's nothing."

"I don't know, Wolf, okay? I spent my entire life being taught to trust no one. You knew that. Lord made sure I would be protected from everyone and everything, and then you showed up, and you—you—"

"I what?"

"You know damn well what you did." My voice cracked, and I tightened my grip on his shoulders as he did the same to my waist. "You made me care for you in a way I had never cared for anyone, and it nearly got me *killed*."

"I swear to you, Huntress, I'm getting us out of this."

My chest heaved, and I let him pull me even closer. "How? Your father will kill me if I don't do what he wants."

His eyes searched mine. Desperate. Needy. "I need time. But I swear to you on my own life, I'll figure it out."

I stared at Wolf, the damned ale making me forget all the reasons I was supposed to hate him. He made it easy with his dark hair and his electric eyes. He made it so fucking easy to forget the pain, the agony, the betrayal.

But there was a wall up now, constantly protecting my heart, a shield I was certain I would never lower again.

I owed myself at least that much.

"I want to go home," I whispered.

His hand slid up my waist to the side of my face, caressing me lightly. "I know you do."

My throat tightened. Tears I thought I buried deep, deep down began to surface. I was so fucking tired. Tired of being strong. Tired of being betrayed. Tired of *hurting*.

I leaned forward and rested my head on Wolf's chest as he

continued to sway us to the smooth music. He wrapped his arms around me, holding me to him.

To be honest, I would have stayed there all night. Days, even. Because as much as I fucking hated it, I still found the smallest sliver of safety in those arms.

Someone shouted outside. Wolf tensed and stopped dancing as I lifted my face from his chest and turned to the door. "What is—"

"*You!*" Jessiah stormed into the pub. "I've been looking for you two everywhere! What do you think you're doing? He'll kill you if he finds out you took her here!"

Everyone in the pub stopped, staring at us now. Even Voiler watched us with wide eyes.

"It's not a big deal, Jessiah," Wolf sighed. He turned to his brother but slid his hand into mine and held tightly. "Nobody here will say a thing. We're safe here."

"And what about her?" He didn't even look at me as he said the words. "You thought bringing her here would be a good idea?"

I looked to my feet, not daring to meet his gaze. Wolf lowered his voice, though, dragging me with him as he stopped two feet from his brother. "Watch what you say here, brother."

"Right," he said. "You have no problem taking the *blood queen* out in public, but as long as nobody knows who she really is, she's safe, right? Tell me, brother, what if they did know? It's not hard to piece together why he is so obsessed with her. She's his coveted weapon. *Everyone* here is a danger to her."

They spoke in hushed tones, but it was too much, too exposing.

"Let's just go," I sighed. "You're causing a scene. We were about to leave anyway."

The brothers looked at me. Hells, they both had that same concerned look in their eyes. I knew why Wolf cared so much, but Jessiah?

I wasn't entirely sure I could trust him yet. He may love Wolf, but so far, he was loyal to his father.

"Come on," Jessiah said, turning around. "You're lucky I'm the one who found you here. One of Father's men would have her locked back up in that dungeon without a second thought."

Yeah, lucky. I glanced at Wolf, but he didn't meet my gaze as he pulled me out of the pub and onto the dark, vacant streets.

CHAPTER 6
WOLF

I lay on the floor of my bedroom, listening to the low pounding of her heart. She fell asleep an hour ago, wrapped in the soft linens of my bed. I could smell her too. The subtle scent of my soap lingered on her perfect skin. *Pine and sweet, sweet cherries.*

This was my own personal form of torture, to have to stay this close to her, unable to touch her. Not able to kiss her lips, to hold her in my arms.

Still, tonight was a step in the right direction. She finally looked at me without disgust and hatred. It was likely the ale, but still. I missed the way she smiled, the way her eyes lit up.

I heard footsteps approaching from the hall outside.

I immediately sat up, careful not to make a single sound as I rushed to the door, waiting. The footsteps grew closer, closer, closer before stopping right in front of my door.

I twisted the doorknob and threw the door open before my visitor could knock.

Luseyar stood in front of me, his hand on his hip, his chin raised. "Your father summons you," he said.

"Right now?" I whispered. I glanced back to make sure Huntyr was still sound asleep. "What about her?"

"Leave her here," he insisted. "He only wishes to speak to you and your brother."

The hair on the back of my neck rose, but I nodded once before grabbing my shirt and slipping out into the hall.

Jessiah was exiting his room at the same time. He clearly just woke up, with his golden hair messy and his shirt in wrinkles.

There was no way he knew where we were tonight. If he thought for even a second that I took Huntyr to that pub, he would have me in shackles.

It wasn't entirely unheard of for Asmodeus to summon us like this. He was chaotic and had no sense of schedule, but usually, this meant he had a new idea—good or bad. I still remembered the way he summoned me to tell me I would be going to Moira to find the girl who would end everything.

My brother gave me a reassuring nod. He did that often, and the older I got, I wasn't sure why. It's not like he could really protect me. Not against our father, anyway.

We both started down the hall after Luseyar in silence. Every step I took away from her felt wrong. I hated leaving her side; even in the dungeons, I hated it.

"What does he want this time?" I asked once we were away from the bedrooms.

Luseyar glanced over his shoulder. He wasn't a bad guy. He was stuck in this trap with Asmodeus, same as everyone. But he would do anything to protect himself, and that included hurting either one of us.

That included cutting my damn wings off.

"You'll find out soon enough," he said with a sigh.

Great. We were going in totally blind.

Father was the one who told us to observe The Golden City anyway. If anyone had seen us out, I had a perfectly good excuse for walking the city with Huntyr. There was something else. I could feel it.

"This way." Luseyar turned toward the door to the gardens. The *dead* gardens, rather. "He's expecting you both."

He waited at the door while Jessiah and I both entered. This place used to be beautiful and lush. Greenery used to cover every stone out in this garden. But it had been years since any plant dared to bloom here. I didn't blame them. The death and decay was much more fitting.

My father sat on a stone bench in the middle of the dead vines and black roses, waiting. "There you two are," he said. "Finally. We have much to discuss."

"It's the middle of the night," I added, and Jessiah gave me a warning glance as he walked forward.

"It is, and that's why I've summoned you both here now. I find it difficult to sleep at night, knowing the queen of the blood kingdom is in my grasp, and yet I still have no control over her."

"I'd say you've got pretty great control, actually. She's still here."

A flare of his magic fluttered through the air, forcing my chest to tighten on instinct. "Do not test me, boy. I will not hesitate to take what is mine, no matter who gets in my way."

"And she's in your way?" Jessiah added.

Asmodeus took a long breath. "If she's not willing to help us, then yes."

Jessiah and I shared a glance. "She's coming around. I need more time to earn her trust back." *And to think of a way to get us both far, far away from here.*

"Time is precisely what we do not have," he retorted.

"She'll be a mature vampyre very, very soon. If my sources are correct, she'll be turning twenty-five in a few days."

"Your sources?" I stepped forward. "Who are your sources?"

"That's none of your concern," he said. "But it won't matter if she becomes too powerful to control—which is why I have a new plan."

I crossed my arms over my chest and tried to steady my breathing.

New plan? This could not be fucking good.

"Huntyr will marry one of my sons. One of you will become king of the blood kingdom by marriage. *Then,* we will have control."

A second of silence passed. I could have sworn the crows stopped cawing in the distance.

And then we both asked, "What?"

He raised his head to look at us for the first time since we'd entered. "One of you will marry Huntyr. I do not care which, but the ceremony will be on the day of the equinox."

I took a long breath, pushing aside the absolute delusion that my father fell victim to. Marriage? As if that would help anything; as if that would somehow allow him to get closer to Huntyr.

"That's impossible," I insisted. Panic crept up my body and tightened my voice. "How is marrying her supposed to give us more control? Nobody even knows she is the blood queen!"

"They will," he said. "We will make the announcement then, after it's done. We'll gather the vampyres and rebuild Scarlata one by one, with *our* family in charge."

Fucking hells. He had a track record of insane, chaotic ideas, but this topped them all.

"She'll never agree to that," I pushed. Jessiah stood with his arms crossed and his mouth shut, but I could practically feel the arguments inside his mind.

"She'll agree to it, or she'll die," he insisted. "And when she begins to fully mature into her vampyre heritage, she'll be more willing to accept her role as their queen."

This was so, so wrong. Huntyr was never going to agree to that. She already made it very clear she would die before she helped him. A forced marriage? Goddess above, we were about to rip apart every ounce of freedom she had left.

"You are dismissed," he ordered. "Keep an eye on her. I will prepare for the equinox. You have eight weeks."

Eight fucking weeks. I had eight weeks to figure out how we were going to escape this fate, how we could shut Asmodeus down before he became drunk on his own power.

If it wasn't already too late.

"Let's go," Jessiah whispered as he turned. My father went back to pretending we weren't even there, weren't even in front of him.

A new wave of hatred washed over me. He never cared about Huntyr, that much was obvious. All he cared about was the power she could give him. But to blatantly use her like this?

"Keep walking," Jessiah whispered, shoving my shoulder lightly. As soon as we were out the door, Luseyar slipped in and shut it, leaving me and Jessiah alone in the dark hallway. "Do you have a damn death wish?" he asked. "You know better than to question him like this!"

"This is fucking insane!" I clenched my fists, looking for something I could punch to get this anger out of me. "He wants to marry her off like she's nothing! What then? He'll lock her up and force us to rule the vampyres?"

"Think about this, okay? If you really care about her, this is how you'll keep her safe. You marry her, satisfy this current outburst of delusion, and the two of you can think of a plan later. Okay?"

I stopped pacing and shook my head. "She'll never marry me, Jessiah."

"That's not what it looked like when I found you in the pub tonight. If it's this or death, I think she'll—"

"You don't know her like I do." I inhaled shakily. "I'm telling you, it will never happen."

"Fine," he sighed. "Then I'll do it."

I pinned him to the wall before he could take his next breath. "You absolutely will not," I growled.

He lifted his hands in surrender. "Okay, okay, calm down! I'm only trying to find a way to get us all out of here alive, Wolf. Think with your damn head!"

This was so messed up. "I can't think of this right now," I sighed. "If she's becoming a vampyre *next fucking week*, I'll worry about that first. Keep your mouth shut about the marriage thing, okay? It'll only piss her off more. I need some time."

"Time?" His laugh was menacing. "You've got eight weeks, brother. Good luck with that."

led Huntyr to a small, overgrown clearing behind the main castle of The Golden City. It was secluded here, private, but it also gave her a break from those suffocating walls of her confinement.

"It's important you don't lose what you learned in Moira. Your magic will be getting stronger as you transition."

She didn't even look me in the eye. Her gaze had been that way lately—vacant, cold, like she was always somewhere else in her mind, never here.

I didn't blame her, but if she was going to get stronger— strong enough to protect herself—she would have to fight.

"Huntress," I called out, setting a soft hand on her shoulder.

She snapped her attention to me before shoving my hand away. "I heard you."

Doubtful, but I continued anyway. "Let's start with whatever feels easiest. Natural magic, anything you can summon."

She stood with her hands crossed over her chest, practically hugging herself. It wasn't cold outside today, but she wore one of my long tunics that practically drowned her. She had on the same dirty, black boots she always wore, and even though they were falling apart, they reminded me of the old Huntyr. The fighter.

"I don't feel anything," she said, mindlessly kicking a small stone with her boot. "There's really no point, anyway. If I allow my power to grow, he'll force it out of me even faster."

"That's not true." I stepped forward but kept my voice calm as I pushed. "You need to be able to protect yourself, especially here. Don't think about this being for him. Think about this being for you."

She rolled her eyes, but at least she finally looked at me.

"Fine. But unless my magic has morphed into some world-destroying essence, I'm not sure it will help me here."

Okay, I ignored that comment. Huntyr had no clue how powerful she was fated to become. She was the blood queen, the heir to the Scarlata throne.

If what I tasted in her blood was true, she really could have the power to destroy worlds.

Which is something my father could never find out.

"Start with something small. Simple."

She closed her eyes and took a breath, the only sign she was trying to summon her magic. I felt a stir in my stomach through our bond, my own magic reacting to hers.

Her eyes snapped open. "Stop doing that."

"I'm not doing anything."

"You are. I can feel it."

I dipped my head to hide my smile. "My magic can feel yours through the bond. I promise you, I'm not doing anything on purpose."

She rolled her eyes and scoffed. "It's distracting. If you want me to use my own magic, put yours away."

Even though I wanted to remind her that the entire point of the bond was to share magic, I kept my mouth shut. I was keeping my mouth shut about quite a lot of things lately.

She was going to fucking hate me for it.

"Fine." I held my palms up and took a step backward, giving her space to breathe. "I'll put it away. Try again."

I pretended not to hear the slur of curse words beneath her breath. She let her eyes flutter closed, her dark brows furrowing in concentration as she tried to summon the magic.

Wind picked up around us, the sky growing darker and darker. I forced my own power down in my chest as it reacted to hers. Hells, she was so damn powerful, and she didn't even know it. She cut herself off, shoved her own magic down to be safe. To be secure, unseen.

I knew the feeling.

"Stop holding back," I ordered.

She huffed in response, but held her hands out before her as the wind whipped around us. Even the barren plants around us reacted to her, vines reaching toward her.

"I'm not holding back."

"You are. You know you are."

Her eyes snapped open, hands dropping back to her sides. The wind ceased, plants stilled. "Maybe it's because it's not safe for me to show my magic here. How do I know you aren't trying to train me so I'm ready for your father whenever he takes my magic?"

Goddess above. She was going to be the death of me, one way or another. "I can't force you to trust me, Huntress, but I don't know how else to make you believe I'm trying to help you. Your power will grow. You'll become very, very strong. You barely touched your abilities in Moira and you almost burned that place to ash, so if you'd rather lose control entirely and have no way to summon your own magic on command, be my guest."

She glared at me with dagger eyes. "I'd love to lose control. I'll take you all with me when I go, too."

I stepped forward. "You wish you could be so lucky." I waited for a response from her, but none came. I pushed forward, "Be angry, Huntress. Be entirely pissed off. Let that fuel you, let that fill every single one of your bones as you train. But *train*. Wield your magic. Become strong." I took another step forward so I could smell the sweat glistening on her skin. "Become unstoppable."

If Huntyr didn't trust me, that was fine. That was something I could live with. But right now, I silently begged for her to understand me, to feel how important it was that she learned full control of her current abilities so I could get us both out of here at the first possible opportunity.

By the kind grace of the goddess above, something I said must have stuck, because Huntyr took another deep breath, spread her feet in another bracing stance, and summoned her magic again.

And again.

And again.

Even though we both felt the strengthening of her magic, we said nothing. I pushed her until an hour passed, then two. Huntyr didn't fight me again, didn't argue as I helped her pull more and more and more of her gift.

Good.

If she was willing to fight, there was a chance. If she was willing to get pissed off, we may be able to make it out of here alive.

CHAPTER 7
HUNTYR

"You have to eat something," he argued, pushing the soup closer. I clutched my stomach, willing the pain to go away, but it was no use.

This had been happening for days now. It started as a constant wave of nausea, the inability to keep food down, and now, I was repulsed by everything.

I was sick, probably something I picked up in those disgusting dungeons, but Wolf kept telling me I was becoming a vampyre. I refused to believe that, refused to believe this was already happening.

"Leave me alone," I argued. "I'll be fine; I just need a few days."

"It's not going to get any better," he said. "You've missed training now for five days. You're in denial."

I pushed myself up on his bed and shot him a death glare. "It's not denial, Wolf. Can you just leave me alone for one damn minute so I can get some rest?"

This became our thing. Wolf would bring me food, and when I didn't eat it, he would insist I needed blood. But there was no way I was going to drink blood willingly. Even the thought of it made me gag more than the thought of eating this food.

"Fine," he said. "Suit yourself. But my father is throwing a party for you tomorrow night, and you're going to suffer if you can't even stand up straight."

This caught my attention. "What did you just say?"

"It's your birthday, Huntress. Tomorrow's a celebration." He stood up and walked over to the door, leaning against it effortlessly with his arms crossed over his chest. Even without his wings, he looked like a smug bastard.

"I don't want to celebrate," I groaned. "And how does he know when my birthday is?"

"He's the archangel. He has his ways, apparently." Wolf looked at me a second longer before turning to exit, leaving me alone in my misery.

I spent the rest of the day trying and failing to ignore the nausea wrecking my body. I was losing my damn mind, that much was certain. I could barely stand up straight without hunching over and clawing at my stomach.

Is this how I would feel every day until I had blood? What if I had blood and turned into one of those monsters? What if I couldn't control it—what if I killed someone?

Hells, Huntyr. Get your shit together. You can't find a way out of here if you're too busy suffering.

Besides, the soup Wolf brought didn't look all that bad. I held my breath and picked up the bowl, shoving a spoonful into my mouth before I could change my mind.

And another bite.

And another.

Three bites in, I practically threw the bowl across the room. That would have to be enough for now.

I forced myself out of bed and walked over to the door that led to the hallway. I pressed my ear against it, waiting.

The last few days, I had done this. Wolf thought I was too sick to even stand, and for the most part, he was right.

But he was an idiot if he thought I would lie back, complacent, waiting for my own demise.

A minute passed, then another. I heard nothing in the hall, no voices, no footsteps.

The coast was clear.

I threw on my black boots and stuffed a bag I found in Wolf's wardrobe with the extra bread I hid over the last few days. The smell of it threatened to make me throw up that damn soup, but I choked it down. I would need energy, even if the smell of it repulsed me.

I was getting the fuck out of here today.

I tip-toed back to the door and double-checked that the coast was still clear before I put my hand on the knob.

And twisted.

Unlocked. They really did think I was a weak, pathetic female who would sit around and accept my fate. Asmodeus didn't know me at all, did he?

I peeked my head out the door, checking both directions of the dark hallway. The sun was beginning to set, which allowed my fae eyes to see just enough to escape in the darkness.

We had come from the left. The left was where the dungeons were, where the rest of the castle resided. The left was likely where Wolf, Asmodeus, and Jessiah were. So, I turned right, down the hallway that grew skinnier and skinnier. There were no windows this far down the hallway, but I slid my hand along the stone wall to guide me as I navigated further and further from the prison of Wolf's bedroom.

At the very end of the hall, there was a stairwell hidden in the shadows, narrow enough for my body to slip through. I stepped through and descended the stairs.

With adrenaline pulsing through my veins, I all but forgot the torturous hunger I felt. My heart pounded, every single one of my senses on high alert.

My boots didn't so much as squeak as I descended the stairs and peeked around from the bottom of the stairwell.

It exited to the street.

How stupid were they? They kept me in a room this close to the street, unguarded, with not so much as a lock on my door?

I pulled the hood up on my cloak and double checked that I was totally alone before I stepped into the night.

With the towering buildings, there was no light to help me navigate. Still, I wasn't about to let that stop me. I wasn't sure how many more chances I would have to escape. Wolf was always around, lingering, and if it wasn't him, it was that brute of an angel—Luseyar—watching guard.

This could be my only damn shot.

I didn't have a plan. Actually, my plan was to get as far away from that place as fucking possible. Voiler seemed to have good friends. Maybe if I stayed hidden enough, I could find her. She would help me. She might even know a way out of this wretched place.

I couldn't go back to Midgrave; that was out of the question, but I could at least let Lord and Rummy know I was okay.

And then, I could sneak off, living my life in the forest. I always liked the forest anyway. It would be peaceful there. Quiet.

The streets were a maze, but I didn't slow down, didn't

falter. I moved forward, one foot after the other. The air was eerily silent. Not a single animal called to the moon. I heard no voices. No laughter. No music.

Just...silence, the kind that made you look over your shoulder every three feet.

I reached to my hip where my dagger was typically strapped, only to find it vacant. It was an old habit, but it forced me to realize how vulnerable I was out here without my weapon.

But I couldn't let fear stop me. Not anymore.

The castle disappeared in the streets behind me. I tried to remember each path I turned down, each odd building or unique marking in the stone I came across in the dark night. Soon enough, the buildings became shorter, the narrow streets opened up, and more empty space littered the area around us.

I was getting somewhere. *Keep going.*

I turned one more corner when I slammed into a large body.

"What the fu—"

I shut my mouth when I realized it wasn't a man's body, but a vampyre's. I could tell by the look in his eyes that he was a hungry one, and he had just run into a warm, blood-filled body.

Shit.

I scrambled backward, once again reaching for my weapon that wasn't there.

I could run, sure. Maybe he wasn't as fast as the others. I could try to fight—I had decent skill in hand-to-hand combat —but this vampyre was large, larger than most.

I backed up around the corner, retreating the same way I came. "It's okay," I said to the monster. "Just turn around.

Plenty of fresh bodies the other way." What was I trying to do? They couldn't understand me. They couldn't understand anything, actually, except their constant craving for blood.

A gruntled growl escaped his mouth. I could smell the rot and decay coming from the creature before his eyes locked onto me and narrowed.

Fuck.

I turned and ran as fast I could, not giving a fuck if I was heading back into the city, not caring where I was going, as long as I got away from this beast.

He was fast, but nowhere near as discreet as I was. I heard his every footstep pounding after me desperately as I maneuvered the empty streets.

Where the fuck was everyone?

"Need some help?" a male voice asked as I rounded another corner, panting.

Wait, I knew that voice.

I screeched to a halt, hiding behind a half-crumbling wall just around the corner.

"Unless you want me to be vampyre dinner, then yeah, some help would be nice!" I shouted.

Jessiah stepped out of the shadows, his white wings glowing in the moonlight. His sword was already drawn from its sheath, and he intercepted the beast just as he was about to reach me with his decaying fingertips.

I choked back a gag as Jessiah cut the head from the body in one swift motion, making sure to back out of the way before the body could touch him.

And then, it was over. I crouched down, bracing my trembling hands on my knees as I sucked in breath after breath.

That was too fucking close. Weeks being held captive weakened me more than I realized.

"Thank you," I panted. "He was about to kill me."

Jessiah tsked, wiping his sword on his trousers before sheathing it again. I watched his feet move closer as I remained in my crouched position.

"What was your plan here, exactly, Huntyr? To run away into the forest and live happily ever after?"

Yes. "Pretty much."

I could feel the disapproval seeping from him. I waited a few more moments before standing up and meeting his gaze. "Did you expect me to just sit in that room, waiting for your father to kill me?"

"He's not going to kill you."

"He will if I don't give him what he wants. We both know that."

Jessiah glanced around us before stepping closer. He looked much more similar to Wolf when he was angry. The same muscle in his jaw tensed as he crossed his arms over his chest.

"How thick-headed are you if you can't see that Wolf is trying to help you? All this does is make things harder for him. Do you want to go back to the dungeon? Is that it? Because the second Asmodeus finds out you ran, that's where you'll end up. Wolf took responsibility for you, Huntyr. Would you take the cold, rotting floor of the castle basement over a warm bed and hot meals?"

I blinked back my surprise. Of course I would rather stay in Wolf's room than the dungeon, but how could he not see how desperate I was to get out of this?

"I can't," I stuttered, taking a step back. "I can't go back there, Jessiah. I'm rotting away in that room." My throat burned again, tears springing to my eyes. Another wave of nausea hit me as the fresh blood from the dead vampyre wafted into the air. "You can't take me back there."

"You know I don't have a choice." he sighed, sounding bored. "I can keep my mouth shut about this, but you have to come back."

"Why?" I pushed. "Why do you care so much if I stay or leave, huh? What's in it for you?"

He turned his head toward the sky and smiled wickedly. It was the first wicked gesture I had seen from Jessiah. He was typically lighter than Wolf. Kinder. Gentler. He was *good*.

But when his eyes met mine again, they held only malice. "What's in it for me? How about the fact that I've already watched my brother suffer for you? He went to Moira for you. His wings were cut off because of you. Do you know what that means for an angel, Huntyr? Do you know how badly he's suffering right now?"

My breath hitched. "If you want me to apologize for any of that, you're wasting your time. It's not my fault Wolf pulled me into this disaster."

"No, it's not, but it's not Wolf's fault either. Asmodeus will get his way whether Wolf is there to help you or not. Trust me, my brother may put on a front of being an arrogant asshole, but he cares. He cares about you, too much for his own damn good. It's dangerous, and it's risky. If my father was smart enough to pay attention for even a second, he would see how Wolf looks at you."

My chest tightened. "Yeah, well, he betrayed me."

"Did he?" Jessiah stepped closer, and I backed up until I was stuck, pressed against the brick wall behind me. "Did he betray you, or did he do everything in his power to keep you safe?"

My mind spun. It didn't fucking seem like he was trying

to keep me safe. There were so many times in Moria where he could have told me the truth, could have told me—

A wave of pain hit my stomach. I doubled over, wrapping my arms around myself as I stifled a groan.

"Not to mention the fact that he's trying to help you mature as a vampyre, and you're blowing him off every chance you get."

"I'm not ready," I grunted.

"Then get ready. Wolf is the only one who knows what you're going through. Get help from him or die, Huntyr. I'm tired of playing these games."

He reached forward, aiming to grip my arm, but I yanked my body away. "Wait." I took a few settling breaths and righted myself against the wall. "I want to visit Midgrave, just for a few hours. If you let me do that, I'll go willingly with you. I won't run anymore."

Jessiah laughed. "You think Asmodeus will let you out of here? There's a reason it's nearly impossible to get out of The Golden City."

"Nearly, but not impossible. You know the way."

His jaw tightened. "No, it's too risky. Not happening."

"Just think about it, Jessiah," I pushed. "If I run away again and get killed by a vampyre, it will be you and Wolf who take the punishments for me. Help me with this one thing, and I swear I'll help you."

He eyed me carefully. Jessiah was smart, calculated, and this was risky.

But I couldn't sit around and wait to be played like some card in a game.

"Flying all the way to Midgrave will take hours," he started. "They'll notice if you're gone, Wolf especially."

I cursed under my breath. "Then we'll go when he's

distracted. It doesn't have to be tonight. I can wait. But if you promise to take me there the second you can, I'll go along with Asmodeus's plans."

He cocked his head to the side. "You have no idea what Asmodeus has planned for you, do you?"

I could picture a few things. "I'm a smart girl, Jessiah. I can figure it out."

His chest rose and fell inches from me. He eyed me like he was trying to decide if he could trust me or not, like he was trying to decipher the code in all my lies.

But the truth? The truth was that I wasn't lying. If I could get back home and let Lord and Rummy know I was okay, I could live with this fate. I could live with my death, even.

"Fine," he said after a while, uncrossing his arms and shoving them in his pockets. "But don't mention a word of this until the coast is clear. And you'll stop fighting Wolf. He's a fucking idiot when it comes to you."

I ignored the way my chest tightened at his words. He might care for me now, but it didn't matter. Everything he did to me, everything he lied to me about...

If I wanted to survive, I couldn't trust him. Not again.

I made that mistake one too many times.

"Deal."

CHAPTER 8
WOLF

My father had a thing for large parties. When I was younger, I loved them. It gave me an excuse to run away for a while, to sneak wine and ale and eat the nicest foods from all over the kingdom.

But now? It made me sick to see the corrupt, evil archangel and his closest companions celebrating and drinking as if they had no problems in this world, as if they weren't the sole ones responsible for people dying and starving all around Vaehatis.

I gave Huntyr time alone to prepare. My father, of course, required her to wear a certain dress that he made specially for this event. She had gone from his prisoner in the dungeon to his prized possession in his castle.

How fucking fitting.

Of course, all of this was another ploy in his sick, twisted games. He didn't care about Huntyr's birthday. He sure as all hells didn't care about celebrating her or making her feel special tonight.

This was all for him. He had something to gain from this,

and every nerve in my body tensed when I thought about what that could possibly be.

I knocked on my bedroom door twice. I wasn't usually one for knocking, but tonight felt different. Huntyr wasn't just in there rotting away, waiting for me to come back with a bowl of soup so she could yell and fight again.

When she didn't answer, I cracked the door open. "Huntyr?"

I found her in the doorway of the bathroom, staring at herself in the mirror that hung from the wall. She wore a floor-length gold gown that covered her arms in long strings of draping jewels. Much of her back was exposed, as were the scars that lingered there. Her hair was tucked up, showing her neck and the delicate skin of her shoulders.

"I don't want to do this," she said, barely a whisper.

I stepped into the room and shut the door behind me. I approached until I was behind her in the reflection, able to look into her eyes from behind. "That makes two of us."

She scoffed. "Don't pretend like we're in the same situation here, Wolf."

"I'm not pretending at all. I don't want to see you go through this, either."

She adjusted the straps of her dress. Fuck, she was so beautiful. I stepped closer, unable to stop myself, and lifted a finger to trace one of the scars that wrapped around her right shoulder.

She shivered as our skin made contact but didn't back away.

"I'll protect you tonight, Huntress, no matter what."

She smiled softly in the mirror. "I really wish I could believe that."

My stomach dropped. Of course, she couldn't actually

believe that. After everything I did, how could she possibly expect me to protect her?

"And if all else fails, there will be plenty of wine," I added, ignoring her diss of a comment.

"What do you think he wants with me tonight, anyway? Why go through all the trouble?" She turned to face me, her arm brushing mine. "He could just as easily keep me locked away until my full powers manifest."

"I think keeping you locked in a dungeon was clearly a bad idea, so he's doing whatever it takes to swing things in the other direction. I think he'll try to impress you, try to win you over."

"Like that will ever work."

"I know you, Huntress. You have to play this smart." I dropped the smile from my face and lifted her chin with one finger, making sure she really heard me. "He won't allow you to embarrass him tonight."

"How could I possibly embarrass an archangel?" She sucked in a breath, eyes wide.

"By defying him. By speaking out against him. Trust me, however much you hate him, you have to be careful." *Don't speak up. Don't be the sexy, stubborn, tough woman you are.* "He wants to have all the power. All of it. If he thinks for even a second that you have a leg to stand on, he'll—"

"I get it," she interrupted, tearing herself away. The scent of her washed over me as she moved to the other side of the room. "Keep my mouth shut and do as he says. I have some practice with powerful males, you know."

I tightened my fists at my sides. "That's not making me feel any better."

She glanced over her shoulder. I waited for some sort of remark on how it wasn't her job to make me feel better or some other quip, but she only smiled softly, something like pity etched onto her face. "Let's just get this over with so we can figure out how we're going to get out of it later, okay?"

I nodded. "Yeah, okay." She headed toward the door, but I stopped her. "Wait."

Her large, perfect eyes looked back at me, waiting. "What is it?"

I walked over to her slowly, taking my time as I closed the distance between us. "It's your birthday," I started.

She rolled her eyes. "Please don't remind me. I'm finally not on the verge of vomiting for once and I don't want to ruin it."

"It's your birthday," I said again, ignoring her interruptions. "I want to give you something."

She eyed me carefully as I approached, coming to stand a breath away from her. *Those fucking cherries.* She was damn near irresistible, and I hated that my father was going to parade her around the court tonight like his possession.

Huntyr wasn't someone to be contained. She was wild, free. Unstoppable.

Seeing her like this tonight, it wrapped a fist around my heart and squeezed. I knew what it felt like to be forced into this world, to be forced under his rule. There was no freedom. There was no independence.

Not until we found a way out of it.

"Here." I reached into the back of my belt and pulled out the dagger—Venom. Since Asmodeus dragged her to the dungeon, she hadn't asked about it.

She sucked in a breath as the metal came to view. "What —how did—"

"It has been safe with me this whole time. I wanted to give it to you sooner, but I didn't know if Asmodeus would search your things. I think tonight's a good night to have it back, though, wouldn't you agree?"

Tears welled in her eyes as she glanced between me and the dagger. "I can't believe this," she whispered, hiccupping a laugh. "I thought she was gone forever! I thought surely he would have destroyed this."

"I would never let that happen." It felt dramatic, this bold remark over a weapon, but we both knew Venom was much more than just a weapon. It was a reminder of home, of where Huntyr came from, of how much was at stake here.

A reminder to *live*.

Her fingers moved to curl around mine. "I don't know what to say, Wolf. Thank you."

A single tear escaped her charcoal-lined eyes, and I reached up to swipe it away quickly with my thumb. "Happy birthday, Huntress."

"Will you help me hide this in my dress?" Her voice suddenly became more hopeful than I had heard it in weeks.

I couldn't help but laugh. "Promise me you won't go stabbing Asmodeus the first chance you get. You know he can't be killed with this, right?"

She turned toward the bathroom. "It wouldn't hurt to try."

She braced herself over the counter, waiting for me. I sauntered after her, taking in every inch of her beauty before I reached up and unlaced her delicate bodice.

My body buzzed at the feeling of my hands brushing against her skin. Being this close to her always had that effect on me, always caused my heart to beat faster, my senses to lock in on her.

Ever so slowly, lace after lace, I untied her dress.

I stayed focused on my task, eyes not wandering to her

breasts that became more and more exposed as I further unlaced her.

She remained silent.

It wasn't until I unlaced her dress down to her waist that I finally looked in the mirror, only to find her looking back at me. A wave of emotion hit me though our bond. The last few days, it had been rare to get even a hint of what she was feeling.

It was as if she opened the floodgates, no longer hiding behind those walls she built.

I sucked in a breath as sweet longing and lust hit me. I ran my finger down her bare spine, feeling it even more.

"Huntress," I whispered, eyes fluttering closed.

She spun to face me, still leaning against the counter but looking directly into my eyes now. "Why did you do it?" she asked.

Through the lust and longing and want of the bond, I felt something break through, like glass shattering. It was hurt, pain, but not physical. This pain was deeper, darker, the kind you couldn't see.

And it was ten times worse.

"Do what?" I searched her eyes, looking for her beneath the sudden clouds in her features.

"You know what. Don't make me say it again."

Why did I betray her? Hurt her? Turn her in? Tell her I loved her and go back on everything I said? "I thought, once I completed the job for my father, I would get my white wings back. I thought he would allow me at least that for returning from Moira with you. I was naive back then, and I hadn't met you yet."

She waited, eyes wide. "You did this all for wings?"

I lifted a hand and ran my pointer finger down her jaw.

She tilted her head further, giving me more access as she closed her eyes briefly.

"I meant what I said earlier. He can take my wings ten times over if it means keeping you safe. All of that—the agreement with him, the plan to bring you back here—was before I knew you. Before I fell for you. Before I had a reason to fight for anything more."

Her eyes opened, glistening with fresh tears. "And now? He takes your wings and you do nothing but sit back and watch?"

"I'm waiting for the right time," I answered. "My time will come, Huntress, and I swear to the goddess above, I'll put a stop to this."

Her chest rose with a breath. "I don't want to get hurt again. I can't."

"I know."

"I'm afraid to trust you again."

A breath lingered between us.

"I know."

Her gaze landed on my mouth, and for a torturous, immaculate second, I thought she might kiss me. But that sharp dagger of pain shot through our bond again, the harsh reality that she was the one living with what I had done.

I did far more than simply betray her.

I was no worse than the male who spent his time giving her those scars.

She spun around, facing the mirror again before I could do something stupid like run my thumb across her perfectly plump lips or nuzzle my nose into her neck and inhale the intoxicating scent of her. "Put it here," she said, signaling to the side of her bodice. She held the front tightly against her as I maneuvered the metal against her skin.

"Are you sure about this?" I asked. "If someone sees that you have a weapon, it could end badly."

She stared at her own reflection in the mirror then, eyes glazing over as she answered, "Sharp blades and even sharper teeth. Weren't you the one who taught me that?"

I didn't answer, didn't trust myself to. Hells, when had I grown so soft? When had I let this woman crawl into the deep cave of my chest and funnel there, warming my icy heart from the inside out?

It didn't matter. I finished lacing her dress for her—even though we both knew she could do it herself—and led her to the door.

Huntyr would have my heart forever now, even if she would not accept it.

CHAPTER 9

HUNTYR

For the dark, colorless castle that Asmodeus lived in, he knew how to make a party look grand. There was still a massive lack of color, but large, pointed black pieces of art lined the perimeter of the ballroom, creating a terrifying yet beautiful wall around the crowd.

"There you are," Jessiah called, stepping forward out of the crowd. "I was starting to think you two bolted."

Wolf's bicep tensed under my grasp. "And miss a great party?"

Jessiah and him both smiled, but I was starting to pick up on the slight differences in their behavior when they were in public, as if they spent their entire lives creating a second personality that would secure their survival in front of their father.

My stomach tightened, lurching. Nerves, I told myself, not the constant hunger I had been fighting on and off.

Jessiah turned to me and held out his hand. I slid my palm into his but was surprised when he pulled my hand to his lips, kissing my knuckles gently. "Happy birthday, Huntyr," he whispered through thick lashes.

I could have sworn I heard Wolf growl, but Jessiah only laughed at my blush and dropped my hand. Charming bastard.

"Father is waiting for you both," he warned. He dropped his voice so only the two of us could hear as he added, "And he's been drinking plenty. Don't let her out of your sight."

Wolf nodded, guiding me further into the room. Twinkling lights lit up the ceiling at least two floors above us, creating a subtle glow of light among the crowd. I glanced around, taking in the slight glittering of everyone's marvelous attire.

It was a show indeed.

"Who are all these people?" I whispered to Wolf.

"Mostly angels, some fae. These are the people who support my father, either because he gives them money, or because he lets them continue their crimes and bad behaviors here in The Golden City. You can't trust anyone here, Huntyr, not a single person."

"You included?"

He chuckled lightly but bent over and whispered against my ear, "Careful, Huntress."

The crowd separated as we parted, but not because of me. Nobody even bothered looking at me. Everyone's eyes were glued on Wolf as we passed. Even without his wings, he was a force. A predator. A leader.

And these people envied him. I could see it in their eyes— the greed, the hunger for power.

It was no wonder they were ready to do whatever Asmodeus ordered.

We waltzed slowly through the crowd, past a group of musicians who filled the room with a pleasant melody.

Did these people all know Asmodeus was the evil bastard he was? Or were they living their lives in ignorance, pretending everything was okay? Pretending darkness wasn't swarming the entire world because of him?

That made me even more nauseous than the thought of swallowing mouthfuls of blood.

"Remember what we talked about," Wolf whispered. I shivered as his breath hit my cheek. "You're playing their game now. You can't win if you don't play by their rules."

"How could I forget? It's my damn life on the line."

I felt him stifle one of his arrogant laughs as we made our way to the front of the crowd. A massive wooden table was set up, spanning nearly the entire length of the ballroom. Black glasses of wine and black and gold plates of food lined the entire thing. It was grand; I couldn't believe that these luxuries even existed.

Was this what the entire city looked like before Asmodeus corrupted it all?

"Ah, there you are." Asmodeus pulled himself away from a female angel and walked over to us. Wolf rolled his shoulders back and lifted his chin. I did the same but held on tighter to his bicep. "Enjoying your party so far?"

I forced myself to meet his cold, uneasy gaze. "It is indescribable." My smile took all the energy I had left.

"It is, isn't it?" When he smiled, his teeth reflected the red wine he had clearly been drinking. I held onto Wolf even tighter to stop myself from backing away. "Sit, sit. Now that you are here, we will begin the feast!"

He turned to the crowd of people filling the ballroom.

"Everyone sit!" Spit flew from his mouth along with the words. "Our guest of honor is here! The party may finally begin!"

Asmodeus turned and ushered us to the head of the table. We walked around to the backside, Wolf pulled out the chair beside Jessiah. "For you, Huntress," he whispered. I blushed at his sultry voice but nodded, taking the seat. At least it was Jessiah sitting next to me and not a total stranger.

Wolf took the seat to my right, putting a barrier between me and the head of the table where Asmodeus sat. Luseyar and another angel I had seen before sat across from us, not even bothering to glance in our direction.

I sat in silence as the rest of the guests funneled to the massive table. I couldn't have seen them all if I tried, the table far too grand to accommodate actual conversation.

"Attention everyone!" Asmodeus pushed himself to his feet as everyone else sat. "I would like to thank everyone for coming to celebrate our special guests. You see, Huntyr is not simply a fae who survived Moira."

Starting with a big speech about me. Great. Both brothers shifted uncomfortably beside me.

"No, Huntyr here is someone special." His snake eyes landed on me as the room of people fell eerily silent. "Huntyr is only half-fae. Isn't that right? Half fae and half something else. Half something powerful."

This could not be happening. I rubbed my palms on my thighs and tried to stay calm. Why would he announce this here? Why now? I still had no strengthened powers, nothing to prove I really was the blood queen.

"Hyntyraina Fullmall Gawerula, Queen of Scarlata Empire."

Silence fell.

Then, the room erupted in chaos. Men further down the table began shouting, asking Asmodeus if it was really true and what I was doing here.

"Scarlata has fallen!" someone yelled. "What are you going to do with her? Kill the blood queen! Kill the blood queen!"

A wave of nausea hit me again, and I feared this time, it had nothing to do with my hunger pains.

"Enough!" Asmodeus said. "There is no need to kill the blood queen! Not when she is here in our kingdom, ready to give us her power."

Another wave of men shouting questions. I tried to tune it all out, tried to focus on my breathing, on picking up the chalice of wine in front of me and taking one small sip.

My hand shook. I nearly dropped the glass.

Wolf's hand slipped over to my knee, squeezing gently and not moving.

"How do I plan on securing this power?" Asmodeus continued with his speech, pausing to take more drinks of his wine and nearly falling over as he stood. "Well, that part is easy. I am not blind. I know she is a risk to us on her own, which is why I plan on changing that. Huntyraina here will be marrying one of my sons, and our bloodlines will forever be merged as one!"

What. The. Fuck.

I replayed the words in my head over and over again, making sure I hadn't missed something. Surely, I heard him wrong. Surely, he wasn't being serious.

"Right, boys?" Asmodeus asked. Wine sloshed over the edge of his cup and splattered on the table.

I turned my attention to Wolf, then to Jessiah. They both sat there with guilt dripping from their features.

"You knew about this?" I hissed to Wolf. "You knew he was going to force me to marry?"

Wolf tried to reach for my hand, but I pulled away. "Don't touch me," I snapped. "Tell me the fucking truth for once, Wolf. How long have you known?"

He couldn't meet my gaze. "Not long."

This was unbelievable. All of that before about helping me? About playing the game? All of that was so he could marry me for himself, take all the power I had to offer, and deliver it straight to his father.

Betraying me once a-fucking-gain.

I pushed myself up from the table, desperately trying to put space from myself and, well, everyone in this damn castle. I scrambled away from the tightly packed dining table but tripped over the long dress, crashing down on my hands and knees. Asmodeus laughed. Wolf and Jessiah both moved in an instant, coming to either side of me and lifting me by the elbows. "Leave me alone!" I hissed.

Laughter only increased, not just from Asmodeus, but from everyone in the ballroom. Taunting me. Enjoying the fucking mess that was my life.

Asmodeus tsked behind me. "You hadn't told the blood queen of her future wedding day?" he said through a fit of laughter. "Well, well, let me be the first to congratulate our beautiful blood bride."

He walked over to me, both brothers still flanking my sides. The amused smile faded from his lips as he announced, "You will marry one of my sons. I care not which you choose, but come the equinox, you will marry. My family will rule the blood kingdom, and I will rebuild Scarlata to be my kingdom of loyal, deadly warriors."

I grimaced at the words. *Play the game by their rules,* Wolf had said. Meanwhile, he knew all about this. He knew, and he didn't even think to warn me.

Heat flushed my cheeks—humiliation, hatred, all of it. I couldn't control it anymore, couldn't hold back the wave of brutal demise that fueled every single one of my senses.

Nausea threatened me. I had been suppressing my hunger for some time now, but all this emotion, all this heat in my body, only added to it. I sucked in a hiccupped breath, smoothing down my now-wrinkled dress. I needed...I needed...

"Come with me," Wolf whispered.

"Like hells! I'm not going anywhere with you." I heaved another breath.

"I'll take her." Jessiah stepped in, holding his hand out.

I slid my hand into his. He was part of this too, but at least he wasn't Wolf. At least he hadn't been lying directly to my face. *Again.*

"Over my dead fucking body," Wolf growled, his eyes lighting up. He wrapped an arm around my bicep and yanked me away from his brother before I could protest.

Then, we were moving, though I could only comprehend some of what was happening as Wolf dragged me through the room now filled with chants and laughter and taunting.

How could this be happening? And why did I care so much?

A sob crashed through my body as Wolf pushed open the doors to the hallway. He dragged me a few more steps, my feet barely hitting the ground as he navigated us to a more private area of the castle, an area where I could no longer hear the sick angels and fae in the other room.

Tears were already falling down my cheeks by the time Wolf stopped walking and released me. "Let me explain, Huntress."

"Explain?" I hiccupped another pathetic breath. "Explain what, exactly? How you've been promising me an escape when, this whole time, you knew I would have to marry one of you?"

He came closer, reaching out almost as if he were about to touch me. I flinched away, watching the hurt slide over his eyes. "It's not like that, and you know it. He just recently told us his plans to marry you off. I swear to you, I've only known for a few days."

"I should have been the first fucking person to know!" I was crying hysterically now, unable to keep everything suppressed. I pressed myself against the wall, running my hands across my wet face and through my mess of hair. "I can't do this. I can't fucking do this."

"You can. You can because you have to, do you understand me? You *have* to do this."

"I don't want to talk to you right now. I don't even want to look at you."

"I swear to you, I am going to get us out of this."

"What do you think he'll do once we are wed?" I blinked through the tears to glare at him. He stood with his hands on his hips now, his chest rising and falling with each rapid breath. "What do you think his plan is once that is done? He's going to control me for the rest of my life, Wolf. And you and Jessiah are helping him!"

He lowered his voice as he said, "We are not helping him."

"But you'd gladly marry me to please him? You'll gladly follow his orders when it suits you, is that right?"

"Is that so fucking terrible, Huntyr?" he pushed. "Of everything that has happened to you, of everything you've been through, that is what disgusts you the most? Is it so bad that you'd have to marry *me* to survive? Because that's what it's between, Huntyr. It's marrying me or death. But I can see how much that decision makes you sick."

"I will *never* marry you. You—" My throat stung through shaking breaths. "You have betrayed me again and again and again. Every time I think I can trust you, you—" I couldn't even finish the words. My tears took over, a mixture of crying and hysterics. "If I must marry, I choose him."

Electricity buzzed around us, and I became very aware of my own heart beating, of the sound of my broken breaths filling the air.

Wolf dipped his chin and laughed beneath his breath.

He moved too fast. He stormed forward and gripped my arm, yanking me toward the door. I tried to pull myself free, but it was no use. Wolf moved with a power mixed with anger and lust, and I felt every frivolous emotion through that damn bond as he continued dragging me down the depths of the hallway.

"Let go of me," I demanded.

He only laughed again, with even less humor than the last time. His fingers dug into me until I was sure they would bruise, and then he spun me around and shoved me against the wall.

"You think I will let you marry my brother? Is this a game to you, Huntress? Is this one of your tricks?"

His eyes flickered with lightning as he snarled. I tried to flinch away, even further back into that wall, but there was nowhere to go. He released his tight grip on my arm and boxed me in with his body.

"I don't care what you think," I muttered, voice wavering. "I'm not marrying you."

"So you'd rather share a bed with him? You hate me that much?"

The air thickened between us, almost crackling. My breath hitched as I stared into his eyes, searching for my answer. Yes, I hated him. I hated him for betraying me.

I would not sit back and play into his plans without a fight.

"Yes, I do. I'd marry a complete stranger before I trusted you again."

Something dark flashed across his features before he bent down and picked me up with my waist flung across his shoulder.

"Wolf!" I yelled. "Put me down!" He didn't hesitate before storming in the direction of our bedrooms. His footsteps were fierce and aggressive, his strong hand clinging to the back of my thighs. A few seconds later, he was kicking open his bedroom door and carrying me inside. The smell of him hit me instantly, enveloping us both in pine and smoke.

"Hells, Wolf! What are you doing?"

He dropped me then, flinging me against the back of the door with hardly any effort.

"You forget, Huntress." He paced the room, running his hands through his unruly hair with tense movements.

"Forget what?"

He stopped to look at me, chest rising and falling with heavy breaths. "You forget that you *are* mine. Nobody else can have you, even if you hate me."

Was he serious? Could he truly not see that he didn't get a

say? "If your father is forcing me to marry, it won't be you. You don't get to control me like this. Not anymore."

He crept forward and put both hands on the wall behind my head. "He will not fucking touch you, Huntyr. You can hate me all you want, but I'm not going to watch you marry my own brother."

"Why not?" I tilted my head to the side, tears still streaming down my face. "Is it because you care so much about me?"

He answered through gritted teeth, "Yes."

I laughed then, and Wolf flinched slightly at the sound of it. "You're a fucking liar, Wolf."

"You *will* marry me."

"I absolutely will *not*."

"I'm not above forcing your hand, Huntress. You haven't seen me possessive yet." The intensity in his voice sent a shiver down my body.

"You can force me to the altar all you want, Wolf, but it will be your brother I swear my life to."

Without warning, both of his hands landed on my neck, lifting my mouth to his as he pressed a fierce, rushed kiss onto my lips. It was hard, aggressive, filled with anger and envy and lust and violence. His entire body pressed against me, pinning me to the wall.

I wasn't sure what the fuck got into me, but I kissed him back just as angrily. I pulled his lower lip into my mouth and bit, but he only growled and kissed me harder, squeezing my neck lightly as I threw my arms around his waist.

The thin fabric of my dress did nothing to hide my own body's betrayal to him. With one hand applying pressure to my neck and holding me still against the door, the other slid up the slit of my dress to the aching apex of my thighs. "Does my brother touch you like this, Huntress?" His fingers teased me over the fabric of my panties before he slid a finger beneath the hem and ripped them off completely.

I gasped as the cool air hit my wetness, but Wolf only growled in approval as he felt how much I needed him.

He took his time kissing me deeply as one finger dipped inside. Fuck, I needed him. I needed him *now*.

I fought the urge to grind my hips against his hand, but fighting it became damn near impossible. My legs trembled as he moved his thumb in circles against my sensitive peak.

"Answer me," he demanded against my mouth. "Does my brother touch you this way?" He added another finger, pumping deeper inside me until I crumbled in his grasp.

"No." My eyes fluttered closed. "No, he doesn't."

"Good girl."

Before I could fall apart entirely in his hands, he dropped to his knees before me, forcing one of my legs over his shoulder and breathing against my exposed core. But he didn't stop there. He held me up against the door with his hands while he flicked his tongue against me, feasting on my body and pulling his name from my lips before I had a chance to fight it.

He only moaned in satisfaction, lapping his tongue harder and faster until I was trembling, shaking.

I would have said anything to chase the release that only he could provide me. Goddess fucking help me. Wolf didn't stop until my climax wrecked my body, and even then, he held me against that door until he was satisfied with himself, until he tasted enough of me.

Slowly, he let my leg slide off his shoulder. Slowly, he stood back up to face me.

"Nobody else gets to touch you, Huntyr. Get that through

your thick fucking head, because if you have to marry anyone to stay alive before I can get us out of this mess, it will be me."

And then he stormed off, leaving me crumbling in the shadows of the bedroom, lips swollen and face wet, wondering what the fuck just happened.

CHAPTER 10
WOLF

Light simmered in my palm. Alone in the dark shadows of the vacant wing of the castle, I took a long breath, watching the way my power moved and flickered across my skin.

I spent so much of my time suppressing my full potential, and it was a relief to come here and let it seep out of me, like running out extra energy.

My magic was growing. I didn't want to accept that being near Huntyr affected my power, but it was true. I noticed it in Moira, and ever since we bonded during the Transcendent, it was undeniable.

Huntyr's power growing was changing me too, which was why I needed help.

I quieted my senses and let my ears focus on the castle around me, ensuring no other living being was in this wing of the castle. My knees grew sore against the stone floor beneath me as I let my head fall back.

To anyone else, I surely would look sadistic, and that was *before* what came next.

I pulled out the small dagger I kept in the sheath at my hip and sliced my palm. I didn't even flinch as the blood pooled there, dripping down to the floor.

Drip.

Drip.

Drip.

At least Moira was right about something: drawing blood was the quickest way to access your deepest pools of magic.

But for me, it could access something else too. I'd been able to speak with Era herself since my father sacrificed my soul. She came to me in dreams on occasion, but this time, I needed to speak with her on *my* terms. I had been patient long enough.

I closed my eyes and let my magic flutter around the spilled blood.

And then, I waited.

I didn't know why I felt this connection to Era. I only knew that this was all happening for a reason, a reason she kept me hanging on for but never divulged.

I was getting sick of anticipating her next move.

With my eyes tightly shut, I felt my power swirling around me. It started slow but picked up second after second, until the air in the room created a whirlpool of magic and light and power.

Era was answering my call.

I saw her in the depths of my mind before she said anything. This was how she always appeared to me—always in my mind, never in the flesh, which was why I became so skeptical of what she really wanted from me.

"You summon me, boy?" she asked. Her words were smoother than honey, but the back of my mind twitched with the power I knew she possessed.

This was the Goddess of Vaehatis. She was more powerful than any being in existence, my father included.

"Yes, I do. I need to know what your plan is. What do you want from me? What do you want from *her*? I was fine with staying in the dark before, but things have changed. There's not much more she can take." The words rushed out of me in a desperate force.

Era became clearer in my mind, the smoke of power fading as she stepped forward. "Everything is happening as it should."

It was always riddles and half-truths with her. Before, that was fine, but now, I required more.

Era read my mind easily, listening to my thoughts before I had a chance to speak. "You worry for the girl."

"Yes, I do. She thinks I am betraying her."

"The only way to save her life, to save everyone you love, is to follow my orders carefully. Your father is a powerful man who has been corrupting this place for a long, long time. Patience is required to have ultimate peace, Wolf."

I took a long breath. Arguing with the powerful goddess was likely not the best idea, but this still wasn't helping me.

I needed to understand why. Why did Era want to use me as a pawn? Why did she want me to protect Huntyr, to stay here with my father?

"All in due time, child." Her voice faded slowly, and the picture of her perfect face in my mind began to blur. "You and the girl are both much, much stronger than you believe. I need you both. Do not give up when we are so close."

"So close to *what*?"

But it didn't matter how much more blood I spilled, how much I called out to her. Era, the Goddess of Vaehatis, was gone.

"She's refusing to marry you, isn't she?" Jessiah teased. Two days passed, two days of avoiding my bedroom at all costs, of lingering outside the door, too afraid to enter.

She needed time to accept this. Once she realized she had no other option, she would get on board.

But that was only one of our problems. Huntyr's cravings were growing. She kept our bond closed as much as she could, but every so often, I could feel the pain wrecking her entire body.

Hunger. It was a different type of pain, not one similar to stabbings or other physical injuries. It was something dull and unavoidable, something that tortured you slowly until you lost your mind.

She would have to feed, and soon. Eventually, she would reach a point where she could no longer refuse, where her body would need blood to survive. Feeding would be just the beginning.

From controlling her feeding, to a new rush of magic, to new strength and speed and vampyre abilities, her entire reality would change, and this was all while we were navigating Asmodeus and everything else he wanted.

"She'll come around," I added. My father waltzed into the room lazily, his long, white robe trailing behind him.

Still, his teasing smile didn't leave his face. "Trouble in paradise, son?"

My face heated. Yes, there was trouble. There was also the

messy new complication of Huntyr's taste still lingering on my tongue, burned into my memory. "It will all be fine soon enough."

"Good," he said. "Because there's something I need from you. Both of you, actually."

Jessiah shifted in his seat across from me at the breakfast table. "What's going on?"

"Scarlata is still crawling with vampyres, but I plan on sending some of ours that way to begin rebuilding while our blood queen is still stepping into her power."

"You want us to go to Scarlata?" I pushed. "Isn't that dangerous?"

"Yes, it is, but you'll be bringing her with you."

Bring Huntyr to Scarlata?

"What exactly do you want us to do there?" Jessiah asked. "Scope out grounds?"

"I need a good idea of what's left—buildings that are still standing, anyone living there who is sane, remaining fae in the area, anything."

I leaned forward. "Can't you send some of your other men there? Huntyr's weak since she isn't feeding. She won't survive an attack if we encounter hungry ones on the journey."

My father pulled out a chair and sat down, leaning back and stroking his own chin in thought. "No. This is going to be your kingdom to rule, son. One of you, anyway." Another teasing smile. "Bring her with you. Perhaps it's the last bit of motivation she needs to finish her transition and become who she was born to be."

"When?" Jessiah asked.

"Start packing," he said. "You'll have to take the horses, as only one of you has wings." Again, not a single speck of guilt laced his words. It would have been nice if he at least acknowledged that he was to blame for my missing wings, but that would require him to care. "You'll be on your way by nightfall. It's a three-day journey on horseback, so you'll need to get started as soon as possible."

"Just us three, then?" I didn't know whether I was relieved or annoyed that he wasn't sending a single guard on this trip with us. The journey was dangerous, but if time taught me anything, it was that my father had an ulterior motive here. He was always testing us, pushing our limits.

This was no different.

My father's cold gaze met mine. "Doubting the task, son?"

I shook my head, pushing myself from the breakfast table. "Nope. We'll be on our way come sunrise."

"**A**re you fucking kidding me?" Huntyr asked. "You want me to travel three days with you and Jessiah into vampyre territory?"

I stayed near the door, not wanting to risk moving any closer to her. I thought about our kiss every damn minute of every day since it happened. It was impulsive and reckless and stupid as all hells, but she actually kissed me back.

Something in her still cared for me, if that's what you'd even call it. Something in her wanted me, enough to kiss me back, at least.

And that was all the hope I needed.

"We don't exactly have a choice, Huntress. Besides, you've

spent your entire life tracking and killing them. We'll be perfectly safe."

"And Jessiah? He's okay with storming into vampyre territory?"

"He's skilled with a sword. It won't be a problem."

She threw herself back onto the bed and groaned. I felt another wave of her hunger threaten the bond.

"You'll need to eat, Huntress. You won't survive the journey like this, and we both know it."

"I'm not hungry." She threw a hand over her eyes, blocking out the sun.

"I'm not talking about food."

She stilled, freezing for a second before lifting her head and looking at me again. "I don't need blood."

"You do, and the sooner you realize it, the better. You can't run from your cravings forever. That's how they control you. That's how you become one of the hungry ones."

"I'll never become one of them."

"Agreed, which is why you need to feed now." I took the risk and stepped closer, slowly putting one foot after another until I stood at the edge of the bed. "I can help you, you know."

"I don't need your help."

I stepped even closer, moving to the side of the bed where she laid. "It's not just my help I'm offering."

I kept both hands clasped behind my back, but her eyes landed on me once again. She knew what I meant. If it was my blood she wanted, she could have it. All of it was hers; all of me was hers.

"I'd rather starve to death than feed from you, thanks." She flashed me a sassy, don't-fucking-talk-to-me smile and rolled over in bed.

"Suit yourself," I said, stepping away. "But at this rate, I'd give you two more days of this. You'll continue to suffer until you feed."

"Suffering isn't a foreign concept to me, Wolf. I think I'll be fine."

I clenched my jaw, forcing my anger down. "We'll leave at sunrise. Be ready to go then. And don't do anything stupid. Luseyar will be waiting outside your door until then."

She mumbled another response that sounded something like *fuck you*, but I was already heading out the door.

The next three days would be worse than any test in Moria, worse than the Transcendent, even worse than all of it.

But my purpose didn't change. *Keep Huntyr alive.* That was my goal, always, and it was about to get very fucking difficult.

CHAPTER II

Huntyr

I knew that there had to be another way in and out of
The Golden City. At Moira Seminary, we were forced to
believe that the only way in was through the Transcendent. But Wolf left. The angels were not stuck in this city
forever. *There had to be another way.*

Even though I saw just how difficult it would be to
somehow get over this damn wall, it was guarded. I tilted my
head to the sky, squinting as I took in the handful of soldiers
who patrolled the top of the towering structure.

As if anyone could get that close. I wouldn't be surprised
if Asmodeus used his magic to extend an invisible wall even
higher than the stone, killing anyone who dared enter.

Still. Wolf had gotten out. Others surely left if they were
permitted to. There was another way out of here.

And I was about to see it.

What I wasn't expecting, though, were tunnels.

Fucking *tunnels.*

There was no magic path, no ominous route through the
wall, no ladder to climb over the towering structure. "This is

it?" I asked as we approached the back of The Golden City, just feet away from the edge. "This is what gets us out of here?"

Wolf knelt ahead of us, pulling the large stone away from the entrance. To anyone else, it looked like part of the stone road that led throughout the entire city. But as he opened the entrance, I saw what really hid beneath. A long, dark, underground passageway.

"After you," Jessiah said from behind.

I hesitated. "What's the trick here? What's the catch?"

"No catch," Wolf answered. His face was straight. Serious. "These tunnels take us beneath the wall."

I still couldn't get myself to move. My mind was spinning, trying to find the obvious flaw in this logic. "You're kidding, right?"

"Not at all, Huntress." Wolf straightened before lowering himself into the entrance, landing at the bottom and ducking to stare up at me. "Are you coming? Or would you prefer to stay here?"

Anger flooded my senses. "You're telling me that we had to *die* to get in here the first time, when there were fucking *tunnels* that would have led us inside?"

Jessiah shifted uncomfortably behind me, but I kept my eyes glued on Wolf. His jaw tightened, his nostrils flared. Surely, he was trying to form some sort of lie, some sort of story to cover this all up.

"It's not that simple," he said. "And we don't have time to explain right now." He turned and started down the dark passageway.

I jumped in after him, the air instantly cooling as I maneuvered my body. I could stand fully, but Wolf hunched ahead of me to avoid hitting his head. "You're not getting off that easy," I yelled. "Why did we have to die? Why couldn't we use these the first time? Hells, Wolf! You died, too!"

I was half-running to keep up with his long strides, but he stopped in an instant, spinning to face me so quickly that I nearly ran straight into his chest.

"Because that wasn't the plan, Huntyr." Wolf's breath hit my face as his chest heaved. Jessiah was re-adjusting the stone over the entrance of the tunnel, cutting off any sunlight that would have filtered through. "The plan was to die. The plan was to trust Era, okay? Besides, we couldn't have found the tunnel from the outside without help."

He turned to continue walking, but I gripped his bicep and forced him to stop. "What plan? Asmodeus's plan?"

"No." My eyesight was getting stronger. Even in the darkness, I saw the way Wolf's gaze flickered over my shoulder to Jessiah before he chose his next words. "Era told me, okay? She told me we had to pass the Transcendent like everyone else. So we did. And we're both still alive, so there's no use discussing this now."

When he spun out of my grasp again, I didn't stop him.

My mind spun with the information, trying to pull apart Wolf's words.

"Don't think for a second that you can get through these tunnels without us," Jessiah added from behind me. I finally forced myself to keep walking. It only took a minute or two to reach the other end.

"And why is that?"

Wolf pushed open the exit above our heads. Sunlight flooded in, followed by the lush scent of fresh air.

"Take a look for yourself," Jessiah answered.

I ignored Wolf's outstretched hand and crawled out of the tunnel, squinting as my eyes adjusted to the light. I pushed myself to my feet and brushed my dirty hands on my trousers before fully taking in our surroundings.

Jessiah was right. We weren't just out in the forest, free from The Golden City. We were standing just feet away from the massive, towering wall, but in front of us stood a small, wooden building that appeared to be horse stables.

"Welcome to the stables," Wolf said, stepping up beside me.

It all looked so normal, like this building existed here for decades in the peace of the forest.

"How is this possible?" I asked. One of the horses grazed freely in the grass a few feet away.

Neither of them answered. Instead, they turned toward the door of the stables that slowly opened, revealing a cloaked figure stepping toward us.

Nobody spoke as the man approached.

But then he stopped a few feet away from us, pausing for a moment before removing the cloak. He was a few decades older than us. A long gray beard hung from his face, and tanned skin wrinkled around his face as he scowled, unmoving. "I don't believe my damn eyes."

My heart stopped, adrenaline pushing into my limbs from the wave of unknown. I was ready to fight. I was ready to draw Venom and prepare for an attack.

But Jessiah stepped forward, closing the distance between them in two swift steps and throwing an arm around the man.

To my surprise, the man hugged him back.

"It's been years, Griffith!" Jessiah greeted as he pulled back, letting Wolf walk up and greet the man just as warmly. "I didn't know if you would still be here!"

"Of course, I'm still here," Griffith replied. "Who else is going to make sure these beauties survive out here?"

Wolf stayed quiet, but I could feel the small trickle of joy filtering through our bond. Whoever this man was to them, he was important.

I found myself standing awkwardly while the three reunited.

The man—Griffith—paused when he noticed Wolf's lack of wings. "I heard the whisperings, but I didn't want to believe it myself." The air stilled. The birds even seemed to stop chirping.

"Don't worry about me, old man," Wolf replied with a smile. "I've missed these horses, anyway. Who needs wings when you've got a four-legged creature willing to take you anywhere you need to go, right?"

Another beat of silence lingered. Jessiah glanced down at his own feet and shoved his hands in his pockets. I fought the urge to do the same.

But eventually, Griffith smiled. "That's damn right, son. Let's get you boys set up with the best animals we've got."

Griffith winked at me—his only acknowledgement of my existence—and turned toward the stables. Jessiah followed quickly after him, but Wolf lingered back, waiting for me. I could tell in his pleading gaze that he didn't want me to ask any questions.

And even though I was still pissed off and confused, I kept my mouth shut.

Wolf walked in after me, holding the stable door open until I was inside. It was small but tidy. Griffith had his own living space in the corner, covered in blankets and pillows and lanterns. The horses had individual stalls inside the building, each one clean and spacious. I could tell he deeply cared for these horses, it was more than a job to him.

I liked Griffith already.

"Wolf, you still remember the ropes around here?" Griffith asked as he walked to the end of the stables.

"I sure do," Wolf answered.

"Good. You can help your friend here get adjusted. I'll take your brother to one of the new mares outside. Meet us out there when you're ready."

The way they spoke was so familiar, like they had known each other for years. Griffith said nothing else as he opened the far door to the stables and led Jessiah back outside.

There had to have been ten horses here at least. The fact that they were protected here for so long with just one man...

"We're within the protection of The Golden City," Wolf said in a low voice. He busied himself with greeting the horses in the stalls around us. "The hungry ones can't touch anyone here. Nobody gets in unless Griffith lifts the magic to this place." He answered my unspoken questions without even looking at me.

"Griffith controls the magic of the wall?"

Wolf shrugged. "Only to these stables. The tunnels take us here, and Griffith can let us out from this point. But the only way back is also through him."

I stayed quiet as Wolf ran his hand down the nose of a beautiful white horse. He was good with them. He whispered to them softly, greeting each of the three horses inside the stables before finally opening the stall door to one of them.

"Here," he said. "This one's for you. She's calm but quick." He led the beautiful horse over to where I stood. Something in her eyes held power. Confidence.

This horse was a warrior.

"Have you ridden before?" Wolf stared at me with arrogant, amused eyes as I approached the large animal.

She blew a puff of breath into my face as I reached out and grabbed her loose reins. "Yep," I lied.

"Good," Wolf said. "I was over here thinking you *hadn't* ridden a horse before, considering you were raised in *Midgrave*, and that you would have to ride with me for your own safety, but it looks like I was wrong."

"You were very wrong." I slid my hand down the horse's long, white neck. She really was a beauty. Hells, I *wished* we had been lucky enough to have horses in Midgrave. Nobody there could keep them fed, though, much less safe. "I won't be needing your assistance. Or your attitude, for that matter."

Wolf smiled at me in the shadows of the stables and leaned back onto the wooden wall, crossing his arms over his chest. "That's great." He smirked as if he knew I was lying, but I wasn't going to give him the satisfaction. "Hop on, then. Jessiah will be waiting for you out front."

I mean, Wolf could do it. How hard could it possibly be?

I walked to the side of the horse, moving my hand from the soft, silky fur to the thick saddle. *Just hoist yourself up. It won't be that bad.*

Yeah, I was very, very wrong about horses. As soon as I gripped the saddle and hoisted myself up, the massive beauty beneath me moved. She took a few steps forward, then backward, and when I pulled on the reins to try and gain control, she bucked completely, lifting her front two legs off the ground and sending me tumbling backward. I landed in a thin pile of hay, not nearly enough to break my fall.

"Shit," I mumbled under my breath as I tried to force air back into my lungs.

"Dammit, Huntyr." Wolf was at my side in an instant, hands on my head, my shoulders, my torso. "Are you alright?"

I forced a smile. "What? No snide remark on how I can't ride a horse?"

His brows furrowed as I winced. A shooting pain came from my back, just behind my ribs. I shifted, but Wolf was already on it, inspecting the area. A few seconds later, he yanked a small piece of wood free from the wound.

I nearly punched him in the face. "Dammit, Wolf! You could have warned me!"

"*You* could have told *me* you couldn't actually ride a horse. Do you know how dangerous that could be? Especially on a three-day journey! Hells, you could have died trying to ride her!"

"Sounds plenty better than riding with you for three days straight."

A sharp pierce of emotion flooded our bond before Wolf shut the window between us. It was rare of him to hide his emotions from me, I realized. At first, I thought it was because he wanted me to feel how sorry he was, but now, he started to hide more and more.

"Come on," he said, standing. "We'll get you bandaged up before we start our journey. The last thing you need is an infection from the stables."

I let him pull me up but didn't miss the way he avoided my gaze as he led me to the back of the horse stables and began rumbling through the spare medical supplies.

The more steps I took, the more the wound in my ribs stung.

"Lift up your shirt," he ordered, sounding more annoyed than anything. I did as I was told, rolling my fitted black tunic up just above the wound.

His jaw clenched as he studied it. "This is going to hurt," he warned.

He wasn't lying. I hissed in pain as he poured alcohol over the wound, catching it with a clean cloth and wiping the skin dry.

I tried not to flinch with every touch as he pulled out every small piece of hay. "Sorry," he mumbled so quietly, I barely heard him.

"You can't just heal me with your magic? Wouldn't that be faster?"

He stilled, eyes widening. "Don't say things like that around here. It isn't safe."

"What isn't safe?"

His voice was hardly audible as he whispered, "I don't have healing magic, Huntyr. I've never healed before."

The lie rolled off his tongue effortlessly. Chills rose on my arms at the solemn tone of his voice. He could heal, I'd seen it.

But he let the wounds from his severed wings take weeks to heal. For whatever reason, he was serious about keeping his magic a secret.

He bent over, adjusting his gaze on my wound as he blew on the skin. Not only was his breath a nice relief from the stinging pain cursing through my torso, but his warm hands fell on my hips to hold me still.

I couldn't control my body's reaction to him—the goosebumps that flooded me, the wave of need. Too late, I secured the shield to our bond so he wouldn't know what I was feeling.

But if he noticed, he said nothing. He worked in silence as he eventually pulled away and secured a bandage around my torso. I was still torturously aware of the brush of his knuckles as he lowered my shirt. "There," he sighed. "That's going to be sore tomorrow, but at least it will be clean. Now, let's go. Jessiah's waiting." He stormed off, leaving me scrambling after him through the stables.

Wolf's horse was much different than mine. The animal wasn't white and feminine like my horse had been. No, Wolf's horse was a shadow, sleek and black and absolutely massive.

"Holy shit," I mumbled as Wolf led us to him. "That animal is huge."

Wolf finally smiled, and I hated the way my chest twisted. "The biggest horse we have. I've had her since she was a baby. I haven't ridden her in a while because, well, with my wings, there wasn't much need."

Guilt cursed through me. Fuck, I should *not* be feeling sorry for him. He was the one who betrayed me. He was the one who did this to himself.

Still, I dropped my gaze when he looked in my direction.

"Need help getting on?"

I approached the god of an animal slowly, making sure he warmed up to my presence. "I–" I took a long breath. "Yes."

I could have sworn I felt something else through the bond then—something like relief. "Come on, Huntress. Up you go."

The saddle was too high for me to hoist myself up. Wolf knelt down and gripped my foot, wrapping an arm around my leg as I pressed up on his shoulders to reach the horse's back. Even in the cool morning air, I felt the heat through his shirt, felt everywhere his body touched mine as I swung my leg over the animal.

Wolf immediately backed up and gripped the reins, making sure to control him. "Good," he muttered, more to the horse than to me. Then, he walked back over and hauled himself onto the saddle just behind me, like it took no effort for him at all. Aside from his thighs brushing against mine, he kept himself as far away from me as possible.

I didn't care. In fact, I preferred it. Hells, I didn't want to ride with Wolf in the first place, but I knew it took a lot more effort to keep himself away from me on that small saddle.

Wolf led the horse out of the stables into the morning light, where Jessiah waited for us on his own brown horse. "There you two are. I was starting to think you left without me."

"Of course not," Wolf joked, his chest barely brushing my back as the horse halted. "We need you to feed to the hungry ones if we get attacked on our way to Scarlata."

"Very funny," he replied dryly. Griffith finished securing the saddlebags on the back of Jessiah's horse. "And I hope you both ate, because there is no way I'm letting you take my blood if we starve out there."

"Like you could stop me." The vibrations of Wolf's laugh radiated through my body.

"Are you both ready?" Griffith asked, stepping between us. "You have what you need?"

"We're ready," they said in unison.

Griffith nodded, but I could see the concern that weighed his features. He cared for these two. He cared what happened to them. "Good," he replied. "Be safe out there. I'll see you when you return."

And then he waved his hand toward the forest. I couldn't see a damn thing, but I could *feel* it. A small area of that invisible, protective shield that surrounded the entire wall of The Golden City called out to us, pulling us forward.

"Always a pleasure, Griffith." Wolf kicked our horse into a trot, barreling toward the forest. The sudden speed of the horse forced my body back into his, but Wolf stayed perfectly upright, maneuvering the reins around my body with ease.

Jessiah caught up to us a few seconds later, his white angel wings falling on either side of his brown horse.

And then we were off. The horse ran for a few minutes before eventually slowing to a walk. I turned to peer over Wolf's shoulder, but the stables that had just been there were gone, hidden by the thick magic that protected the entire city.

I said nothing as we marched away from the wall, deeper into the thick, lush forest that separated us from the ruins of Scarlata Empire.

Hours passed. My legs ached from the trotting of the horse, and my body all but screamed at me any time I tried to pull myself away from Wolf. Eventually, I let my body relax into his, no matter how much he tried to stay away from me. But he didn't seem to mind. He just kept us down the straight path in the woods, the sun filtering through the canopy above and the birds chirping at our arrival.

After an entire day of riding through the forest, I had to admit it was a nice contrast to the absolute dungeon of The Golden City. I found myself turning my head up and staring at the tall trees. They relaxed me. Mesmerized me.

It reminded me of the forest back home in Midgrave. Quiet, except for the community of everything else that lived out here in peace. Green, lush bushes coated the area around our trail. I pictured what it would be like to slip off this horse, to run away, to live out here forever.

"You're smiling," Wolf said. It was the first time he'd spoken to me since we left.

I cleared my throat and refocused my attention forward, where Wolf couldn't see my face. "I'm just thinking."

"About killing me?" His voice finally held that teasing tone I didn't even realize I'd missed.

"That seems like it would fix a lot of my problems, actually."

His mouth came close to my ear as he whispered, "Careful, Huntress."

A shiver rattled my bones. I made sure our bond was closed completely, but this close to him, it was hard to separate ourselves, our emotions.

As if on cue, a roll of hunger wrecked my stomach. I hunched over, groaning in pain. "Fucking hells," I muttered.

"Jessiah, hold up!" Wolf called ahead of us, and Jessiah's horse stopped instantly, backing up to us.

"I'm fine." The words were followed with another wave of hunger, another moan I couldn't keep in. Goddess above, is this how vampyres felt when they were hungry? Are these really my vampyre cravings?

The last few days, they came and went. I was happy to ignore them, especially when I still wasn't ready to accept that I was one of them, one of the creatures I spent my entire life killing.

I mean, how messed up could this get?

"No, you're not fine," Wolf sighed. He slid off the saddle before grabbing me by the waist and hoisting me down. "You have to feed, Huntyr. Soon."

"Just give me a damn minute." I tried to stand up straight but immediately doubled over, wrapping my arms around my waist again as if that could fix me, as if that could stop the pain that threatened to break me.

"You don't need a minute. You need to *feed*."

Jessiah slid off his own horse. "Maybe this is a good place to rest for the night. You two clearly have some things to discuss." He pulled both of our horses through the forest, getting lost in the green foliage.

Wolf's hands were on me, hovering, searching for a way to help.

But he couldn't help me, not like this.

"I'm not drinking blood," I said before he could argue. "I'm not ready, Wolf."

His face contorted in pity. "You're never going to be ready. Nobody is ready, especially somebody who just recently found out they are a vampyre."

"*Half* vampyre," I corrected.

"Right. *Half* vampyre."

I took a few long breaths, willing the hunger to pass, before I finally pushed myself to stand. This hunger, this wicked thing inside me, would *not* be the thing that broke me. I would not allow it to be the *one thing* that brought me to my knees after all of this.

"You might not be ready," Wolf added, "but your body is." He slid a hand up the side of my neck, rubbing his thumb against my cheekbone.

My breath hitched. "I need more time."

Wolf's eyes softened as he tilted his head to the side. "Time is something we don't have." The moon glistened above us, giving us the smallest amount of light in the eerily dark forest, just enough light to see the way Wolf pulled his hand from me and removed the blade from his hip.

Then, he sliced his own forearm.

"You once offered me your own blood when I needed it the most. Consider this me returning the favor."

CHAPTER 12
WOLF

She was already backing away, but even as she shook her head and held her hands between us as a barrier, I could see it in her eyes.

The hunger. The want. The need.

I knew the feeling all too well. I also knew how disgusted she would be by this, how much she would hate herself once it was done for the first time.

The shame, the hatred. It was unavoidable. But at least I could help her through this. I could guide her through this.

"Listen to your body, Huntyr."

"Get away from me." Her words were merely a breath, and as soon as one breeze blew across my dripping blood and caressed her black, curly hair, she stopped backing up.

Her dark pupils widened.

"I can help you."

I stepped forward, putting only inches of space between us as I held out my bleeding forearm.

"Wolf," she sighed, begging. "Please."

"Please what?" I asked. "Please stop? Please leave? Please

116

clean the wound and leave you starving, suffering?" Her breath hitched. "You forget that I can feel this," I put a hand over her stomach. "I can *feel* the hunger, Huntyr, even if you try your best to hide it from me."

"Wolf," she repeated, eyes darting between the blood and my face.

Tears threatened her eyes now, welling at the red rims. "Let me help you, Huntress."

Her eyes fluttered closed, and I watched as she took a long, painful breath. When her eyes opened, the fight was gone.

"Okay," she sighed.

Her hands reached for my forearm, but I pulled away at the last second. "Just one thing I need from you."

"What?" Her eyes widened in panic.

"Marry me," I demanded. "Tell me you'll be mine, and you can take it all."

She whimpered, and the sound alone nearly brought me to my knees.

"I'm not marrying you," she argued.

I took a step back, taking my blood with me and clicking my tongue once. "Still so stubborn. Fine; then you'll have to find Jessiah to help you, though he may not be as willing."

I moved to turn away, but she stopped me with a hand on my bicep. "Wait."

Silence lingered, heavier than any weight. "Yes, Huntress?"

One thick swallow. "I'll do it."

"I need to hear more than that." Blood dripped down my elbow, landing on the forest ground beneath us. "I need to hear you say it."

"I'll agree to marry you." She spit the words out as quickly as possible. "I'll do it."

I couldn't stop the smile that spread on my face, the satisfaction that rolled through my body at the sound. Yes, this was all forced, but those words...

Huntyr would be mine. Not Jessiah's, not my father's. *Mine.*

"See?" I teased, holding my forearm back between us. "Was that so hard?"

"You're still just as big of an asshole as ever. How do I–" She paused and looked away in shame.

I used my free hand to caress the back of her head, gently urging her forward. "You know how. Trust those fiery instincts of yours."

I let my hand fall to her neck, feeling her rapid pulse as I rubbed my thumb over the vein there.

Fuck, Huntyr was so perfect. Everything about her, even this part of her that she hated so much, that she tried to avoid so desperately, was perfect. Watching her mouth slide closer and closer to the blood on my forearm...

I was in deep, deep trouble.

Her lips made contact with my wrist first, barely brushing over the single trail of dripping blood. It was as light as a feathered kiss, but I sucked in a sharp breath anyway.

A wave of desire rolled through me, and I let Huntyr feel it through our bond, let her feel how much I *wanted her to drink.*

She kissed my wrist again then, fiercer than the first time, more confident. She kissed me again and again until her tongue slipped out and slid against my skin.

My cock throbbed in my trousers, and I fought back a moan. Then, she was pushing me, keeping my forearm to her mouth with one hand while guiding me to lean against the nearest tree with the other. She licked the dripping blood until there was none left, and then she paused.

"Well?" I breathed, voice hoarse. "How is it?"

Her chest rose and fell with rapid breaths, and then her wild eyes met mine. "Do you want to feel?"

Her emotions slammed into me, delight and pleasure and *want*. But under it all was the same dark, creeping creature that lurked in me, the sleeping beast that came out only in these moments.

"Huntress," I gasped, but she was already pulling my forearm back to her mouth so I could feel that, too, until her own pleasure mixed with mine.

Her teeth brushed my skin, hesitating.

"It's okay." I snaked my free arm around her waist, pulling her to me until she was flush against my body. "It's okay."

She moaned as fangs protruded from her teeth. It wasn't painful for fangs to appear, but her mouth would take time to adjust each time she fed.

"I won't let you lose control, Huntress. Feed."

And then, she fed.

Her teeth slid into my skin with a satisfying pinch, and she kept that bond open so I could be distracted by the wave of euphoria within her. I hardly noticed the pain, hardly noticed the blood she took as her mouth moved against me.

"Fuck," I moaned. A wave of lust hit her too, fierce and uncontrollable. She slid between my legs, grinding herself against my length and making me throw my head back against the tree bark. "You're trying to kill me, aren't you?"

She drank more, and I let her. I let her take and take and take until that pang of hunger was gone, until that beast within crawled back into the deep, dark hole it came from.

I didn't have to tell her to stop. She pulled away, dropping my forearm. I picked up my thumb to brush the drop of blood from her bottom lip, but quickly let it fall.

Fuck it.

My mouth crashed against hers fiercely, unapologetically. She stiffened at first but quickly wrapped her arms around my neck, pushing the rest of herself against me. I tasted my own blood against her lips and made sure to lick them clean, scraping every last drop from her mouth.

"You're so fucking perfect, Huntyr," I mumbled against her mouth. Her chest heaved against me, but she pulled my face down against hers, kissing me just as hungrily as I was kissing her. I didn't care what this meant. I didn't care if she forgave me, if this was going to change anything.

I was just happy to be here with my wicked Huntress in my arms.

"Are you two done?" Huntyr yelped in surprise and shoved herself away from me at the sound of Jessiah's voice. "Because I'd actually like to get some sleep before we're all killed by vampyres. I'm glad to know I won't be the one Huntyr feeds from in my sleep, though."

His words were joking, but I watched as Huntyr lifted a finger to her mouth.

The high of feeding was euphoric, but the crash would wreck you.

That was when the realization of it all set in.

"Oh, goddess above."

"Don't," I pushed, stepping forward. Huntyr stumbled away from me like I was fire. "Don't you dare start to feel guilty. You solved your hunger. That's *it*. You don't even have to think about it again for days."

She couldn't look at me. She pulled herself away from the bond, shutting herself off entirely.

"Huntyr," I whispered.

Her voice shook as she answered, "I'm fine. I just need some sleep."

Jessiah busied himself with his bed roll, and Huntyr moved to do the same.

Guilt wrecked through me. Should I have let Huntyr feed from someone else? *No,* the thought alone nearly made me sick.

She might hate me. She might be marrying me out of force. She might only feed from me because she was near starvation, but she would *never* feed from anyone else.

Did that make me possessive? Insane? Unhinged? I didn't give a fuck. All I cared about was Huntyr standing there with *my* blood dripping from her lips.

CHAPTER 13
HUNTYR

There was absolutely no way I was going to sleep after that. My heart pounded so hard in my chest, I knew Wolf could hear it. Jessiah too, though he was fast asleep on his bedroll just feet from me.

Wolf took the first watch, which I was somewhat grateful for, because at least that meant he was on the other side of the clearing and not sleeping beside me.

But that also meant he was over there in the darkness, using his half-angel eyes to watch me. Every single ounce of my body buzzed with a new energy, an awareness of him, a thrill.

I shut my eyes and tried to count backward, tried to force myself to sleep.

Tried to force myself not to listen to Wolf's breathing from a distance, tried to force myself not to reach out through our bond and see what he was thinking, feeling.

Dammit, Huntyr. You know what he feels. If that kiss was any hint...

I rolled over on the thick blanket and ran a hand down my face as I took a long, cooling breath.

Time passed, though I lost count of the hours. I tried and failed time and time again, but it was no use. My racing heart would not slow. My rapid breath would not calm.

"If you're going to toss and turn, you might as well keep watch." Wolf's voice slid through the air, as smooth as the breeze.

One glance at Jessiah told me he was still fast asleep. His wings cascaded around him, blocking out the rest of the world as he snored quietly.

That would be fucking nice right about now.

I pushed myself up and stormed in Wolf's direction, wrapping my arms around my stomach to try and fight off the cool breeze of night. He sat against a tree trunk near the trail, using his dagger to sharpen a random piece of wood. He didn't stop as I approached, didn't take his eyes off what he was doing for even a second.

"How's your arm?" I stood awkwardly a few feet away, not sure what to do with myself, not sure it was safe to allow myself any closer to him.

He stilled, dropping the now violently pointed stick. "My arm is not what I'm worried about."

I took one step closer and paused. "You don't have to worry about me."

"Yes, I do," he answered without a breath.

I closed the distance between us, moving to sit beside him, resting my back against the same rough bark. His shoulder brushed mine gently, and neither of us moved away.

"Well, I don't know why. I can take care of myself."

His laugh was silent, but I felt his shoulders shaking beside me. I snapped my eyes to his. "What?"

"You think I don't know that, Huntress? You're a wicked, violent little thing. I know you can take care of yourself just fine."

"Then what's with the act? What's with..." I waved my hand between us. "What's with all of this?"

"This?" he asked, turning his body to face mine. Below the moon and the stars, his eyes nearly glowed. He was only inches from my lips, so close that I could feel his breath as he spoke. "You mean me sharing my blood with you?"

"That, and then there's the kiss."

The smirk fell from his face. My stomach dropped.

"I shouldn't have done that," he whispered. "I'm sorry."

I bit my lower lip. "I didn't bring it up so you could apologize. I brought it up because—because I'm *confused*." I pulled my knees up to my chest and wrapped my arms around my shins, dropping my forehead to rest against them as I took a long, calming breath. "Why is this all so damn difficult."

Wolf didn't respond with a snarky comment like I expected. He just leaned his own head back against the bark and twirled his dagger in his hands. "I don't know."

I lifted my head. I wasn't sure why; maybe it was the way his voice broke just a little, or it could have been the way his brows wrinkled in worry as he focused on his own hands, but I couldn't stop myself from reaching out and pushing back his thick, dark hair. It had grown so much since we met. It now fell in waves, nearly long enough to tuck behind his ears.

He froze at first, then leaned into my touch slightly, jaw clenching.

"You're feeling a lot of things right now," he whispered. "The feelings that come with feeding can be a bit sensual."

"Does it always feel like that? Even with others?"

His eyes snapped to mine in the darkness. "No, Huntress. It does not."

"And when you fed from me?" Heat flushed my cheeks. "Is that what it felt like for you too?"

He smiled. "Are you asking me if I enjoyed it?"

"I guess I am."

"Yes, Huntress. I enjoyed it. I enjoyed every goddess-damned moment of it."

My chest cracked. My stomach dropped. I didn't want to fight with Wolf. Not anymore. Not after everything.

I mean, hells, I had lost so much. *But so had he.*

Tears came rushing forward. I wasn't sure why, but I couldn't stop them. I couldn't even begin to control them as they spilled over my cheeks, dripping down my chin in a sudden rush. Wolf didn't say anything; he sat beside me silently as I cried and cried.

I wasn't even sure why I was crying.

"Wolf," I said, though a sob cracked my voice half-way through. "I'm really sorry about your wings. I never wanted, I mean, if I knew that he would—"

He spun his entire body to face me and pulled me into him, wrapping his arms around me and rocking us back and forth. "Shh," he whispered. "Don't even think about that, Huntress. My wings were not your fault, okay?"

His voice cracked too, and I could have sworn I saw his own eyes glistening, but perhaps I only imagined it.

"If I would have just given your father what he wanted— if I would have trusted you—"

"Don't." He stopped rocking us and twisted me around until he could look at my face, holding my chin with both hands. "Don't you dare give in to him. I don't care what he takes from me; do not give in to him. Understand me?"

More tears came. More tears fell. "How? How do you let him control you like this?"

Something dark washed over his features. "A lifetime of hatred will make you do crazy things, Huntress. He can take from me now, but I'm working on a lifetime of freedom, a lifetime he can't take away from me."

"Tell me how." I pulled Wolf's hands into my own. "Tell me how you're going to stop him."

I could see the debate in his eyes, of whether or not he should tell me. "You're already risking too much. I won't put you in more danger than you're already in."

"I don't care what I'm risking. I want to help you. I can't— I can't keep living like this, not knowing who to trust, not knowing what's going on. I'm trapped in this life, Wolf. I'm trapped in this life, and I can't get out, and I'm fucking terrified."

He pulled my body to his again, and I let him guide me until I rested with my back against his chest, settling between his legs.

"I know you don't want to trust me," he mumbled against my mess of hair. "I know I betrayed you. I know I broke your fucking heart, and trust me, mine broke that day, too. But I will never hurt you again, Huntyr. This marriage, this trip, this kingdom we're heading to, Asmodeus is wicked, and he is powerful. He can make us do all these things like we are his little puppets for now, but when this kingdom rises, when things change, when people start seeing you as the powerful, unstoppable queen you are, you will not be denied. Not by anybody, and certainly not by my father."

A chill ran down my body. Not from the cold of night this time, but from the raw power of his words. What he was saying...it was...

"But you don't have to think about all of that right now," he continued. "I've already put you through enough. All I want is for you to stay alive. Because I can fight. I can plan and I can kiss ass and I can be the pawn of the kingdom, but without you?" He choked on his words. "Without you, none of this matters. Without you, I don't give a fuck what happens to me or this kingdom."

I put my hand to my mouth and stifled a sob. Things were so messy, so screwed up. How did we get here? I was a vampyre, for fuck's sake. How had I fallen so far?

I leaned back onto Wolf, reveling in his warmth, not caring that I was supposed to hate him, not caring about any of it, actually. Not caring about anything at all.

The next day was just as uneventful as the first, thankfully with no insane cravings for blood, no reason to feed from Wolf, and no attacks from vampyres in the woods.

It was all very calm.

Until it wasn't.

"Are you sure we're heading in the right direction?" I asked. "Have the two of you been here before?"

"More times than I'd like to admit," Wolf answered from behind me. "These trails are supposed to be confusing. It keeps us all safer when hungry ones and other creatures get turned around in between our kingdoms."

Interesting. After last night's kiss, there was no need to pull my body away from Wolf's. He leaned against me too, whatever grudge he was holding yesterday was long, long gone.

We didn't talk about it. We didn't talk about the blood, either, and neither did Jessiah, which I was grateful for.

I didn't need anyone to mention the fact that I was undeniably a vampyre. I couldn't hide it anymore, couldn't pretend it wasn't actually happening. This was all very real. It was happening. There was no going back now.

"Do you feel it yet?" Wolf asked, breath brushing against my ear.

My senses flared. "Feel what?"

"The surge in your power. Your abilities heightening."

I took a quick scan of my body. My abilities were always very dull. Even in Moira, I could barely feel my magic unless I was absolutely desperate. That had been an afterthought so far; using my magic or even thinking about it was no use in the house of the archangel.

"I don't think so," I admitted. "I feel exactly the same."

He laughed quietly, his broad chest shaking against my shoulders. "Focus here." He snaked an arm around my body and pressed his palm against my stomach. "What do you feel?"

My entire body became aware of his hand pressed against me. "I feel *you*."

I couldn't see him, but I could practically feel the way he smirked. His fingers tightened, pressing deeper into me. His thumb brushed my ribs just below my breast, and his smallest finger reached down to my pant line. "What else do you feel?"

I took a deep, calming breath of the fresh forest air and tried to think about what else I felt, if anything. Yes, I felt him. I felt his warmth, his presence, *him*, but as he moved his fingers slowly, as he pressed his hand deeper against my body, I felt something else, too. Something deep stirred within me, like excitement and adrenaline mixed together in a seed deep within my body.

"*That*," he whispered. "*That* is your power awakening, Huntress. Since you fed, you'll be gaining more and more strength each day. You're changing."

My breath hitched. He didn't move his hand. I knew my power would grow once I fed, once I completed that transition into a vampyre. I did notice the way Wolf's blood healed my wounds overnight. It pulsed through my body with a new wave of strength, and I didn't realize just how badly I craved just that. It was as if I could finally take a full breath, like I finally felt fully energized.

But that all came from Wolf's blood. I was still terrified of what would happen from my own magic awakening. "What if I don't want to change?"

"You will," he replied. "Especially when you're powerful enough to summon your own wings."

Wings? I twisted around so I could see his face. His eyes lit up with a teasing level of amusement. "Are you kidding? You think I'll be able to fly?"

"You are descended from the most powerful vampyre bloodline. There are much weaker vampyres that have no problem summoning wings. All it takes is magic, which you already possess. I don't doubt it for a second."

I couldn't stop the smile that spread over my face or the laughter that bubbled from me. *Flying.* With wings, I could fly far, far away from here. I wouldn't be a slave to my feet, wouldn't be trapped riding horses or spending days on any one journey.

I could go home.

I could go anywhere in the world.

"Don't get too excited," Jessiah called from ahead, clearly eavesdropping on our entire conversation. "We have to survive the next few days first."

His voice had gone cold, worried.

"What's wrong?" I asked.

He shook his head, his eyes scanning the thick trees of the horizon as he slowed his horse. "I don't know," he answered. "But something doesn't feel right."

Wolf slowed our horse too, immediately stiffening. "You've still got Venom, right?" he asked. I loved that even he called her by her name, out of respect more than anything.

I nodded.

"Good." His hand moved from my stomach to my waistline, where Venom was strapped to my belt. He slid her out of the sheath seamlessly and moved it to my hands.

I took it without question.

Jessiah descended from his horse without a sound. His white, feathered wings were tucked tightly behind his shoulders, ready for a fight.

Wolf started to do the same, quietly guiding himself onto the ground.

I stayed on the horse, peering into the forest around us. Jessiah was right—something was off. The birds should have been chirping, the wind should have been blowing the trees and rustling the leaves.

Instead, there was only silence. An eerie, blood-curdling silence.

But then, I smelled it: the same stench that lurked in my nightmares since I was a child.

Hungry ones.

CHAPTER 14
HUNTYR

The three of us stopped. Both horses felt the tension, felt the threat nearby.

My pointed ears flickered, listening for the next sound of danger.

Hungry ones were deadly, yes, but they were not exactly stealthy. The next snap of a twig to our right gave them away within a second. Jessiah and Wolf were already pulling on the horse's reins from the ground—not to run away from the bloodsuckers, but to run toward them.

Just a few feet through thick trees and brush, and we were on them. There were three. They looked fresh, like they had yet to fall into the rotting life of living for nothing but the taste of blood.

But then, we heard the voice.

"Stop!" someone yelled. "Stop! Please!"

The two horses, along with Jessiah and Wolf on the ground, boxed in the three hungry ones, but the voice was coming from somewhere else.

"Who's out there?" Wolf yelled. "Show yourself!"

I tightened my grip around his waist on instinct. Who would be out here with the hungry ones? Who would be *defending* them?

What we weren't expecting, though, was a young girl to step out of the brush.

Jessiah pointed his sword at one of the creatures that got too close.

"Who are you?" I asked.

The girl looked no older than twelve—starving, clearly, and also terrified, but not of the hungry ones.

"Just stop," she said. "Don't kill them, please."

"We have to kill them," Jessiah explained. "Or they'll kill us all. You understand that, don't you?"

The young girl took a step toward the hungry ones. How the hell was she still alive, anyway? How had they not killed her already?

The girl looked at us with a brave face. "I swear to you, they are not hungry ones. They were fine just yesterday. They're just sick. They're just—"

"They're not sick," I said, lowering my voice. "They would eat Jessiah right now if he lowered his sword. And then they would eat us, and they would probably eat you."

A single tear fell down her dirt-stained face. Hells, she looked so tired. Had she been following them this whole time? It wasn't possible, was it? I mean, it—

"How are you still alive?" Wolf asked before I had the chance to intervene. He guided the horse a step in her direction, careful to avoid the three hungry ones that were now frozen—almost dazed, as if they were confused on what to do next. I'd seen hungry ones practically crawl over each other to get access to fresh blood.

These hungry ones seemed calmer, not on the verge of

tearing into each of our throats. In my entire life of killing these creatures, I had never seen anything like it.

"How have they not killed you?" he asked again when she didn't answer.

The young girl's eyes flickered between the hungry ones and Wolf, like she was looking to them to help her.

That was when it clicked for me.

"That's her family," I said. "She's with them because they're family."

The largest hungry one—her father, I assumed—chose that moment to let out a low growl and take a step in Jessiah's direction. The tip of his silver sword pressed into the chest of the creature until blood beaded at the surface. "Tell me what to do here," Jessiah mumbled in a low voice. "I can't say I feel great about killing them in front of her."

I prepared myself to get off the horse and comfort the girl, considering these two men likely had no practice with sensitive matters, but Wolf beat me to it. He took a slow, tentative step toward her. He even hunched his shoulders inward, like he was trying to make himself appear smaller to keep from frightening her.

"What's your name?" he asked.

The girl's eyes widened, gluing themselves to Wolf. "Abigail."

"Abigail," Wolf repeated. I couldn't see his face, but I could hear that he was smiling. "Your family is very sick, do you understand?"

The girl nodded.

"Good. And this type of sickness, it doesn't have a cure. Your family is going to become dangerous, and if you don't leave them now, they might hurt you."

Abigail sniffled but kept her eyes on Wolf. Brave, brave

girl. My heart twisted in my chest at someone so young having to go through this. I never thought about the hungry ones like this—as real people with families and loved ones, as monsters who eventually turn on their own children.

"They won't hurt me," she said. "Mother would never do something like that."

Mother crept a little too close to my leg and I had to kick her shoulder to keep her back. Her eyes were already sunken voids in her skull. Any remaining pieces of her soul were quickly dwindling as she morphed into one of them.

We learned in Moira that vampyres turned into hungry ones after losing control of their blood lust, but this was particularly strange. Why would three family members all lose control at the same time?

"Abigail," Wolf continued, "you need to come with us if you want to stay alive."

The three hungry ones grew impatient. They could clearly smell the blood pumping in our veins, and although they might have been holding onto the smallest amount of restraint, they were quickly losing it.

"We need to go." The horse beneath me took a step away from the monsters as if it, too, knew we were running out of time. "Now."

"Agreed," Jessiah added. "Let's take the girl and go."

"No," the girl cried. "I can't leave them. I can't leave them!"

"I'm sorry," Wolf said, stepping closer to her like he was willing to kidnap her to keep her alive. "But you have to."

Instead of staying put and letting Wolf pick her up, she darted past him, catapulting herself and wrapping her arms around her mother's waist.

Fuck.

The hungry ones were losing control. She may have survived this long, but she had about five seconds before they ripped her flesh from her bones.

"Abigail!" Wolf yelled.

The mother stilled, void eyes turning to her daughter. The other two stopped moving as well. One sniffed the air.

Jessiah and Wolf were unmoving. There was little we could do as we watched the horror play out in front of us.

My power reacted before I could even comprehend the situation. One second, the mother was looking at her daughter with an open jaw and teeth lowering to Abigail's flesh.

The next second, my magic catapulted around them.

The three hungry ones froze. Not metaphorically, either, but actually *froze*, like their corpses were now statues.

"Huntyr," Jessiah called out from his horse, "are you doing this right now?"

"I have no idea," I answered honestly.

"Nobody move," Wolf said. "Huntyr, don't you dare fucking stop whatever you're doing right now."

So I didn't. I still had no idea what was actually happening. I mean, was I controlling this? Did my *magic* make the hungry ones stop?

It didn't matter. What mattered was getting Abigail out of there alive.

Wolf crept forward, into the danger of the frozen hungry ones, and grabbed Abigail's hand, pulling her to him. He guided her to Jessiah's horse and lifted her onto the saddle in front of him. She wasn't objecting anymore. She was smart enough to understand that her mother had been seconds from tearing into her flesh.

Once Wolf was settled back onto the horse behind me, he

said, "Let's get the fuck out of here before we have to kill them in front of her."

So we did. I didn't lessen the flow of power leaving my body as our two horses ran away from the hungry ones, from the girl's parents, from the atrocity she almost witnessed.

It wasn't until I was sure we were far, far away from them that I pulled my magic back to myself, taking a deep breath as my body adjusted to the expended energy.

Jessiah rode in front, but he glanced over his shoulder every few seconds, almost waiting to see if I would admit what just happened.

"That really was me, wasn't it? My magic did that?"

"You are the blood queen, Huntress. I have no doubt in my mind that your power could be capable of such things."

"I don't even know how that happened. I just—I just wanted to save her." Abigail was shockingly quiet for the next few hours of the trip. She did not cry. She did not ask to turn around, to be reunited with her family again. I even forgot she was there until we took breaks and I saw her climbing off Jessiah's horse.

But she remained quiet. Calm.

I was glad, because I was silently freaking the fuck out.

Even the next day, as we rode through the forest in silence, my thoughts trailed back to the way my magic made those hungry ones freeze. My magic *controlled* them. This was what Asmodeus wanted, right? He wanted me to control them. He wanted me to build him an army of blood-hungry monsters who would stop at nothing to destroy, destroy, destroy.

Wolf's breath fell on the back of my neck, making me shiver, finally distracting me from my dark spiral of thoughts. "You're panicking," he whispered. "I can feel it." He pulled our horse back far enough that Jessiah and Abigail couldn't hear us.

"I wouldn't say panicking," I replied. "Just realizing I actually might be capable of everything your father wants from me."

"I always knew you were capable," he replied. "But that doesn't mean we're going to play into his plans. You're safe with us, Huntress. Jessiah won't say anything, you have my word."

"How do you know? You two are brothers, but he doesn't seem to hate your father as much as you do. He could be more loyal."

Wolf laughed quietly, the shaking in his chest vibrating through my back. "I just know," he answered. "Very few people truly want to see my father with even more power than he already has. If you trust anything, trust that."

Fair enough. Jessiah was a good man, even though he was the child of the evil archangel. That wasn't his fault, though, was it? We had no control over who our parents decided to become. I had a hard time believing Jessiah had a single evil bone in his body. To sit by while his father took over kingdom after kingdom?

It wasn't right. Jessiah wouldn't stand for it.

But I also knew that trusting others got me into trouble on more than one occasion. Now, they knew I ultimately had more power than I was showing.

I would have to be very, very careful moving forward.

Trust no one, and I *might* make it out of this alive.

CHAPTER 15
WOLF

Scarlata Empire was as creepy and dark as I remembered. It was as if the sun never actually shined on this place, constant cloud-cover kept the city dim and gray. Fitting for the blood kingdom, the kingdom of death.

My chest tightened with each step our horses took. Witnessing the destruction from a distance was nothing compared to the crumbling ruins up close. Huntyr stiffened in front of me, taking in our surroundings in silence.

There were no vampyres in sight, but they would be lurking, hiding. The kingdom fell, yes, but not everyone left that day after the war. Vampyres and hungry ones lurked in these shadows, living their lives in secret.

I didn't blame them. The fae absolutely slaughtered them. Vampyres were forced into hiding, pretending to be dead all this time.

Hells, maybe they were all dead, the hungry ones especially.

My voice seemed much too loud as I whispered, "We'll let

them go here," pulling my horse to a halt. Jessiah did the same, helping Abigail off first before unstrapping our bags.

"What?" Huntyr asked. "We let the horses go?"

"It's not safe for them to remain tied up here. We must let them go if they want to survive. They'll find their way back to Griffith, don't worry. They always do."

I could do nothing to soothe the worry on her sharp, pale features. She was right to be worried. One couldn't even leave a horse tied up in this kingdom without waking to find them drained of blood.

Huntyr would have to be careful. We all would.

Jessiah and I busied ourselves with unpacking the horses, taking everything we needed from the animals before removing the harnesses and sending them on their way. This wasn't their first journey to Scarlata, and it wouldn't be their last. But watching them trot back into the darkness of the forest never got any easier.

I cleared my throat and turned my attention back to the crumbled kingdom. "It's getting dark. Let's get to the tower before the sun is gone."

Jessiah agreed, grabbing the young girl's hand and taking the lead as he led us across the scattered cobblestone, now half-overgrown with tall grasses and greenery creeping in from the forest.

Every few feet, though, I spotted broken grass, crumpled dirt.

We were not the only ones here. Huntyr walked a step ahead of me, Venom drawn and her knuckles white from gripping. She was prepared for an attack, always. As much as I hated it, her inability to trust any situation would keep her alive here.

A few minutes later, we made our way to the tall tower

that still stood in this wretched place. It was ten stories high, maybe more. In the height of Scarlata, this would have been one of the smaller buildings, but the war destroyed everything, buried every building, every home. Now, this was one of the only places left.

"What are we going to do with her?" Huntyr asked, looking at Abigail.

Fuck. I had to be very careful about this. Huntyr knew very little about what really existed here in Scarlata. I still wasn't sure she would be ready to know the truth. "I have a plan," I answered honestly. "There's someone here who can take care of her."

Huntyr nearly tripped over her own feet. "You know people living here?"

I squinted and gripped her arm, stopping her from walking. Jessiah and Abigail kept moving forward, oblivious to our conversation. "It's complicated, but yes. I can't tell you anything more without putting you in danger."

She nodded, still skeptical. "Does your father know?"

"Absolutely not, and it's going to stay that way." I stared into her deep eyes, silently begging her to understand everything I wasn't saying. Yes, I knew others living here in the ruins. No, my father didn't know.

And I would die before I let him find out about them.

"Okay," Huntyr said after a few seconds, turning her attention to Jessiah and Abigail. "As long as she's safe."

"She'll be much safer here than back in The Golden City. I think we both know that." My words were harsh, but true. Here, she could be with her own people, other vampyres who would raise her as their own, who would keep her safe. Back home, she'd be exploited for everything she was. Hells, I wouldn't be surprised if my father killed her on sight.

Without another word, we followed the others through the rubble and ruins. I knew where they were heading, the same place Jessiah and I always stayed when we visited here. We walked until we made it to the base of the tallest standing building in Scarlata.

"Is anyone in there?" Huntyr whispered, turning her head to the sky.

"Not anymore," Jessiah answered, pushing the door open. "They know we're here. They always know when we are coming."

"And they just leave us alone?"

My brother and I shared a look. If we were lucky, yes, they would leave us alone. Sometimes, we were lucky. Other times, we were met with *unwelcoming* surprises.

"Keep your guard up," was all I said. "It has been a while since we were last here."

The little girl was as silent as a shadow, lurking near the wall and keeping her wide, innocent eyes on everything that moved.

Smart girl. She might actually have a chance at surviving.

We walked through the arched doorway that led to a tall, narrow staircase. We started the ascent to the top floor—just as we did each time we visited these ruins. It was the safest spot, but it also gave us an advantage to see what had been going on since we last visited. We could see any buildings that were rebuilt, any gatherings of vampyres, anything.

The stairs creaked beneath our weight, but we kept moving. One by one, we climbed those stairs in silence. Nobody said a word until we reached the top floor.

Jessiah pushed the already-open door open further, ducking inside with his sword drawn before giving us the signal. The room was clear. I let out a breath I was holding then followed Huntyr inside, shutting the iron door behind me.

Each time we made it to this room, it looked nearly the same, but there were small things, little details, that told me people had been here. Not fae or angels, but vampyres. We had no idea if they were our friends or our enemies, no idea where they were in this world or what they wanted, but they had been here, rummaging through the few rations we kept, sorting through clothes and supplies, leaving a trail of their mixed scents behind.

The top floor was the largest in the entire tower. Someone noble must have lived here, the furniture left behind was certainly grand. Expensive, too. A gold-rimmed couch sat near the large window at the back of the room. Two bedrooms flanked each side, each with a large bed and plenty of clothes left.

There was a kitchen with a large table, plenty of space for us every time we visited, but running water hadn't existed here for quite some time now. That, I missed.

Huntyr paced the perimeter of the room, scanning the furniture, pushing the torn, white-lace curtain aside and peering out the window. "Why does it feel like we're being watched?" she asked quietly, more to herself than to either of us.

Jessiah and I set our bags down before trailing behind her to look out that same window. "It always feels this way," he answered. "Whoever is out there, they know we're here. We just have to hope they're smart enough to leave us alone."

"I can't believe your own father sends you here."

I bit my tongue. Of course, he sends us here. He couldn't give a shit if we lived or died. All he cared about was the fact that we would get the job done.

"He trusts us," Jessiah said, always the fucking kiss ass. "And he knows we're strong enough to defend ourselves if anything happens."

"Still," she argued. "He doesn't even send Luseyar to help in case there's an attack? It's reckless."

"As reckless as being sent to Moira?" I asked, voice suddenly dripping in a bitterness I wasn't expecting.

She spun to face me, eyes sharp. "Excuse me?"

"I'm going to leave you two to figure out whatever this is. Come on, Abigail. I'll show you the super cool room you'll be staying in tonight." Jessiah led a very exhausted Abigail into one of the bedrooms, shutting the door behind them before Huntyr let out another breath.

"You have no right to say things like that. You have no idea why I was sent to Moira."

"But do you?" Wolf pressed. "Is it any different than why we were sent here? Was Lord any different than—"

"Yes," she spat. "Lord loved me. He actually cared about my wellbeing."

I rolled my eyes and turned away from her. She was still so brainwashed, so naive. She actually thought a man who hurt her like that could love her.

That was not love.

The hatred that washed over me was a result from picturing those scars on her back, from picturing how they got there.

"Stop that," she said.

"I can't." I couldn't close the bond all the way, couldn't keep out that anger and hatred.

"He took care of me, Wolf." Her voice was softer now, and I felt her approaching from behind me. "He saved my life."

"He hurt you."

A thick pause.

"So did you."

I spun to face her, finding her staring at me through those long black lashes. "Huntress…"

"Don't apologize again. Don't say anything." She held her hand out, almost reaching for me, before dropping it. "Just don't ever let me get close to you like that again."

I wasn't expecting the words, and they hit me hard, cracking my chest open. "But I want you close," I admitted. "I want you closer than ever."

Her jaw tightened. She lowered her eyes and retreated. "I can't protect myself and love you at the same time. Not again. Not after everything."

"Then don't." I stepped forward, reaching for her. "Don't give me your love, Huntress. Give me anything. Give me the tiniest fucking piece of you. Give me the shreds, all the pieces you hate, I don't care. I'll take anything you give me, and it will always be enough."

Her eyes glazed over. "I already gave too much."

Huntyr slept in the second bedroom, Abigail in the first. Jessiah passed out for a couple hours on the couch, his massive white wings barely fitting, before waking up.

"Hells, brother," he groaned, pushing himself to a sitting

position. "You're sitting there watching me sleep? That's creepy, even for you."

I threw an apple at him, huffing when he caught it instead of letting it plummet onto his chest like I intended. "I can't sleep here. I never can. You know that."

He nodded, taking a bite of the apple and falling into silence with me.

Jessiah and I came here for the first time as children, right after the war that ended Scarlata. Back then, The Golden City was still good, still elite, still upholding its values and protecting the people inside.

That's what they said, anyway. That's what they told everyone on the outside. But *they* were the ones creating the mass fear against the vampyres. They were the ones spreading the rumors that vampyres were monsters, unable to control their thirst.

What a load of shit. There were very few times in my life that I was hungry enough to lose control, and I never needed to drain someone completely of blood. Just a few mouthfuls would be enough to fuel me entirely.

Vampyres weren't monsters. Vampyres weren't a danger to society. But The Golden City started that frenzy, started the narrative that the vampyres had to go.

There was so much fucking irony in that. My father was behind so much of the misinformation, yet he turned me into one of them years later, after he placed the fear of the blood-suckers in everyone's mind.

Vampyres were very similar to fae. They even had magic like the fae and angels did, though it was rare.

The hungry ones, though...

The hungry ones were still a mystery to me. In Moira, we were taught that the hungry ones were created when a vampyre lost control of their thirst, but I had a very, very hard time believing that, especially when all of the vampyres I met were in total control.

Even the vampyres here, living in hiding—they seemed just as afraid of the hungry ones as we were.

But I was only half vampyre, and I wasn't even born one. The truth existed somewhere, I just had to find it. There were whispers about a cure to the hungry ones. After what I saw today with Abigail, I was questioning everything. They had enough sense to try not to kill Abigail. I had never met a hungry one with any ounce of restraint, but those ones? What if Abigail was right? What if it was a sickness, a disease?

And what if there was a cure?

I needed to find it before my father did. He would make sure the cure to the hungry ones—if it existed—was never found. He wanted more hungry ones, more chaos, more destruction. He wanted to keep everyone else weak and afraid so he could stand on top.

"You're scowling," Jessiah interrupted, taking another loud bite from his apple.

I took a breath and shook those thoughts away. "Just thinking about what we saw in the woods." I tilted my head toward Abigail's bedroom.

Jessiah nodded. "She *stopped* them. I thought Father was insane when he thought Huntyr would give him the power he desired, but this? This changes everything."

The pit in my stomach—the same one that had been there since I saw Huntyr in that dungeon—grew. "He can't know. *Nobody* can know, Jes."

"I won't say a thing," Jessiah replied, and I believed him. It wasn't the only secret he had been keeping, and I was certain it wouldn't be the last. "But I really hope you have a plan here, brother. One that doesn't end with all of us getting royally fucked over."

I let my head fall back on the chair. I had a plan, yes, but Jessiah didn't know about it. Nobody did, nobody except the very few trusted individuals who would die for this cause.

I had been planning for weeks. The fewer people who knew about it, the better.

"I don't ask questions about what you do when we come here, brother, never have. But are you sure Abigail will be safe? Are you sure we can trust them?"

I appreciated that about Jessiah. The first few years we came here, we were on the same side as my father. We killed the survivors. We reported back what we saw. We scavenged the land, ensuring nobody was rebuilding this place.

We ensured Scarlata was still fallen.

But that was before my father sacrificed me, before he turned me into one of them and turned my wings black.

Fallen angels in The Golden City didn't exist. Once you fell—which was rare enough—you were cast out, unable to live with the elites.

It made me fucking sick. Why was *I* fallen, when power-hungry monsters like my father were still living with their pure white wings?

Why me? Why fucking me?

I guess it didn't matter anymore. My wings were long gone, along with any proof that I was a fallen.

Now, I was nothing. A vampyre with some extra magic. Magic I tried my best to keep secret.

Huntyr knew I could heal, but I learned at a very young age my father was not someone I could trust. I saw him use and throw away angels with far less magic.

When I woke up as a vampyre, I felt it. It was a spark

inside of me that grew over time. Nobody knew. Nobody suspected, even when the lightning in my eyes grew. They all attributed it to my temper, to my wild lack of control when it came to my emotions. I let them think that. I felt it, though. I felt that I was given this extra power for a reason.

It was almost as if the goddess wanted to compromise for turning me into this, for taking my white wings away from me.

And the day I met Huntyr in Midgrave, it sang in my chest, buzzing to life like a hibernating animal coming out to play.

When we returned to Scarlata together after I became a vampyre, things changed. I couldn't kill them blindly anymore, and neither could Jessiah.

It was years before I spoke to the survivors here, and even longer before they actually trusted me. But now, with everything we had planned, our trust was the one thing we held on to. The survivors needed me, and I needed them.

"Yes, we can trust them to keep her safe. If anything, they'll be grateful we brought her here instead of dragging her back home with us."

His nostrils flared before he said, "Things are changing, I can feel it. Something big is coming."

The hair on the back of my neck stood straight up. "You're right about that, brother. Something very, very big. If we're lucky, we just might end up on the right side of this mess."

CHAPTER 16
HUNTYR

I dreamt of Wolf's blood that night. Not in the hypothetical, nice way. No, I *actually* dreamt that I could drink more of it, that he was in that bed with me, offering me the warmth from his veins.

I woke up sweating with a dry mouth, trying to get myself under control. The faint sun was already pouring through the windows, breaking up the vast darkness in the tower. I pushed myself out of bed, attempting to smooth down my hair before opening the door to my bedroom.

"Morning, sunshine," Jessiah sang from the small kitchen, holding out a piece of dried meat. My stomach tightened.

"Where's Wolf?" I glanced around the empty suite, taking in my surroundings in the daylight. "Where's Abigail?"

"He's taking a stroll around the ruins to see what he can find, and he took Abigail with him. There are people here who will take care of her."

I stepped forward, accepting the piece of dried meat. "He's handing her off to random vampyres?"

149

Jessiah avoided eye contact with me. "I wouldn't call them random, but yes. She'll be safer this way. Trust me."

Okay. I had a feeling there was a lot going on here that both Jessiah and Wolf were keeping from me. I didn't blame them. This was all very eerie, very secretive.

"He knows people here, then? A lot of them?" I was pushing the boundaries, looking for any hint that could piece this all together in my mind.

"I stay out of it, and you should too. This is Wolf's business. It's safer if you don't know anything." He got back to rummaging through whatever supplies were left in the kitchen.

"And he went alone? Is that safe?"

Jessiah shrugged. "Wolf can take care of himself. Plus, he needed to feed. I think he prefers to go alone."

Feed. My chest tightened at the memory of Wolf sinking his teeth into me, of him caressing me, of him taking away the pain with his lips, with his body. I clamped my thighs together, my body betraying me in ways I couldn't even begin to control.

I *didn't* want Wolf to feed from me, not after he betrayed me. But then why did it piss me off so much that he could be out there somewhere feeding from some random person? I didn't want to picture his mouth on someone else's neck, the moans likely leaving their lips as he pulled them close, sucking the blood from their veins and pulling the sustenance into his own body.

"You okay?" Jessiah asked, interrupting my thoughts. I cleared my throat and made my way to the large window, peering outside at the dim daylight.

"I'm fine," I replied. "Just not sure why we came all this

way if Wolf was going to leave us here alone while he did all the dirty work."

Jessiah sighed loudly then came to peer out the window just a few feet behind me. "I figured we could think of something else to pass the time."

I spun to face him. "Something else like what?"

A slow, mischievous smile splayed on his mouth. I was beginning to see the fun side of Jessiah, the side that wasn't so wound up by his father, wasn't so worried about punishment or being perceived by the angels in court.

"We're all alone in this massive tower. What better time than right now to learn how to summon your wings?"

My jaw dropped, but my body lit up at his words, like I was secretly waiting for this moment my entire life. "Are you kidding?" I asked. "You can't possibly think I can learn to summon my wings today."

"Why not?" he asked. "You have to learn eventually, and Asmodeus isn't here to watch over your every move as soon as you start wielding your magic again."

I scoffed, turning away. "I didn't have much magic to begin with."

Jessiah clicked his tongue. "That's what you might think," he said, "but you are the heir to the blood throne. You have very powerful blood in those veins of yours, Huntyr. Not to mention what happened in the woods with the hungry ones. You might as well start trying to access your own magic."

I took another bite of my dried meat. The ability to fly would definitely come in handy, but was he kidding? I could barely use basic blood magic in Moira without burning the entire school down. What happened in the woods with the hungry ones was a fluke, an accident. There was no way I could naturally summon my wings out of thin air.

"I know it seems impossible." Jessiah's voice softened behind me, all jokes missing from his tone. "But you have to try sometime. Let me help you. I swear, I'm a better teacher than Wolf."

That pulled a smile from my lips. Wolf actually wasn't a bad teacher at all, but now was clearly not the time to bring that up. "That, I don't doubt."

"Good." He held his hand out, motioning toward the doorway. "Then follow me. Some fresh air is exactly what we need for your first lesson on flying."

I scarfed down the rest of my food as I made my way through the door of our suite in the tower. Instead of heading down the stairs, though, Jessiah led us further up the hallway, where a small, broken window led to the roof.

"The roof?" I questioned. "Is this safe up here?"

Jessiah scoffed, pulling his white angel wings tight behind his shoulders so he could maneuver through the window. "What?" he teased. "Never been on a roof before?"

I bit my cheek to keep from smiling. Of course, I had been on *many* roofs before. Rummy and I practically built our entire relationship lounging on roofs, staring at the stars and pretending we were literally anywhere else in the world.

"All I'm saying is that if I fall and die, you're the one who has to answer to your father."

Jessiah scoffed. "Please. I'll blame Wolf, and Asmodeus will believe me in a heartbeat."

I faked a gasp, putting a dramatic hand over my chest. "Jessiah, maybe you are the evil one."

We both laughed as I slid through the window, straightening myself on the other side and taking a deep breath of fresh air. "Wow," I said. "Even in ruins, this place is much more beautiful than The Golden City. Maybe this is where we should all be fighting to get into."

Jessiah put his hands on his hips as we both looked out at the land surrounding the tower. "Aren't we, though?"

My stomach dropped. He was right. We were fighting over these lands, and this was just the beginning. If I agreed to become Asmodeus's pawn in this game, we should be unstoppable.

But what would that mean for this place? Standing on the roof of the tower, I could see the entire kingdom—what was left of it, anyway. Massive hills surrounded us on three sides, leaving just one side to enter and exit through the forest without the steepness of the land. It was tragically beautiful, with vines overtaking the crumbling stone walls and covering the old ruins in lush greenery.

A bird chirped in the distance, the start of a beautiful, peaceful song.

"It doesn't look like anyone lives here," I noted. Aside from a few barely cleared out paths amongst the overgrown forest and crumbling ruins, there was nothing. No rebuilt homes. No clearings in the kingdom. Just...nothing.

Jessiah took a few seconds to himself before responding. "You would be surprised at how well people can hide when their life is on the line."

I glanced at him. "Wouldn't it be our lives on the line?"

Something like anger flashed over his features. "The fae were the ones who killed the vampyres, Huntyr, not the angels. The fae were the ones who brought war to this kingdom, who created the massive rift between the people. Vampyres are the ones everyone fears, yes, but they fear the wrong species. We should be fearing the people in power, not the vampyres."

I shook my head. Lord told me about this, about the war and how the people outside The Golden City were forced to protect themselves. "Fae *had* to wipe them out. It was the only way to get the vampyres to stop killing everyone."

He turned to face me. "Do you really believe that, Huntyr? The hungry ones are dangerous, yes, but what about all the other vampyres living in this kingdom? Ones just like you? Just like Wolf? Do you really think they're capable of uncontrollably ripping apart entire kingdoms just to get to fresh blood?"

An eerie feeling crawled over my skin, clawing up my neck.

"Why would the fae kill the vampyres here if they weren't causing any problems?"

His lips tightened into a thin line. "Fear. Fear will make even the sanest creature do insane things, especially for survival."

A soft breeze blew through the air, caressing my skin and sending one of my black curls loose across my face. There had to be thousands of vampyres living in this kingdom at one point, everyone going about their lives every day in peace, doing their part to keep this city thriving.

It was hard to imagine the fae taking over, killing them all, slaughtering an entire species with nothing to stop them, the angels jumping in line to help.

"I didn't realize the fae were that powerful," I said. "It looks like the vampyres didn't even have a chance."

Jessiah craned his neck downward, looking toward the bottom of the building. "Fae are powerful, yes, but it's the archangels who hold the most power. Magic and blood, that's what really matters around here, Huntyr."

Another chill ran through me. "And my blood? My magic?"

His eyes glistened when he looked at me. "Your blood will change the world."

"You're not even trying," Jessiah called from the other side of the roof. I kept my eyes closed as I dropped my hands to my sides and let out a long sigh.

"I am trying! I told you I don't have strong magic! Wolf can attest to that."

He stood up from his lounged position, making his way over to me. "Except you *do* have strong magic. Wolf has attested to that part *many* times."

"Well, he doesn't know what he's talking about then. I've only used my magic a handful of times, and none of them were controlled. It only became useful after Wolf and I——" I stopped myself from finishing the sentence.

"Bonded?" Jessiah finished for me. I cursed under my breath. "We all know. It's not like it's a big secret."

"Still," I pushed. "It's not something I'm particularly proud of. We did what we had to do to survive, but that was before Wolf betrayed me. If I knew then what I know now, I may have reconsidered."

Jessiah paused a few feet away from me. "Everything he has done is to keep you alive, Huntyr. My brother is an arrogant prick, but he cares about you. He cares about your safety."

I rolled my eyes. "Can we not talk about this right now?"

"Fine," he said. "We don't have to talk. You can summon your wings instead."

Anger flooded my senses. I stood on that roof trying to summon those damn wings for hours now, and I felt nothing, not even the slightest sensation on my back.

"I told you, I can't do it. Maybe I'm not strong enough to have my own wings."

Jessiah took one more step closer, coming just an arm's length away. His white wings flared out on either side of him, and I had to stop myself from staring. Even the sheer size of them, the sheer strength, was enough to tell you just how powerful he was, just how close in heritage he was to the almighty archangel.

"Why are you so afraid?" he asked, cocking his head to the side.

"I'm not afraid," I spat.

"You are; you're blocking yourself from unleashing the full potential of your power."

"That's ridiculous." I turned away. "The only thing blocking my full potential is my lack of power."

He stepped closer. I backed up naturally, coming even closer to the edge of the roof. "Maybe you just need to feel it," he said. "Maybe some motivation will force you to unleash it."

"Motiva—" My words were cut off by Jessiah hauling himself toward me then catapulting both of us over the roof's edge.

A scream built in my throat, but as the tower disappeared from beneath my feet, Jessiah wrapped his large arms around me and held me. Tight. I gripped his shoulders with all my strength, slamming my eyes shut.

But we didn't fall.

Not even slightly.

A few wooshes of his powerful wings, and we were going higher, lifting into the sky.

Jessiah held me effortlessly, his arms around my waist. "See?" he pushed. I finally lifted my head from his shoulder, peeking slowly. "This is what you've been missing this whole time. This is what you're holding yourself back from."

He pumped his wings again and again, launching us even closer to the dark clouds above the kingdom. I opened my eyes fully, taking in the surrounding forest and the sheer beauty of it all.

A giggle bubbled in my throat before erupting outward, blending with the sound of air gliding against Jessiah's feathers.

I had flown with Wolf before, but this was different. This was a window into what my future could look like, into what I could accomplish.

"Goddess above," I mumbled. "This is incredible."

"Is this motivating you at all?" Jessiah adjusted me in his grip before diving down, lowering us to skim just the tips of the crumbling buildings. My stomach dropped out, and I laughed again as I clung to Jessiah's neck.

"It might be," I answered through laughter. "But if you drop me, I'll kill you."

I felt his own laugh in his chest. "If I drop you, I'm sure Wolf will beat me to it."

The air caressed us, kissing our bodies as Jessiah demanded we go higher, lower, around the blood kingdom and through the ruins. It had to have been ten minutes that passed, maybe more, before Jessiah finally returned us back to the roof of the tower.

My legs wobbled as he set me down, but he made sure I

could stand on my own two feet before removing his arms from my waist. "Next time, that's all you."

I met his eyes and smiled—a genuine smile, not one of teasing or jokes or sarcasm. Jessiah made me feel like someone in this world actually cared about me, and I needed a friend more than anything right now.

The hair on the back of my neck stood straight up. I didn't have to turn around to know that Wolf was back.

"What the fuck do you two think you're doing?" Each word was a dagger thrown through the air.

Jessiah backed away in an instant. "Relax, brother. I was just helping Huntyr learn to fly."

"Yeah, it looked like you two were having a great fucking time flying all around the kingdom. Do you know how dangerous that was? You could have gotten hurt or Huntyr could have been killed, Jessiah!"

Wolf stormed forward, seething in anger. His clothes were wrinkled and dirty, his hair a mess. It looked like he didn't sleep at all last night. He came just inches from his brother, staring at him like he was the enemy.

"We were perfectly safe," I interrupted.

"Right," Wolf answered without looking at me. "Jessiah had things under control, didn't he?"

I stormed forward and put myself between the two brothers. "Calm down, Wolf." I placed a hand on his chest and pushed him back a step. "What is going on with you? Why are you freaking out? I was just trying to summon my magic."

"I don't want you flying with him." His eyes still didn't meet mine.

Was he kidding? "And why is that? You don't think I can handle myself?"

"This has nothing to do with you," Jessiah answered. "Wolf here has a jealousy problem."

Wolf's jaw clenched, and I pushed on his chest again to keep him from killing his brother. "Watch what you say next," Wolf seethed.

"Am I wrong?" Jessiah asked. "Get over yourself, brother. Huntyr needed someone to teach her how to fly. Did you expect it to be you?"

My own stomach tightened as I watched Wolf's face drop.

Jessiah kept pushing. "I hate to break it to you, but you can't help her, Wolf, not the way she needs to be helped right now."

"Jessiah," I hissed, spinning around. "Why are you suddenly being so cruel?" This was not the Jessiah I had seen, wasn't the brother who smiled and laughed and wanted to help me.

He scowled at Wolf with fierce eyes and brows drawn together. "You haven't known our family long, Huntyr, but Wolf is not the victim he portrays himself to be."

"I do not portray myself as—"

"Yes, you do. It's *poor you* for being sacrificed to the goddess, for turning into a vampyre, for being sent to Moira. *Poor you* for being the chosen one. *Poor you* for being the one with all the attention, with all the skill, with—"

Wolf stepped forward and roared, "My wings are *gone*, ripped from my damn body! Would you prefer that fate, brother? Would you prefer to be the one who is tortured, who is killed, who is manipulated, who is–"

A wicked, dull laugh cut through the air. "At least you are *seen*." Jessiah's voice dropped as he walked away from the conversation. "I would rather be a vampyre, have a purpose, have a damn kingdom, than live in the invisible shadows of others for the rest of my life."

"What are you talking about?" Wolf asked. "You are safe and protected in The Golden City, Jessiah. You and your perfect white wings, your spotless reputation."

Jessiah looked down at his feet. "Do you know what Father and I talked about when you were gone? When you were in Moira, when you were with Huntyr all those months?"

Wolf blinked.

"We talked about you, brother. Every meal, every conversation, every topic. It was all you."

"I'm sure Father had no shortage of horrific things to say about me."

Jessiah took a few steps toward the broken window that led to the staircase. "Not horrific things, brother. Not horrific at all."

CHAPTER 17
WOLF

"You shouldn't be so angry with him," Huntyr started. I waited until I heard Jessiah's footsteps enter the suite, until I heard the door click shut behind him.

"I am not angry with him." I turned away from her and stared out amongst the ruins of the kingdom. "I am furious."

"Because he was teaching me to fly?" She sounded like the words were so damn ridiculous.

"*Yes.*"

She sucked in a breath, waited a few seconds, then followed me. Her warm hand came down around my forearm. "He was just trying to help me, Wolf."

I clenched my jaw and forced down the wave of emotion that threatened to drown me. I was very fucking aware of the fact that Jessiah was only trying to help Huntyr. That's what he did. He helped. He supported people. He cared about others and looked after them. That's all he was doing for Huntyr, too.

But when I looked up and saw her in his arms, saw her

laughing and clinging to him like they had no cares in the world, I nearly lost control.

It was bad enough that I spent my morning hunting down the *others* and handing Abigail off to them, but I also had to drink from a deer in the forest to keep my cravings at bay. The last thing I needed was the vision of Huntyr with another male.

"It should be me." My voice betrayed me, wavering slightly. "I should be the one helping you, not him."

A soft breeze blew the scent of her in my direction. I inhaled deeply—*fucking cherries*. My chest tightened, my entire body reacting to the smell of her.

She stepped even closer, not helping in the slightest. "You've already helped me enough," she said. "Too much, in fact." Her eyes flickered away as she said the words. She kneaded her hands in front of her, pulling lightly on each knuckle.

"I told you my blood is yours," I reminded her. "I meant that."

"That doesn't make it any easier."

"Well, it should. You never have to feed from anyone else, Huntyr. Not ever." It was my turn to look away, to take a deep breath and swallow the anger and jealousy that came with picturing her drinking from someone else.

"But you do?"

My eyes snapped to hers. "What are you talking about?"

"Where were you just now?" She sucked her bottom lip between her teeth. "Jessiah said you went out to feed after you made sure Abigail was safe."

"I'm a vampyre, Huntress. I have to feed."

She blinked a few times, tension filling the air. "And you

didn't think to ask me? You didn't think I might return the favor?"

I couldn't meet her deep, oval eyes, not when her voice sounded like that. Not when I could nearly picture the tears welling there, could picture the rare vulnerability she almost never showed me anymore.

"I didn't want to put you in that position," I said honestly. "Not after everything I've done."

Another beat of silence. I didn't look at Huntyr, but I could feel her. Fuck, I could feel her, like every single ounce of her body had a map in my soul, like I would know each of her movements before she made them.

Like she belonged to me.

"You could have asked."

My breath hitched in my chest, and I turned away so she wouldn't see. Fuck. I wanted her to forgive me so badly, I wanted all this shit to be put behind us. I wanted her forgiveness, but I never expected it. I wasn't blind to how much I hurt her.

Sharing her blood with me was the most vulnerable thing she had ever done, and I betrayed her. I was never going to touch her veins without her permission. I would starve first; it would be a much easier death than living with that shame.

But I had to admit, her jealousy over thinking I fed from another person was turning me on.

"Jessiah shouldn't have told you." I changed the subject as I paced the perimeter of the tower. "I wanted to get back before you noticed, but I got a little distracted at the sight of you two flaunting our presence in the blood kingdom."

I sharpened my words to cover up the pain that welled in my chest.

"He's your brother, Wolf," she sighed. Her voice softened

in a way I hadn't heard since Moira. "I didn't think you would mind."

I walked to the ledge of the roof and sat down, letting my feet dangle over the solid edge. Every one of my senses locked in on the fact that Huntyr did the same. Her body moved closer to me until her arm brushed against mine.

"He is my brother," I said, "which is why it fucking sucks so much."

She looked out on the horizon too, kicking her feet slightly back and forth in the air. "He seems to think you're the favored one in the family. I can't say I would've guessed that."

I coughed a laugh. "Yeah, I wouldn't guess that either. My father hates me. Anyone with two fucking eyes can see that." Too much venom spilled into my words, but I couldn't stop it. Jessiah was wrong. What kind of a father sacrifices their own son to become a vampyre? What type of a father cuts off his own son's wings after he was already fallen?"

My chest welled with a new emotion, an emotion I had been shoving down for some time, ever since I was a child.

"It's not fair," she said.

My attention snapped in her direction. "What isn't?"

She shrugged. "None of this is fair."

We sat like that for a few minutes, not talking, barely touching, taking in the surroundings of her future kingdom.

"This is all going to be yours," I said.

She stayed silent for so long, I wasn't sure she heard me, but then she said, "I don't deserve it. I don't belong here."

Another silence.

She didn't think she belonged here, but what she didn't know was that she was the one who belonged here the most. These were her people. Her kingdom. Her ruins.

All of this—the crumbling, tragic glory of it all—it was all for her.

"Come with me," I said, pushing myself to stand. "I want to show you something."

T fought the urge to slide my hand in hers, fought the urge to wrap my arm around her waist, to keep her body as close to mine as possible while we maneuvered through the streets of Scarlata Empire.

Everything about this place kept me alert. The trusted ones I handed Abigail off to surely were not the only survivors living here.

Huntyr and I were both vampyres, but to them, we were outsiders. They had no reason to trust us, and us them.

Besides, the vampyres who lived in hiding weren't what we needed to fear. It was the hungry ones, the masses of uncontrollable killers that would bombard us from anywhere.

We walked for a few minutes, making our way to the back of the kingdom. "Stay close," I whispered back to her. She nodded, her hand hovering near her hip where Venom lay.

When we made it to the catacombs, I stopped. The iron gate had been ripped off, leaving it open to any passerbyers. Steps led underground, covered by dead leaves and sticks and dirt. If you didn't know what was there, you would walk right past it.

But I knew. I had spent many hours in this place, learning. Studying. *Feeling.*

Huntyr deserved to see it too. It was part of who she was. It always had been.

"Here," I said, kicking some debris to the side. "Take my hand."

She did, and I carefully guided her down the steps into the small underground tomb.

"What is this place?" she asked. Normally, I would need lantern light to see down here, but at this hour, the sun filtered in just right, creating a small trail of vision for both of us, enough that we could see the small, semi-circle perimeter of the room and the massive throne that sat within.

"I've wondered that myself," I admitted, "but I'd guess this is where the queen hid during the war."

Huntyr didn't seem affected by my words, just craned her neck upward to look at the crumbling stone, taking in the walls, taking in the debris. "You mean my mother?" she asked. "This is where my mother would have hid."

I shoved my hands into my pockets and leaned against the wall near the entrance. My eyes locked onto her every movement, traced her body, memorizing it. "This is her throne, after all. But her bones aren't here, which makes me think she would be up there fighting with her people until the very end."

Huntyr approached the iron-clad throne. It was black as night, somehow still untouched by dust, even as the entire underground area drowned in it. She reached up and traced a finger against the long armrest, following the line up to the sharp, gate-like headrest of it.

It was the throne of the blood queen, hidden here all these years.

"Does your father know this is here?" she asked.

"No."

Her eyes slid up to meet mine. Shock, questions, doubt. "Why wouldn't you tell him? I'm sure he'd love to have the blood throne in his possession."

I shrugged, holding her gaze. It was the same question I asked myself for years. "It didn't feel right. The throne isn't his."

Her chest rose and fell, her face grew serious. "Tell me more about her," she said. "What was my mother like?"

Hells, her eyes were so hopeful, so innocent. It took her weeks to even accept the fact that she was a vampyre. She had been through so much, yet she still had so much to learn about herself. "I never knew your mother."

"But you've heard stories of the blood queen." It was a statement, not a question.

"Yes, I have."

She stepped closer. "Tell me."

I looked away as I let my mind wander. I heard stories of Huntyr's mother from when I was a child, from when the war ended and her death was declared. Many of the stories came from my father, but I heard other stories too. Whispers around the town. Legends, even.

"The blood queen was the fiercest warrior of these lands. She was brutal, a trained killer. Nobody stood against her, not even the king of fae."

When I finally looked at Huntyr, she stood with wide eyes and brows drawn together, waiting.

I continued. "But she was the protector of the people. She was a force to her enemies, but she was the mother to all who lived here. She took care of the weak, defended them. I heard stories of her working with the hungry ones, trying to find a cure, trying to prevent her people from losing control."

"A cure for the hungry ones?"

I shrugged. "From what I've heard, she was trying to find a way. She couldn't stand it when someone who grew up in her kingdom became one of them. It devastated her every time. They were her people, afterall. I'd imagine that would be gut-wrenching to watch."

Huntyr took a half-step forward. "Did she ever find a way to cure them?"

"Not that I know of, no. But she was one of the few willing to try." Hells, anyone else who claimed there could possibly be a cure for those creatures would have been laughed at. My father would have made sure of that.

Her gaze flickered to the floor. I pushed myself off the wall and closed the distance between us, using my finger to lift her chin. "The blood queen was brutal and treacherous, Huntress, but she cared about her people. She would do anything to protect them, anything to unite them."

"The fae killed her," she said, eyes watering. "Your brother told me that the fae killed all the vampyres who lived here, not just the hungry ones. It was a massacre."

I cleared my dry throat. "He's right."

"And I—" She ripped her chin away from me and turned, running her hands down her face. "I spent my entire life doing the same damn thing."

"Hey." I chased after her and spun her around, both hands on her shoulders. "You were protecting your town from the hungry ones. That's different, Huntress. That's not the same thing as slaughtering good people because you are afraid."

"Isn't it, though? I killed everyone he told me to, Wolf. Everyone. There were even times when I—" She stopped herself as tears welled in her eyes.

"I see you, Huntress. You don't have to feel shame around me. You don't have to feel guilty for things you've done in the past." I took a breath to calm my heart that now beat rapidly, shaking my bones. "You don't have to prove to me or anyone that you are good. I feel you." I slid my right hand down to her chest and felt the harsh thud. "I feel this."

I waited for her to swat my hand away, but it never came. My thumb touched her skin just above the neckline of her shirt, and I swear, my entire body reacted to it, electrified from that single brush of skin against skin.

Huntyr's own breath hitched. "I don't want to be like them." A tear fell down her face. "I don't want to be like Asmodeus, either."

"You're nothing like them. Do you understand me?" My hand moved from her chest to her neck, my thumb brushing her sharp jaw. "You are the blood queen, my violent Huntress. You are the one who will rebuild this kingdom. Not him. Not my father."

She waited a second longer, staring deep into my eyes, before breaking our connection with a sudden burst of laughter. She didn't pull away, though, not as she said, "This has been your plan all along, hasn't it?"

"What pla—"

"You want me to become the blood queen and stand against the angels. You want me to stand against your father."

I prepared to defend myself, prepared to convince Huntyr I was doing the right thing, that I was doing this to protect her, but I didn't have to.

Because Huntyr closed the distance between us and jumped into my arms, slamming her mouth against mine before I could take my next breath.

CHAPTER 18
HUNTYR

Wolf wrapped his arms around me and held my body to his chest as I kissed him. I latched onto him, pulling him as close as possible while our mouths clashed. He kissed me back, just as hungrily, just as needy. Just as fierce.

I wasn't sure what changed, wasn't sure when I started viewing myself as one of them, as one of the vampyres...

But Wolf? Wolf had a plan this entire time. Wolf knew all along what he was getting us into. It was why I had to marry him, why he couldn't tell me any of it. He wanted me to become the blood queen, yes, but he had no intention to give his father the power.

Wolf gripped my hips and dug his fingers into my skin as his mouth moved against mine, his tongue pushing into me and pulling me closer, creating an addicting spell I couldn't break.

This. This felt right. For the first time in fucking months, something actually felt good. I could sense it in my chest, could feel the happiness I had been missing for so, so long.

Wolf broke our kiss and pulled away. "Are you sure about this?" he asked, eyes wild.

I answered him by gripping his hair and pulling his head back down to mine. I wanted to forgive Wolf for some time now, but I couldn't get over that fear, the fear that he was keeping more from me, that he was going to betray me again.

But this was *Wolf*. I knew in my bones that he was good, that he was mine, that he was true.

Wolf backed me up until I was forced to sit on the armrest of the iron throne. He gripped my waist again and hoisted me backward until my back met the cold metal, and then he nipped my lip between his teeth. "You belong here, Huntress," he mumbled against me.

I gripped the front of his shirt and pulled him tighter, needing his body closer. "We both do," I mumbled back. Wolf's chest rumbled in response, a low growl slipping from him as he continued to kiss me, to ravish me.

His hands gripped my thighs as he spread them, making room for his own body between me and wrapping them around his waist. His body blocked the entrance of the tomb, blocked out the rest of the world. There was only him. There was only us.

Hot emotion built in my chest.

Wolf halted. "Do you feel that?"

My breath echoed off his. "Feel what?"

A second passed.

Then another.

"It's your power, Huntress."

He smiled against me but didn't kiss me again. I tried to focus on what he was talking about, on the hot fuel that burned inside me, that pulsed with excitement.

I couldn't help it. I found myself smiling too. "Do you think I'll be able to summon wings with this power?"

Wolf raised an eyebrow. "What's stopping you from trying?"

I pushed him away with one hand while focusing on that pull of power, focusing on the feelings Jessiah told me about earlier. We were in the depths of the ruins, deep in the blood kingdom, surrounded by possible enemies, but I hadn't felt this at home in a long, long time.

I gave in to that power, let it pull around my body, let it pulsate.

And then, I focused on my back, on the presence of wings, on magic.

I closed my eyes, not sure what to expect. Hells, what was growing wings supposed to feel like? But I could sense Wolf's presence. I could feel him near, could identify his own power through his bond reacting to me, almost as if it was trying to help me.

"Huntress," he said after a minute.

I opened my eyes. "What?"

He didn't have to answer. His eyes went wide as he backed up a step.

It wasn't until I saw the massive, leathery black wings flanking over both my shoulders that I realized what just happened. *Wings.*

I actually summoned my own vampyre wings.

"Holy shit," I breathed before I laughed. "Holy shit!"

Wolf laughed too, genuine joy dripping over his features. "You're fucking magnificent," he breathed.

In that moment, I agreed with him. I could hardly believe it. There was a strange awareness I had in my back, but otherwise, they felt completely normal, like they were meant to be there all along, like I was meant to have these wings.

It felt fucking good.

"What does this mean?" I asked. "Does this mean I can fly?"

Wolf's smile never faded. "Why don't you test them out a few times before you go catapulting yourself off the building with Jessiah?"

"Noted," I argued. "I guess you'll have to get your wings back so you can teach me how to fly without getting all jealous."

Wolf huffed a laugh, but then, his smile fell.

"What?" I asked. "There has to be a way to get them back, right? I mean, you could heal them, or, I don't know, use your magic to—"

"It's not that easy," he interrupted. His voice was still light, like he was trying to hide his true emotions from me. But even in the chaos of summoning my own wings, I could feel him. The real him. The him who felt disappointed as all hells that he couldn't be the one teaching me to fly.

"Why not?"

"My wings weren't cut off in normal circumstances. Sure, angels who lose their wings to injury or battle can visit a healer and try to regrow them. Magic helps, of course, but this..." He turned away from me.

"Don't do that." I gripped his bicep and forced him back. "Don't hide from me."

"I'm not hiding from you; I just don't want any more of your pity."

When he wouldn't turn to face me, I stepped around to meet his gaze. "Pity?" I questioned. "You think I *pity* you, Wolf?"

His eyes searched mine, the dull lightning now flaring with emotion. He didn't answer me, though; he just stood there with a set jaw.

"It is not pity I feel for you, Wolf. It's—it's—"

"It's what?"

"It's *guilt*." The words rushed out of me like they couldn't stay inside any longer. "I feel guilt. I feel shame. I feel fucking hatred for you and myself and for all of this."

He blinked but didn't move. I stood there before him, chest heaving, throat burning.

"You feel guilty?" he questioned.

Yes. "Every fucking day."

"*You* feel guilty?" He took a half step closer. "You have *nothing* to feel guilty over, Huntress. You're not the one who ruined everything. You're not the one who—"

"I'm the reason your wings are gone, am I not?"

"*My father* is the reason my wings are gone."

"I'm the reason you've been forced to live as your father's servant for your entire life. It's all been for this." I held my hands out, flaring my new wings as far as I could, stretching them. "Is this what he wants? Because fuck, Wolf, I'm half-tempted to just give it to him so you could have your life back."

His eyes darkened. "Don't say that."

"I don't want to say it. Fuck, I don't want to *think* it, Wolf, but that's the truth! I'm not good at this!"

"Good at what?"

I started to respond but stopped myself. I took a long, calming breath and tore my eyes away from him so I could answer, "I'm not good at acting like I don't care about you."

Wolf closed the distance between us gently then slowly

brought his hands up to my chin, forcing my eyes to his. "Say that again."

I bit my tongue. I already said way too fucking much. "I hate you," I breathed. *An obvious lie.*

He smiled, glancing down to my lips. "My violent, violent Huntress." He brought his lips down to mine—just a breath away from me but not touching. He didn't quite kiss me, just teased me, taking me in as if he was seeing me for the first time, as if he was holding me for the first time. "I never thought you would care about me again." His voice cracked. My chest tightened.

"I didn't want to," I breathed. "Not after everything. I never thought I would let myself trust anyone again, especially not you."

Only the faintest touch of pain flowed through our bond, but I moved my hands to his waist and felt the rush of something else cover it.

"I do not deserve you," he whispered, the same thing he whispered to me our first night in The Golden City, before his father. Before the wings. Before everything. "But I will gladly spend the rest of my life making it up to you."

I thought he was about to kiss me, but he stopped and smirked. "Now turn around." He backed up, and I instantly missed the heat of his body. "You have many admirable features, Huntress, but these..." He whistled quietly as he surveyed my wings. "*These* are impressive."

I turned to face the wall so he could look at them. They were nothing like Wolf's wings. Wolf's angel wings had been brutal and muscular, but also soft and caressing.

No, these wings were sharp. There was nothing soft or caressing about them. I felt my power moving through them, and I used my breath to force that power out, expanding the wings even further until I felt the stretch at the base of my spine.

Wolf's fingers trailed the waistline of my pants, toying with the hem of my shirt. I sucked in a breath when his other hand came down on the tip of my left wing.

It was a sensation I had never come close to feeling before. Every touch from his hand sent my nerves into a frenzy. The wings didn't have much feeling, but they were sensitive to his touch, like they were made only for him.

"Let me feel how I touch you," he whispered. I instantly knew what he meant. I lowered the mental shields to my bond, forcing the delicate sensation through it.

Wolf laughed under his breath. "Now I'm going to show you how you tortured me all those times with my own wings."

"How did I—" I was cut off by Wolf's right hand slipping under the back of my shirt. His palm slipped up between my shoulder blades, narrowly skimming each base of my wings.

Heat immediately pooled between my thighs.

Then, he pushed—lightly, guiding me forward until I pressed my own hands against the wall for support.

"That's my girl," he whispered.

Then, he ripped the shirt off entirely.

I gasped, starting to turn and face him, but he kept his hand solid on my back. "Let me look at you like this," he said, his breath tickling the back of my neck. "Let me see how fucking powerful you are."

The low growl in his voice sent a chill through my entire body. I stood before him in nothing but a thin chestwrap, one that did very little to cover anything that mattered.

But Wolf's entire body was large enough to cover mine. The cool breeze disappeared as Wolf put both hands on the back of my neck, encapsulating me in his warmth. Then, ever so slowly, he slid those hot hands down my bare back.

"Wolf," I warned, clenching my thighs together. "You're teasing me." His fingers barely brushed the base of my wings, sending flares of heat through my entire body.

"Yes," he chuckled quietly. "I am. And you're going to be a good little Huntress and let me."

My words were ripped from my throat as Wolf gripped my back. His hands were large enough that the tips of his fingers nearly brushed the sides of my breasts while he massaged me, working his palms through my muscles and covering me with his heat.

I didn't even realize I moaned until the breath of Wolf's laughter hit my bare shoulder.

"Wings can be very sensitive," he teased. To prove his point, he let his fingers trail up the delicate surface. I shivered in response, but he didn't stop there. He ran his hands all the way to the top of them, back down to the very bottom. "They're especially sensitive to light touches, like the wind."

Then, he blew on them, making every muscle in my back tense.

But his hands were on me again, pressing me to the wall, holding me still while I trembled in his grasp.

"I don't remember torturing you this much," I sighed. "I left your wings alone."

My breath hitched when his lips landed on my shoulder, kissing me lightly before moving further down my back.

I couldn't see my own wings, but I was sure they tightened, flexed, clenched. "Wolf," I moaned.

He didn't stop. He moved his hands across the length of my wings, fully massaging them now, fully palming them.

"Yes, Huntress?"

He touched the very bottom of my back again, then trailed his fingers up to the base of my neck.

"You know you ruined my shirt," I manage to mumble.

I couldn't see him, but I could feel him as he peeled his own dirty shirt off his body.

"Here," he said. I turned to face him, finding him shirtless in the small trail of light. "Take it."

I didn't cover my exposed body as I leaned forward and reached for his outstretched shirt, but he pulled back at the last second.

"Really?" I asked. "You want me to run around here shirtless?"

His eyes trailed down my entire body. "Maybe I do."

"Fine," I said, propping both hands on my hips. "You have it your way, then. I'll head home to Jessiah."

I started out of the underground cave, barely making it two steps before Wolf shoved his shirt over my head from behind.

I stumbled but quickly straightened and pulled the shirt the rest of the way on, stretching my wings as the fabric settled around them.

"What?" I teased. "Change your mind?"

When my eyes met his, I shivered. Something hungry, depraved, possessive lingered there, waiting. All this time we spent together, it was easy to forget how much of a predator he really was.

"I'm the only one who gets to see you like that," he growled. "Only me."

I opened my mouth to respond, to pretend to argue, but Wolf's eyes snapped to something behind me. He was now shirtless, but his sword remained strapped at his waist, always ready.

The look in his eyes at whatever he saw behind me sent my hand reaching for Venom.

My body shot to life, adrenaline pulsing, ears tuning in. Even with this new wave of power controlling my wings, I looked to Wolf for guidance.

He was watching something behind me. I heard the stick break next, then another.

I spun around, pulling Venom from her sheath as I raised my hand, ready for a fight.

But we were not met with daggers and violence. No, standing before us was a group of males and females, all dressed in black, all with red paint smeared across half their faces.

"What are you doing here?" the male in front of the group asked.

Wolf stepped forward, draping a protective arm across my shoulder. "We're only here on a visit. We mean no harm."

I straightened, trying my best to flex my wings as the group sized me up, taking in my new wings, my dagger, my everything. Hells, it felt like they stared directly into my soul.

"Not you," a woman in the back asked. "Her."

I opened my mouth to defend myself, but Wolf gave the back of my neck a light squeeze. "You know why she's here."

The group in front of us—all vampyres—just stood there, observing. Not one of them reached for a weapon. Not one of them even looked to be on the defense.

"We're ready," the male in front said. "We've been waiting for months now."

"We wed on the summer equinox," Wolf answered. I snapped my attention to him, wondering what in all hells was going on and why he suddenly knew these random vampyres. Were these the same ones who took Abigail? "I expect my father will be here in full force the next day or two."

Wolf was the one who spoke, but still, all the eyes lingered on me. I didn't trust myself to speak, didn't trust myself to move.

"Is she as powerful as you say she is?" the male in front asked.

Wolf smiled softly, rubbing a thumb against the back of my neck before answering, "She is even more powerful than we could have dreamed."

My breath hitched in my throat. I wanted to turn, wanted to run, wanted to scream. Why were they talking about me this way? And who in all hells were these people?

Vampyres, yes. The ones here in hiding, I was starting to guess.

The ones Wolf was sent here to scope out.

Unease washed over me at the thought of it. I didn't know who to trust. Wolf was playing both sides. This was more than sneaking around. It was more than standing up to Wolf's asshole father.

This was a rebellion against the archangel.

All thoughts ceased as the female in the back of the group took a knee. Another one did the same. Then another—all kneeling until the entire group before us bowed, lowering their heads.

"What's happening?" I asked.

Wolf bent over to whisper in my ear, "All hail the blood queen."

Wolf led me back to the tower, back up the massive staircase that led to the top floor, to the suite where Jessiah waited for us. He didn't so much as glance at us as we approached, just kept his focus on the ceiling as he splayed across the sofa, his white angel wings relaxed on either side.

My chest tightened when I saw it. Wolf used to lounge that same way, his black wings a force to be reckoned with.

"We're back," I announced. Wolf walked straight past me and into the room I slept in last night.

Clearly, he wasn't speaking to Jessiah.

But Jessiah didn't seem to notice or care. His eyes widened when he finally turned to face me. "Well, well, well," he cooed. "Did somebody finally learn some control of their magic?"

"I don't know," I pushed my power out, using all the control I had left to flare my wings. "Why don't you tell me?"

He smiled and flung himself off the sofa, taking in my wings with his jaw hanging open.

"Hells," he sighed. "These wings are massive. That's damn impressive for a vampyre, Huntyr, even one of your lineage." He stepped to the side to take them in fully, nodding slowly in approval. "I haven't seen fae wings like these in years. Your magic is...it must be *strong*."

"It's incredible," I sighed. "It feels so normal, like I should have had wings this entire damn time."

He smiled lightly. "Would've made your life a lot easier, huh?" His face slowly dropped, my small window into the cheerful Jessiah slowly vanishing.

They were both hurting. I knew that. It didn't take a genius to see that their father had really done some damage on both of them. Still, Jessiah wasn't the asshole, but he had no right to pile on Wolf the way he did.

"Don't say it," he said.

"I wasn't going to say anything!"

"You were. I can see it on your face." He turned and flopped back down on the sofa.

I propped a hand on my hip. "And what, do tell, was I planning on saying?"

Jessiah got comfortable on the sofa before answering in a high-pitched voice, "You were a big asshole to your brother, Jessiah. You should apologize. It isn't fair that you said those things, etcetera, etcetera."

I took a step backward. "Sounds like you have a guilty conscience. Maybe that's your heart telling you to apologize. I don't know about you, but I wouldn't stand in the way of fate —" My words were cut off by him throwing a dusty pillow in my direction. I dodged it quickly, tucking into my bedroom for safety and shutting the door behind me.

The energy in the room changed instantly.

"You don't have to ignore him," I said. Wolf lay on his back, waiting for me on the bed. I kicked off my dirty boots, unclipped my dagger from my belt, and joined him, flopping onto my stomach.

The sun was still up outside, and I was exhausted. I hadn't done much at all since I was taken by Asmodeus. The travel, the exploring, the wings. The new wave of exhaustion rolled over me heavily, relentlessly.

"I'm not ignoring him," Wolf whispered, making sure to keep his voice quiet so only I could hear. "I just don't trust myself to not drive my sword into his shins the next time he speaks."

"Right," I answered. "So, ignoring."

I let my eyes flutter closed for just a second. My eyelids were heavy, pulling me deeper and deeper into the exhaustion.

"Retract your wings," he said. "You'll replenish your magic quicker."

I could feel the power within me beginning to flicker, like I drained the well of magic deep in my soul. *Retract.* Like it was that fucking easy. I felt frazzled and uneven; the very last thing I felt was control over my emotions.

"Here." Wolf's hand landed on my back, splaying over the base of both wings through his large shirt. "Relax here."

I let out a breath and tried to relax the muscles Wolf touched. It was hard, though, when his touch affected me like that.

"They're just hiding out there," I whispered. "They're waiting."

A few beats passed. "They're waiting for you."

I took another breath and let my shoulders relax further. "Do they know I can't help them?" My throat burned at the words. They looked so hopeful kneeling before me, like I really would be the one to save them, like I really would be the one to rebuild their kingdom.

His hand began to move in soft, soothing circles around my back. "Deep breath, Huntress. Pull your power back to you."

I did as he ordered, trying my best to pull everything back to my center. I focused on the tendrils of power that flooded my body and, one by one, I pictured them crawling back to my heart, retreating.

"How can I possibly help them?" I continued. "I can't even control my own damn wings."

His hand made another circle then paused. "You don't give yourself enough credit."

I didn't realize what he was talking about until I blinked my eyes back open and saw only the room around me where the large wings should have been.

Hells. "I didn't even feel that."

"That's good," he said. "That means it's natural."

"If I had years to practice with them, if I had years to sharpen my magic, practice with my blood, maybe I could—"

"You don't need years. You're perfect exactly as you are."

I turned my head on the pillow so I could see him. He was already staring at me, eyes dark in focus as he traced the spot on my back where my wings just were.

"They're going to fight for us, aren't they?" I asked.

His jaw clenched. "Not *for* us. *With* us."

"Does he know?" I glanced toward the bedroom door. "Does he know what you have planned with them?"

Wolf lowered his gaze again. "It's safer for him if he doesn't, but I'm confident that when the time comes, he'll choose the right side."

Sleep came swiftly.

Wolf's hand never left my back.

CHAPTER 19
WOLF

"The mission was uneventful," I lied, doing my best to sound as bored as possible. Luseyar and Asmodeus sat at the far end of the large table, both demanding answers to questions Jessiah and I couldn't answer.

It was always the same damn thing.

"You didn't see anyone else in Scarlata?"

I shrugged. "The place was overgrown by the forest. There's no sign of anyone living anywhere in the ruins. It was silent."

Luseyar busied himself with looking anywhere but at me. *Still.* But Asmodeus glared at me for one too many seconds before sliding his gaze to my brother. "And you agree with this?"

Jessiah leaned back in his chair. Even after our long journey home, he looked confident and put together. Hells, he was such a damn good liar, I couldn't help but wonder what else he lied about in his life.

"I agree," Jessiah added. "We scouted the entire kingdom's ruins and the surrounding areas. There was no sign of anyone, not even the hungry ones. They must have moved on."

Asmodeus tapped a finger against his chin. "They're out there somewhere. If they're not in Scarlata, they're somewhere else, waiting for us."

I took a long breath, making sure to exhale loudly.

His gaze snapped to me. "Apologies, son—are we bothering you?"

I rolled my eyes. "I'm simply exhausted from our journey, and I have much better things to do than stand here and tell you—once again—that our trip was uneventful."

He considered my words. It was risky, but he would usually rather dismiss me than deal with my attitude on a regular basis.

"Fine," he snapped. "You must prepare for the wedding, anyway. The equinox is coming up, and I want to know everything there is to know about Huntyr's power before then. Find out what she can do. My patience is growing thin. I assume she'll be more forthcoming with you than she will be with one of my men forcing it out of her."

In the corner of my eye, I saw Jessiah shift.

"If you don't start showing me what she's capable of, I'll be forced to get the information another way. Understood?"

I nodded, biting my tongue and clenching my fists until I was sure my palms bled. "Understood."

"What the hells is that supposed to mean?" Huntyr asked. "I show him my wings? I draw blood and burn the place down like I nearly did in Moira? I turn more hungry ones into statues when we're about to die?"

"You've matured as a vampyre now," I explained. "Your magic is going to be much more powerful than it was at Moira."

"Great," she mumbled. "Because that wasn't terrifying at all."

"You summoned your wings, right?" I pushed myself away from the door. "That was magic you didn't have access to until you drank my blood."

She paused. "You must think very highly of your own blood."

I took another step closer. "It could have been anyone's blood you drank. But it was mine, because it will *always* be mine."

"How is that fair?" Her big, round eyes looked up at me from her seated position on the edge of the bed. "You drink from other people. You've drank from *a lot* of other people, I'd bet."

The possessive flare inside me heated up. "That was different. You didn't know what I was; I couldn't exactly feed off you to survive."

"And now?" Her smirk dropped. "You've been feeding since we arrived in The Golden City. It certainly hasn't been from me."

I clenched my fists and reminded myself to breathe. Hells, even thinking about her blood sent me into a freaking whirlwind.

"Would you rather I fed from you?" Thick tension clung to the air. "Do you want it to be your blood that keeps me alive, Huntress?"

A lustful gaze flashed through her eyes, but she blinked and cleared her throat. "I don't know what to think, not anymore."

Pain stabbed me in the chest. I took a step back.

I knew that would be the answer. I hurt her too badly; I betrayed her trust too much. What happened in Scarlata between us... the kissing... the everything, it still wasn't the same.

Because I could never go back in time and take back everything I said to her, everything I did, everything I used her for. I couldn't go back in time and fix things between us.

I took another step back, putting more distance between us. "Exactly," I mumbled. "My blood is yours anytime you need it, Huntress." I couldn't look at her as I said the words. "But you won't have to worry about who I'm drinking from, so long as it's not you."

I felt our bond, tried to sense any emotions coming from the other side. I got the slightest whisper—like a scent wafting in the wind—of grief.

"Anyway," I started again, "we need to continue training your magic. We have to show Asmodeus something, so it's better we plan for it now than get blindsided at the equinox."

I turned around and reached for the doorknob.

"Wait," she started, "you mean right now?"

"We only have a few weeks to find the true strength in your blood. Time is a luxury we do not have. Follow me, Huntress."

To my surprise, she followed me without arguing. Perhaps she understood how dire this situation was, how little time we had to get her magic under control before Asmodeus took matters into his own hands. And this time, I didn't hold back. I pushed Huntyr as far as she would allow, both mentally and physically.

Something in the air shifted. The lightness, the joking around the situation was long gone.

It wasn't just about us anymore. It wasn't simply Huntyr and me, our conflicts, her own fight for survival.

Others were counting on her to survive. Others were counting on her to fight back.

CHAPTER 20
HUNTYR

Wolf and I trained together in Moira, but nothing like this. It was as if something deep within him unleashed, as if he was holding back on his own power the entire time we were in that academy working together.

The first few days, I could barely get out of bed in the morning. Not only was Wolf challenging my body by throwing lessons of tactical training in every so often, but he absolutely drained my magic every single day.

I thought my magic was supposed to be growing. I thought there was supposed to be something special about my blood, about what I could do.

It certainly didn't fucking feel like it.

"I need a break," I gasped. I bent over and put both hands on my knees, supporting myself. "Hells, I don't remember this being so difficult."

"That's because you barely even touched your magic in Moira. What they taught you there was hardly even the basics."

"Really?" I pushed my black hair aside and looked up at him. "That's not how I remember it."

Wolf scoffed, putting both hands on his sweaty waist. "I hated being there, watching you struggle to learn what they were teaching you. They barely had any idea what they were talking about."

I took a few more big gulps of air, finally catching my breath. "How? How can Moira possibly exist when this is what's waiting for us on the other side of the Transcendent? How do they not know they're sending everyone to their deaths?"

Wolf shrugged. "They trust the archangels. That alone is probably the most dangerous thing anyone can do."

"Careful," I warned. "You never know who could be listening around here."

Wolf stepped closer, eyes darkening. "I'm always very aware of who may be listening."

I knew what it was like to grow up in a place that wasn't safe. I knew what it was like to look over your shoulder for danger at every damn turn. "It must have been hard here, living as a vampyre."

He dropped his head, mind escaping somewhere I could not follow. "It was isolating, confusing. My father already brought vampyres into this kingdom, but nothing could prepare me for what would happen when he sacrificed me to the goddess."

My breath hitched. "How could Era let that happen? How could the goddess allow him to turn you into a vampyre?"

Wolf shook his head. "She spoke to me that day. I thought it was a dream at first, but then..." He paused, clearing his throat before continuing, "she told me I would understand eventually, and that she was doing what had to be done."

Those words made me pause. "Strange," I mumbled.

"What's strange?"

"She told me something similar during the Transcendent, after we both—after I thought we both died." I didn't exactly want to tell him that Era told me to stay with him, especially since everything that happened afterward was so fucking awful.

"I wonder if this is what she meant," Wolf continued. "Your blood could change things, Huntyr. Your power could change things."

I thought back to the passages in the books left in Wolf's bedroom. "I read something about this, about the powerful one with blood who could end the hungry ones. What you said about my mother looking for a cure, and now this..." I stared at Wolf, waiting for some sort of reaction, but the tight clenching of his jaw was the only thing that indicated he heard me. "It's me, isn't it? Your father thinks I am the one who can do all of that, who can control them."

Wolf didn't answer me. He didn't have to.

"He's wrong," I continued, voice wavering only slightly. "You know he's wrong, Wolf."

"No, I don't." His eyes met mine in a hungry glaze. "What I tasted in your blood—I've never tasted anything like it, Huntyr. You have something special. I mean, hells, look at your wings. When's the last time you saw someone with wings like that?"

I stiffened. "We both know what happened when the hungry ones attacked us in the forest. I saw it. Jessiah saw it."

"It was an accident. Hells, who knows if that was even my power? You were the one who said we needed to keep it a secret, Wolf. You were the one so adamant on protecting this." I didn't understand him! One second, he's swearing me to secrecy about what we saw in Scarlata, and the next, he's wanting to exploit me.

"Things have changed, Huntyr. We need to prepare to show him what you can do before he becomes impatient."

"You're kidding, right? I can't show him any of my magic, Wolf! Not with what he can do to me!"

"We don't have a choice. If I don't get it out of you, someone else will."

"We *always* have a choice!" Emotion leaked into my words. "This is too far, Wolf. I'll marry you. I'll pretend to be on his side, but I will not show him my power. He'll use me. He'll make me... Hells, I don't even know what he'll do with my magic once he finds out!"

I felt the presence of the archangel before I saw him. He sauntered into the room behind Wolf.

And then, a slow clap came from Asmodeus.

Wolf stiffened, eyes snapping to me in warning.

"Good work, son," Asmodeus said. "It seems you know a few things you have yet to share with me. Care to rectify that? Or shall I?"

Wolf's posture instantly changed. "I was planning on telling you," he said, "as soon as she was ready."

What the fuck was happening?

"I knew you were the one I was looking for." He stepped forward to stand beside Wolf, his disgusting eyes flickering over my body. I fought to keep my chin up, even as everything in me wanted me to retreat from his gaze. "I just needed something to confirm it."

"You can't prove anything," I spat.

"Maybe not," Asmodeus pushed. "But my son here seems to think you're worth protecting, which means you truly are powerful."

I didn't dare look at Wolf. This was a completely different version of him than I saw in Scarlata. Was he doing this to protect me? Fuck that! Fuck protection! This was much deeper than him and me now.

Scarlata changed everything.

"I have amazing things planned for you, Huntyraina. Powerful, great things."

I said nothing as I stared back at him, even though the panic started to claw at my chest, begging to take over my body.

"That's enough for now," Asmodeus announced. "Go back to your room and rest, Huntyraina. With what we have coming, you're going to need it."

I didn't think twice. I shoved past both of them and bolted back to Wolf's bedroom, grateful he didn't follow.

Was this his plan all along? To make me trust him then deliver me right back here to Asmodeus? Did he know Asmodeus was listening to us back there?

Tears poured down my face as I ran into the room and slammed the door behind me.

Trust no one.

Why the fuck did I keep forgetting that?

CHAPTER 21
WOLF

I knocked on Jessiah's door warily. Between Huntyr and my brother, I figured it would be easier to make up with my brother.

Besides, Huntyr needed some space to cool off after what happened earlier today.

Jessiah answered the door within two seconds, stepping aside so I could enter. "Mind if I hide here for a bit?" I asked.

His face softened immediately, and he shut the door behind me as I made my way inside. "I take it she wasn't so thrilled about showing some of her magic?"

"Not in the slightest."

"Did you tell her it was to keep her safe? Who knows what he was planning to do with her if you gave him nothing. You did the right thing, brother."

I sat on the edge of his bed. "Well, she's officially pissed at me."

"Can you blame her?" he asked. "She has been betrayed time and time again. She may want to trust you, but her life is on the line here. If she thinks for even a second you have other intentions with her, she'll pull back."

He had a point there. "I hate fighting with her. Things were so much easier when—"

"When she thought you were only a fallen angel? When she thought she was only a fae?" Jessiah scoffed. "Isn't it better for her to know the real you and hate you for it, than to love the fake version of you?"

"That's easy for you to say."

Jessiah took a long breath. "After everything you did to her, she was still willing to forgive you. To trust you again. To try. That says a lot, brother, even if we are still operating under the grasps of Asmodeus and his plans for power."

I thought about it then, about telling him what was really going on, about telling him the plan I had to put a stop to the insanity of Asmodeus and his hungry search for power.

But Jessiah was loyal, and right now, I wasn't sure how loyal he was to me and how much of his loyalty still held for our father.

"Listen," I started, shifting uncomfortably. "I need a favor from you."

A smile curled his lip. "This should be good."

"I need you to help Huntyr learn to fly. She can summon her wings now, and she's getting stronger every day. She just needs someone to get into the air with her, and we both know it can't be me."

I glanced away before I could see the shock in Jessiah's golden eyes. "I was under the impression you didn't want me anywhere near Huntyr, especially if we were to go flying."

"Things have changed."

"What, exactly, changed? Because I know you're still in love with her, if that's what you're referring to."

I ignored his comment and ran a hand through my tangled hair. "I realized I was wrong. She needs to learn to fly. It's the best way to keep her safe. I can't teach her, but you can. This goes beyond me and my selfish intentions of keeping her to myself."

He eyed me carefully. "There are other people living in The Golden City who could teach her. It doesn't have to be me, brother. Plenty of fae and angels would be more than willing—"

"It has to be you," I interrupted. "I don't trust anyone else with her."

"But you trust me?"

I finally looked at him. "Of course I trust you, you damn idiot. You're the only one in this entire kingdom I trust besides Huntyr."

"Well, then there's something you should know."

I froze. "What is it?"

Jessiah shifted uncomfortably, looking anywhere else in the room but at me. "A few weeks ago, I caught Huntyr trying to sneak around in The Golden City. I brought her back, of course, but I gave her a bit of a hard time for being so mean to you. She told me she would agree to marry you and she would go along with our plans if I promised to take her back home for a night."

I processed his words very, very slowly. "Are you joking?"

My brother threw his hands in the air. "I only agreed because I wanted her to get her ass back to the castle. I never intended on bringing her back there, especially without telling you."

Fuck. Midgrave was a long way from here. It would take hours just to fly there, and that was if she managed to get out of The Golden City alive, which was a challenge already.

"Absolutely not," I stated. "Huntyr visiting Midgrave, even for a night, is the worst thing she could do right now."

"Agreed," Jessiah said innocently. "I just wanted to tell you about it now that we're trusting each other and everything."

I rolled my eyes at him. Huntyr *would* ask Jessiah to take her back. Honestly, I expected her to make a break for it a long time ago.

I wasn't mad about it, but it couldn't happen, not if we wanted to keep her safe.

A long silence filled the air between us. "I won't let anything happen to her," he said. All jokes left his voice. This was serious. He meant those words.

"I know you won't. Just watch your hands, okay? She might not know where we stand, but nobody else gets to have her." *I was only half-joking.*

"No need to worry, brother." Jessiah clapped me on the shoulder. "My romantic interests lie elsewhere. Even if they didn't, I can see the way Huntyr looks at you, not to mention the fact that she's pissed at you every other day."

"What? That's supposed to be a good thing?"

Jessiah laughed quietly. "Oh yes," he said. "That's a good thing."

The entire day was spent avoiding my bedroom. I went on a run through The Golden City, careful to avoid any hungry ones, and ate in the dining hall alone, taking my sweet time. Huntyr would not want to talk to me today, not after what happened.

But she would have to understand that this was all to protect her. We were playing the long game. We couldn't defeat the evil here if we were all dead.

It was a give and a take; show Asmodeus some of Huntyr's power so he would be happy, and then we would have space to plan our next move.

Why couldn't she understand that?

I was on my way back to my room a little after midnight when I felt a flare of Huntyr's emotions through our bond. I was just passing the long hallway to the empty training rooms, my bedroom much too far away to feel through the bond.

I turned.

Huntyr was close.

I kept my footsteps light and the walls to our bond up. I didn't want her to know I was coming. If alone time was what she was looking for, I didn't want to interrupt that. I just wanted to know she was safe.

Besides, it wasn't like her to be creeping through this castle alone. She hardly left our bedroom.

Suddenly, I felt a rush of frustration in my chest. It felt warm and intense, just like the rest of Huntyr's emotions. I was growing more and more accustomed to them, though. Her emotions, mine—they blended together, and I felt different without the mold of both of them. It was like I needed them both to feel whole again, to feel normal.

The hall grew darker and darker. I kept my ears sharp, but I didn't hear anyone else in the vicinity. I just felt Huntyr.

And then, I heard her. I heard subtle grunts, low moans of frustration.

Was she down here training?

I made sure my every move was silent as I approached the doorway of the training hall. Darkness helped conceal my presence as I peeked into the room.

Huntyr was training. Sweat coated her body, her black tunic—*my* black tunic—clung to her as she knelt on the ground.

She had her hands out in front of her, summoning a small flame over and over and over again.

I went to step into the room but stopped myself.

Huntyr wasn't just training, wasn't just sweating from exertion.

She was crying. Her face turned slightly, moonlight pouring into the dark room and reflecting off her wet skin.

Fuck. My chest tightened, and I had to remind myself to keep my bond closed.

They were not silent or peaceful tears, either. They were violent ones, angry ones. They wrecked her body, wrecked her magic.

She dropped her hands as a sob shook her, raised them again with a determined breath, and summoned the flame once more. What she was trying to do was beyond me.

But clearly, she thought she was failing.

"Dammit!" she half-yelled in a hushed whisper. She dropped her hands again and crumpled entirely, her arms wrapping around her body.

Then, her wings appeared.

They appeared quickly, likely in response to her emotion.

She didn't seem to notice at first as she cried in her crumbled position on the ground. But when she did notice, she paused.

Took a breath.

Then she looked up.

Her throat bobbed in the moonlight as she gasped through tears. "Why?" she whispered. "I'm so fucking tired. Why does it always have to be me? I don't want to fight anymore. I don't want any of this." Her eyes flickered closed, but she remained that way—knees on the ground, wings hanging from her shoulders, tears dripping from her chin. "Please, please, help me."

I never took Huntyr for the type to worship the goddess, but here? On her knees? She *begged* for help.

For a break.

I pressed my fingernails into my palms with restraint, forcing myself to back out of the room. Huntyr was strong, I was the first person to know that, but we all had a breaking point.

Had Huntyr finally hit hers?

I made my way back through the hall, back toward my bedroom. I kept the walls of my shield firmly shut. I didn't know what would leak through the second I lifted them, the second I relaxed for even a second.

I thought I knew pain, but seeing Huntyr like that exposed me to a brand new definition of the word.

Before I could stop myself, I was pounding on Jessiah's bedroom door.

Thud, thud, thud. I waited a few seconds before lifting my fist again. *Thud, thud, thud.* "Jessiah!" I called out. "I know you're in there, Jessiah! I need to talk to you! Now!"

When I went to knock again, the door swung open.

"Hells, Wolf, what? What could possibly be so damn important?"

"Take her home," I said.

His face remained blank. "What?"

"Huntyr asked you to take her back home to Midgrave. I want you to take her."

"Are you kidding?" he asked. "You seriously want me to fly her all the way there with her new wings?"

"You can teach her to fly tomorrow. She's a fast learner, she'll be fine." My throat tightened, but I clenched my fists at my sides.

Jessiah ran a hand down his face. "You don't think that's dangerous?"

"I'll make sure you're not caught. The day after tomorrow, after you teach her how to use her wings. Wait until the sun is set."

I was ready for him to argue, to tell me how insane this plan was. But he just blinked at me before nodding. "What's with the sudden change of heart?"

"She's losing hope," I answered, turning my back on Jessiah so I didn't have to look at his face when I said, "It might be the only thing she has left to hold onto."

CHAPTER 22
HUNTYR

I crept through the dark halls of the wretched castle, making sure I didn't run into a single soul as I made my way back to Wolf's bedroom.

It took me hours to train until I was exhausted, hours to realize I was never going to be as strong as I needed to be.

A fucking queen. A leader. A vampyre. I couldn't be those things. I couldn't lead people to freedom, couldn't raise a dead kingdom from the ashes.

That wasn't me.

Those people—everyone who counted on me—they were wrong. They were wrong to put their faith in me.

My magic rattled my bones, clattered inside me, but I could never control it. Not in the way I wanted to.

I wanted to be better. I really fucking did. But I felt so weak. So powerless. So incompetent.

I was no queen. I was no savior.

The sooner everyone realized that, the better.

Wolf slept with his back to me as I entered the bedroom, and I was grateful for it. I didn't need him inspecting every emotion on my face, didn't need him questioning my sweaty body or my flushed skin.

I just wanted some peace.

I kicked my boots off and made my way to the bathroom door before Wolf said, "Jessiah is teaching you to fly tomorrow first thing. Don't be late."

"What?" I asked. "I thought you—"

"I changed my mind," he said. "You deserve to know how to fly. He's the one who will teach you." He didn't turn around, didn't face me, just let me walk to the bathroom without another word.

If I hadn't felt so damn empty, I might have actually been excited.

Jessiah and I stood awkwardly on the roof of an abandoned building on the edge of The Golden City. The sun had fully risen, but the place still felt grim and shadowed.

"This doesn't feel safe," I said.

A cool breeze tickled my skin.

"That's because it isn't, and that's even more reason for you to learn how to fly."

"Shouldn't I be learning to fight? To protect myself and my people?"

Jessiah flapped his own wings. "If you're in the middle of battle, sometimes it will be up to you to gauge the advantage point, to see things your weaker soldiers with no wings cannot see. Very few vampyres and fae possess magic strong enough for wings, Huntyr. You have a gift. You must learn to use it."

My chest tightened. I hated that he was right. I also hated that I didn't *want* these wings. I didn't *want* to bear this burden.

But that wasn't going to fix the problem. These wings were mine, no matter how hard I wished them away, no matter how often I cried to the goddess about it.

"Fine," I said. "So what's next?"

"Well," Jessiah smiled softly, "you can summon your wings now. That's the hardest part. Now, we just do this."

I should have seen it coming, but Jessiah catapulted himself forward and gripped me around the waist, flinging us both into the air.

This time, however, I had wings.

"Try!" he yelled through the air. His grip on me loosened but didn't disappear entirely as I flapped the heavy leather now attached to my body.

It was much harder than it looked. My body felt too heavy, wings flapping at an uneven beat.

I didn't make it a few seconds before we started to descend toward the city.

"Jessiah!" I yelled—shrieked, rather.

"I've got you." His arms tightened around me, nearly cutting off my breath as they dug into my stomach. His own wings flapped up, sending us back toward the sky. "Do it with me. Act like you're flying alone."

"It doesn't feel right!"

"It never will until you get used to it. Think of it like a child learning to walk."

I choked down the wave of frustration and did what he asked, pumping my wings repeatedly to match his.

Soon, our wings were moving in unison. We soared through the sky, but I didn't have time to worry about our height or how quickly I would die if I crashed toward the ground.

Hells, could I die by falling? Vampyres were much harder to kill than fae. Their bodies could handle more, could survive more than—

"Focus, Huntyr! I'm going to let go now."

"No!"

"I'll be right here," he said. His hands started to loosen, and panic crept into my chest. "Don't change a thing. I won't let you fall."

It was now or never.

Jessiah's hands slowly left my body.

And then, I was fucking flying.

I half-expected to plummet toward the ruins below us, but when my wings actually held my body in the air, I burst out laughing.

This. This was everything I could have dreamed of. This was *freedom.*

Jessiah cheered behind me, but I barely heard him over the sound of my own laughter. Joy bubbled in my chest—a feeling that had become foreign to me.

Did I want my wings? Did I want this burden? Did I want to be the most powerful vampyre, heir to the blood throne? Definitely not.

But this was making it worth it. This was finally giving me something to work with.

"You're doing it!" Jessiah yelled from above me. I flapped my wings again and again, soaring higher into the sky. I could see the walls of The Golden City below us, heavily guarded with weapons I had never even seen before.

I made sure to turn before we got too close. The last thing I needed was to be shot out of the sky on my first day of flying.

Still, it was hard to care when I was this ecstatic.

The rest of the day was more of the same. I flew until my back screamed at me, took small breaks to recover, and got right back out there. Learning the limits of my own wings and pushing my body harder and harder had me panting for breath and collapsing onto the roof by the time the sun began to lower on the horizon.

"Alright, alright," Jessiah said, standing over my collapsed body as I lay on my back. "I think we can consider this a successful first day of flying lessons."

I smiled, still too breathless to reply.

He approached and sat beside me, relaxing backward on his hands and extending his legs out in front of him. "Wolf will be thrilled for you," he started.

Ugh. I really tried to *avoid* thinking about Wolf all day. It gave me fucking whiplash every time I did. Hells, I didn't understand him or his reasoning. He wanted to help me save the vampyres, but now he wanted me to show his father my power?

When I didn't respond, Jessiah continued. "He's doing it all to help you, you know. Everything he does is to keep you safe."

"It really doesn't feel that way," I spat.

"Our father threatened to torture you again if we didn't show him something. Wolf would die before he let those men touch you again, Huntyr. Showing Asmodeus a small amount of your power was the compromise."

Well, shit. Why hadn't Wolf said that? He could have started with *Hey, Huntress, my father's going to hurt you if we don't give him something, so let's work together and figure out what we're going to expose.*

Instead, he let me believe he had ulterior motives for gaining his father's trust.

Again.

"Your brother can be a huge asshole," I replied. "It's hard to trust him when he's changing direction every five minutes."

"He always has a plan. He's always thinking of the greater good. I may not know the details of it all, but I can promise you that he is trustworthy. He's doing his best to get you out of this, even if we don't know the specifics."

The guilt started to creep in again, but I shoved it aside. I had nothing to feel guilty for. Wolf shouldn't be surprised I expected his betrayal again.

Even if, this time, he had his reasons.

We laid there on the roof for a few more minutes, watching the sun lower until darkness shadowed around us. I was beginning to see more and more of Jessiah, of what type of man he was. He was loyal to his brother, even when he had no clue what Wolf had planned for us.

And Jessiah was smart, calculated. He surely had his reasons.

"Come on," Jessiah said after a few more minutes, wiping sweat on the back of his arm and reaching down to hoist me up to my feet. "We deserve a drink after that."

CHAPTER 23
WOLF

The second ale was much easier to drink than the first, and the third was even better. One after another, I let that bitter liquid slide down my throat. The air was starting to warm, and this liquid was everything I needed.

"Careful," the barkeep warned. "I won't be the one carrying you through these streets back to the castle tonight."

"Who cares about the damn castle?" I muttered. "Nobody would notice if I didn't show up tonight."

She placed a fresh drink in front of me. "Maybe not, but the last thing we need is more angels creeping around this place."

A large hand fell onto my shoulder. "I've got him from here." Nathan pulled himself into the seat beside me. "I've got some catching up to do with my old friend, anyway."

I turned and faced him, using all my energy to pull a smile onto my face. "Nathan," I greeted. "Shouldn't you be off planning the world's demise?"

He laughed but eyed me carefully. "Even I deserve a cold drink every now and then."

I held my mug up to him in salute. "That, I understand."

We both drank, letting the low buzz of conversation in the pub surround us. My senses were comfortably dulled, and I was beginning to feel the relaxation I had been searching for since I arrived here tonight.

Ah, the power of a few ales.

"You look worried," he started. He leaned toward me and lowered his voice as he said, "Word around the street is that you were sent to Scarlata not too long ago. Anything note-worthy we should know about?"

Normally, I would shut him up immediately, push away any conversation of the blood kingdom in public. Nowhere was safe to discuss such things with him, not even here.

But I was tired. I was frustrated. And I was growing damn tired of keeping secrets. "We were there for a day or two," I answered. "Same as usual."

He waited for more, but even he knew I couldn't say much. The chattering of the pub lowered.

When I didn't say anything else, Nathan added, "I also hear a celebration is in order."

"A celebration?"

A large, stupid grin spread across his dark face. "You're getting married." He broke out in laughter, and dammit, he almost made me forget what was so bad about the entire thing.

Yes, I was getting married.

If only it was under better circumstances.

"That I am," I said. I clinked my mug against his when he held it out. "In a few days, I'll be a married man."

"She must be a very special girl if she can chain down the infamous Wolf Jasper."

I wanted to smile, but my chest ached at the thought. "Yeah," I mumbled. "Yeah, she is special. More special than anyone could imagine." I didn't tell him how terrified I was. I didn't tell him that I was very close to losing my shit entirely.

No, I let him buy me another drink, let him clasp my shoulder once or twice more, let him tell jokes of our past and dull the thoughts in my mind.

I wasn't sure how much time passed, but the sun no longer filtered through the piece of fabric we called the door. Fewer and fewer conversations filled the air around us. Nathan's words began to slur until I was certain he was just as drunk as I was.

In fact, when he started elbowing me in the ribs, I thought he was just falling out of his seat.

"Wolf, look."

The room blurred together as I lifted my gaze to the front of the bar.

My stomach dropped.

Huntyr walked ahead of Jessiah, eyes wide and hair a mess. She glanced around the entire room—which only consisted of two or three other parties—before her eyes landed on me.

She stiffened.

The smile fell from her face.

I barely noticed Nathan moving away from my side to greet my brother. My eyes were too focused on Huntyr.

She stood still for a few more seconds, not moving at all, before finally taking one step in my direction.

Then another.

Her wings were hidden now, summoned away. Good,

because everyone in this tavern would have dropped to their knees at the sight of those glorious things. She made her way over to me, though, and I took a deep breath of her.

Wind and cherries.

Fucking addicting.

"I didn't expect to see you here," she said. She stood at the bar beside my tall stool, her arm just barely brushing against mine.

"How was flying?" I asked. Maybe she'd forgotten she was angry at me. Maybe, by the grace of the fucking goddess, she'd understand why it was all so important we let Asmodeus think he was winning.

She looked down at her hands, blushing.

Then she smiled.

She tried to hide it, tried to bite her lip and suck in her cheek, but it was undeniable. The grin spread across her entire face until it reached those perfect eyes of hers.

"It was incredible." Her voice was barely a whisper. "I never thought I would experience anything like that. I felt so... so free."

Thank the goddess for the ale numbing my senses. "I remember those moments," I admitted. "Flying can be the most freeing thing in the world."

Her eyes finally met mine, smile fading. "I'm sorry, I shouldn't have said anything, not when you..." She didn't have to finish the sentence.

"Don't," I whispered. I turned in my stool and adjusted my legs so she was standing between my knees. To my surprise, she didn't move away. "You don't have to hide things from me. I want to know all of it."

"Still," she whispered. "It's bad enough that you didn't want Jessiah teaching me to begin with."

She tried to look away again, but I stopped her. I reached out and pulled on a stray piece of her black, curled hair. It was windblown now, wild. I liked it like that.

I liked her like that.

"Wolf." Her eyes twinkled. I liked it when they did that too. "Are you drunk?"

"Yes. And you are beautiful."

She sucked in a breath. "There are people watching." She went to turn around, to look at goddess knows who else, but I gripped her chin with my hand.

"You just spent an entire day in the arms of another man. Don't look at anyone else." My voice got too low, too possessive, but I didn't care. "You only look at me."

The fucking ale. It made me reckless. Or maybe it was her. She tended to do that, tended to make me forget about this fucking disaster of a city.

"Careful," she teased, leaning in. Fuck, was *she* drunk? "You sound jealous."

"I am jealous." I snaked an arm around her waist and held her body against mine. "I am jealous of anyone who gets to spend a single ounce of time with you. It should be all mine."

"What should?"

"All your time. It should all be with me. I can't fucking think straight when you're with someone else."

"Is that why you're here? Drunk at the pub?"

I scanned her face. Perfect. Sharp. Strong. "I'm here because I thought you would be going home, and I didn't think you wanted to speak with me." At least it was the truth.

The teasing smile disappeared.

"Am I wrong?" I pushed.

A handful of torturous seconds passed. I could hear my own heart pounding in my ears. "No," she answered. "No, you're not wrong. I wasn't sure I wanted to speak with you either."

My stomach dropped. "I wanted to apologize to you—"

"Don't." She placed a hand on my chest. "Don't bother, okay? Enough apologies. Enough of all this."

I pushed toward her bond but felt nothing. She had her walls up, the bond entirely shut off.

"You deserve an explanation."

"No." Her eyes sharpened when they met mine. "I deserve loyalty. I deserve to never be betrayed, to never be stabbed in the back."

I fought the urge to pull her even closer.

"What's done is done," she whispered. "You father is your father. I thought we both hated him the same amount, but I see you have lingering loyalties."

The growl from my chest surprised us both. "I do *not* have lingering loyalties."

"Really?" Both of her hands came to my shoulders. Hells, it had been so long since she touched me like this. Or maybe that was the ale talking, too. "Because you were simply training me for my magic so you could take the information back to him, right?"

"I wasn't going to tell him everything."

"But you were going to tell him I had magic."

"He isn't a fool, Huntyr. He already knows you have magic. He just wanted me to get it out of you instead of torturing it from you, alright? This way was less painful for both of us."

She tossed her head back and laughed quietly. "*Both* of us? You have no idea, Wolf."

"What would you like me to do?" I pulled her closer until she caught herself against me. I wrapped both arms around her back, holding tight. "Would you like me to tell him you aren't cooperating, that you aren't coming any closer to being convinced to help him? That you have not a single ounce of magic in your veins, that you aren't the powerful heir to the blood kingdom he thinks you are?"

Her eyes flickered to my lips. "That would be helpful, yes. At least he wouldn't be forcing me to—"

"Yes, he would be. He would be forcing you into everything, just as he's doing now. Only now, he at least is giving you the illusion of some freedom. That illusion won't last if he isn't satisfied with the results, Huntress."

Her jaw clenched. "Don't call me that."

"Why not? That's what you are. My wicked, violent huntress."

"I'm not your *anything*." She tried to pull away, but I tightened my grip on her. She fell back into my chest with a light gasp.

"You are my *everything*, Huntress, and like it or not, you'll be my wife."

An emotion I couldn't read crossed her features. "Only because we are forced to wed."

"Still. If you must marry, I'm glad it's me."

She shook her head. "It could have just as well been Jessiah."

"Don't say that. Don't say anyone else's name when you're in my arms, Huntress. Only mine." I leaned up so our lips were only a breath away. "Only me."

I reached for her through our bond but felt nothing. Hells, I would have given anything to know what she was thinking right then. Did she want me like I wanted her? Was she as aware of the tiny sliver of skin on her back that my fingers brushed? Or was I the only one going completely mad by even the smallest touch from her?

"Stop looking at me like that," she said.

"This is how I always look at you."

"I know, and it's becoming a problem."

"A problem for who, Huntress?"

"You're drunk." When she pulled away, I let her, though a deep, deep part of me wanted to throw her over my shoulder and take her out of here.

"Hardly."

Huntyr was just turning back to the bar when someone outside screamed.

My blood ran cold. Nothing in the world could have sobered me up faster.

Shit.

They're here.

CHAPTER 24
HUNTYR

"What was that?" I asked, looking to Jessiah and Wolf's friend, who stood near the front of the bar.

Wolf was already pushing himself up from his chair and attempting to step in front of me. Venom was in my hand within a second, every single one of my instincts burning.

Jessiah held out a hand. The music and conversation of the pub ceased. Nobody moved. Nobody spoke.

"Huntyr," Wolf warned from behind me, gripping my arm. "Stay here."

"What's going on?"

Jessiah pulled his sword from his belt and shared a glance with Wolf.

"Vampyres," Wolf answered. He tried to step in front of me, but I stopped him.

Another scream echoed through the buildings outside. "What are you going to do?"

Wolf seemed to sober up pretty quickly, and his brows

drew together with conflict when he gazed down at me. "What you spent your whole life doing, Huntress."

Shit. I knew The Golden City wasn't safe, and I had only seen the smallest amount of proof. This was what happened to the people here—they lived in fear. "Are they hungry ones?" I asked. "They must be, right?"

"Goddess above, I hope so."

Darkness flashed over Wolf's eyes before he pushed away from the bar and crept toward the entrance. Jessiah did the same, as did Wolf's friend.

Wolf was going to kill his own kind? My stomach dropped at the thought of it. I hated that I was conflicted. I hated that I cared about it at all.

This was what I spent my entire life doing, there was no denying that. But knowing what I knew now, would I do it all again? Even the hungry ones—who tried to kill me on many different occasions—held a soft spot in my chest now.

It was the nerves. I was absolutely certain it had to be the nerves stirring inside my stomach, creeping up my chest, pulling a reaction from my magic.

Wolf felt it through the bond, and he spun to make eye contact. "Huntress," he growled.

The room around us stilled. I knew exactly what he was thinking. If I do anything, if I even attempt to stop these things with my magic, everyone will know.

The secret would be out. I'd have confirmed what everyone else had been wanting me to be the entire time.

Voiler appeared beside me, stepping out of the shadows. *Had she been here this whole time?*

She slipped her arm around mine, securing herself at my side before whispering, "This could be a test sent from Asmodeus. Let them handle it."

Shock sent a wave of chills down my body. *Voiler knew.* "How do you—"

Another scream interrupted us, closer this time.

Wolf turned his attention back outside, following the others through that front door.

"She's right," he said without looking at us. "Stay here with Voiler. For all we know, he's doing this to test your power."

Voiler became the only thing anchoring me inside that damn tavern as the others rushed outside, swords drawn. "That sick bastard *would* risk innocents just to push you into using your power," she mumbled. "Every time I think I can't hate him any more, he proves me wrong."

I did a double take, realizing just what Voiler was saying. "How much do you know, exactly?" I kept my voice below a whisper, very aware of the lingering ears, though most were distracted with whatever lurked outside.

She didn't even look at me, just kept her gaze glued on the door and her arm hooked through mine as she answered, "I know enough to know he will regret every fucking thing he's done to you. We're going to make him pay."

If we weren't in public, I would have pushed her further, but something deep in my gut told me to keep this to ourselves.

She knew more than she was letting on.

Who else in this tavern did? Who else here was acting against Asmodeus?

Did she know about what happened in Scarlata too?

A few seconds later, the screams ended, and the sound of swords slicing flesh ceased.

Wolf, Jessiah, and the others returned without so much as a drop of sweat beading across their foreheads.

A few hungry ones were no match for a group of trained men, I knew that much. If Asmodeus was truly trying to lure out my power, he was going to have to try a lot harder.

"Just a few stragglers," Jessiah explained. "Nothing to worry about."

Everyone else seemed to accept this, but my attention locked on Wolf, who gave me a tight smirk. We both felt the truth—those hungry ones creeping this close to the tavern wasn't an accident.

But the barkeep went back to serving drinks. The other patrons warily returning to their tables as we all tried to act like we *weren't* almost just slaughtered by the beasts lurking in the streets.

"It would've saved me a lot of time in Moira if I knew this was what we were trying so hard to join," Voiler sighed.

Her relaxed tone eased some of the tension, but I had so many questions—like why was Wolf eyeing her from across the room, and why did she know so much about Asmodeus and his plan?

"I should go," she said, letting go of my arm and stepping to the side. "We'll talk soon, okay?"

Before I could even begin to ask what she knew, she was gone.

An hour later, after three more ales courtesy of Wolf and Jessiah, we made our way back to the castle.

I had to admit, the slight dull in my senses was exactly what I needed to finally relax for once. Even Wolf seemed to relax a little, which seemed damn near impossible.

For once, it felt like we actually had a step up. If Asmodeus really was trying to draw out my power, he failed.

We had control here, and we were going to keep it that way. Even if I had to show Asmodeus some of my power to keep him off our backs, I could choose when, where, and how much. He wasn't going to exploit me for everything I had, that was for damn sure.

And now, I could fucking fly. I could hardly believe it, but my tangled mess of curls was a nice reminder that just a few hours ago, Jessiah and I were soaring above this damn castle.

"What are you smiling about?" Wolf asked, bumping my shoulder with his.

"Nothing, just thinking about earlier today."

"She was incredible, brother. A natural." Jessiah stepped forward, taking lead down the long hallway that led to the two bedrooms.

I turned to Wolf, half-expecting him to be secretly upset he wasn't able to join us again. But he just stared back at me, beaming. Literally *beaming*. The lightning in his eyes practically glowed in the darkness.

"I didn't doubt her for a single second."

My chest fluttered, heat rushing to my cheeks. *Fuck.* Lord would literally disown me if he knew how much I swore I would never trust Wolf again.

And how much I forgot about that when Wolf looked at me like *that*.

Jessiah stopped walking abruptly ahead of us, the smile from Wolf's face falling in an instant. "What's—"

"I'd like to speak to our guest alone." Asmodeus stood in the hallway, half-hidden in shadows, aside from his massive wings glowing in the darkness.

Jessiah stood still, like he could really be the barrier between us and him.

Wolf stiffened at my side. "I don't think that's—"

"It's okay." I smiled at Wolf. "I'll be fine."

I felt a flare of his pure disgust through our bond, all the emotions toward his father he was very, very good at hiding. For survival, I guess you had to be good, especially in a place like this.

Wolf waited a few more seconds before huffing under his breath and walking to his bedroom, shooting Jessiah a look that ordered him to do the same. "I'll be waiting inside," he said.

Leaving Asmodeus and I alone together in the dark hallway.

I forced my hands to unclench and relax at my sides. Asmodeus wanted something from me. I possessed everything he desired, and he wasn't going to hurt me, not when he was this close to getting everything he ever wanted.

"Busy day for you, I take it," he started, taking a casual step in my direction. In this empty hallway, his voice echoed.

I forced a smile on my face. "Compared to being locked away in a dungeon, I suppose so."

His grin sent a chill down my spine. "I'd like to remind you, Huntyraina, that not a single thing happens in this kingdom without me knowing about it."

"I'd sincerely hope not."

"That includes your escapades through the skies with my

son, and that includes the little establishment you and your friends like to drink ale at."

I swallowed, not trusting my own words. It wasn't a surprise that he knew what we were all up to, but Wolf was under the impression that Asmodeus didn't know about the tavern. I wasn't going to be the one to prove his suspicions.

"You're a smart girl," he said, stepping even closer to me. He was still multiple feet away, but I had to resist the urge to step back. "You don't care about your own safety, that much you've proven, but what of your friends?" I clenched my jaw to stop myself from grimacing. Was this bastard really threatening Voiler? "What about them?" He motioned to the bedrooms behind him.

"What do you want from me?" I asked. "So far, I've done everything. You want me to marry one of your sons, and I'm doing it."

"Are you?" He crossed his arms over his chest. "Because I can feel something in the air, Huntyraina. I feel something coming."

Once again, I kept my mouth shut.

"Just remember," he continued, "it is not only your life and your freedom on the line here. Everyone you love is at my mercy. *Everyone.* It would be very wise for you to remember that before you go off and do something you may regret."

He stared at me for a handful of seconds, really ensuring I heard those words, before leaving down the hallway, narrowly missing my shoulder as he passed.

Holy fucking hells.

Just when I thought there was a semblance of hope, it was ripped away. It was naive of us to think we could do anything without Asmodeus knowing. I was putting everyone in danger by even thinking of standing up to him.

Jessiah's door opened first. "Hey," he said. "You alright?"

I nodded, throat dry.

"Good," he answered. "You can't let him scare you, Huntyr. You can't let him get in your head and control you with fear."

"But he—"

"It doesn't matter what he said." Jessiah took a long breath, glancing once at Wolf's door before adding, "You and I had a deal. I think it's about time I take you back to Midgrave."

My heart stopped beating. "Are you serious?"

He shrugged. "As long as your wings can handle the flight."

"They can!" My words rushed out of my mouth. "I swear, they can!"

"Good. Meet me here tomorrow when the sun goes down. We'll be back before anyone notices a thing." He slipped back into his bedroom without another word.

Adrenaline pulsed through my veins, but I took a long breath before allowing myself to follow Wolf into his room. He stood on the other side, shoulders tense. "I hate him," he sneered.

"Really?" I teased. "I hadn't guessed."

"I'm serious, Huntyr. I hate that he gets to order us around. I hate that we're stuck here, pretending like he owns us. What did he say to you?"

"He saw me flying today," I said. "And he made an ominous threat against everyone I care about. Nothing new."

Wolf cursed beneath his breath and ran his hands through his hair. "I'm so sorry, Huntress. You don't deserve this."

I kicked my boots off and made my way to the bed. "You

don't have to apologize for him. I can handle it, really. He wanted to test me today, and he's pissed that I didn't walk directly into his trap."

"It was stupid of us to spend so much time at the pub. He was going to find us there eventually."

I pulled Wolf's blanket up over my body, adjusting the soft pillow under my neck as I watched him pace the room. "But you have a plan, right?"

He stopped pacing and faced me. "Oh yes, Huntress. I have a plan. Now sleep. Your body will be exhausted from all that flying."

I couldn't even keep my eyes open long enough for him to join me in the bed. Wolf was right about the exhaustion. Every ounce of my body craved sleep, and after the additional ales at the pub, I was in no position to fight it.

CHAPTER 25
HUNTYR

I waited all day for Wolf to come back to the bedroom, to find me sneaking out with Jessiah, to ruin the entire plan.

But none of that happened.

My nerves grew and grew as the night approached, but nothing was going to stop me from flying home. Nothing was going to take this one chance away from me.

Wolf never showed up, which made it easy for me to slip on my worn boots and meet Jessiah in the hallway.

He was already waiting, his jacket tight across his shoulders as he leaned back against the wall with his arms crossed over his chest, looking just like Wolf but much less smug. Always less smug.

"Are you sure this is a good idea?" I asked, suddenly feeling like we were going to get caught any minute.

"No." His voice echoed off the small hallway. "It's definitely not a good idea. But I made a deal with you, and I'd rather we get this over with now, while things are calm."

I nodded. "I swear I won't stay long. Just enough time to

see some people, and we'll be back here before anyone notices." *Lord and Rummy.* If I could just lay eyes on them, if I could just tell them I was alive, I could at least go through with this damn plan knowing they were at peace with it.

My heart ached in my chest.

"If we hurry, we'll be back before the sun comes up," he said, pushing himself off the wall. "But it's going to be risky. Come with me."

I followed him as he crept through the dark hall. He descended the stairs of the small, hidden staircase, careful not to make a single sound with his boots. I did the same. Jessiah's white angel wings were tucked tight behind his shoulders, the only way his large frame would fit through the bottom door.

The cold air fluttered across my skin, tickling my nerves.

I lost hope of ever going back home. Even after my conversation with Jessiah, I never thought he would actually risk taking me back there, but I was learning, day by day, that Jessiah was a man of his word. He was loyal and kind, and if he made a deal with me, he would keep it.

We walked outside in silence, but the street began to look familiar as we made our way to the very back of The Golden City.

"Are we taking the tunnel out of here again?" I whispered. "Won't Griffith tell Asmodeus that we left?"

He turned and looked at me, letting his wings fan out on either side. "When you live in this place long enough, Huntyr, you learn a thing or two about how loyalty works."

I did the same, summoning my wings and flaring them on either side of my body in preparation as we walked.

"That doesn't make me feel better about this."

Jessiah just laughed under his breath as we found the

same large stone that covered the entrance to the tunnel. "Griffith has known Wolf and I since we were children. He loved us more than our own father did at times. As long as we return before we are noticed, he'll keep our secret for us."

I froze, hesitating at the tunnel's entrance. "You're sure about this?"

Jessiah's smile faded. "I'm sure that Griffith won't announce our departure, yes. But if you're having doubts, we can always turn back. We have a long journey ahead and you need to be sure."

"No," I interrupted. "I want to go." I didn't give it another thought. I jumped into the tunnel and made my way toward the other end, where Griffith and the stables would be waiting. Jessiah was right. I was sure about this. It was worth the risk.

Jessiah followed behind me, reaching up to push the exit door open. "You owe me for this," he whispered.

"And you owe me for assisting in holding me captive, so I'll consider us even for now."

He rolled his eyes, but I was already crawling out of the tunnel above. I waited for him outside, crouching near the entrance in the darkness.

It looked much, much different here than it did during the day. Griffith's lantern from inside became the only visible light filtering toward us.

But Griffith was already awake, waiting. I jumped in surprise when I saw him leaned against a tree to my right.

Jessiah stood beside me as Griffith stepped forward. "This is dangerous, even for you," he said to Jessiah.

"We know it's risky," Jessiah replied. "We wouldn't be going if it weren't absolutely necessary."

Griffith practically ignored me the last time we came here

to gather the horses, but not this time. He stared me up and down, his intense eyes beating into me like they could see my every secret.

"You put all of us in danger by leaving, girl," he said. "It isn't just your life on the line here. It's mine. It's Jessiah's."

I stiffened, rolling my shoulders backward. I was getting tired of hearing that. It *was* selfish for me to leave like this, but couldn't they see the situation I was in? Couldn't they see how desperately I needed this? "I'll never speak of this again, and I'll never ask this of you again." I met his eyes with the same intensity. "I swear it."

Griffith looked at me for what felt like hours, but then he swallowed and turned to Jessiah. "Hurry up, then. The sooner you're back, the better." He turned and left, walking into the stables like he wanted no part of this.

"Are you sure this is okay?" I whispered to Jessiah.

"It's fine, he's just protective." Jessiah sounded like it was no big deal, but every inch of my body lit up with nerves.

Griffith was right. It wasn't just my life on the line. I was putting everyone else in danger by leaving tonight.

Which made it so much more important.

I stayed silent as Jessiah led us away from the stables. I felt the protective magic of the wall the second we passed through. It was as if the air itself shifted from the danger we were now exposed to, but I loved it.

We were finally free again.

"Stay as low as possible until we're away from the wall. Then we'll rise." I nodded, spreading my wings and preparing to jump. The trees would be tricky, but there was a gap wide enough for both of us and our wingspans.

Jessiah nodded at me one more time, offering a reassuring smile before launching into the air.

I stayed directly behind him, mimicking his movements as he guided us up and up. It took only a few minutes before we could not see the remainder of The Golden City behind us.

I never knew angels could fly so fast. We were not simply moving through the air; we were soaring. Wind roared in my ears as we catapulted through the night sky. Thank the goddess that Jessiah knew where we were headed, because I had absolutely no clue. The moon glowing above us became the only light illuminating the treetops.

We could have flown for an hour. We could have flown for three. I lost track of time as I soaked in the clean, night air.

It was peaceful up here.

Safe.

"We're close," he said eventually, his low voice slicing through the wind. "You stay hidden. See who you came here to see, nobody else. The last thing we need is all the citizens of Midgrave announcing they saw an angel flying through the sky."

Fair enough. Especially because until Wolf, nobody here would have believed angels still existed.

The crumbling, half-eroded city of Midgrave slowly came into view as we approached the ground. Jessiah led us down until we both landed with no more than the sound of crunching sticks below us.

I immediately found my footing, retracting my wings, then stepped toward the border of my old town.

Jessiah caught my arm, forcing me to face him. "I'm serious, Huntyr. The second you're done, we leave."

I had never heard him talk so sternly, almost as if he... as if he was afraid.

"I know." I put a reassuring smile on my face. "I'll just be a minute."

I wanted nothing more than to run back to Phantom and find Lord, but Rummy's small unit was closer. I would stop there first, talk to her for just a few minutes, and then go find Lord.

The streets were darker than I remembered. The entire town slept; nobody dared to creep through these alleys at night. Not unless they wanted to be food for the hungry ones, anyway.

I kept my footsteps light, half-running in the shadows as we got closer and closer to where Rummy lived. Jessiah followed behind me, but he stayed back far enough that we wouldn't be seen together unless he wanted to be seen.

He was sneakier than I anticipated.

When we approached Rummy's building, I stopped, turning to face him. "Wait here," I said. "I'll be back in a few minutes."

"Absolutely not," he argued. "I'm not taking my eyes off you in this place, Huntyr. Where you go, I go."

I guess I should have expected as much. He wasn't going to give me free rein in my old town. The last thing he needed to deal with was me running off, leaving him to answer to Asmodeus for why his blood queen went missing.

I couldn't say the thought didn't tempt me.

"Fine," I said. "But these people have never seen an angel before. Try not to look so intimidating."

The smirk on his face definitely reminded me of Wolf. "I'll try my best."

My heart beat faster and faster as I ascended the stairs to Rummy's building. I reached out to grab the handle, still hardly believing I was actually here. I was actually home. For the first time since I went to Moira, I was back where I belonged.

Her door was locked. Go fucking figure.

"Let me," Jessiah said. He stepped forward, pulling a tiny knife no larger than my palm out of his belt. He stuck the tip into the side of the door, jiggling it for only a second before the door slid open.

Damn, he was good. "Thanks," I whispered, quietly pushing it open in the darkness.

My eyes had gotten more accustomed to the dark, something I was certain I had my newfound vampyre traits to thank.

But Rummy's bed in the center of the room was empty.

I felt the cool blade on my neck a second later. "Tell me who the fuck you are, or you die right now."

I didn't have time to answer. Jessiah swept into the room, pinning Rummy and her threatening blade to the wall before I could even blink.

"Rummy," I whispered. "It's me! It's Huntyr!"

She stopped struggling against Jessiah's massive body, mouth falling open as she squinted in the darkness.

"Hunt?" she repeated. "Holy shit! I almost fucking killed you!"

Jessiah gently slid the knife from her hand before letting her go.

I half-shoved him out of the way and pulled my best friend into my arms.

I wasn't sure how long we stayed like that. I didn't care. This felt real. This alone would give me the fuel I needed to get through another damn month in The Golden City. This alone reminded me why I was still fighting, why I was still living.

"Goddess," she breathed, pulling back to take me in. "I thought you were dead. We all thought you were dead."

"You have such little faith in me?" I asked.

She smiled, finally turning to look at Jessiah.

And his massive angel wings. "Holy hells. He's a—a—"

"He's an angel. Yes, they still exist. There are even more of them inside The Golden City. Jessiah here is helping me," I explained quickly. "He took me back here so I could talk to you, but I'm not staying. I wish I had more time to explain, but I have to go back tonight."

Her eyes lingered on those wings before they shot back to mine. "You're going back? Why?"

"It's complicated, Rummy. I can't explain it all, but there are some things I need to take care of before I can come back."

There are some people I need to kill. There's an entire evil archangel I need to get free from. But I didn't tell her any of that. She had enough to worry about already.

"Are you alright?" she asked. "You survived Moira? You made it to The Golden City?" Her voice held so much hope, but why wouldn't it? She still thought The Golden City was the great, magical place I could live my luxurious, perfect life in after completing Moira.

So, I smiled anyway, nodding my head. "I survived. I made it."

She hugged me again. Hard.

"How are you?" I asked. "Tell me how you've been. What's been going on around here?"

The smile faded from her face. She looked away, glancing down at her feet. "I don't know, Hunt. Things are different. I can't explain it, but it's just a feeling. I'm on edge all the time; everyone is. It's like we're all afraid now."

"Afraid of what?"

She shrugged. "Vampyres? Ourselves? I really don't know, but the longer you're gone, the worse it gets."

When I didn't respond, she shrugged. "But I'm sure I'm just being paranoid. We've all been a little on edge since the last attack."

"Have there been more since I left for Moira?"

"Only one. The Phantoms took care of them this time, but we're all waiting on the next attack."

Even hearing her say *Phantoms* sent the hair on the back of my neck raising.

She picked up on it instantly, eyes softening. "He isn't here."

I stiffened. "What?"

"Lord isn't here. I saw him go into the forest yesterday with a travel pack. I haven't seen him since."

My stomach dropped.

"Lord left?"

Jessiah's features softened too. He had no idea who Lord was, had no idea how much it meant to me that I would get to see him again, would get to tell him I survived, that I made it into The Golden City and I could finish what he started by sending me there.

"Maybe he's back and I missed it," she offered. "Or you could stay here with me and wait for him."

"Not an option," Jessiah interrupted from the shadows. "We're running out of time already."

He was the whole reason I got into this mess.

He was the whole reason for everything.

I slowly stepped backward. Maybe he returned. Maybe he snuck back in tonight and Rummy didn't see his arrival.

"I have to go check," I said. "I have to see for myself."

Rummy reached out and gave my shoulder a squeeze. "I'm coming with you."

Jessiah, to my surprise, didn't stop Rummy from coming

along as we slipped back onto the shadowed streets of Midgrave and headed for Phantom. Nobody said a word as the cave entrance approached. Nobody spoke as I stepped inside, eyes vigilant, listening for any signs of Lord.

But the cave was empty. Nobody was here.

"He could be home," Rummy whispered. "There's one last place you could check."

I nodded, immediately moving my feet in the direction of my old dwelling.

Rummy locked her arm through mine as we approached the run-down building. I had never been embarrassed of my home until now, until Jessiah stepped through the rat-covered entrance of the building, ducking so his wings could fit through the door.

The door to Lord's unit was unlocked, and I pushed it open without a sound.

But the room was empty. His bed was made. The moonlight filtered in through the window, exposing just how little Lord really owned.

Everything was gone.

Panic started to creep through me. I spun and stormed in the direction of my own unit, just above Lord's.

The door wasn't even shut. Someone forced it open, breaking the handle and leaving it ajar.

"Hells," I murmured. The place was a disaster, worse than the normal, run-down home I grew up in. Someone had been here, had ransacked the place, had searched through every single inch.

Not like I had anything I cared about here. I had nothing of value to lose.

"You lived here?" Jessiah said, taking in the room.

My face heated. "Yes. Much different than the luxuries of The Golden City, I know."

But Jessiah's face held no judgment, no disgust. Only a deep, unmistakable sadness.

"I'm so sorry, Hunt," Rummy whispered. "I know how badly you must have wanted to see him."

I choked down my tears. I would not cry. Not here. Not because of this. "It's alright," I lied. "At least I got to see you."

She placed a hand on my shoulder. "I'll tell him you came. I'll tell him you're alive."

I nodded, not trusting myself to speak.

"We need to leave," Jessiah said after a few moments. "We've already risked too much by walking through the entire city."

I didn't look at the room again, didn't look at this sad excuse for a home that I was leaving behind. Because it didn't matter how shitty it looked to Jessiah, how disgusting it felt, how unsafe it was, how unlivable.

This was home. I was coming back here one day; I swore to the goddess I would.

"Thank you, Rummy." I pulled her in for one final hug. "I will come back again. I swear to you, I will."

The tears in Rummy's eyes reflected the moonlight. "I know you will. I know it."

Jessiah said nothing, nodding respectfully at Rummy as we made our way back outside. She didn't ask any more questions, didn't question why this stranger of an angel had taken me back here in the middle of the night, didn't question why I had to go back, why I couldn't stay here.

She was a good friend for that, never questioning, always supporting me like the one stable thing I had in my life.

"I love you, Hunt," she said as Jessiah spread his wings.

"I love you." My voice cracked. "Take care of yourself. I'll see you soon." The words felt heavy—like a lie—as they left my mouth, but I couldn't bear to imagine not seeing her again, of not coming home again after this.

This was my home. Rummy was my home.

"Ready?" Jessiah asked.

I nodded, summoning my own wings with a gust of magic. *No,* I would never be ready. Nothing in this entire world would make me ready to go back to The Golden City.

But Lord would know I was alive. Rummy knew I was alive.

Still, as we flew into the night sky and made our way back to the prison of The Golden City, I let the silent tears fall.

I would fight for them. I would survive this for *them.*

No matter what Asmodeus forced me to do in the meantime.

CHAPTER 26
WOLF

I fought every fucking instinct in my body that told me to go after them. I made peace with my lack of wings. I accepted it for what it was, because anything else would be torture.

But knowing that Huntyr was out there with my brother, flying across the kingdom all the way back to the crumbling, vile town of Midgrave?

And knowing she was going to see *him*—the male who put those scars on her back?

That was its own form of torture. Even the scars on my back itched, urging me to go after them, to fly into the night sky and protect her, no matter the cost.

I could do nothing but sit in the bed that reeked of her and wait for them to return.

Asmodeus was thoroughly distracted, spending his time bottle-deep with Luseyar in his study. I made sure they wouldn't be looking for Huntyr or Jessiah at any point tonight so the two could make it out during the night and arrive before anyone noticed they were missing.

But the sun approached the horizon. They were running out of time.

I returned my attention to the book in my lap and tried to focus on anything else. It was the same book Huntyr had been reading, and she folded one of the pages in the corner to keep her place. I scanned the page, inhaling every word.

A lot of it, I heard when I was younger. I never read these specific books, but I remembered a few details from stories the maids would tell us as children.

Never when my father was around, of course. He never wanted us to hear of such things. The less we knew, the better. It was one of his many tactics to keep us at his mercy.

The book talked of the vampyre history, but it also talked of the hungry ones.

The hungry ones had been around for centuries, but never in such high numbers. The book explained their origin, how the first vampyre to lose control of their blood lust was cursed, a reminder to everyone of what would happen when one lost control.

But then, the curse grew and grew.

After a few decades, it did not matter if you lost control of your thirst or not. Vampyres of completely sound minds were at risk, and the curse spread through the kingdom like a wild-fire in the valley.

Nobody was safe.

Nobody would be safe until the curse was broken.

I flipped the page, expecting to see more about the curse and *how* it was supposed to be broken, but the page had been ripped out.

Ripped out.

Anger immediately flooded my senses. I knew exactly who would do something like this. If there really was a way to break the curse, to cure the hungry ones, my father would ensure nobody else knew about it.

The cheating fucking bastard.

I threw the book from my lap and sauntered to the bathroom, pacing back and forth a few times as I tried to calm my temper.

He wanted us to be so weak, it made me sick. I didn't even have to ask myself if he would be capable of such a thing. I already knew the answer. Someone who sliced their son's wings from their back was capable of anything.

I pulled off my shirt and turned around in the mirror, glancing over my shoulder to see the massive, hideous scars that remained. My chest tightened. I didn't give myself time to think about my missing wings after it happened. All I cared about was Huntyr—getting her out of that dungeon alive.

That was still my main focus.

If I had to lose my wings to keep her safe, so fucking be it. I meant what I said. I would cut them off my own back if it meant protecting her.

But looking in the mirror right now still sent a cold shudder of disgust through me. My black wings were bad enough. They were an anomaly, a signal to everyone that I was unworthy. But to have no wings at all?

My eyes burned, tears clawing their way to the red brims. I didn't have time to pity myself.

If I did, if I gave in to the pain and betrayal and fucking sadness, I didn't think I could pull myself back out.

What is an angel without wings?

What is a monster without teeth?

I didn't notice the bedroom door opening until it clicked shut behind me. Huntyr stood there, back pressed against the wall as she eyed me carefully.

I cleared my throat and wiped at my eyes, praying to the fucking goddess she didn't just see me gawking at myself. I stepped out of the bathroom casually, looking her up and down. She wasn't hurt, something my magic would've picked up on immediately.

But her face was blank.

"Where have you been?" I asked. I walked to the bed and picked up the book I had been reading, twisting it in my hands to avoid looking at her.

I felt her cock her head to the side as she stared at me. "Don't act like you didn't know," she breathed. "Jessiah would never take me out of here without running it by you first."

I tensed but said nothing, keeping my attention on the book in my hands.

"It was fine," she started. "Good, actually. It was—" Something tight filtered through our bond. It was enough to make me finally look at her. "He wasn't there. We made it all the way there, but Lord wasn't there."

"Fuck," I muttered. "I'm sorry, Huntress."

She stepped forward, hands in front of her, almost as if she was going to reach out to me. "Don't apologize. You're the one who made this possible, and I—" She swallowed before she continued. "I don't know how to thank you for this. I know how much it must've killed you."

I tore my gaze away, suddenly feeling very vulnerable in front of my violent Huntress. Yeah, it did fucking kill me, but nothing was more important than her. If she needed a few hours back home to survive this mess, it was worth it.

"It was nothing," I replied.

A long silence fell. "Yeah, well. Thank you anyway." She waited a few more seconds before making her way to my bathroom. "And Wolf?" She turned and glanced at me over her shoulder.

"Yeah?"

"A wise man once told me, 'Just because your back may hold those physical scars doesn't mean you can't rewrite that story.'" She dipped into the bathroom before I could answer, and I was damn grateful for it, because the tears rushed back to my eyes as I settled into my space on the edge of the bed.

I said those words to her in Moira after I'd seen the scars on her back. Fucking hells. *I guess we both had stories to rewrite.*

A few minutes later, the bed shifted where Huntyr's body slid between the sheets. She always tried so hard to stay as far away from me as possible, but it never mattered. I always woke up with her head on my chest and our limbs intertwined.

It made it that much harder to untie myself from her grasp every morning without waking her, but there were certain boundaries I still wasn't willing to cross. She already fought with her emotions plenty. I didn't plan on adding more to that mix.

For now, I would accept as much of her as I could get.

Even if it meant torturing myself over it.

CHAPTER 27

HUNTYR

I slept for a day and a half before I finally pulled myself from bed. Wolf brought me food, but eating was the last thing on my mind.

The wedding was tomorrow. We were officially out of time.

I looked at my reflection, taking in my mess of curls and the sharp bones of my face. Wolf had a plan, yes, but it seemed as though Asmodeus was still getting everything he wanted.

The blood queen was marrying his son.

"You're nervous." I jumped at the sound of Wolf's voice from the bedroom behind me.

I scoffed and shook my head. Of course, I was nervous. I was getting married against my will tomorrow, and I was supposed to use that union to give the evil archangel power over the entire vampyre species.

Nervous was just the beginning.

"More like terrified," I admitted. "I spent my entire life learning to kill, learning to protect myself. But this? This political mess is out of my skill range. I don't know how to navigate this."

Wolf sauntered into the bathroom, coming to stand behind me as I stared at my reflection and tried desperately to recognize the person before me.

"Once this is over, we begin our path to freedom, okay? Once tomorrow is behind us, we can finally breathe."

"You seem sure about that."

"That's because I am." He stood close enough that I could feel the heat radiating from his body, but he didn't touch me. He just hovered so close that the smell of pine and maple trees filled the bathroom.

My ability to scent him seemed to grow stronger and stronger now that I awakened my vampyre senses. Aside from a heightened sense of smell, I was faster. Stronger. My magic grew more and more powerful and it was getting easier to control. I also had yet to set the entire castle on fire, which wouldn't exactly be an awful outcome, but still.

I was actually *proud* of myself, although I was still learning to process the fact that I spent my entire life killing vampyres, only to learn I was one of them.

I didn't want to be a monster. I didn't want to be those vile, blood-sucking creatures I heard about in tales from Lord.

I just wanted...I just wanted *peace*.

"I keep thinking about Lord. I keep thinking about why he sent me here, about what he really wants from me."

Wolf went still. "How do you know he wanted anything from you at all? What if he thought he was sending you here because you deserved to be one of the elite?"

My chest tightened. "That would be unlike him."

"He raised you, didn't he? He's practically your father.

Why wouldn't he want you to get out of the slums of Midgrave?"

I dropped my head, finally looking away from the reflection I didn't recognize. "He wanted me to be strong and fierce so I could survive with him. In Midgrave. If he wanted me to leave, he would have just told me."

Wolf considered these words. "It's okay to miss him. It's okay to miss your entire life in Midgrave, actually."

"I do miss it." Hells, the words stumbled out of my mouth before I could even think. "I miss Lord. I miss the damn bakery every morning. I miss..." My throat closed up. "I miss all of it."

Wolf leaned in closer, forcing the hairs on the back of my neck to stand up straight.

"I miss having freedom."

"Did you ever really have freedom, Huntress?" His breath hit my bare neck when he spoke. "You were living in the shadows, never knowing who you really were."

"It was better than this, than being forced to live in this castle with *him*."

Wolf's eyes darkened. "I'm going to make this up to you. I swear it on my life, you'll be the happiest damn vampyre in all of Vaehatis very, very soon."

I tried to smile, but my face felt stiff. *Happiness.* The thought seemed so foreign. Unfair, even. Why would I, of all people, deserve to feel happiness? Why would I get the chance to live a free, peaceful life?

No, things like that didn't happen to me.

I had a destiny. I had a fate. *I was the damn blood queen.*

But when Wolf placed his hand on my shoulder, I forgot about all of that for one second.

I leaned in.

"I never thought I would get married," I said aloud. "But if it's required of me, I guess I'm not entirely angry it's with you."

His smile didn't reach his eyes. "Music to my fucking ears, Huntress."

CHAPTER 28
WOLF

Huntyr fell asleep before the moon was high. I waited, listening to the soothing sounds of her breathing until I was certain she wouldn't wake up.

She was a damn light sleeper, too. I learned that much in Moira.

The castle was quiet as I snuck through the empty halls. Being the night before the equinox celebration, everyone was likely resting to prepare. The equinox celebration sometimes lasted three entire days and nights, with way too much drinking and dancing and very little sleeping.

It was what made this plan almost possible.

I reached the main entrance of the castle and waited, not yet revealing myself, not yet approaching those large doors.

Tonight, I wouldn't be navigating through The Golden City. No, I would be walking through the underground tunnels.

I made sure the coast was clear, made sure I didn't hear

footsteps or conversations lingering from the guards outside, and I ducked to the right.

There was a small hallway here that was almost never used. Servants to the archangels used it back in the day, back when The Golden City was actually a home for the elite fae and angels of Vaehatis. But servants here were now very few. Luseyar was one of the only my father allowed in his presence, and he was mostly used as a bodyguard.

These small, dark hallways were abandoned now, which made them perfect for me tonight.

My feet were light and silent, these tunnels much easier to navigate now that I no longer had black wings scraping the stone walls on either side. Still, every one of my senses was on high alert. My ears strained in the silence, looking for any threat.

My heart raced too. I wasn't one to get nervous easily, but this?

This wasn't just about me. Huntyr's life was on the line. Jessiah's life was on the line.

Hells, the whole damn kingdom was at stake.

Because when the equinox began tomorrow, when Huntyr prepared to swear herself to me and I to her, it wouldn't just be the wedding.

The rebellion was going to kill Asmodeus.

I made my way further and further into the tunnels, until the stone under my feet turned to dirt and sand, until the air went dry, unmoving, until spider webs and insects littered the walls.

"Took you long enough," Nathan started. "I was beginning to think you changed your mind."

I walked into the room with dimly lit lanterns, the same room Nathan and I had been meeting in since I got back from Moira with Huntyr.

It was safer than the pub, safer than anywhere else in the city with wandering eyes. It was certainly the only place safe enough to plan something so damn idiotic.

"Change my mind?" I questioned. "This is the only way to protect the kingdom, Huntyr, myself, and every damn person living within the walls of The Golden City. I'm not changing my mind; you can count on that much."

He eyed me for a second longer before nodding. "Good, because we have a lot to talk about tonight."

"Is everything ready on your end?" I asked. "You have the rebels ready?"

It sounded so barbaric, but as Nathan and I talked about the safest way to get Asmodeus out of power, that's what we became.

Rebels.

"They're ready and eager. As soon as the ceremony is in full swing, we'll wait for Asmodeus to be distracted, and then, we'll attack."

"Good." I kept my voice strong and unwavering. Nathan did too, although I could hear how fast his heart was beating now that we were discussing the attack.

We spent months planning this, waiting for the right moment, hiding it from everybody.

It was time to act or risk all of us dying before we got another chance.

"What about you?" Nathan asked. "You're really ready to kill your own father?"

I looked him in the eye so he would understand me clearly when I said, "I've been ready to kill that man since he laid eyes on her."

Nathan nodded.

"Please tell me you know for certain that this will really end him. Archangels are tough to kill for a reason."

Nathan pushed himself back and began pacing the dark room. Orange light cast shadows on his dark face as he thought, hands tightening on his hips. "My people have gone to the damn edges of Vaehatis looking for the right answer. All our sources say the same thing. Huntyr's magic combined with the angel sword will do the trick."

Huntyr's magic, we had, but the angel sword? There was only one I knew of in existence, and Luseyar wielded it himself. It was the same sword that sliced my wings from my body. How the rebels planned on retrieving it, I had no idea.

"And if you're wrong?"

He stopped pacing and looked at me. "If I'm wrong, we're all dead. But we're running out of options here."

We stood for the next few minutes in silence. Nathan continued pacing near the back wall while I leaned against the cold stone with my arms crossed over my chest. Goddess help us if we were wrong about this.

The ways to kill an archangel were anything but common knowledge. Most of my life, I thought it impossible to kill them. They were stronger than angels. Older. More powerful.

But the way my father was continuing had to be stopped. This evil could not continue in this world any longer, and I couldn't fucking live with myself if I let it.

"You protect her at all costs, Nathan," I said after a while. "She's the key to all of this. She has to stay alive no matter what."

He faced me with serious eyes. "She's our queen. All of us will gladly protect her with our lives, Wolf. Trust me on that."

I bit my cheek to stop the stream of threats that lingered in my mind. He *had* to keep her alive. No matter what happened, no matter if we succeeded tomorrow or failed, Huntyr would live.

CHAPTER 29
HUNTYR

"You're kidding me." I stared at the dress—or lack thereof—with my jaw falling open. "This has to be a joke."

"It won't feel so bad once you have it on, I promise." Wolf carried the dress to the bed and laid it out flat.

"Easy for you to say. You're not the one who has to parade around here practically naked."

He smirked. "I'll be wearing less clothes than usual, if you're looking for an excuse to see more of me."

I sighed. "This is hardly the time for jokes."

"But it might as well be." He took two steps toward me, hands out, almost as if he wanted to touch me, but he stopped himself. "The angels have much different traditions than the fae, or even the vampyres. This wedding will be... well, it will be unique, at the very least."

"And wearing this damn dress is something that's required of me?" Hells, I could see the dark color of the bedsheets through the dress.

"If I could stop this all from happening, Huntress, you

know I would do it in a heartbeat." His softened tone made my chest ache.

"I know you would. I'm just not ready for this, I guess."

"But you are." My breath hitched as he reached out and brushed a knuckle against my cheekbone. "You're more ready than you could even know. You'll walk in front of a group of drunk people who only want to party and celebrate the equinox, we'll exchange some words in front of my father, and the hard part will be over."

"That seems painfully mundane."

"It is." He smiled. "That should be a relief. In vampyre culture, they drink each other's blood, you know."

My eyes widened, but he was already laughing. "Relax. My father would rather not have a wedding at all than bend to vampyre culture."

"Who knows," I added. "He tends to be a bit impulsive. What if he decides to kill us both at the altar?"

"Then he'll have no queen and no way to access the power of the blood kingdom."

My face fell. "Right."

Jessiah pushed the door open and peeked his head inside. "Brother?" he asked. "You're needed in the throne room."

Wolf glanced at his brother and nodded before returning his gaze to me. The soft smile that lingered before vanished, replaced by a stiff tenseness. He looked *nervous*.

"Everything alright?" I asked.

Jessiah left, closing the door behind him. "As good as it could get on a day like this," Wolf replied through gritted teeth. "I'll be fine. Try to relax a little while you get ready for the equinox. If we had a single female servant I trusted working here, I would send them your way, but—"

"I'll be okay. I'll be fine on my own. I'll see you at the ceremony."

Wolf's face tightened as he took a step back. "Right," he said. "Good luck, Huntress. It'll all be over soon."

He turned and walked out the door without saying another word.

It wasn't just the look on his face or the tenseness in his shoulders. The deep, growing pit in my stomach also told me something wasn't right.

But I was marrying Wolf under Asmodeus's hand. Of course something wasn't right.

Wolf had a plan. I could trust him, right? After everything, I could trust this. I could trust that he hated his father just as much as I did, that he was willing to do what it took to protect these people.

I walked back into the bathroom and let the hot water fill the porcelain tub.

It felt so fucking foolish, getting ready for an event I was forced to attend.

What was Asmodeus going to do to me, anyway? Wolf was just trying to make me feel better about the whole thing. This was not going to be a nice, quaint wedding between two lovers.

This was a damn war ritual, and I was the prized possession.

I stripped my clothes off and left them in a pile on the floor while I stepped into the water. I used Wolf's soap, letting the pine scent wash over me and infiltrate my senses.

This was all happening so we could free the citizens of The Golden City and protect the vampyres from Asmodeus's rule.

Where was he going to stop? Someone like him wouldn't

halt until he had the entire kingdom under his fist, ready to do anything he said.

This was for them. For the people of Midgrave who were too weak to fight for themselves. For the ones slaughtered by the fae who feared them too much.

This was so they had a chance to fight too.

After scrubbing my body until my skin felt raw, I started on my hair. I dunked the thick black curls into the soapy water, running my fingers through it until it felt somewhat manageable.

I wasn't even sure why I cared. I could show up covered in dirt and wrapped in chains, and it wouldn't make any difference.

This wedding wasn't for me or Wolf. It was for him. Asmodeus.

I waited until the steam of the hot water dissipated, until it cooled to too light of a temperature, and I finally pulled myself out.

Next was that damn dress.

You've got to be fucking kidding me. Asmodeus was a sick, sick man.

I tried not to think about all the other brides who could have worn this before me. It wasn't new, that much was obvious by the tattered hem and the softened fabric.

I dried myself off before stepping into the dress, pulling it up over my hips and securing it across my breasts.

That was the extent of it. The dress had no straps, which felt neither practical or necessary, and it fell all the way to the ground. A tall slit exposed the skin of my left leg all the way to my mid-thigh.

The fabric itself was a bright, cherry red, but it was so

thin, it left very little to the imagination. Every inch of my body was draped in red and on full display.

Great. Just great.

I prayed to the goddess that everyone would be too damn drunk at this thing to notice.

My bare shoulders contrasted deeply with the bright dress, making me look younger than I looked in a long time.

I didn't like to feel exposed. I liked to feel prepared. Ready. Powerful. I liked to wear all black and training leathers and layers and layers of clothing.

Not this.

I was just starting to hear voices outside as I secured my hair in a braid straight down my back, letting the shorter curls around my face hang loose.

Asmodeus wanted a damn show for this equinox celebration, and I had a bad, bad feeling that was exactly what he would get.

CHAPTER 30
WOLF

The castle was in full celebration mode. Normally, the equinox was a massive excuse to celebrate, but this year was even more so. Throw in a wedding—a royal wedding, at that—and you had every single worker in The Golden City preparing.

I forced myself not to think about Nathan, about everything that could go wrong tonight, about the danger we were all in if we failed. That wasn't going to help anyone.

Instead, I marched myself through the fully-decorated throne room, looking for my father.

But it was not my father who greeted me.

"Luseyar," I stated. "Did you ask to see me?" I straightened instinctively, though I hated myself for it. Luseyar was nothing more than the right hand of my father. It was nothing personal that he had to cut my wings off; it was simply business for him. He wasn't going to hurt me unless it was ordered again, which I certainly did not put above him.

"I did," he replied. His voice was low and sharp. I rarely heard him speak and certainly never so freely. "I want to talk to you. Warn you, really. Your father doesn't know we are speaking, and it would be best if you kept it that way."

I stepped forward, eying the angel. "Okay..."

"Your father—as rash as he may be sometimes—is not an idiot, Wolf."

"I'm aware." I kept my face blank.

"Are you?" His tone sharpened as he stepped forward, keeping only a few strides between us. "Because I have a very bad feeling about tonight, and I want to warn you that if you or your betrothed do anything to jeopardize this ceremony, there will be consequences."

I opened my mouth to lie to him, to convince him that there was nothing going on, but he held a hand up to stop me.

"He ensured that if you or Huntyr decide to go against this marriage, he would force you into it himself. Do you understand?"

Force us? What else could he do to force us into this? We were already willing to oblige. Nobody was dragging us to that altar against our will. Not physically, anyway. "Not really, no."

Luseyar dropped his hand, taking a long breath. In the years I had known this man, I hardly ever saw worry on his face, and certainly not like this. "Let's pray to the goddess you don't have to find out. Keep it together, Wolf. Don't try anything tonight. It will be much worse than taking your wings, I can promise you that."

He stormed out of the throne room, smacking my shoulder with his own as he left. Crowds were already gathering in the hallways of the castle. Voices streamed into the room as he opened the door, shutting it behind him.

It was a bluff.

It had to be a bluff.

There was nothing my father could do to make either of us back down, to not fight back.

Besides, he had no idea what we had planned. If he did, I would already be dead.

It was fine. It was all going to work out exactly how Nathan and I planned.

Fear crept at my chest and shortened my breaths, but I quickly swallowed it away.

Fear or not, Asmodeus was going to die.

Fear or not, tonight would change everything.

CHAPTER 31
HUNTYR

Asmodeus was the one who knocked on my door. I expected Wolf or Jessiah or literally anyone else, but no. The archangel stood at my door with his formal clothes. It was shocking to see an angel—an archangel —so put together, so mundane.

He wore all white, the fabrics draped over his shoulders and around his body like they were perfectly made for him. His sword was sheathed in a gold case, hanging from the top of his hip and nearly hitting the floor.

"Hello, Huntyraina."

"Asmodeus," I replied, keeping my chin lifted and my tone short.

"I believe you will be very pleased with tonight's events. The equinox is a celebration that most of our people look forward to every year. There is much, much to celebrate."

Yeah, like the fact that you thought you were about to gain power over an entire abandoned kingdom and use it for yourself.

I smiled tightly. "Then let the celebration begin."

His eyes slid over me, and I fought off a shiver. He held his arm out and I took it quickly, trying my best not to act absolutely disgusted by the closeness of him.

I hated Asmodeus. I hated everything he was, everything he stood for. It shocked me that two men like Wolf and Jessiah could come from the same bloodline.

"You look radiant this evening as well. I'm sure Wolf will appreciate this dress."

Gross. "You are a great father, truly. He must appreciate you looking out for him this way, making sure his bride has a beautiful dress. Chains and rags would have worked just fine."

He shook his head and tsked. "Now, now, Huntyr, there is no need to be sour. You see, I have a surprise for you. Consider it a wedding gift."

We continued walking, but my blood ran cold. "A wedding gift?"

"Right this way." He led me down another set of hallways, ones I didn't remember navigating before. The dark halls of the castle were decorated with hundreds, if not thousands, of candles, giving the shadows of night a glittering glow.

In any other scenario, I would have thought it beautiful.

Right now? I was creeped out.

I kept my face calm and forced myself to relax as Asmodeus pushed a door open and guided me inside. A million possibilities raced through my head. He wouldn't just kill me right now, right? He needed me alive for this entire charade to play out. Perhaps it was something as simple as jewelry.

He led me into an empty, quiet room, one that had not been decorated for the celebration.

My heart stopped beating.

I coudn't believe my fucking eyes.

Lord stood on the far side of the room, gazing out of the small, barred window.

He spun to face me when the door closed behind us, a rare smile on his wrinkled face.

CHAPTER 32
WOLF

Something was wrong with Huntyr.

At first, I thought I was getting sick, but I quickly realized the deepening pit in my stomach was Huntyr's. Her emotions poured through the bond, quickly sharpening my every sense.

"What's wrong?" Jessiah asked. We waited at the doors just outside the gathering room where the ceremony would take place.

I pushed myself away from the wall and tried to pinpoint where the emotions were coming from.

"I don't know," I said. "But there's something wrong with Huntyr. I feel it."

Jessiah didn't have to say a word. He just nodded, understanding exactly how important she was to me, how important today was.

"Let's go," he said. "You check the right wing; I'll check the bedroom in case she's still there."

I was already moving, already following that small thread through the castle, trying to get closer to Huntyr.

She was feeling a tornado of different emotions: fear, betrayal, hope, relief.

What could possibly be happening right now? Unless she was just teasing me, unless she just lowered her bond to play games before we were officially wed...

But something deep in my chest told me that wasn't the case.

Jessiah turned the hall and bolted toward our bedrooms, but I went left, into an empty hallway that wasn't decorated for the celebration.

"Come on, Huntress," I mumbled. "Where are you?"

CHAPTER 33
HUNTYR

"Lord," I breathed as Asmodeus stepped away from me to stand by him.

I was staring at a damn ghost.

He looked the same, but different. His slicked back hair was messy and in disarray. His normally black clothes were gone, replaced with a white outfit that looked shockingly similar to Asmodeus's.

But he was here.

I had missed Lord for so long, whatever that meant. He was my home. He was the man who raised me. No matter how horrible Wolf thought he was to me, he was my everything.

And he was finally *here*.

"I'm sorry it took so long to get to you," he said. "I've been meaning to come see you for some time now."

"I don't understand." I stood near the door, afraid I would collapse entirely if I took a step. "How are you—what's happening? How did you get in here?"

Lord and Asmodeus shared a glance, one that made me want to vomit.

Fuck. Panic crept into my chest, climbing over any relief I felt at the sight of Lord.

This wasn't right. He shouldn't be here. They shouldn't be looking at each other like that.

"Someone please tell me what's going on."

Lord stepped forward, apprehensive at first, almost like he was going to be gentle with me. But then he shoved his hands behind his back, clasping them tightly and lifting his chin while he cleared his throat.

Right. Always a show. Always a mask. Never the real Lord.

"I wanted to tell you the truth, Huntyr, but I needed you to learn so much on your own first before you could truly understand."

I folded my hands together to keep them from shaking. "Before I could understand what?"

He took a long breath. Asmodeus stood silently in the corner, a smug grin on his face that made me hate him more than I ever thought possible.

"I did not randomly find you after the war, Huntyr. I knew who your mother was. I knew who you were."

I was going to throw up.

"You knew who I was this entire time." My voice sounded foreign. Not mine. Dazed.

The door burst open behind me, and I found Wolf standing there, flabbergasted and winded, eyes wild as he took in the situation.

"What in all hells is going on here?" he spat.

"You might as well join us," Asmodeus chimed in from the back. "Huntyr was just getting acquainted with the male who raised her. It's a joy, really! A reunion to celebrate!"

Wolf looked at me.

Then Lord.

Then me again.

Lightning erupted in his eyes, and all chaos broke loose.

CHAPTER 34
WOLF

I was moving before I could think. Before I could breathe. Before I could focus.

My power flared around me, stronger than it had been in months, fueled by the anger and hatred and confusion I felt at the sight of him.

I knew who he was before Asmodeus opened his mouth. The way he looked at her like she was his property, the way Huntyr looked at him like he just ripped her heart out and shattered it to pieces...

I launched myself at the pathetic excuse of a man, my magic flaring all around me, buzzing in the air. Huntyr screamed as I tackled him with my hands at his throat. We both fell, but he rolled me over until my back was to the ground, my still-healing scars pressing into the stone.

"You better learn how to respect visitors in your own damn house, boy," Lord hissed.

I grunted, my power cracking in the air around us as I flipped him over, regaining control. "What in the hells do you know about respect?" Huntyr was screaming something, but I heard nothing over the roaring in my ears. "Only a sick son of a bitch would hurt a woman like that."

Lord laughed beneath me. "I *made* her strong. I *made* her who she is."

I squeezed tighter, forcing the air from his lungs. I wanted him to die. Fuck, I waited on this moment for so damn long.

But pain split through my temple. I lost my concentration for a single moment, long enough for Lord to push me off him and scramble back up to his feet.

"Enough of this," Asmodeus chimed in. His hand was held out toward me; he was the one inflicting this piercing pain in my head. "Can we all discuss things like the mature adults we are? Or would you rather us ruin the entire damn equinox celebration?"

I didn't dare mention that I didn't give a fuck about the celebration. Neither did Huntyr.

I pushed myself back to my feet and glanced at her, but she didn't look at me. Lord, either. She stared somewhere between us, neither here nor there, with eyes glossed over and lips parted slightly while she breathed.

"What is he doing here?" I asked. I could barely fucking look at him. I wanted to make him suffer for every scar on her perfect, pale skin. I wanted to make him feel every ounce of the pain he inflicted upon her.

"I came here to support Huntyr," Lord answered.

"And how do you two know each other exactly?" I motioned to the space between Lord and my father.

Huntyr's emotions overpowered the bond—her hurt, her betrayal, the sheer sickness she felt in the pit of her stomach. It was all mine now too, all of it mixed together in an unstoppable force.

It was like Huntyr already knew the answer to the question.

"Listen," my father started. "Lord wanted to ensure Huntyr would be protected."

"Bullshit," I started, but my father held up his hand and sent another wave of pain in my direction. I flinched slightly but shut my mouth. Fucking archangels.

"As I was saying. Lord ensured Huntyr's safety since she was a child. I sent him a message when it was time for her to join us here in The Golden City."

"You knew I was a vampyre?" Huntyr's voice crept through the air. "You've been training me and lying to me since I was a child?"

"It was all to protect you." Lord kept his voice steady. Strong. "Every single thing I did was for you, Huntyr, so you could grow up to be the powerful queen we all knew you could be."

Her breath grew shallow, panicked. "What was the point of all this?" She stepped beside me now, finally looking Lord in the face. "Wouldn't it be easier to kill me and take the kingdom for yourself?"

The air thickened. "*You* are the blood queen," Asmodeus pushed. "Nobody will raise the vampyre kingdom better than you can, my dear."

"Don't call her that," I pushed. "Don't talk to her at all, actually."

My father and Lord looked at each other and laughed. *Laughed.*

"Did you know about this?" Huntyr asked me. A brand-new wave of pain pierced my gut.

"I swear to the goddess, Huntyr, I had no idea. I never would have let this happen if I knew."

She still didn't believe me; I could see it in her eyes. She was betrayed time and time again. Even Lord—the one male she actually trusted with her life—was lying to her this entire damn time.

Fuck, I wanted to kill him.

"Why?" she asked, facing Lord again. "Why train me to kill my own kind? Vampyres? Are you a—a—"

"I am a fae, child," Lord pushed. Even the low, gravelly sound of his voice made me sick. "Asmodeus found me just before the attack to put this plan in place. I was a trained vampyre killer before you were even born. It made me strong. It protected Midgrave. You needed to be strong too."

"No." She staggered backward, and I stopped her with a hand on her back. "I don't believe this."

"It's difficult to understand, I know, but—"

"You were supposed to protect me!" Huntyr let loose those damning emotions, let them pour into her words as she screamed. "You were the one person I trusted with *everything!*"

I kept my hand on her back, supporting her.

"I *did* protect you."

"You delivered me to this! This is all your fault! Do you even know what I went through in Moira? Do you have any idea what I've been forced to endure?"

Lord took a long breath. Hells, he didn't seem the least bit conflicted that the woman he raised was this distraught, that she was put in so much danger time and time again.

"Look at you now." Lord stepped forward, and so did I, putting a barrier between him and Huntyr. "You're strong. You're powerful. You're half vampyre, half fae, rarer than you could even imagine. Most fae don't survive becoming a vampyre, you know. When it's time for them to mature and feed on blood, they starve. But you..." He looked her up and down, and I clenched my fist to keep from killing him right there. "You are stronger than all of them, Huntyr, because *you* are the vampyre queen. *You* will unite the vampyres once again. *You* will give them power."

"I'll be giving *him* power," she spat toward Asmodeus.

"Enough of this charade," Asmodeus interrupted. "The celebration is beginning, and it would be rude to make our guests wait any longer."

He started toward the door. "I'd like to speak to Huntyr alone for one minute," Lord called out.

Huntyr leaned onto me, just slightly.

"Absolutely the fuck not," I seethed. I wrapped an arm around Huntyr's waist, pulling her to my body. Lord waited one more second before sighing and giving up, eventually following Asmodeus out the door.

I waited for a few seconds before turning and looking Huntyr in the eye.

"What. The. Fuck?"

CHAPTER 35
HUNTYR

Luseyar led us to the grand ballroom. He said nothing. I said nothing. Wolf said nothing, though his presence was the only damn thing holding me together.

Lord was working with Asmodeus. He *had* been this entire damn time. It sounded like a sick, twisted joke, one that should be appearing in my nightmares, not right here in the flesh.

"This will be over soon," Luseyar said without looking at us. "Don't do anything stupid." The warning from the angel shocked me, but I was out of any emotions to feel. I became a shell, a void in this body.

The closer we got to the ballroom, the louder the space around us became. Voices flowed through the air, music followed, and then there was the rapid pounding of my heart that I knew was louder than all of those.

"This can't be happening," I mumbled to myself.

Wolf stopped walking when we made it to the large doors. He turned to face me and put both hands on either side of my face, forcing me to look at him.

"Hey," he started. "Don't you dare lose it now, okay? You're stronger than any of them. You're the damn blood queen, and people are counting on you to survive this. My father wants to shake you up. He's doing all this to get a reaction from you. Don't let him see you break."

I was way beyond breaking. I was ready to crumble entirely into a pile of ash. The fact that Wolf put up with his father for so long was a damn miracle to me. That man was pure evil, and the only person I hated more than him right now was Lord. Fuck, I couldn't even think about him right now. "I don't think I can do this, Wolf."

"You can because you *have* to." His words were sharp, but they pierced that wall of grogginess and fog that clouded each of my senses. "Do you hear me, Huntress?"

Darkness crept around my vision, caressed my entire body, wanting to pull me under, but Wolf was right. Asmodeus wanted to show me that he was in control, that he was the powerful one.

He wanted to show me he controlled *everything* since I was a damn child, but I wasn't going to let him break me. I wasn't going to let him be the reason I finally cracked, not after everything I'd done to spite him.

I didn't trust myself to speak. I nodded in Wolf's hands, feeling the wave of relief roll through his body at the sight of it.

"Good." Wolf straightened, letting go of my face and slipping one of his hands into mine. "Focus on me. Don't think about anybody else. I'm going to get you through this."

I closed my eyes and took a long breath, letting the reassurance from Wolf's bond cascade through my own body. He was forcing it, I was sure, but it still helped. His calm, determined essence washed around me until I opened my eyes again.

"Alright," Wolf said to Luseyar without taking his eyes off me. "We're ready."

Luseyar put a large hand on the door ahead of us, paused, then opened it.

The music and voices halted the second we came into view. I instantly spotted Jessiah waiting at the head of the room right next to Asmodeus.

And Lord.

I tore my eyes away from them, though, and just focused on Jessiah's figure ahead.

One foot in front of the other. *I could do this.*

I could fucking do this.

I had to do this.

Wolf's hand never left mine as we were led forward.

A few people whispered as we passed, but I didn't dare lose focus. *Get this over with. Get this over with. Get this over with.*

Wolf was pushing as much love and peace through our bond as he could. I knew it was for me, I knew he was doing this to help me. There was no way he wasn't also freaking out over what just happened, over Lord being here and working with Asmodeus, especially if he didn't already know about it.

One step forward. Keep your head up.

We made it to the front of the room before I felt like my legs might finally give out beneath me.

"Welcome, everyone!" Asmodeus announced, moving to stand ahead of us.

Wolf turned, the two of us facing the crowd while he clasped his hand around mine.

"Today, we will witness the union of a century. Wolf

Jasper, son of the archangel, will marry Huntyraina Fullmall Gawerula, heir to the blood throne. Together, they will rule Scarlata Empire. They will rebuild what was ripped to shreds. They will build this power, not in solitude, but alongside us! With time and discipline and loyalty to the crown, we will have the entire blood kingdom bowing before us!"

The crowd erupted, and I bit my cheek to keep from vomiting.

Asmodeus lifted his hand, and the crowd silenced.

"Let us begin the traditional marriage ritual of the angels."

He turned around, now facing Wolf and me. "First, you both will draw blood to signify the eternity of life."

Focus on Wolf. Focus on Wolf.

Wolf gripped his blade, running the sharp tip down the center of his palm, then doing the same to mine.

Someone shouted in the back of the room, followed by more frantic screams, but I barely heard it. I was frozen, stuck. Unraveling with every passing second.

Wolf's eyes ripped away from mine and widened, the only sign of panic as screams spread and spread.

I finally turned to look.

Smoke filled the air, spreading further into the ballroom, closer and closer to us.

"What is that?" Wolf asked. "Where is that coming from?"

My stomach sank.

Fire.

The damn castle was on *fire*. It seemed to be coming from the hallway we just entered from, but there was no other exit to the grand ballroom. The dozens of fae and angels who came to witness this marriage were panicking, shoving, screaming, desperate for a way out.

It all happened so fast.

"Enough!" Asmodeus yelled, but he couldn't be heard over the roar of screams in the ballroom. "Enough, everyone! We must complete the ceremony!"

"The castle is burning!" Wolf screamed. "We need to get out of here!"

Asmodeus faced us with rage over his features. "Finish the ceremony *now!* You must marry!"

"But it could be a—"

"*Now!*"

The entire room shook with the force in his voice. I squealed in panic, quickly taking Wolf's bloody hand in mine. I squeezed my eyes shut, focusing on my magic, calling it forward how Wolf taught me.

More people screamed. Luseyar was yelling something now, louder than the roar of voices. It sounded something like an attack, but I quickly shook the thought away.

We were not being attacked during the damn wedding. This wasn't fucking happening.

"Finish it!" Asmodeus yelled.

Wolf began reciting words in a language I didn't understand, and I opened my eyes to find him breathing hard, head tilted back as he fought to finish what his father started.

Asmodeus cared so much about this damn union that he would risk being stuck in this castle during an attack? He wanted us to be united *that* badly?

My senses flared to life, becoming too aware of the absolute chaos surrounding us.

A large boom shattered Wolf's concentration, and we held onto each other tighter as the floor shook.

Was the damn castle crumbling?

Asmodeus let out a roar of anger, animalistic and terrifying. I thought I had seen that man angry, but this was something else entirely. This anger was mixed with a desperation I could hardly fathom. "*Is it done?*"

"It's done!" Wolf screamed back. Panic laced his words now, and he gripped me like he would never let go again. "It's done!"

Instead of running out of the ballroom like the rest of the crowd, Asmodeus turned to Lord. "Bring the girl out here!" he ordered. "Hurry!"

Lord disappeared into the chaos quickly. *The girl?* Who could he possibly be so worried about? The damn castle was burning!

"We're going to get out of here," Wolf whispered to me. "Don't worry, Huntress. I'm getting you out of this."

Jessiah was barking orders too, some at us, some at the others. He was trying to get everyone out before we were all killed, I realized.

The room grew hotter with every passing second. Did none of these powerful individuals have the magic to put this damn fire out? *Nothing could make this any fucking worse.*

Another scream, closer this time. Familiar.

I glanced over to find Lord returning through the crowd, shoving and elbowing as he forced his way. But he was not alone.

My stomach sank to the floor.

Rummy, bruised and bloodied, was being dragged at his side.

CHAPTER 36

WOLF

I didn't know who the girl was, but by the way the blood rushed from Huntyr's face, it wasn't hard to guess. Panic rushed at me through our bond, followed by Huntyr's anger.

"Huntyr," I warned, pulling at her hand. This was what he meant when he said he would ensure our obedience, I realized. This was what my father planned all along. "This is a trap, Huntyr. Don't fall for it."

"Rummy!" she called out. The girl—Rummy—stilled immediately, no longer fighting against Lord's grasp. She was covered in dirt, and dried blood clung to her lip. Her clothes were worn and ripped at the hems. Whatever journey they had here, it was not kind on her. "Rummy!"

I gripped Huntyr's arm to stop her from running to them, but she fought against me. "Let me go!" she yelled. "Let me go, Wolf!"

"He's only doing this to hurt you!" I reminded her.

"I don't care! I'm not leaving her!"

Asmodeus stepped between us. "If you want your friend to remain safe, you'll come with us."

A burning pillar fell from the ballroom ceiling in the distance. Jessiah froze, too, as he realized what happened.

This was no random fire. We were under attack.

I had a vague idea of what was happening, but Huntyr had no clue. All she knew was that we were about to fight for our damn lives to get out of this mess.

My mind snapped back to the girl still tight in Lord's grip. "Let her go!" Huntyr screamed.

"Come with us, and she'll be just fine!" Lord yelled.

Huntyr was glancing between us and the front of the ballroom, where most of the crowd now funneled out. "This is a trap," I whispered against her ear.

"I don't care. I don't have a choice, Wolf. They'll hurt her."

She pushed her bond open, flooding me with the terror and dread that came with the simple thought of leaving her friend behind. Whoever that girl was, she was important to Huntyr. "We can't leave her," she whispered.

My eyes searched her face as she took a deep breath, jaw clenched. "Fine." I turned my attention to Asmodeus. "Let's get the fuck out of here before this place crumbles to the ground!"

Then we were moving. Jessiah and Luseyar came with us, pulling us to a tunnel located in the back of the ballroom. Not everyone was going to make it out of the fire. The smoke was thick, almost too thick to breathe. Tears rimmed my eyes, blurred my vision.

I darted toward Huntyr's friend, but Lord dragged her ahead of us, not letting her go for even a second as he followed Luseyar through the small, dark tunnels.

Asmodeus tailed behind us, and Jessiah caught up to us at

the first turn. "Is everyone alright?" he asked. "What is going on out there? Are we being attacked?"

Luseyar didn't slow down for a second. We turned right, then left, then another right.

"Where are we going?" I asked when nobody responded to Jessiah. "Where are you taking us?"

"Somewhere safe," Luseyar answered. "Somewhere we aren't being attacked."

"Why would anybody attack us here?" Huntyr asked. "I thought people wanted this union to happen!"

We reached the end of a tunnel and Luseyar stopped. He turned so quickly, we all almost ran into each other. "Why don't you ask Wolf?" He pushed open a door above him, one that opened to the outside. The sun was just setting, which left plenty of light for us to see.

Luseyar jumped out first. Lord lifted Rummy next, and she didn't resist as Luseyar pulled her from the top.

"Here," Lord said to Huntyr. "I'll help you up."

"I don't think so," I answered. Jessiah stepped forward.

"You go," Jessiah pushed. "We'll help her." Damn him for being so calm in a situation like this. Damn all of them, actually.

That was our one fucking chance at getting out of this.

Lord hoisted himself out of the tunnel. Jessiah went next, then leaned down to offer Huntyr a hand. I lifted her from the waist while he pulled her up.

I moved to push myself out of the tunnel, but a hand came down on the back of my neck.

"Is this your doing?" my father asked, voice sharp. "Did you plan an attack on the castle to try and escape the wedding?"

"No," I answered. "I'm not a damn fool, Father. I would never put Huntyr in danger like that."

He considered my words for a second as I tried to swallow down my fear. I wouldn't put it above my father to slice my throat right now for even thinking I might be involved in an attack like this.

But he knew about my bond with Huntyr. He knew I would do anything to protect her.

"Go." He let go of my neck and I pushed through the door.

Huntyr was already rushing over to Rummy and pulling her into her arms. Lord stepped back for just a moment while they held each other.

My chest tightened. They dragged that woman here to ensure Huntyr would obey. Why my father's cruelness still effected me, I wasn't sure. I stopped being surprised by his actions long, long ago.

Still. Seeing the two of them cry together put a sinking feeling in my chest.

They didn't deserve this. Neither of them fucking did, and I wasn't sure how much more Huntyr could take.

"Are you alright?" Huntyr asked, pulling away just enough to examine her friend.

"I'm fine," Rummy answered. She tried her best to calm Huntyr, to brush off her own injuries. "I've just been worried about you. I didn't know if you—I didn't know if you were alive or dead this whole fucking time."

Huntyr smiled. A real smile. "I'm not that easy to kill, apparently."

Fuck. I was going to do whatever it took to get us out of this.

"What was that back there?" Jessiah asked. His voice was low, and he spoke only to me.

"I don't know," I answered, but I shot him a low glare. *Not now.*

Jessiah knew nothing of the attack. He knew nothing of the rebels, or of what we were building in the blood kingdom.

But he was my brother, and he cared about Huntyr too.

Now would be the time to test his loyalties. The truth would come later.

"We have to keep moving." Asmodeus closed the latch to the underground tunnel. "We don't know who's following us."

"The castle is under attack," Luseyar said from the back of the group. "Should we not return and fight whoever is responsible?"

Asmodeus shook his head. "If the castle is under attack, they are only after one thing. And we have that one thing right here in our possession."

"What? Huntyr?"

Asmodeus looked at Huntyr.

Then to me.

"The blood queen and her king."

CHAPTER 37
HUNTYR

I could handle my own pain. I could handle my own fear taking over my shaking body. I could handle being forced to marry one of Asmodeus's sons. Hells, I could even handle being the damn blood queen if that's what was required of me.

But to handle seeing Rummy—my longest friend—being dragged through the dirt by the one male who betrayed me most in this world?

It made me fucking sick.

I thought my weaknesses were already exploited, but I guess I was wrong. Because as soon as I laid eyes on Rummy, I knew I was going to do whatever it took to protect her.

Attack on the damn castle or not.

I kept my mouth shut as Luseyar guided us quickly through the surrounding land. We were no longer in the city, but the trees around us were so thick, I could not tell if we were inside or outside the walls. There must've been other tunnels that led under the wall, not just the ones in the stables.

284

By the looks of it, I imagined we were outside.

I tried to inch my way closer to Rummy, but Asmodeus ensured there was a safe distance between us. "Once I know we are safe and there is no longer a risk of attack, you two can speak to each other." Hells, I fucking hated him. I hated him for dragging her here, for using her like she was a damn tool.

Rummy was strong. She was fierce and bossy and had an attitude that scared nearly everyone in Midgrave, so to see her like this, it broke my fucking heart. But she still wore a brave face. That hadn't broken her. Not yet.

Which was another reason why I couldn't crack. Rummy needed me to survive. She needed me to fight, so I was going to fight for my damn life.

"This looks familiar," I said after a while, quiet enough so only Wolf could hear. He glanced around and surveyed the trees, the thin path we were on.

And then, his large, bright eyes met mine. "This is the path to Scarlata Empire."

Something like fear laced his words, but I didn't let that get to me. The fact that Asmodeus wanted to make the trip through the forest to the blood kingdom with no protection, no horses, and no food was downright insane.

He must have been truly worried about the attack on the castle, which meant there was actually a threat to him.

I wanted so badly to talk to Wolf alone, to ask him if he knew anything about the attack or who could have been behind it, but I knew better than to ask him those types of questions with so many ears around us.

And I was almost sure I could guess what his answers would be.

So, we kept walking. My feet grew tired quickly. I wasn't in the clothes to be making a long trip through the forest.

Hells, without horses, the journey would take more than a few days.

But there were no signs of slowing down. Even as the sun fell behind the horizon, even as darkness took over, shadowing the path and everything around us, we kept moving forward.

We kept going.

Rummy walked ahead of me with her back straight. Lord eventually moved to the front of the group, leaving Jessiah to guide Rummy, which immediately made me feel better.

I didn't want that lying bastard anywhere near her.

I knew the type of pain Lord inflicted on me. If he so much as laid a fucking finger on Rummy, he was *dead*.

Wolf's hand fell to my back. "You must be getting cold," he said, interrupting my thoughts.

I kept marching forward. "I'm fine."

It was a shit lie. The cool night air quickly infiltrated the thin fabric of my dress. The hem dragged along the dirt, adding dampness to the fabric and weighing it down more than necessary. My feet already blistered, but the heaviness of our situation was enough to distract me from my discomfort.

"Here." Wolf pulled his tunic over his head. He wore a thin undershirt, certainly not enough to keep himself warm, but when he handed me his shirt, I accepted it.

"Thank you," I mumbled. "This is going to be a long journey without proper supplies."

Rummy stumbled ahead of us, nearly falling to her knees. Jessiah caught her at the last second and hoisted her back to her feet.

"We can't keep going like this!" he announced. "We need to take a break. Regroup. This is a dangerous journey as it is."

Luseyar stopped walking and turned to face Asmodeus, awaiting orders.

But when I looked at Asmodeus, he was staring directly at me, brows drawn, eyes dark.

"Fine," he said after a handful of moments. "We'll stop here and rest, only for an hour. The faster we get to Scarlata, the better."

Wolf shook his head. "We're in no condition to make the journey by foot."

"We've all endured worse. Wouldn't you agree, son?" Asmodeus stepped forward, and I fought the urge to step between them, to shield Wolf from his father's inspection.

Wolf only stared directly back at his father, eye to eye. "I suppose since we cannot all fly, it will have to do."

His words held no emotions. Only facts. Asmodeus waited a second more and then smiled. Ruthless bastard. He would be the first one to become food for the hungry ones.

"Better rest up," he ordered. "It's a long journey ahead."

Asmodeus disappeared into the bushes, walking around the group to speak with Luseyar privately.

A thick eeriness hung in the air. The journey wasn't exactly pleasant last time, but we had the horses to guide us, and there had been a near peaceful sense in the forest as we traveled through it.

Very different from this time around.

It felt as if we were being watched every step of the way.

"This doesn't feel right," I said to Wolf, but I didn't take my eyes off Rummy. I tried to take a step toward her but Lord cut me off.

"You heard Asmodeus," Lord said before he clicked his tongue, shaking his head. "I thought I raised you better than that. Disobeying orders so soon?"

Fiery rage consumed me.

"Do not speak to her," Wolf said. "We're out here in the middle of the damn forest. Talking to Rummy isn't exactly a threat."

"No, it's not," Lord answered. "But Huntyr requires a punishment for her actions."

"Me? What exactly did I do that requires punishment?" I stepped in front of Wolf, finally facing Lord with the rage that built inside me. "I did everything you asked of me, every single fucking thing!"

He actually looked bored with what I was saying. Rummy shifted behind him, but I kept my attention on Lord.

"And yet, you still disappoint me. Do not try to speak to Rummy again. It will not end well for you."

And then he, too, disappeared into the thick trees.

My chest rose and fell, rose and fell. I could feel my power responding to the emotion, looking for a release, for a target.

I wanted nothing more than to direct all of it in his direction, to let him know exactly how powerful I really was.

He couldn't talk to me like that anymore. He had no fucking control over me.

Still, tears stung my eyes. Jessiah separated me from Rummy, guiding her to sit at the base of one of the trees on our path.

Wolf's hands fell on my shoulder. "Hey," he whispered. "Everything's going to be okay."

"How can you say that? This is... Hells, this is so much worse than I thought today would be."

He glanced around, making sure nobody else was listening before leaning in and kissing my cheek. He kissed me slowly, working his mouth toward my ear before whispering, "I have a plan."

CHAPTER 38
WOLF

It wasn't a complete fucking lie, but there was no way we were all making it to the blood kingdom alive.

The rebels would be on our trail. Surely, they found that tunnel by now. Surely, they would be tracking our every move.

They were the ones who could kill Asmodeus. They would be here soon, and I prayed to the fucking goddess this wouldn't last a single more day.

Huntyr rested against me, her head on my chest as her eyes drifted shut. Her feet were covered in blisters. Her body shook from the cold, even with the added layer.

My father was idiotic, but to drag us all after him like this? We could have *prepared* for this trip. We could have gathered supplies, clothes, food, anything.

Every rustle of a leaf caught my attention. Luseyar was awake, keeping watch a few feet away through the thick trees.

But otherwise, the clearing was quiet.

Huntyr relaxed when Jessiah was near Rummy, and for

that, I was thankful. There was no way we were getting Huntyr out of here without her.

She wouldn't leave her friend behind.

And now, neither would I.

The forest was dark, even for an angel. I could see the shadowed figures of the others sitting to my left. Jessiah's head fell back against the tree bark just an inch away from Rummy. At least she had a leather jacket on. It would be enough to keep most of her body heat in.

Even in her sleep, Huntyr shivered.

She kicked off her shoes, wrapping her legs up around mine to keep them warm. I would have taken the shoes off my own fucking feet for her if I thought it would help.

The blisters on the backs of her heels were starting to bleed. She would heal with her new powers, but not before we had to continue walking.

We couldn't continue like this, not when her body had already taken this much of a hit.

I slid my hand down her calf and stopped at her ankle.

Nobody would see. Nobody would know. Everyone was too busy sleeping or listening to the forest around us.

Huntyr wasn't going to make it an entire day like this. Besides, I was using too much of my energy to keep moving every day. The bond between us was open at full force, and I could practically feel each painful step she took.

She didn't need to ask me to heal her. She never did. Never would.

I closed my eyes and focused.

Healing wasn't something I did often. Hells, before I healed Huntyr in Moira, it had been years.

There had always been a force in my mind urging me to keep it a secret from my father. Even now, my ears strained in the forest, listening for any rustling, any sign that he might be awake.

Still, Huntyr was the only one who knew I could heal.

She stirred softly as my magic touched her skin, caressed her body. An electric sensation washed through me as my magic healed her, something that never happened before.

It felt like my power belonged to her, like it recognized her, like it *wanted* to heal her.

"Sleep," I whispered against her temple as she leaned into me further. "Sleep, Huntress."

The next day was uneventful, aside from the fact that I was damn hungry. The group of us traveled together in silence, nothing but the subtle complaint or the rare command from Asmodeus to keep us going, to walk faster.

But that familiar, dull aching in my stomach grew. It sat in my body like a rock at the bottom of the river.

Huntyr and I walked together in the back of the group, just feet behind Rummy and Jessiah, while the others marched ahead. She surveyed her sore feet in the morning but said nothing, though she did send me a glance and wink before we were ordered to keep walking.

"Stop that," she whispered as she stepped over a fallen log on the thick forest path.

"Stop what?"

"Stop thinking about blood. I don't need that distraction

right now." She crossed her arms over her torso and hugged herself.

I took a long breath. "It *has* been a while. I can't exactly control the hunger, Huntress. You of all people should know that."

She shot me a sideways glance. "Unless you're planning on sinking your teeth into one of them," she motioned to the front of the group, "you'll think of something else."

We walked for hours. The sun rose to the peak in the sky, beating down on all of us with a subtle fierceness that, on most days, would be nice.

But not today.

"We'll stop here for water," Asmodeus called out as we reached a river. "Just a few minutes, then we'll cross and be on our way."

I immediately glanced at Huntyr. Unless something drastic changed between when she nearly drowned in Moira and now, she couldn't swim.

But she just lifted her chin and clenched her jaw, eyes shooting daggers at Asmodeus, who quickly dropped to his knees by the running river.

It wasn't too wide, but the river ran roughly with the new rain from the last storm.

"You'll be fine," I whispered to her. "Jessiah will fly you across. Save your wings for when you'll need them."

"Yeah," she whispered back. "This entire situation is *just fine.*"

Jessiah and Rummy knelt by the river a few feet away, enough distance between us and the others that they wouldn't be able to hear us talking unless they strained for it.

Huntyr eyed her friend. Her gaze changed from anger and hatred to sadness. Kindness. Grief.

"Go on," I ushered. "Nobody is paying attention now. Kneel beside her and pretend to be drinking."

Huntyr's eyes sparkled with rebellion. "Are you sure?" she asked. "He won't like it if he sees us talking."

I nodded. "What's the worst he can do to you, anyway? He already mentioned he needs you alive."

She waited a second longer before nodding and scurrying to kneel beside her friend at the river. Only a few feet away, she turned her head slightly to speak while she knelt and cupped the water in her hands.

They both looked so damn tired.

My father would pay for this. They all would.

Jessiah stood and sauntered over to me. I pressed my shoulder against a tree, trying my best to look casual. Bored. Unaffected by the events of the last day.

"How are you holding up?" he asked.

"I'm surviving."

Jessiah had at least been wearing his sword when the attack went down. At least he had that to protect himself with. I only had a small dagger, as did Huntyr.

Hells, we were *severely* unprepared.

"And Huntyr?"

He turned to glance at her. She still murmured quietly.

"What about Huntyr?"

"Is she doing okay with all of this? That attack was unexpected."

I surveyed his words and tried to find any hint of accusation beneath them, but there was nothing there, nothing but genuine concern.

"She sure as hells was not expecting Rummy to be dragged here as collateral. And Lord..." I stopped myself before my anger took over.

Jessiah eyed me. "I take it he wasn't exactly a kind and loving caretaker?"

I coughed a laugh. "Something like that, sure." ·

The two of us stood there by the tree, a wave of unsaid words hanging between us. I wanted to tell him about the attack. I wanted to tell him about my plan, about Huntyr, about everything. But even if I wanted to, there was no way we were getting away from Asmodeus, Luseyar, and Lord long enough. They could hear every damn word, and that was something I wouldn't risk.

Soon enough. Soon, he would learn the truth, and I prayed to the goddess he would be on my side.

We stood there for a few more moments until Lord stormed into view, eyes locked on the girls. "What did I say about obeying my orders?"

CHAPTER 39
HUNTYR

With the harsh snap of Lord's words, I was back in Midgrave, back in that crumbling house. Back at his mercy.

How many times had I given in? How many times had I let him strike me, let him paint me as weak and unworthy?

It all happened so damn fast.

Rummy scrambled away as Lord marched in my direction, fist raised.

Normally, I would have shut my eyes and braced myself. I would have awaited whatever punishment Lord thought I deserved, because he knew best. He always knew what I needed, and he was the one who saved my life, who raised me out of the goodness of his heart.

But that all changed.

I no longer looked at Lord as my savior, but as my enemy. He was working with *them*, the evil angels who corrupted The Golden City, who wanted to take over Scarlata Empire.

No. I wouldn't put up with that anymore.

Lord raised his hand to strike me, but I moved faster. I pulled Venom from the sheath at my thigh—grateful for the long cut in my dress—and sliced at his shins.

He lost his balance and stumbled, but before he could regain his position on solid ground, I launched Venom up at his torso.

And pushed.

Blood sprayed as Lord stumbled into the running water of the river.

Fucking bastard. He got away with hurting me for far too long.

He resurfaced a second later, gasping and howling in pain.

Asmodeus and Luseyar appeared out of nowhere. "What in all hells is happening over here?"

"He attacked me," I explained, heart pounding. "I had to protect myself." For *once*, I wasn't going to let him hurt me.

Wolf shook with anger as he rushed forward. The river pushed Lord a few feet down the riverbank before he caught the edge and hoisted himself up.

"You ungrateful swine!" Lord spat through gritted teeth. "I told you what would happen if you were caught talking to her!"

Lord hoisted himself to his feet and looked at Rummy, but Jessiah quickly sidestepped, putting himself between the two of them.

You won't fucking touch her.

"I'm growing tired of these antics," Asmodeus said. The smell of Lord's blood wafted through the air, but it was neither appetizing nor pleasant. It was sour, disturbing. I wasn't sure if it was because I hated him so much or because he was truly such a vile, evil being that even his blood wasn't any good in this world.

Wolf's hand fell to my back. "Are you okay?"

"I'm fine." I glanced over my shoulder at Rummy, who stared at me with a set jaw and glittering eyes.

Even just a few seconds of speaking to her settled my heart. Dirty clothes, a bruised body, exhausted spirit, but she was still a fighter, still the badass, unstoppable Rummy I knew in Midgrave.

Maybe we would survive this shit after all.

"Water break is over," Luseyar announced. He waved his hand toward the other side of the river. "Let's keep moving."

Of our group, Asmodeus, Luseyar, and Jessiah had wings.

And me, but Asmodeus was waiting on me to display more of my magic, and I wasn't about to summon my wings with him watching. I wouldn't give him that satisfaction.

Asmodeus was already expanding his white-feathered wings, ready to launch himself across the flowing water. Luseyar, however, eyed our group.

"I'll take care of them," Jessiah announced before Luseyar could take a single step in my direction. "You worry about that one." He nodded his head to Lord, who busied himself with the wounds on his body.

They could have been worse. I could have pushed that blade in a lot deeper.

"Fine," Luseyar said. "But do it quickly."

Rummy was first. She hesitantly put an arm around Jessiah's neck as he pumped his wings once, twice, then launched them across the river. She let out a shaking squeal as they landed.

Just like everyone in Midgrave, she had never seen an angel. Not before Jessiah. There was no magic in Midgrave, no reason for angels or even powerful fae to stick around in those slums. Hells, they didn't even know angels still existed.

Luseyar and Lord went next, and damn, it was satisfying as all hells to see the two men struggling to grasp each other well enough to fly.

"Promise me you're okay," Wolf whispered now that we were alone on this side of the riverbank. His hands fell to the small of my back as his breath hit my ear from behind. "Promise me we're going to make it through this."

I leaned back into him, reveling in his touch. "I promise."

My fucking *husband.* My life. My other half. The wedding may have been for Asmodeus's plans, but something felt different between us now. Something changed. And it wasn't just the wedding ceremony—it wasn't just the words Wolf had chanted to bind us together for eternity.

Jessiah landed back on our side of the river with a thud. "Ready?" he asked, holding a hand out to me.

"Not just yet," Wolf answered for me. He spun me around by my hips, fast enough that I caught myself on his shoulders to steady my feet.

Then he kissed me. Harsh and fierce, his mouth pressed against mine with a million promises he could never say out loud. It was a promise for the future, a promise that we would survive. A promise that he would fix all of this.

And dammit, I kissed him back.

It only lasted a couple of seconds, but my entire body felt lighter at the gesture. I didn't realize just how badly I needed this, just how much I missed Wolf and I together.

He pulled away too soon. "Something to think about when you're wrapped in his arms," Wolf teased. "You're *my* wife. Don't forget that."

I rolled my eyes and pressed against his chest, pushing

him away before turning to Jessiah, who only stared at us with an eyebrow raised.

"Not a word," I ordered.

He held his hands up in defense. "I wouldn't dream of it."

I snaked an arm around Jessiah's neck before he scooped my legs up under my knees, pumping his wings again and launching us both into the air.

My magic called to me, pushing me to extend my own wings, but I fought the urge. My body wanted to fly. It was the most natural thing in the world for me now, to extend my wings, to soar into the sky.

But Asmodeus was too close to seeing my magic. He wanted it too badly, and frankly, so did Lord.

It only took a few seconds to fly across the river.

Jessiah landed gently before dropping me to my feet right beside Rummy.

Luseyar attempted to help Lord wrap up the wounds on his shins and his torso with extra fabric from his shirt. Hells, he deserved those. He deserved much, much worse. He deserved to have his back whipped over and over and over again after any slight mistake or failure.

Would he think of this as a failure? Would he hate me for who I had become? For the magic I now possessed?

Probably. It would never be good enough for him. *I* would never be good enough for him.

Suddenly, my stomach sank. Memories of my childhood flashed in my mind, memories of Lord taking care of me. Of him feeding me. Of him smiling and even occasionally laughing.

But those were quickly replaced with cruel, nonstop moments of violence. Torture. Hatred.

And the killing.

So much damn blood dripped from my hands. I killed and killed and killed at *his* orders.

I blinked the memories away and shook my head. I couldn't go back to that place, not when so much mattered right here, right now.

I brushed Rummy's shoulder as I turned and watched Jessiah launch himself back across the riverbank.

Hells, it hurt that Wolf couldn't fly himself across. I knew every single time he had to watch Jessiah fly me instead, he felt the pain of those wings being taken over and over again.

Asmodeus would pay for what he did to Wolf. He would pay for all of it.

The roar of the river drowned out whatever the brothers were saying to each other.

"Hurry up!" Asmodeus yelled.

But the brothers ignored them, turning their attention to the forest behind them.

"What is—" My words were ripped from my mouth as an arrow pierced the air, flying above Wolf and Jessiah, landing just a few paces away from my feet.

CHAPTER 40
WOLF

"What is that?" Jessiah asked as we both ducked. His wings splayed out, protecting us from the arsenal of arrows being launched across the river. They all missed his wings but landed *much* too close for comfort.

My magic buzzed beneath my skin. "*Rebels.*"

I didn't have time to answer questions, didn't have time to explain to Jessiah everything that fucking happened from the time I was sent to Moira until now.

"Draw your sword," I ordered. "We have to get Huntyr and Rummy."

"They followed us this entire time?" he asked, unsheathing his sharp sword from his waist. "What the fuck are they after? What do they want?"

I pulled my small dagger, waiting for the rebels to show themselves. "They want what we want."

Even over the roar of the river, I heard my father yelling. One glance over my shoulder told me Huntyr and Rummy were safe from the first hit of arrows.

Were they fucking shooting blind? Those arrows landed way too close. One wrong step, and Huntyr could have been hit.

"Fly back!" I yelled to Jessiah as I stepped toward the forest, away from the river. "Protect them. Avoid the arrows, your angel blood won't heal you if you're hit by one of them. I'm going to find the rebels!"

Jessiah gripped my arm and spun me around as I tried to push forward. His eyes were chaos, wide with fear, adrenaline, and confusion. "You're working with them?"

He didn't need my answer. "*Protect them,*" I repeated. "I'll find you when it's done." *When Asmodeus is dead.*

His jaw tightened, his eyes darting between myself and whoever may have been hiding in the thick trees of the forest.

But then, he nodded. "With my fucking life."

I didn't look to see if Jessiah made it across the riverbank in one piece, didn't look to see how Asmodeus and Luseyar were reacting.

This was going to be our only fucking chance to finish what we started before we made it to Scarlata Empire.

I ran as fast as I could into the foliage, limbs and branches slashing at my body as I pushed through.

"Nathan!" I called out. "Hold your fire!"

Arrows continued to spray into the air. A few seconds passed, I kept pushing deeper and deeper into the forest, toward where the sound of arrows slicing the air originated.

Until a solid body slammed into mine. We both fell to the ground with an impact that pulled the breath from my lungs.

"What the fu—" My words hitched in my throat as Nathan's face loomed over me, a warrior's gaze lingering in his eyes.

"Good to see you're still alive," Nathan said. I shoved him off me and we both scrambled to our feet.

"That was fucking reckless! Huntyr could have been hurt!"

"We're trying to get rid of him for good! You've known the plan, you knew there was a level of risk involved. Huntyr is fine, our shooters are careful. Now, grab a bow and help us pin them before they get away!"

He tried to turn, but I grabbed his arm. "Your arrows are too dangerous! Huntyr and her friend, Rummy, are with them. Asmodeus would use their bodies as shields, I'm damn certain."

Nathan looked between me and the riverbank. We could barely make out the bodies on the other side.

"You have the weapon to kill him?" I asked. "You're certain?"

Nathan turned behind him. "Voiler, come here." Voiler, the small but surprisingly strong fae I met in Moira, stepped out of the forest. She survived the Transcendent. She made it into The Golden City, and now, she fought with them.

The rebels.

She held a sword—a sword I recognized immediately—in her hand. It glowed with a white aura, shimmering with its own magic.

This was Luseyar's sword. He *just* had it, he always carried it with him. She must have taken it recently, there was no way he would continue without it.

"That's it?" I asked. "Luseyar's sword is what will kill the archangel?"

Voiler's features were fierce. Confident. Unwavering. Exactly what I needed from someone set to kill an archangel.

"This is it," she answered. "We only have a few minutes

before he realizes we have it. Get me close enough to use it, and it will be done."

Fuck.

"Hurry!" another rebel yelled from the trees. "They're running now! We don't have much time!"

Of course they were running away. My father was always a fucking coward.

"Let's kill that evil bastard."

CHAPTER 41
HUNTYR

"Where is he?" I screamed at Jessiah, who was now ushering Rummy and me into the trees and away from the chaos. "Why didn't you bring him back with you?" I fought against him, not wanting to leave that damn riverbank.

Not without Wolf.

"Don't worry about him," Jessiah ushered. "He can take care of himself. They're not after him."

"What the fuck are they after, then?"

Hells. It all snapped into place so quickly, the pieces finally fitting together in my mind.

The attack at the wedding. This. It was all part of Wolf's plan.

He was working with the attackers and they were here to follow through.

Jessiah watched me as I realized all of this. "Exactly," he hissed. "So we need to get you two as far away from here as possible."

Asmodeus, Luseyar, and Lord stumbled forward ahead of

us. They yelled something about the arrows being harmful to angels, but I could only hear half of what they rambled about as chaos spread through the group.

"Get her!" someone yelled. "Get Huntyr!"

Fuck. I looked at Jessiah, then at Rummy.

Wolf was on the other side of that fucking river, trying to figure out how they were going to kill Asmodeus, and Asmodeus wanted *me* more than anything.

The decision was already made in my mind. "Take care of her," I said to Jessiah. I kissed Rummy's cheek before running as fast as I could toward the water.

I launched myself into the air before my wings fully expanded.

Someone screamed behind me. Maybe it was Rummy.

But as my toes began to skim the cold water beneath me, my wings caught against the wind, launching me up a foot, then another.

Thank the fucking goddess.

I could see the outline of Wolf's body in the trees as I crossed the center of the river. He turned from whoever he spoke with to face me.

Then he ran.

He was only a few paces from me when I landed. My wings grazed the tall grass as I caught myself on solid ground.

"What the fuck are you doing?" he yelled.

"You think I'm going to let you do this alone? You've lost your fucking mind if you thought I was going to leave you!"

I felt Wolf's emotions through the bond, as raw and unfiltered as they came. Anger. Relief. *Love.*

"There's no time to fight about this," Wolf's friend—Nathan—said.

Voiler stepped out of the forest behind him.

"Voiler?"

She held a weapon in her hand, one that buzzed with energy, with magic. It was Luseyar's sword—the angel's weapon practically radiated magic.

She smiled, holding it up. "I come with gifts."

I couldn't hold back the laugh that bubbled in my chest. Arrows stopped flying above, but chaos still ripped through the air. Rebels yelled, emerging from the trees. Ones with wings began to fly to the other side while some dove into the river.

"This is really happening?" I asked.

Wolf's face broke into a wicked grin. "Oh, it's happening, Huntress."

I nodded, taking as big of a breath as I could to manage my nerves. "Great. What do I need to do?"

"**N**o fucking way," Wolf argued a minute later. "It's too dangerous."

"This entire damn thing is dangerous," I argued. "We're killing an archangel! We need my magic and we need this sword. There's no time to sit around and think about this, Wolf!"

Nathan interrupted us. "They're already moving deep into the forest. If we're going to do this before they disappear, we have to move. Now."

Wolf wanted Asmodeus dead just as badly as I did. I knew it was true. It was why he was willing to risk all of this just to get the rebels near him.

"The plan will work," Voiler said, handing me the sword. "It's the only way we're going to get close enough to Asmodeus without being slaughtered."

"He'll know by now that we're working together," Wolf said.

"It won't matter. He needs me to gain power over the vampyres. He won't hurt me."

Wolf's jaw tightened. He knew I was right. The plan was dangerous, but everything was dangerous with Asmodeus still breathing. I was willing to risk it.

I placed a hand on him and felt his heart race rapidly beneath my touch. "We're going to survive this, okay? Let me do this for you." His eyebrows drew together. "Let me do this for us."

A few seconds passed, though it felt like hours. "Fine," he answered. "But if you're hurt for even one fucking second, I'm stepping in."

Protective as always. "Deal."

Then we were moving, catapulting ourselves to the other side of the river to catch up with the archangel. Everyone else —Wolf included—swam across the river, but my wings were summoned and ready to fight. I flew across quickly, not bothering to wait.

They were all leaving, anyway. Nathan, Voiler, and the rest of the rebels would push forward toward Scarlata to prepare the vampyres there. Our plan to kill Asmodeus was too dangerous for them to stick around, especially when my magic was involved.

It would be Wolf and I facing him in the forest alone.

For being a powerful archangel, Asmodeus was humorously slow. The trees created too many obstacles to fly through with any real speed. I was the first to catch up with him. Lord was already running as fast as possible ahead of them, not waiting around to discover his own fate.

Him, I would deal with later.

I dropped to the ground in front of Asmodeus with a thud.

He stopped immediately as he smiled through labored breaths. "Come to play more games, Huntyraina? Unfortunately, I'm not interested."

He moved to keep walking, but I held my hand up to stop him. "Wait." He halted. Luseyar, too. "I can help you. I can get us both what we want."

His eyes narrowed as he watched me. "And why would I believe a single thing you say?"

"Because I would do anything to save the people I love." It wasn't a total lie, which is what made it believable. "If I give you what you want, will you let my friends go?" I stepped closer to him, just a few paces away now.

"You'd give me your power now, after all this time?" He laughed, the sound of it making me flinch. "You are a smart, smart girl, Huntyraina. You always have been."

A chill filled the air.

"Which is why it will be *such* a shame to have to kill you."

Before I could flinch, Asmodeus's power lashed out at me. Pain erupted through the very depths of my mind, paralyzing me as he moved behind me. He gripped my throat with one hand and held a blade to my chest with the other.

By the time his power released me, Wolf caught up to us.

He breathed heavily with nothing but rage on his face. "Get your fucking hands off my wife."

Luseyar finally stepped forward and aimed a small dagger at Wolf's chest. "That sword does not belong to you," he growled. "I thought I warned you not to do anything stupid."

I stiffened.

Asmodeus held me in front of him like a barrier, like a protective shield against his own body. I wanted to shiver from the closeness of him, from the sheer proximity of this monster.

Desperation leaked from his every pore.

"After all I did for you!" he yelled. "After everything I sacrificed so you two could stand in power!"

"You did nothing for us," Wolf argued. "You forced us to act. All you ever wanted was power, and you didn't care who got hurt in the process!"

Asmodeus laughed again behind me. I shut my eyes, blocking out the sound. "Huntyr is a queen, dammit! She is meant for power!"

Tension dripped from the air around us. Nobody moved a damn muscle, not even Wolf. "She'll still be a queen, but she'll rule Scarlata like it was always meant to be ruled: with grace and loyalty."

"And what do you know of loyalty?" Asmodeus argued. "Did you not betray your new wife time and time again? Did you not lie to her about why you met in Moira, about what you wanted from her?"

Wolf's hand was still tight on the angel killer weapon, still ready to fight, ready to end it all.

"This isn't worth it," I whispered. Asmodeus tightened his grip on my shoulders, and I couldn't stop the whimper of pain that escaped.

Wolf roared in anger as Luseyar tensed.

"So protective," Asmodeus tsked. "You've always been loyal, I see," he continued. "Just never to the same person. Do you really think these rebels will protect you? Do you really think they have your best interests at heart?"

Again, I tried to catch his gaze.

Look at me. Focus on me.

But his eyes locked on Asmodeus, blinded with anger, hatred, fear.

"Well, I hate to break it to you," Asmodeus pushed, "but if you want to kill your own father, you'll have to kill her, too."

CHAPTER 42
WOLF

Each second that passed with his hands on her body sent me fuming into a spiral.

She was no longer a stranger I had been sent to collect. She was no longer my roommate. No longer a mission from my father.

She was my *wife*.

This would be the last fucking day he laid his vile hands on what was mine.

The weapon in my hand buzzed, as if it reacted to my anger. It wanted to kill Asmodeus just as badly as I did. It was an extension of me, of what I wanted most.

Luseyar lingered inches from me. He raised the dagger in his hands defensively, but he knew the power of the weapon I held.

His dagger was nothing compared to this massive, magical blade. *He* was nothing without this sword.

Four of us hesitated in the standoff. We were not all leaving this forest alive.

"Wolf," Huntyr whispered before Asmodeus tried to

silence her again. There was such an urgency in her voice, I finally ripped my eyes from Asmodeus and looked at her.

Her features held no fear. No anger, either.

Just a determination that lit my soul aflame.

Asmodeus tightened his grip on her neck until she was forced to claw at his wrist. She tensed against him, but her finger pointed to her head, grazing a strand of her hair that fell loose.

My mind flashed backward to Moira, to the daggers I was forced to throw inches from her head.

I had good aim.

I could do it again.

If Huntyr released her power upon him at the same time, we stood a chance.

My entire body shook with adrenaline, anger, fucking determination to end this fight already.

But Luseyar stood so damn close to me. The second I released that sword, his dagger would pierce me.

Still. It was between my life or Huntyr's, and I would choose Huntyr's every damn time. No question.

"It never had to come to this," I pushed. "There could have been a peaceful ending to all of this madness."

"You're a damn fool if you believe true peace really exists, son. I know I raised you better than that."

I huffed. "You raised me to be a liar. A cheat. A fucking weapon. But I won't help you build your army of vampyres, Father. Not when the true blood queen is standing before us." He opened his mouth to respond, but I cut him off again. "You're the one who made me one of them. You're the one who turned me into a vampyre."

"I did that for *us*!"

"You did it for yourself! Who turns their own son into

this?" I held my arms wide. Luseyar flinched as I motioned to my wingless back, to the sharp fangs that emerged from my teeth.

"I'm going to give you one more chance," Asmodeus said anyway. "Come with me. Come to Scarlata and take your place as the king of vampyres, or die at Luseyar's hand."

Now, it was my turn to laugh. "I hold the weapon that kills angels, and you threaten *me*? You threaten *my* life?"

My eyes locked on my wife.

And I threw the damn sword.

CHAPTER 43
HUNTYR

I prayed to the goddess that Wolf's aim hadn't gotten worse since our time in Moira. He possessed the one item that would kill his father—the only thing that could save us.

We had to try.

I squeezed my eyes shut and threw as much of my magic as I could into Asmodeus. According to the rebels, we needed my powers *and* the blade to kill an archangel. So I pushed and pushed and pushed, forcing every ounce of power out.

I felt the impact ricochet through my entire body. The blade landed right above my shoulder, directly in the middle of Asmodeus's chest.

A roar of pain followed.

Asmodeus's.

Then Wolf's.

I opened my eyes to see Luseyar pulling his own dagger out of Wolf's back then rushing toward us.

As soon as the tight grip on my body lessened, I moved. He fell to the ground behind me as I rushed to get away from the evil archangel and half-crawled to Wolf, who fell to his knees a few feet away.

We fucking did it.

He did it.

"Wolf," I sighed. "Wolf, we need to go. Now."

Blood poured from his wound where Luseyar stabbed him. He pulled his hands away to show me the blood that pooled there, dripping from his fingers.

His face paled.

"No," I sighed. "No, you're fine, Wolf. Come on. We have to go."

I tried to sling his arm across my shoulders so I could lift him, but he grunted in pain and collapsed even deeper into the forest floor.

Goddess above, we did not make it this fucking far to lose everything now. *I did not make it this fucking far!*

"It's okay," Wolf whispered, leaning into me. "It's okay, Huntyr. Go."

That pissed me off. "You've lost your fucking mind if you think I'm going to leave you." I glanced over my shoulder to find Asmodeus on the ground with Luseyar leaned over his body. He pulled the blade out of Asmodeus's chest and sheathed it at his hip.

Luseyar would kill Wolf for this. He would kill us all.

"Can you heal?" I asked, keeping my voice down. "You can heal it, right? You're going to be fine, Wolf, but if you can heal, it needs to be now."

But the blood poured without any sign of stopping. Luseyar's dagger had pierced deep into Wolf's body, and we were all exhausted. It was difficult to kill an angel, even one that was half-vampyre. But this wound was terrifying to look at.

Plus, we had been traveling and fighting without feeding.

Wolf was already low on blood before this goddess-forsaken battle started. His healing had limits.

"I don't think so, Huntress." A soft smile fell from his lips. "You'll be fine. You need to go. Find Jessiah, he'll keep you safe."

I was already shaking my head. "Don't do this to me," I whispered. "You're not putting me through this, Wolf Jasper. Not again. I'm not going to lose you after all of this."

"You'll never lose me, I can promise you that much." Horror filled me as I watched his eyes flutter closed—just for a moment. But when he opened them again, he looked tired.

At peace.

I held his head in my hands and pressed my forehead against his. Blood smeared. Sweat dripped. "I can't do this without you."

Wings pumped through the air behind me. I heard one more deep roar of pain before Luseyar threw himself into the air, taking Asmodeus and the magical sword with him. My stomach dropped. My entire body lit up with adrenaline as we watched the two of them disappear deep into the sky.

They left. They actually fucking left.

"Do you see that?" I asked, half-laughing in pure delusion. "Do you see that, Wolf? They're gone." My voice cracked, squeaked. "It's just us now, okay? We can heal you and we'll be in Scarlata in a few days."

When his eyes fluttered closed again, they stayed that way. His head grew heavy in my hands and his entire body slumped.

The blood continued to pour.

But I wasn't going to give up. That horror—that absolute panic—fueled my limbs. I pulled Venom from my sheath and sliced my own wrist.

There was a time when I swore that Wolf would never feed from me again, that I would never allow *any* vampyre to feed from me. Not after all the hurt, all the betrayal.

But watching Wolf die? That would be the deepest wound of all, the harshest betrayal. There was no coming back from that, no returning to a world he wasn't in.

"Drink," I whispered, pressing my bloodied wrist to his mouth. "Drink, Wolf. You need blood to heal."

For a few painful, terrifying moments, I thought he wouldn't drink. I thought that, maybe, I said my last words to him. That we shared our last moment, our last victory. I thought that maybe, after everything—after falling as an angel, after losing his wings, after all of it—he was finally done fighting.

But then, ever so slowly, his eyes fluttered open.

His tongue slipped out of his mouth, tenderly licking across my skin.

"It's yours, Wolf," I whispered. "Take it."

My entire chest ached as I watched him push himself up, pulling my arm to his mouth. His teeth brushed against me, gently at first, before piercing my skin.

Heat pulsed through my body, but I was too terrified to give into it. *Drink, Wolf. Don't you dare fucking die right here.*

And he did. He pulled a mouthful of my blood into his mouth and swallowed.

And then he stopped.

He jerked his mouth away from my arm. "I can't do this, Huntyr."

"What are you talking about?"

"I can't drink your blood, not after what I did to you."

I gripped the back of his head and practically pulled him back down to my arm. "If you die right now because you refuse to drink this blood I'm offering, I'll never fucking forgive you, okay?"

He resisted at first, still hesitant.

So I did the only other thing I could think of. With the walls of our bond down, I pushed as much emotion through as I could. I sent him the absolute horror and fear and love I felt for him in that moment. He could not fucking die. I would never be okay again, and he had to know that.

"Drink," I said again, breath hitching. "Please."

Something flashed across his features before he returned his attention to my wrist, sliding his teeth into the same puncture wounds and drinking deep.

He didn't hold back this time. He needed blood and we both knew it; I could feel the hunger deep within him through our bond. No, it was beyond hunger now. It was survival.

"That's it." I relaxed against him and let him take whatever he needed. Wolf always had so much control, so much restraint.

Even now, seconds away from bleeding out entirely, his thirst did not scare me. I was not afraid that he would take too much, that he would drain my veins of every drop. The truth was, I never feared that with Wolf.

Even if he wanted to take every drop, I wouldn't stop him. My blood was his, every damn ounce.

Not a minute later, he pulled away. The blood at his side slowed as the healing effects began to kick in.

Thank the fucking goddess.

I wasn't sure how much more panic I could have taken in that moment. If that didn't work...

"Thank you," he whispered softly, voice sounding like he just woke up from a ten-year slumber. "You didn't have to do that, Huntyr."

I met his gaze as I answered, "Yes, I did. We both know it."

He smiled and dropped his head. Was he blushing?

"It worked," I said. "It fucking worked, Wolf. Asmodeus was hit." I used my hand to lift his chin up. His tired eyes searched mine, finally showing me the lightning that came out every so often.

Beautiful. He was fucking beautiful.

"Good," he said. "Because I don't think my aim is good enough to do that all again."

I shoved his shoulder lightly as I pushed myself up. "Can you walk? I'm not convinced Luseyar won't come back and kill us both for what just happened."

With a grunt of pain, he stood. He lifted his arm and surveyed the wound at his side.

It was ugly, but it no longer poured with blood. It was actually healing, thank the fucking goddess.

"Good as new," he teased. "Your blood is perfect, Huntress. Fucking perfect."

We stared at each other, locked into this magical gaze that neither of us could escape from. Everything disappeared around us—the trees, the violence, the weight of the fucking war we were about to start. All of it washed away.

There was only Wolf and me. Only the two of us, without any of this other shit that weighed us down.

Then, I was stepping closer, or maybe it was him, drawn to each other by forces we could not explain or control.

I knew I was still pushing my own emotions through the bond, the fear and horror and love and excitement, but so was he. He was showing me his own love, his pure gratitude, his overwhelming joy and light.

This was Wolf. This was the fallen angel who was sacri-

BLOOD SO BRUTAL

ficed to become a vampyre. Who lost his own wings for me. Who killed his own damn father.

So much darkness followed him, but this was pure love, pure light.

We were merely inches away. Wolf's hand came up to trace the side of my neck, my jaw, my earlobe. "You don't have to worry about me." His breath kissed my temple. "I'm not leaving you again in this lifetime. You'll have to kill me yourself if you want me gone."

I leaned against his touch. His thumb brushed my cheekbone, wiping away a tear I didn't realize had fallen.

"Don't tempt me. If you refuse my blood while you're dying again, I really might have to kill you."

I tilted my chin up, eyes flickering down to his lips.

But his brows drew together. "You know I never wanted to do that again. I never wanted to take from you, not after everything else."

"That was before."

"Before what?"

"Before I realized how messed up all of this was. Before I realized you didn't have a choice."

He tried to pull away, but I caught his wrist and stopped him. His eyes fell to the ground. "I always have a choice, Huntress. Always."

"Then choose me now. Choose this life."

Silence fell between us. Wolf kept his gaze on the ground for a few torturous moments before dragging his electric blue eyes up to meet mine. "Choose you?"

I waited, unable to say anything else.

He shook his head as if dumbfounded by my words. "I'll choose you every damn day for the rest of this life. The next one, even. There is nothing I wouldn't do for you, Huntress, nobody I wouldn't kill for you." He pulled himself back to me and pressed his forehead against mine as he added, "I choose you forever."

I pushed onto my toes and kissed him softly, testing the waters of whatever weight now hung between us.

Choose me.

Wasn't that what I wanted all along? I wanted someone to love me. To protect me. To care for me. I didn't want someone to simply love me out of convenience, only to turn their back on me when things got hard.

Lord never chose me. No, he chose power over me every damn time.

I didn't think Wolf had chosen me either. There were times when I hated him more than anything in this entire fucking world.

But here? Now? I believed every single word he said. I could feel it trickling through that tether between us with hot, searing light.

He kissed me back, firmly but softly, being patient with his movements as he slid both hands up to my neck and held me there. Blood smeared across both of us. It tainted our skin and trickled down our limbs, but I didn't care.

That was what we were, wasn't it? Two blood-soaked vampyres, desperate and clinging onto every last shred of hope.

Wolf pulled away slightly, both of us breathing heavily, trying to process what just happened. My hands remained on his chest. I held him like I never wanted him to leave, like I couldn't comprehend life without him.

It was true, I realized. I didn't want to live life without Wolf.

And that was fucking terrifying.

"We should get going," I said. "It'll take time to catch up with the others and the rebels will be worried."

He nodded, eyes flickering down to my lips once more before he finally stepped back. "You're right. We don't want to be here when Luseyar comes searching for us."

Together, we started down the thin path, clothes soaked in blood and lips swollen.

Our kingdom awaited us.

CHAPTER 44
WOLF

An entire day passed and we still hadn't caught up with the others. I wasn't worried. I saw signs of them every so often, and Jessiah was making his path known to us with assembled rocks or branches pointed in his direction.

It was something we did as children, leaving markers that only we could identify, like our own secret language away from Asmodeus.

I couldn't think of him right now, couldn't think of what I fucking did to him. The weight of the situation would come crashing down at any fucking moment, and it would be so damn heavy.

Asmodeus was dead because of me. I killed my own damn father, and the worst part? I didn't even feel bad about it.

Would Jessiah hate me? He seemed to be on board with my plan in the moment, but what was he thinking now? We sent him away with Rummy and practically forced him to run. When he found out what happened...

I shook my head. Jessiah would understand. He had to understand.

Huntyr's walking slowed. We would never catch up with them at this rate, but I was as worn as she was. My wound was healing because of her blood, but I still felt the pain with every step.

Hells, the memory of her blood sent another wave of heat through my veins. Cherries and fucking perfection. Goddess above, I'd planned on never again tasting anything so divine in my entire life, but when I tasted that hot liquid from her body again, I was practically pulled from the shadows of death.

"Stop that," Huntyr said from behind me.

I immediately pushed up my mental shields so she couldn't feel what my thoughts were doing to my body.

"Trust me, Huntress, I'm trying." Okay, I was sort of trying. *Think of literally anything else. Think of Jessiah. Of Asmodeus. Of how fucking angry Luseyar is going to be when he hunts us down to kill us.*

Maybe Huntyr would share her blood with me again once more before I died. Death would not be so bad with her blood on my lips.

"*Wolf,*" she warned.

"Sorry!"

"Are you doing that on purpose?"

I laughed quietly. We spent the last couple of months practically ignoring what the bond meant for us, but things were more intense after the wedding ceremony. We were bonded now in more ways than one, and it was getting harder and harder to keep my thoughts and emotions to myself.

"Is it so bad that I enjoy the taste of your delicious blood?"

I felt her own emotions then, hot and sweet at my words.

Instead of answering, she put her head down and grunted. "Just keep walking."

So I did. The two of us walked and walked. We would be a fucking sight to anyone passing us by. Huntyr's dress from the wedding ceremony ripped above her knees and split down her back. The tunic of mine she wore hung off her, now caked with my dry blood and covered in dirt.

My own shirt was ripped and tattered. My pants and boots thickened in blood—some mine, some not.

And we had days left of this journey.

Still, the scent of cherries wafted through the air.

And it smelled fucking *good*.

I turned right as soon as I heard the soft stream of water running down the hill. Hours had gone by, and the blood covering our bodies was now so dry, it cracked and flaked with every torturous movement.

A fucking bath was exactly what I needed.

Huntyr too, though she didn't seem nearly as excited as I did as we made our way to the shallow trickle of water.

I instantly dropped to my knees and scooped up a handful of the liquid, pulling it into my cotton-dry mouth and throwing it over my head.

I kicked my boots off quickly and slipped into the water. Fuck, it felt amazing, a close second to tasting Huntyr's blood.

The water was deeper than I thought, coming just above my shoulders as I stood.

Huntyr tentatively fell to her knees too, taking a drink before sitting back and watching me.

"What?" I asked. "Get in here, Huntress. It feels fucking amazing."

"I'm sure it does."

She looked down at her hands and picked at her finger-nails before she shifted to stick her feet in the river. "I'm fine here."

"Like hells you are."

I took two strides through the water before reaching her. I gripped her legs beneath her knees and pulled. *Hard.* She slid off the land with a squeal.

But I didn't let her go far. I snaked an arm around her waist and pulled her body to mine. She sucked in a sharp breath and clung to me, arms tightening around my neck. Her face looked pissed, but I could feel her relax as I pulled us both into the flowing water.

"Dammit, Wolf," she muttered under her breath. "Just when I think I could get used to you."

She looked at me, just inches away, water dripping from her thick, black lashes. Hells, she was beautiful, and the only thing separating her perfect body from mine was a very, very thin layer of soaking wet fabric.

If she knew what I was thinking, she didn't show it. She leaned back in my grasp and dipped her head into the water, using one hand to run her fingers through her thick curls.

"I'm teaching you to swim one of these days," I whispered, watching her. I couldn't take my damn eyes off her if I tried.

"Maybe," she replied. "But today is certainly not that day. I'm not even sure I have enough energy to make it all the way to Scarlata."

Her legs wrapped around my waist while her ankles locked behind my back. I moved my hands to grip her thighs, holding her body against me effortlessly as she bathed herself in the stream.

When she pulled herself back up, her face was clean. Blood no longer covered her perfect, pale skin. I could even see the faintest signs of freckles.

She stared at me for a second before dragging a handful of water up to my face. "Here," she said as she rubbed my rough skin gently, using her thumb to wash away the dirt, grime, blood, violence. Her eyes grew serious, her face focusing on the task at hand.

I watched her while she washed my face, closing my eyes momentarily when she demanded it. My entire body grew hot as she used her finger to wipe away the smeared blood on my bottom lip. Then, she moved to my hair. She used her torturous fucking hands to pull at the long strands.

I wasn't sure how much time passed. It could have been ten minutes. It could have been two fucking hours.

Huntyr relaxed against me, trusting me entirely as I held her body in the flow of the river.

Eventually, we were both clean. The water no longer ran red, my hair no longer heavy with caked substances.

But still, we remained in the stream.

"I should dry these clothes," I said, voice hoarse. Huntyr's eyes clung to my lips when I spoke.

"Yes," she agreed. "That's a good idea."

She did not smile, did not joke. She adjusted herself slightly so she could grab the bottom of my shirt, using her legs to hold herself against me while she pulled it up and over my head before throwing the wet fabric onto the dry riverbank.

I reached down and unbuttoned my own pants, pushing them off without letting go of her.

I was already so fucking hard just from holding her body to mine. Any chance of hiding that was long gone. I threw my pants onto the land, underwear following.

Huntyr said nothing.

I froze in the water as she leaned back—every movement laced with caution—and pulled the tunic up and over her own head.

She did the same with her dress, though it already bunched around her waist. She maneuvered it off, her breasts falling against me as she tossed the dress to dry.

Leaving only her panties between us.

Huntyr swallowed, and I watched every fucking movement of it, mesmerized by her beauty, barely controlling myself.

"I should let these dry too," she whispered.

"It would be a good idea." Neither of us moved. I didn't fucking dare.

She cleared her throat. "Care to assist?"

Goddess have fucking mercy.

My throat rumbled with a low growl, one I couldn't hold back if my life depended on it. I carried us to the riverbank, eyes locked on her, hers locked on me.

This felt different. Intense. Huntyr made me nervous in more ways than one, but this was something entirely more nerve-wrecking.

I reached the land and set her down with her legs still straddling me.

I took both index fingers and hooked them around each side of the evil fabric.

Her breasts dripped with water, her black curls covering her shoulders so fucking perfectly.

She pressed herself up on her hands as I pulled the panties away.

Her breathing hitched as the air hit her exposed body. I quickly tossed the fabric aside and into the sun along with the rest of our clothes.

Still, we said nothing. We didn't need to. I could feel her own nerves, her anticipation, her longing.

I slowly moved closer, running my hands on the outside of her smooth thighs. "You're fucking perfect, Huntress, and you're all mine."

Her big, brown eyes gazed up at me.

"Will you let me clean you?" I asked.

She hesitated for a second before nodding, pulling her bottom lip between her teeth.

So shy. So perfect. So *mine*.

I stepped back in the water so I could see her fully. I pushed her knees, spreading her open. She glistened against the damn sunlight. She was *that* stunning, *that* incredible.

Controlling myself with her blood was one thing, but controlling myself with her body?

Damn near impossible.

I pulled back even further, lifting her left foot and massaging gently, using the water to wash away any dirt, any lingering blood, until I left only her perfect, clean skin.

She moaned as I worked my thumbs deep into the sole of her foot. I ran my fingers across her heels where I healed the blisters that lingered there.

I cleaned the other foot too, taking my time as I worked my way up her calf.

By the time I reached her knees, she was squirming against my touch.

Hells, I loved the way she reacted to me. I loved the way she could hardly control what her body really wanted.

And I was the one who could give it to her. I was the one who could give her anything, who could make her feel pleasure she would only ever feel by my hand.

Or by my mouth.

I sank into the water and kissed the inside of her knee. I sank even deeper and slid her leg over my shoulder, looking up at her in the sunlight. She really was a goddess, her pale body glittering with drying drops of water as she exposed herself fully.

She didn't try to hide from me, didn't try to cover herself.

She locked her eyes on mine as she reclined backwards, propping herself up on her elbows.

I didn't dare look at her bare center. I knew once I got a view of her perfection, it would all be over. My cock pulsed in the water as I returned to her inner thigh. I washed any remaining dirt away with handfuls of water before covering her wet skin with my mouth. I kissed and sucked and nipped as I pleased, obsessing over the taste of her until I heard her moan again.

"Wolf," she said finally. "Please."

The way she said my name sent a shiver through my body.

My mouth met her center with an electrifying jolt, as if finally, for the first time in fucking weeks, I was giving both of us what we desperately wanted.

I craved this more than blood, more than water.

I craved it like it was everything I ever fucking needed.

Cherries and perfection. I was wrong when I said I could

die happy with her blood on her lips. *This* was what I needed. *This* would make me a happy, happy dead man.

She leaned back, arching off the ground as I slipped my tongue inside her, licking her fully and holding both thighs over my shoulders. I lapped and devoured, never wanting to get enough of her.

Hells, it would be impossible to get enough. I could taste her for weeks straight and still not be satiated, but there was so much more of her body I hadn't tasted, so much more of her I had been craving for the last few weeks.

I licked her apex once more before moving upward. My divine Huntress shivered when I slid her legs off my shoulders and re-secured them around my body as I kissed her stomach and licked her torso until I reached her breasts.

"I can't believe I've been able to stay away from you this long, Huntress." I leaned over her and palmed one of her breasts. Still so fucking plump, so perfect. "I need to touch you every minute of every day. I need to taste you more than I need your blood."

She whimpered as I dropped my head and pulled a nipple into my mouth. I teased her with my teeth, making her shiver again. Fuck, I would never grow tired of that.

I returned myself to the water and tried to regain a single ounce of control. Goddess above, I needed her. I needed her in the next five fucking seconds, or I would die, I was sure of it.

But Huntyr surprised me by following me into the water, sliding off the riverbank and wrapping her legs around my naked body just like before.

"Huntress," I moaned, my hardness throbbing against her entrance. "You're playing a very dangerous game."

Her serious, focused face finally flickered into a smile.

"And what if I want to play?"

She reached down, sliding a hand between our bodies and gripping me. My entire body shook as her warm, delicate palm wrapped around my shaft.

"What if I want you to feel everything I feel?" She pumped her hand up and down. "What if I want you to moan for me like I moan for you?"

Goddess fucking kill me now. I tossed my head back and closed my eyes, using every last ounce of energy to not throw her on that riverbank and fuck her.

"Eyes on me, Wolf. Only me."

Images of our first time together flashed through my mind. *Eyes on me, Huntress. Only me.*

I meant what I said before. I would choose her forever. Every fucking day. Always.

"You have no idea how badly I want to moan your name," I admitted. "Every time I dream about you, I wake up fearing that I've said your name in my sleep. You have no idea how much restraint it takes to be so close to you and not have your naked body in my arms."

She pumped her hand again.

I shuddered against her.

"Then show me how bad you want me, dear husband." She leaned down and ran her mouth across my jawline before nipping lightly at my earlobe.

Any remaining restraint quickly unraveled.

CHAPTER 45
HUNTYR

A growl rumbled in his chest, followed by a mischievous grin that only *slightly* made me regret my demand.

But even with the sun beating down on us, even with my entire body on full display to him, I wanted more.

The hunger in my core was not one for food, not for blood. I just wanted him.

Wolf's hands on my thighs tightened as he aligned himself with my entrance. He was losing control, and I fucking loved it. I loved watching him unravel in front of me, loved watching him lose himself piece by piece as I touched him.

He was mine to torture, mine to pull apart, and I wanted to watch his undoing. I'd been wanting to watch it, I realized, for some time now.

Wolf started slowly sliding into me and carefully adjusting my body to fit his. I held myself up with arms tight around his neck, pressing my breasts into him and letting him move me as he pleased.

I sucked in a sharp breath as he pushed himself all the way in, filling me so deeply that I nearly lost control.

"Is this what you want, dear wife?" he asked. Our breaths mixed in the tiny space between our lips. His words left his mouth and tumbled directly onto mine. "Is this what you want to feel?"

He slid my body up then back down again, growling once more at the sensation.

My breath hitched. "More," I whispered. "I want more."

Wolf smiled, the tips of his lips brushing mine. Water fell from my hair onto his chest as I stared at him, held him.

He moved faster.

Harder.

Moving himself into me perfectly, effortlessly guiding my hips so he slipped in and out with a perfect, controlled rhythm.

Even in the water, I knew I was dripping wet for him. I had been since before we even made it to the damn river, and he knew it.

He tasted it.

"More, Wolf," I demanded, tossing my head back and soaking in the pleasure that spread through my entire fucking body. I wanted more, wanted to feel him all over me, wanted to touch him, to look at him outside of the water.

He understood what I meant in an instant. He took two strides and hauled us out of the water, guiding our naked bodies to a nearby tree. He kept my legs wrapped around his waist as he pressed my bare back against the bark.

"I've wanted to have you like this for so fucking long, Huntress. And now, you're my *wife*." He nipped at my earlobe. "Now you're mine, and I'm never going to let you out of my damn sight."

I moaned in pleasure as he pumped into me again, sending my back grinding against the rough bark of the tree. I pressed my head against it and leaned back to look at Wolf in all his remarkable, gorgeous glory.

Hells, I fucking loved this man.

He fucked me like it was our first time, like he had been starved of me for years, like he never felt anything so pleasurable in his life.

"Drop the bond," I whispered. "I want to feel it."

He slowed only slightly, eyes flickering open and meeting mine, before drawing his brows together.

And then he dropped the walls of his bond, allowing all the emotions to flow through.

I gasped in surprise, not just at the sensation of love and light overflowing in my heart, but at the want. At the longing. At the relief and peace that he felt too.

It wasn't just lust. It wasn't just the primal longing, the act of our bodies together as one. He truly wanted this for some time now, and not just my body.

He wanted me like this. He wanted me to give myself like this to him.

"Is this what you want to feel?" he asked, sending more love, more light, until I was sure my chest would be overrun with emotions. "Do you want to feel how I would burn this entire world for you?" He pumped into me again. "Do you want to feel how obsessed I am with every single thing you do? Every single move you make, Huntress?" More love. More light. More power. "Because I'll let you feel it every fucking day for the rest of our lives if that's what you want. My heart beats for you." He bent down and kissed my neck, sucking lightly on the skin. I moaned his name, louder than was safe in the middle of this forest.

Wolf.

Wolf.

Wolf.

I was speechless, absolutely taken aback by the overwhelm of emotion.

But a few moments later, Wolf paused and pulled back. "Tell me you're mine." I felt it then through the bond—the tiny, minuscule amount of fear that lingered there. "Tell me you're not leaving, that we're in this together from now on."

I ran a hand down his face, over his lips, across his thick, wet eyelashes. *Oh, Wolf.* Did he really think I would do all of this, go through this fucking mess of a journey, defend him, let him feed from me, if I wasn't his? If I wasn't in this with him?

But I knew that feeling. The fear. The desperation that you might lose again, that you might have nothing. Again.

I knew it all too well.

"I'm yours," I said, voice cracking. I dropped my own walls, then, and let him feel the love behind every word as I said, "I'm so deeply yours, Wolf. I've been yours long before the wedding, long before any of this. I've never stopped being yours, even when I was mad as all hells, even when I hated you for betraying me."

He swallowed

"I am yours, Wolf, and nothing is going to change that."

My words unlocked something in him, gave him that final push we both waited for. His movements grew stronger, rougher, as he pumped in and out of me against that tree. The shadows of the leaves cascaded over us, but as my eyes fluttered closed, as I felt the peak of my orgasm rushing through my body, I didn't care where we were or who might be near us in the forest.

I had Wolf, and that was all I ever fucking needed.

He moaned my name as he climaxed too, both of us crashing down and clinging to each other like we were the only ones who mattered in the world.

I was his. It was the truth, and it had been the truth for longer than I wanted to admit.

By the time we made it to Scarlata, I wasn't sure my legs were even working. I was floating on the dirt path, barely alive.

We didn't run into any hungry ones, thank the fucking goddess. There was no way in all hells we would have been able to fight them if we did; there was no way we could have defended ourselves.

Even after he drank my blood, Wolf struggled. His steps grew shorter, slower. He started to limp yesterday, and I truly thought I would have to summon my wings and fly us both the rest of the way to Scarlata.

We would have plummeted to our deaths, certainly.

But that crumbling, ruinous kingdom came into view ahead of us, and I collapsed against Wolf in relief as we entered the clearing of Scarlata Empire.

Our new kingdom.

I saw Voiler and the rest of the rebels waiting, but I was instantly distracted by two figures running toward us. Rummy and Jessiah sprinted to greet us as soon as we took two steps onto the land. I fell to my knees, as did Wolf. Rummy fell in front of me as she gripped my shoulders.

We were both alive.

Jessiah muttered a slew of questions and concerns to Wolf as they surveyed each other too.

"Don't you ever do that again, you bitch!" Rummy yelled, punching my shoulder lightly. "You scared the living shit out of me! What were you thinking? You could have been killed!"

Wolf and Jessiah quieted. Everyone turned to me.

I was so fucking exhausted. Rummy was right—what I did was stupid. But I couldn't stop the smile that spread across my face.

"What?" Rummy asked. "Why are you smiling like that? Did it work?" Her eyes slid between Wolf and me repeatedly as she waited for a confirmation. "Did you kill him?"

"It worked," I said. "It worked."

The four of us laughed together then, Wolf and me all but collapsing as pure relief washed over us.

It worked. It was over. The biggest obstacle to our freedom was gone.

"But we're not out of danger yet," Wolf interrupted. "I have no doubt that my father's men will retaliate. He wasn't the only one who wanted power for The Golden City. They'll come for us." He looked at me. "They'll come for you."

"Then we'll be ready." I gripped Rummy's outstretched hand. "We'll be ready whenever they come."

Jessiah and Rummy shared a glance then both looked at me.

"What?" I asked.

"There's something we want you to see. Both of you."

Wolf walked behind me as we followed Jessiah through the ruins. I wasn't as fearful of Scarlata this time around. The crumbling gray walls, the overgrown foliage of the kingdom it felt oddly familiar now. It felt comfortable, like returning home after a long journey.

"When Jessiah took me here a few days ago, I couldn't believe my own eyes." Rummy spoke with an excitement I hadn't heard from her in, well, forever. There wasn't much to get excited about in Midgrave.

"You're making me nervous," I said. "Tell me where we're going."

She smiled widely, hooking her arm through my elbow. "It's better if you see it for yourself."

My body tickled with nerves. Part of it was Wolf's nerves, too. I could feel every inch of his presence as he walked two steps behind us in silence, following his brother without question.

We reached a portion of the ruins hidden behind a large, stone wall. It looked as if it had once been the central meeting place of the kingdom. I imagined the queen—my mother—summoning her people here to speak. To rule.

We walked around the edge of the wall.

And my stomach dropped.

Dozens—no, hundreds—of vampyres sat waiting.

All of them with their eyes on me.

CHAPTER 46
WOLF

"What is all this?" Huntyr asked. "Who are these people?"

She stood in front of the crowd, not moving a muscle. Rummy and Jessiah froze, too, letting her step forward and survey the group of vampyres.

Some, I recognized. Some, I had been building relationships with for years. Others were new. Still, I knew why everyone came. I knew exactly where Jessiah had been leading us.

"This is Scarlata Empire," I answered from behind her. "This is your kingdom. They're all gathering here for you, their queen."

Huntyr sucked in a sharp breath. "What do you mean they're gathering here for me?"

Jessiah dipped his chin. "When I arrived to find dozens of vampyres here, I admit, I was shocked. But my brother here seems to be very good at keeping secrets."

His eyes slid to me with a message that we certainly would be speaking later.

341

"He has been working to rebuild what was lost, to find the vampyres who scattered after the war."

"These are the survivors from Scarlata?" Each vampyre looked back at her, and I swelled with pride as they tilted their chins up in respect.

This was her kingdom. These were her people. The vampyres here had been waiting for years, never losing hope that the true blood queen was still out there somewhere.

One of the vampyres in the front row—a woman with long, red hair—stood. "We're here to fight for you," she announced as she pulled her own sword from its sheath. "We're here to fight for what was lost."

Many of the other vampyres stood then too, unsheathing their own weapons. Some were older, some young, still children. But one by one, they all stood, announcing their support for the true blood queen of Scarlata Empire.

And then, one by one, they all took a knee.

Silence rippled over the crowd.

I stepped forward until I was sure Huntyr could feel my presence behind her, reassuring her I was there. I would always be there.

"I don't know what to say," Huntyr whispered. Rummy placed a hand on her shoulder and smiled.

"You don't have to say anything," Jessiah added. "Just know that you're not alone in this. None of us are."

"And it's time to prepare," I chimed in.

"Prepare for what?" Huntyr asked.

Another silence fell over us, colder this time. Fiercer. I looked at the faces of the warriors staring back at us. Each one of them had something to gain, something to fight for, someone to protect.

"Prepare for war."

I walked toward the fire with a handful of logs from the forest, Jessiah silently following behind me. The two of us had been doing this for an hour; walking to and from the forest to gather wood.

The silence didn't bother me. I enjoyed it, actually. Huntyr had been catching up with Rummy and Voiler all day, but I made sure to keep her in my line of sight at all times. I wasn't going to take my eyes off her after what we went through.

It wasn't until I threw the third pile of logs next to the bright fire in the ruins of Scarlata that Jessiah finally cleared his throat. "He's really gone, then?"

I looked at my brother, but his gaze was locked onto the burning embers ahead of us. "He's gone," I replied. "Luseyar flew away with his body, but we did it. The sword mixed with Huntyr's magic worked."

He nodded, emotionless. I hated the pang of guilt that followed. My father made us suffer. Not just us, either. He made entire species suffer. He kept the vampyres on their knees at his mercy. He corrupted The Golden City, he went against Era's trust.

He deserved to die for the things he did.

"Thank you." Jessiah turned to face me. His eyes glistened against the flickering fire. "I understand why you didn't tell me about your plan, but know that I'm on your side, Wolf. I support you. What you did couldn't have been easy."

I cleared my own throat and tore my gaze away. Huntyr

found my gaze from where she stood in the crowd. "It was shockingly easy when I assessed what was at risk."

I wasn't sure how long we stood there in silence, watching the fire crackle before us. But that was our tribute. That was our way of saying goodbye to the torture we endured our entire lives.

"Come on," Jessiah said after a while. "You look like shit, you need to eat something."

"You've always had a way with words, brother." I ignored the tightness in my lungs and followed him as he made his way to the others. "I guess some things never change."

"It's about time you two join us," Rummy announced, passing some of the meat that was cooked over the fire. "We were just talking about you."

"Oh really?" I asked. "Rest assured, nothing you've heard is true."

Rummy smiled and nodded to Voiler. "She was telling us that you practically planned the entire attack, that you've been planning this all for months now."

I stiffened, suddenly wishing Huntyr and I were alone so I could explain this all privately. I told her many times that I had a plan, but she never knew the depths of it. She never knew I snuck off to meet with Nathan to plan this entire uprising.

Jessiah nudged my shoulder.

"Some of that may be true, sure." I glanced at Huntyr, looking for any sign of anger, but all I got was a flare of her amusement through the bond.

"I couldn't have done it without Nathan, Voiler, and the others." I quickly deflected the attention. "How did you get Luseyar's sword from him, anyway? He's been glued to that thing for as long as I can remember."

She shrugged. "Going unnoticed is a skill of mine. As soon as the arrows started flying, he was wide open. Everyone was too busy panicking to notice me stealing his weapon."

Everyone nodded. "Very impressive."

She shrugged. "Not as impressive as actually killing the archangel."

I met Huntyr's eyes again, and this time, she beamed with pride. There was no hiding her true emotions, there was no denying that gratitude that lingered there.

"Killing Asmodeus wasn't the end of it. His people will come for us. They'll try to take what we're building here."

"They can fight all they want," Huntyr said. The sound of her voice made my heart race. "But they can't take what's ours."

I only tore my eyes away from her when an older vampyre approached our group. I recognized him instantly, I had seen him around Scarlata for years. He was one of the survivors that stayed here to fight.

"You look just like her," he mumbled. Huntyr—along with everyone else—spun to face the man.

"Excuse me?" she asked.

"You look just like your mother."

CHAPTER 47
HUNTYR

My mother?

I stared at this stranger dumbfounded, waiting for someone to explain.

"I'm sorry," Rummy jumped in, "you knew Huntyr's mother? You knew the queen?"

The man smiled softly and nodded. "It was a long time ago, but yes. I knew her well. She was one of the strongest women I ever met. Brave, too. And she looked just like you when she was your age."

There weren't many survivors that lived long enough to remember my mother, especially when she was my age. My hands shook as nerves began to take over, but I didn't let them control me. This man likely knew more about my mother than anyone else here. I suppressed my questions for long enough. It was time to get some answers.

"Can you tell me about her?" I asked. "What was she like?"

The man smiled again as his gaze got lost in the distance and his mind wandered in thought. "Claudia was very strong.

Stupid at times, too, but always protecting what was right. She was everything this kingdom needed. She had a dream of uniting everyone, of fae and angels living in peace. Her and your father both wished for that."

Even the fire seemed to quiet as he spoke.

"My father?" I asked. I felt someone moving closer and I half-expected it to be Wolf, but relief flooded me when Rummy's hand slipped into mine and squeezed. "Is he still alive?"

The man's smile faded. "No, he isn't. Your father was a good man. He was a powerful fae who lived here with us, proving that the fae and the vampyres really could live together. He fought for your mother until the war. Even then, he still fought."

I said nothing. Rummy squeezed my hand again. "That sounds a lot like Huntyr."

"We all thought you were killed in the war," he started. "If any of us knew you were still alive, we would have fought to get you back. We would have fought for you, Huntyraina."

"Just Huntyr," I corrected. His eyes widened and I instantly regretted the correction, but he wasn't offended. Not in the slightest. His gaze glistened with a pride that made my knees weak. How could someone who knew so little about me support me this much?

"I see them both in you, *Huntyr*," he added. "They would be proud of you. They would be proud of everything you're doing to fight."

I shook my head. "I've been gone for so long. Sometimes it still doesn't feel real. I feel so disconnected from them."

The man reached for my free hand and squeezed it gently between both of his. "Look around you, child. Look at all the people who love you. Look at all the people who are fighting for you." My throat tightened, but I looked around, taking in the hundreds of people littered throughout Scarlata, surrounding the fire, sharing food. "Let this place reconnect you," he said. "Let this place remind you of who you were born to be."

Rummy and I lay back on the roof with our feet dangling over the edge, exactly like all those nights in Midgrave. The clouds that typically covered Scarlata during the day disappeared, leaving a beautiful sea of stars glittering above us.

I took a deep breath, sucking in the smell of Rummy's leather jacket and smoke from the fires below us. "I never thought I would see you again," I whispered.

Her hand found mine in the darkness and squeezed hard. "Please. You can't get rid of me that easily," she joked.

I smiled, but my stomach clenched. Any words in my mind vanished at the thought of actually losing her.

My body had been in fighting mode since we left the wedding. Since before that, even. I had been in shock for quite some time now, still deciphering everything that happened to me. To *us*.

But I was alive. Rummy was alive. Wolf, by a fucking miracle, was alive.

And apparently, the entire fallen blood kingdom was alive, too.

"Hey," Rummy said, turning her head to face me. "Don't

lose it now, Hunt. You're so close to being free. Keep it together until then, okay?"

A fist tightened around my lungs. "I'm trying, but hells, this all feels like a fever dream sometimes."

"I can't even imagine what you've been going through. Being held captive by that crazy bastard while you were transitioning into a vampyre?" She huffed a breath. "You deserve an award. You really do."

"I thought they were all losing their minds at first. It wasn't until the cravings started to hit me that I believed I might actually be one of them."

A few beats passed.

"You're okay, though, right?" she asked. Her voice sounded so young, so vulnerable. The fierce, tough friend I knew rarely showed this soft side. "I mean, you're doing okay with everything? With who you are?"

I shut my eyes and squeezed them tight. I couldn't look at Rummy, couldn't look at the fear and worry I knew would be lingering on her face. I couldn't look at the stars, either. They were the same stars Rummy and I used to stare at when I was a lowly, magicless fae in Midgrave.

"I'm surviving," I admitted. "Wolf's been helping me get through it. Without him, I—" I stopped myself before my voice cracked and took a long breath to settle the rush of emotions that followed. "I'll get through this. These people are counting on me now. That's what I have to focus on. I'll figure out the rest of it later, once these people are safe."

She squeezed my hand again. We remained like that for minutes—maybe hours—before I finally asked, "Do you really think they would be proud of me?"

"Your parents?"

I nodded.

"I don't doubt it for even a second."

"I never really questioned who my father was. I grew up with Lord, and even though I knew he wasn't actually my father, he felt like one to me. It's actually a relief hearing that my real father wasn't a monster."

"Lord was nothing but a pest, Hunt. The fact that you turned out so amazing after everything he put you through is a damn miracle. You are the daughter of greatness. You're a good fucking person, and I know both of your parents would be beaming with pride if they saw you."

Tears threatened my eyes. "You honestly believe that?"

She moved beside me, reaching into her leather jacket and pulling out a new flask. "Well, they might not be proud of *this*."

Hells, I loved Rummy.

We spent the next hour laughing and talking about our lives, passing the flask back and forth as we reminisced on our late nights in Midgrave.

The two of us came so far. We endured so much together. I hated that Lord dragged her here for leverage, but I was so fucking happy she was here with me.

We only shut up when we heard the rustling of movement on the roof behind us.

"Do you think they're sleeping like that?" Jessiah whispered, though not nearly quiet enough.

"Wouldn't surprise me if they were," Wolf replied. "Rummy is just as insane as Huntyr. They probably slept like that every night in Midgrave."

"I can hear you, assholes!" Rummy yelled from beside me.

I laughed then, a real laugh. A laugh that filled my whole stomach. A laugh that wasn't covering dread or fear or grief.

"No offense," Wolf replied. "Can you two maybe not sleep with half your bodies over the edge of the roof?"

Rummy and I looked at each other a second longer before crawling backward a few feet in unison. Wolf approached us and threw me a blanket. "Take this," he said. "We're all sleeping here tonight."

Rummy quickly covered both our bodies with the thick fabric. Wolf sat himself down a few feet to my right while Jessiah settled on the other side of Rummy.

"Are they always this clingy?" Rummy whispered.

I nearly snorted. "Actually, yes, they are."

"I prefer the term protective," Wolf grumbled.

"Or stoic," Jessiah chimed in.

Rummy and I both laughed again. I knew the two wouldn't leave us alone for more than a few minutes, not when we were entirely surrounded by vampyres.

But even though it was dangerous, even though I spent my entire damn life learning to hate these people—to kill them—I felt safe, safer than I had in my entire life.

Because, vampyre or not, these were *our* people. Rummy's too. Jessiah's. Wolf's.

I pressed myself close to Rummy's side, letting my heart fill with this moment.

Tonight, we were safe.

Even if just for a moment.

The sun had yet to fully rise when I blinked my eyes open.

I was no longer sharing a blanket with Rummy; rather, I had rolled to my right and somehow ended up splayed over Wolf's chest.

His eyes were still closed, but the second I tried to gently lift myself away, his hand around my waist tightened, trapping me to him. "Not so fast, wife," he mumbled, eyes still closed. I felt every vibration of his groggy voice. "I'm keeping you here forever."

Rummy had our blanket to herself now, though she ended up much closer to Jessiah than before.

"The sun is rising." I returned my attention to Wolf. "We should get up before the others start to wake."

He growled his objection before pulling me even closer, nuzzling into the mess of my curls. Fuck, I could have stayed there all damn day. Weeks, even. Months. Here on this roof with Rummy, Jessiah, and Wolf was everything I ever needed.

The people I cared about were safe.

And they were *here*.

For now, at least. I pushed myself up and ignored Wolf's groan of protest. We were safe, yes, but that wouldn't last. Not without preparing to fight.

Wolf followed me off the roof and down the stairs to meet the rest of the waking crew below. I spotted Voiler instantly, speaking in hushed tones to a couple other women I hadn't met yet, and Nathan, who I was beginning to recognize as one of Wolf's trusted leaders in this rebellion.

"Rise and shine!" Nathan greeted us as we approached. "You two sleep well?"

"Like a fucking rock," Wolf replied from behind me.

Voiler flashed me a smile.

"Good, because we have a busy day ahead of us."

And he wasn't wrong. Within the hour, everyone was awake, working their asses off to prepare for what we all knew deep in our bones was coming.

First, we prepared a bunker for the untrained vampyres and the children. Keeping them safe would be a priority if Scarlata was attacked. It wasn't hard to find a partially underground room with enough space for all of them. We secured it with a few large stones at the entrance then moved our spare water and supplies into the back.

Then, we gathered weapons, preparing for the fight. Wolf acquainted himself with the other soldiers, got to know their history and their expertise while I took Rummy and Voiler with me to help distribute the extra weapons. We didn't have much, but a welder had been living with the surviving vampyres here in Scarlata, and he managed to build a decent supply of swords and daggers.

The angels would have more—much, much more—but thinking about that was a waste of our time.

Around midday, Wolf sent two scouts into the forest to track the movement of our enemies. It all started to feel very real, like we were all sitting around, waiting for doom to strike.

But when I glanced around the fire later that night, I didn't see scared faces. I didn't see doom or terror or death.

The fire in the center of the ruins blazed bright enough to light up everyone's faces. Children ran around the perimeter, laughing and screaming as they chased each other. A group of males—Wolf included—exchanged war stories to my right. They stood around, sharing cooked meat and listening intently to one another as the light flickered among their features. It didn't matter that they weren't all vampyres. Nathan was fae, Wolf part angel, but they accepted each other fully, understanding that we all fought for the same thing here.

And then, there was Rummy and Voiler, who sat on the ground beside me, whispering to each other about the atrocities of The Golden City.

The two of them had a lot in common. I barely knew Voiler in Moira, but I was glad she was here now. I felt safe around her. Calm. Neither of them left my side for two days, almost as if they knew I would crumble entirely without them.

I started to actually feel at peace here, like this was all supposed to happen. Like we all belonged here, just like this.

That peace stayed with me until the scouts returned from the forest.

The entire group fell silent as the two men stumbled toward the fire, catching their breaths.

"Two days," one on the right muttered. "We have two days until they're here."

CHAPTER 48
HUNTYR

The next day was quiet. Most of the vampyres were gone by the time we woke up. I didn't miss the way Jessiah slept extra close to Rummy that night—the same way Wolf slept extra close to me.

The vampyres were fueling up for the fight.

The thought should have scared me, especially considering we were some of the few people here with blood to feed from, but it didn't. I trusted the others completely, even the ones I hadn't met yet.

Wolf took me to the edge of the ruins to let me feed. I argued with him and insisted I was fine, but he could feel my hunger. He knew my magic needed this if we were going to put up a fight.

And because of our bond, we both needed it.

"The others are feeding off animals nearby, aren't they?" I asked.

Wolf shrugged, rolling up the sleeve of his black shirt. "The others aren't you."

"What's that supposed to mean?"

Wolf stopped messing with his shirt and looked up at me. "It means you're my wife now, Huntress. You'll drink my blood. I don't care if you grow to hate me. I don't care if you travel thousands of miles away. It will be my blood and my blood *only* that feeds you, understand?"

The fierceness in his voice made me freeze. He was completely serious, completely unhinged.

I swallowed then nodded. "Fine."

He stared me down with his darkening eyes for a second longer before breaking into a smile. "Good. Now, drink."

My own vampyre fangs protruded from my teeth, but I resisted. "That hardly seems fair."

"What's not fair?" He stepped closer.

"That I drink your blood while you drink none."

His eyes held mine as he took a long breath. "I told you, Huntress. My blood is yours. All of it."

I held my wrist out then, rolling up my own sleeve. I made this decision long ago, I realized. The thought of him drinking anything else—animal, fae, or angel—made me sick.

He would drink *my* blood.

His eyes flickered to my wrist then back to mine. "You're under no obligation to share your blood with me."

"Aren't I, though?" When he didn't move, I stepped closer. "You are my husband, just as I am your wife. You offer me your blood; I want to offer you mine." I stopped a few inches away. "*That* is fair."

"Fairness doesn't exist here, Huntress. I can easily find blood from—"

"Mine," I interrupted. "You'll drink mine."

I knew why he hesitated. The first time he drank from me,

I went against everything I was raised to believe. I went against my morals, my self-respect. I gave *everything* up so he could feed.

Why? Because I loved him. Because I trusted him completely, even though he was a vampyre.

Hells, so much changed since then. Wolf would never ask to feed from me. He would never put me in that position, the position to compromise myself again.

But everything was different now. Forced or not, Wolf was my husband. Our lives were tied together. All this betrayal, this hurt, it all had a purpose.

Wolf cared about me more than anyone else. It took me a long time to see that, but Lord never loved me. Lord never truly cared about me; he only cared about what I could do as a powerful queen.

With Wolf standing before me, my chest welled. He wouldn't care if I was a queen or not. He wouldn't care if I was fae or angel or vampyre. He would protect me all the same, no matter who I was to him.

His loyalty to me came before anything else.

Something possessive and dark rumbled in him, lower than a growl. "If you're sure," he added. "I can't say I haven't been dreaming of the taste, of what it would feel like again to have your blood dripping from my lips."

Heat pooled in my stomach. "It's better this way. We both need to be strong before the fight."

Wolf leaned back onto one of the short stone walls behind him, tugging my hips forward so I straddled him as he sat on the edge of the wall. The hunger in his eyes funneled through our bond until I couldn't keep his feelings apart from mine.

His eyes flickered to my lips and darkened before I kissed

him without hesitation. Without guilt. Without question. It was soft and quick, but it sent my stomach fluttering all the same.

Wolf held me like my body was made for him. I settled onto his lap, instantly warming at the closeness of him.

He pulled back enough to say, "Can I ask something of you, Huntress?"

I nipped at his bottom lip. "Anything."

He reached up and pulled the collar of his shirt down with his index finger. "Will you bite me here? Will you do me the greatest honor of wearing your mark upon my skin so even our enemies know who I belong to, so even the angels know who I'm willing to die for?"

I wasn't expecting *that*. Tears instantly rushed to the surface as my breath hitched in my throat. I held his face in my hands as I lowered my forehead to rest against his. "If you'll have me," I started, trying and failing to keep my voice steady, "I would love nothing more."

When he kissed me this time, he was not gentle. He was not patient. He ravished my lips with his, slipping his tongue into my mouth and letting me taste him with every last ounce of restraint gone.

And I kissed him back with just as much hunger, with just as much need. I held his face to mine as I kissed him with everything I had. The heat in my body roared, begging for more.

When I moved to tilt his head to the side, exposing his perfect, muscular neck, he easily obliged. His breathing shallowed as I kissed his ear and ran my mouth down his jaw.

His blood called to me, pulled me closer like a siren in his veins. I kissed his neck with a fierce need before letting my sharp teeth pierce the skin there.

The bite mark would normally disappear within a few minutes due to our healing abilities, but I sensed Wolf's magic pulsing through me as he forced the healing to avoid this bite mark. This wound would remain, marking us both forever.

I never wanted anything more.

Wolf hardened beneath me, clearly not affected by the pain of the bite one bit. His blood in my mouth was fucking euphoric. I made sure the bond was wide open as I drank, letting him feel how it affected me.

Blood was one thing. But the taste of his power? It sweetened his blood and tingled in my body as I swallowed.

And swallowed.

And swallowed.

A few seconds later, I pulled back. Wolf was reaching for my wrist, but I stopped him, pulling my hair away from my own neck.

"A mark for a mark," I breathed. I knew blood smeared my mouth, but I didn't care. "I want them to know who I belong to, too."

He smiled, his fangs already protruding. "My wicked Huntress," he teased. "We both know you belong to no one."

He leaned up to kiss me, but I stopped him. The smile fell from his mouth as I said, "My heart is yours, Wolf. It has been since Moira. Mark me here. I want everyone else to know we belong to each other."

A second passed, and I thought maybe he wouldn't do it, that maybe I pushed him too far. He was always so careful about my boundaries, even when I didn't want him to be.

But that ounce of hesitation vanished within an instant, and Wolf was bringing his own mouth to my neck, ravishing the skin there with his lips before biting me.

And then, he was drinking.

I felt the moment he let himself relax, taking what his body wanted. Our bond protected us; I knew he would never take too much, because he could feel how badly I wanted this. Needed this.

He drank from me, I drank from him. Our bodies intertwined under the beating sun in the Scarlata ruins. Thank the goddess we were alone, because a few moments later, when I reached between our bodies and fumbled with his belt, he growled in agreement.

It was a haze of lust and blood and passion, but it was also clear as day in my mind. Nothing ever felt so right.

I shoved his trousers down his thighs, and he did the same to me, not even bothering to take my pants off completely before I slid down onto him. Neither of us cared about anything but *this*. I slid up his length then gasped as I let him fill me again.

His magic buzzed inside me, mixing with the perfection that was this moment. I leaned forward and bit him again, pulling more of his blood into my mouth as I rode him with a rough, eager need.

"Fuck, Huntress." He leaned forward to lick up more of my blood. "Nothing is more perfect than this moment right here."

I moaned in agreement and rode him faster. He guided my mouth down to his. Both of us smearing blood on the other, neither of us cared.

He licked my mouth clean of every last drop, pulling my tongue into his mouth to taste.

I came too fast, filled with ultimate perfection between Wolf pulsing inside me and his blood heightening my senses.

He crashed too, holding me tight against him as he shook with release.

As quickly as it started, it was over.

Neither of us moved for some time. We waited until both our breaths returned to normal, until the buzz of the blood-lust faded.

I sat up and cleared my throat. "Well, I wasn't planning on that."

Wolf loosened his arms around me and helped me readjust my pants to their original position.

I crawled off his lap, giving him space to do the same. My face heated as I glanced around. We just had uncontrollable vampyre sex *in public in the middle of the day.*

"None of that." Wolf stood up and placed both of his large hands on my face until I was forced to look at him. "You don't get to feel ashamed, Huntress, because that was fucking incredible." He leaned down and gave me a wet, sloppy kiss. "And you just might be my saving grace, because now, I can die a happy man."

I gasped and smacked him playfully. Wolf's confidence, his steadiness, calmed me in an instant. He was right; I had nothing to be ashamed of.

Wolf was my husband. I had been fighting this for so long, but why?

Nothing so *divine* could ever be wrong.

"You're not allowed to die," I argued. "I already got pissed at you for it once. We're going to fight those bastards and prove to everyone that the vampyres deserve to live in peace."

He nodded in agreement, leaning down to kiss me again before freezing and looking somewhere in the distance.

Every ounce of my now-fueled senses lit up.

"What? What is it?"

Wolf stood with a calmness and fierceness I only saw on him once before. It was the vision of a warrior. A soldier. "They're coming."

CHAPTER 49
WOLF

The air shifted. The wind warned us of the attackers minutes before I felt it in the ground—the low rumble of horses in the distance, the fluttering of wings miles away.

There was no room for fear here.

No room for hesitation.

I reached out to Huntyr through the bond, reached out to feel her emotions, but she felt no fear either—only a fierce, reassuring determination.

The only option here was to win. Win and survive. Win not only for us, but for every single person with a weapon drawn, ready to fight for our freedom. For our future.

They would never control us. They would never eradicate us.

Asmodeus thought he was gaining an inside man when he sacrificed my soul to Era, when he turned me to this half-vampyre, but he was wrong. He had no idea where my loyalties would lie after that betrayal. He had no idea I would finally find myself here, among these blood-sucking monsters.

They would find out how much of a monster I could be.

They would all find out.

I gripped my sword with steady hands.

Huntyr wasn't far, but dammit if every single one of my instincts didn't urge me to turn around and run after her.

She was a strong fighter. She spent her entire life learning to kill, after all.

But that was why she needed to protect the others. Rummy, the kids, the women—they were deep in the ruins, hiding in the bunker.

It was our job to keep them safe. It was our job not to let those evil, power-hungry bastards anywhere near the kingdom.

I looked to my right. Hundreds of vampyres—females and males both—lined the trees. They created a barricade of bodies, ready to rip apart anyone who dared enter, anyone who dared attack us.

Then, I looked to my left. My chest swelled even further as I saw the same thing—hundreds more vampyres with swords drawn and teeth barred, ready to protect this kingdom.

They weren't going to lose it for a second time.

I wasn't going to let that happen.

Anticipation thickened the air, but not fear. Nobody was afraid.

Fear came when you had something to lose. This? Us? We fought for a chance to live. A chance to build a home. A chance to build a kingdom.

We had no kingdom to lose, no home to savor, and that's what made us dangerous.

I braced myself as the sound of men grew closer and

closer. They weren't even trying to conceal their approach—they were too big-headed. With the magic of the angels, they thought they were no match for us.

The first fae came into view ahead, sword raised and mouth open with a battle cry.

Chaos erupted in the valley.

Violence was not new for me. I did not flinch away from the metal of a sharpened sword. I did not cower from the brute force of warriors, from the strong powers of angels.

I, too, grew up to fight. I, too, had a sharp sword.

And thanks to my father, I, too, had sharp teeth.

My vision blurred as I moved, maneuvering myself with little to no thought as I sliced down every opponent who charged us. My instincts took over with every slice of my weapon, with every body pummeled by my fist.

The army of fighters from The Golden City consisted of fae and angels both. They were strong, yes, but we were angry.

I kicked a body off my sword just before a large male charged from my right. Brutal hatred covered his features, and he ran at me sloppily, sword raised and body exposed.

My sword sliced through his flesh like butter.

Again and again, I cut down our enemies.

Again and again, they kept coming.

It wasn't until I felt the first wave of magic that I paused, stepped back. This first wave, this was the distraction. This was to draw us out.

The powerful angels would be next, and they would not be fighting with mere weapons and fists.

They would be fighting with blood. With magic. With the air itself.

A wave of fire erupted on my right and split our line of defense in two. Heat followed immediately, adding to the already-thick air.

But the fighting did not stop. Our side stood strong, a wall against our attackers.

The hair on the back of my neck, though, rose.

I used my free hand to block an attack from my left side while I stood, waiting. Another vampyre sliced down my opponent for me while I turned my head toward the sky.

Wings.

Swooping straight down for us.

I had only seconds to brace myself before the sheer power of their violence rained upon us. I immediately got to work, aiming for the angels first.

They were hard to kill, I knew that more than anyone. While fae could be killed by any mortal wound, angels healed too quickly. They would need to be wounded fatally with no chance of healing themselves.

But that was easier said than done.

Too many of us were falling. Too many vampyres couldn't take on the force of the angels.

Hells.

For the first time since the fighting began, panic whispered into my senses, but I shook my head and kept fighting. I kept pushing forward, kept aiming for the powerful ones. A few of our attackers started to slip past our line of defense, but I couldn't turn back, couldn't retreat. We had to hold our line steady; it would be the only damn way to protect the kingdom.

It wasn't until I saw *him* that my sword stopped swinging, my muscles stopped fighting.

No, it wasn't possible. It wasn't—

"Hello, son." My father—my father who should have been dead—greeted me. Blood smeared on his face. He carried no sword. He didn't need to. When he took a step toward me, my knees shook. "Surprised to see me?"

CHAPTER 50
HUNTYR

The only sounds in the confines of the half-crumbling underground sanctuary were breathing and rapid heartbeats. Nobody spoke. Nobody dared.

But we all felt it—the rumbling under our feet, the promise of violence coming from above.

A loud boom rattled the stone walls. Rummy and I shared a glance but said nothing. She gripped her dagger with steady hands, as did I.

A few other warriors stood with us at the front of the chamber. We shouldn't have to use these swords, I reminded myself, but if we did?

Nobody was getting through to these innocents. *Nobody.*

My heart swelled as I looked at Rummy. She turned to reassure a female vampyre to her left. Hells, Rummy had not a single ounce of vampyre blood in her body. She was fully fae, fully supposed to stand against us, and these vampyres, according to everything we were raised to believe, should have been scrambling over each other to sink their fangs into her fae veins.

Yet there were no whispers of such atrocities in this sanctuary, only promises of teamwork. Of family. Of union.

We would kill any enemy for these strangers.

I squeezed my eyes shut as the ground shook again. Hundreds—if not thousands—had to be fighting out there to shake the damn ground. Not just with swords, either, but with magic.

I knew firsthand how powerful some angels could be, but these vampyres were skilled too. They didn't need magic to win a fight. The plan would work.

It had to work.

I didn't let my mind wander to Wolf. I couldn't. Even picturing him out there on the front lines would force me to run after him, to protect him. We were supposed to fight together, I knew that.

But I also knew these people needed me.

We were fighting together, just not in the same place.

"It'll be alright," Voiler said to my right. "This kingdom has something to fight for now, something stronger than the lust for power." Her voice was softer than a whisper, but the words rattled inside my skull.

"I hate not knowing what's going on out there," I replied.

She nodded and turned to face the thick, closed door. "Goddess help us," she whispered. "Destroy our enemies. Rebuild what is good." The small group huddled around us turned their attention to Voiler as she repeated, "Goddess help us. Destroy our enemies. Rebuild what is good."

A male warrior—no older than twelve—lifted his chin. "Goddess help us," he repeated with her. "Destroy our enemies. Rebuild what is good."

Goddess help us.

Goddess help us.

Goddess help us.

Chills erupted down my arms until I realized that I, too, repeated those words, recited that prayer as the rest of the bunker joined in.

The ground shook. The sound of screams in the distance infiltrated the bunker.

Still, we chanted.

The words grew as our spirits soared.

Destroy our enemies.

The sound of footsteps rattled the stone over our heads. They were here. This was happening.

I tightened my grip on my dagger.

Rebuild what is good.

When the first sound of fists echoed through that stone door, I turned to the young male warrior beside me. "Use this," I said, curling his fingers around his own dagger. If that door opens, you fight anyone who enters. Understand?"

He nodded.

Someone cried in the back. More footsteps. More shaking. More violence. It was only a matter of time now.

"This is your kingdom!" I yelled to the group of terrified faces. "They cannot take what is ours!"

Voiler's hands were already on that door. She didn't need to speak. We all thought the same thing.

We were waiting to be slaughtered if we stayed here. Our only option was to fight.

"Close this door the second we're out!" I yelled to the boy.

Voiler turned to the group of us in front—the group of us who had sworn to protect these innocents—and said, "Let's make those bastards pay."

Then she opened the door.

We rushed out as quickly as possible, eyes adjusting as we spotted the enemies surrounding us. They could not have what was ours. They could not slaughter these people, not again.

Never again.

I channeled my rage into my weapon, running and slicing and killing. I did not hesitate. Any enemy who charged us, who stood against us with harm in their eyes, would die.

Every last one of them.

Voiler and Rummy flanked me on either side. Rummy was a fast learner, slitting the throat of one fae before ducking under another, using her leverage from below to slice his gut.

She was a natural. A fighter. Just like the rest of us.

We pushed the enemies away from the door, away from our safe haven. They charged us from the forest and poured into the ruins of Scarlata in massive numbers.

But there was no fear in the air. Not from us, anyway. Only determination.

Only grit.

They could not have what was ours.

I wasn't sure how much time passed. Ten minutes? An hour? My limbs did not grow weary. My blade did not falter. Enemy after enemy, we persevered. Fae fell at our feet. Angels were cleaved under our blades.

For a moment, I looked to the kingdom around us, violence everywhere.

Still, my heart swelled with a dangerous amount of hope. I should have known it was too good. I should have known it was too easy.

Because when I felt Wolf's panic flood my bond with every ounce of his being, I stilled. That panic was a beacon, pulling me to him. I made sure Rummy and Voiler were both okay, both safe.

And I bolted as fast as possible toward the trees.

CHAPTER 51
WOLF

I had no words as I faced my father.

He was supposed to be fucking dead. We killed him. I watched that damn sword slice his body.

The violence continued to pour around me, but I saw only *him.*

"Stop this madness!" I yelled at him. "This is not the way to get what you want!"

My father barked in laughter with his head tossed back and his mouth open. When his eyes fell back to me, they held no love of a father. No light. No joy. Something empty and evil lingered there.

"It's a little late for alliances now, son. Wouldn't you agree?" He held his hands up toward me and released his power.

Never in my life had I felt the full force of my father's power. White light blinded my vision, eradicated all my senses, numbed my limbs. I didn't realize I fell to my knees until the light stopped.

The power of an archangel was not one that could be

373

easily categorized. It was not blood or natural magic. It had no boundaries.

I felt every bit of that truth as the pain rocked through my body. Gritting my teeth, I lifted my chin to face him. If he was going to kill me, he could damn well look at me while he did it.

"You cannot stop what is happening," he said, "though I must admire your determination. Look around you, son. You are missing one important piece in this big plan of yours."

"And what is that?" I didn't need to look around to see the slaughter, the corrupt angels under my father taking over with sheer force.

He stepped closer. "True power."

I fought the urge to flinch against his blood-stained hands. Not in fear, but because I knew this would be how I die.

This was it. I did not get another chance.

I wouldn't have another opportunity to fight.

For once, I let my guard down. I let that panic, that desperation, flood my body, and my power reacted stronger than I ever felt it.

My magic. My blood. My instinct.

Light erupted again, but it was not the flare of my father's magic that flashed before us.

It was mine.

My magic cracked the air and pierced the space around us. I felt the impact in my bones as it struck true, landing on my father in full force. I did not hold back as my magic poured out of me. I let him have it, let him feel what I was really capable of, what I had been capable of all this time.

I did not stop until something sharp pierced my side.

Lord stood a few feet away, still holding the handle of the blade launched deep in my gut.

Shit.

"Not so proud anymore, are you?" he seethed.

Lightning cracked again.

More fighters fell around us, more warriors down.

That was the first time I truly began to lose hope.

Live, Huntress, I thought. She was our last hope, our one reason to keep going. Without her, none of this mattered. Without her, we were nothing.

Live.

CHAPTER 52
HUNTYR

I ran as fast as my feet could carry me. My wings would expose too much of me to the violence that spilled on the edge of the kingdom.

My kingdom.

So one foot after the other, I ran closer and closer to him. I used my dagger to slice a few attackers as I passed, but I did not stop, did not waiver.

Wolf was in trouble, and I would stop at nothing to get to him.

My boots crushed stone and gravel before finding dirt and grass, pushing further and further to where I knew the battle started, out in the forest, on the front lines.

I felt our bond strengthening as I got closer, but I also felt it slipping. Weakening, but not from distance—from lack of *him*. He was fading.

He was hurt, and the thing that terrified me the most—he was afraid.

"Wolf!" I called out. "Where are you?"

Chaos ripped through the trees. Fire blazed in the distance. Bodies littered the ground.

Huntress.

It wasn't a word spoken aloud, but in my soul. In my bones. I stopped in my tracks and turned to the right.

Then I saw them.

Asmodeus—I looked twice to make sure it was really him—lay unmoving on the ground a few feet away, but that was the least of my worries.

Lord stood over Wolf, a sword piercing his torso.

Dread flooded my senses. "What did you do?" I breathed, rushing toward them. Wolf was still alive, still kneeling, but Lord did not release the weapon. He pushed it further into Wolf's body as he looked at me.

"I'm doing what I have to do to protect you," he spat.

I stopped for one beat, letting the truth of the situation fall around me. "You've taken *everything* from me!" I seethed. "I will not let you take this!"

Violence was not strong enough a word for what poured out of me then. Rage, betrayal, disbelief. Years and years of being hurt by him, all of it came to the surface as I charged, weapon raised.

I hesitated before, but now? After this?

Wolf fell forward, now struggling on his hands and knees as Lord stepped back.

I would kill him for this.

A warrior's cry escaped me as I pounced, aiming my blade directly at Lord's heart.

But he was no fool. He knew my fighting style better than anyone. He knew each move before I made it, each maneuver before I thought of it myself.

He blocked me with one hand, using the other to shove

me back. "You don't want to do this, Huntyr," he warned. "You don't want to fight me."

"Yes," I choked with emotion, "I do."

I tried again and again, very aware of the fact that Wolf was barely holding on a few feet away. I attacked over and over, but Lord continued to block me.

Think, Huntyr. What moves does he not know? What have you learned that Lord knows nothing about?

It had to be magic. That would be the only maneuver Lord wouldn't see coming.

He was an expert in combat, yes, but magic?

I did not need to bleed into the ground. I did not need to offer my own blood to the goddess to access my power.

It was mine. It had always been mine.

When the familiar rush of fire came from within me, I released it, aiming directly at Lord.

I did not falter as he screamed, did not falter as my entire life flashed before me; all those whippings, all that suffering, all that punishment. All he ever wanted for me was pain. I was a fool before, but I saw everything with clear eyes now.

My power pushed until it reached its limit. When I pulled back, I had no doubts that Lord was dead. His body—charred and unrecognizable—fell to the ground with a solid thud.

I didn't hesitate. My eyes landed on Wolf, and then I was moving, desperate to get to him.

"Wolf." I fell to his side. "Wolf, are you okay?"

He sat on his heels, gripping the dagger in his torso with both hands as he pulled, blood pouring through his fingers.

"Hells," I mumbled. "You're losing too much blood. You won't heal in time."

I surveyed the war around us. The fighting continued, but too much of it pushed into the kingdom, and Wolf knew it.

"You have to finish this," he mumbled. "It has to be you."

"Don't talk like that," I ordered. "I'm not doing anything without you. Can you stand?"

He nodded, only to grunt in pain when he tried to lift himself from his knees. My stomach sank. Not only was Wolf fading quickly, but Asmodeus started to move.

"It has to be you," he said again.

"What?" I looked at him frantically, searching for meaning behind his words. "What has to be me? I can't do this alone, Wolf!"

"You have to kill him. Kill him and stop this."

"We already tried to kill him." Screams rang out in the distance. Goddess help us, we were losing this damned war. "It didn't work."

"That's because it wasn't you. It has to be you, Huntress. You are the blood queen. You are the one with the magic that can end him."

"I'm not strong enough," I replied quickly. "My magic is no match for his, Wolf."

He swallowed, eyes nearly fluttering closed. "That's why you'll take all of mine too."

"No." I was shaking my head before he even finished the words. "No, I won't do that. You won't survive it."

"None of us will survive if he's still alive. This war will end in blood, Huntress. You still have a kingdom counting on you."

How the fuck did we get here again? How did we get to this point again, with Wolf sacrificing himself for me? I was sick of it, sick of having to choose, of having to do the right thing.

I didn't want to do the right thing if Wolf wasn't here. I didn't want the kingdom if he wasn't part of it.

Damn it all.

"I see that look in your eyes," he said, smiling softly.

"What look?"

"The look you make when you're about to do something incredibly stupid. But I won't let you do it, Huntyr. I won't let you try to save me."

He fell forward slightly and threw his arms around me. I was too distracted to notice the way his hand fumbled at my belt, pulling my bloodied dagger out of its sheath.

He was already bleeding, but he sliced his palm deeply before I could stop him, before I even realized what was happening.

"What are you—"

He gripped my arm and sliced my palm before placing our two hands together.

Asmodeus struggled to sit up a few feet away. He drew our attention with a grunt of pain, then anger.

"It's yours now," Wolf said. "It's all yours."

I tried to pull my hand away, but Wolf clasped on. I didn't feel his magic, didn't feel any part of him anymore. He was fading too fast, slipping out of my grasp, just a few seconds away from—

"You will never win!" Asmodeus shouted. I flinched, straightening as much as I could and trying my best to block Wolf from his father.

"You should have died a long time ago." I returned my gaze to Wolf, whose eyes fluttered closed as his body collapsed to the ground.

No, no, no.

"Don't be too upset," Asmodeus said. "You two will be together again soon."

I knew what was next. I knew what came after this.

Asmodeus would blast us both with his power before he blasted the entire damn kingdom, taking over the vampyres and using them as weapons in whatever plan for dominance he had.

He would never stop. These people would never know peace.

Wolf would never know peace.

Wolf pulled on our bond, and I focused on him enough to feel the love, the light, the hope that radiated from him. He was lying here, bleeding out and ready to die, while putting the fate of the world in my hands.

And his father was about to ruin everything.

So, I did the only thing I could think of, the only thing that would give me a chance to get us out of this mess.

I held my hand out to Asmodeus and met his flash of magic with a storm of my own.

Since Moira, I hardly learned the extent of my own power. I had no clue what turning into a vampyre had truly done to me, to my blood, to my magic. But light rippled against light as my magic battled his. It stopped his flash of light, freezing it in the air.

The power of an archangel.

He screamed out in frustration, but I didn't stop pouring everything I had at him.

It has to be you, Wolf said.

This madness, this absolute chaos Asmodeus brought into this world, it ended now. He deserved to pay for what he did. He deserved to pay for what he put us through, for what he put Wolf through.

I did not worry about how much power I was throwing out, did not worry for my own health, for the consequences of draining myself.

And when I felt as though I had nothing else to give, I felt the pull of the bond, the nudge of Wolf's magic ready to replace mine.

Ready to finish the damn job.

I let my free hand fall onto Wolf's body as I took a deep breath, mustering the strength to pull, dragging everything that remained through that dwindling thread of a bond.

A scream left my mouth as I was filled with the electrifying strength of Wolf's untapped magic. I knew he was strong—hells, he was half angel—but this was unlike anything I could have possibly prepared for. Wolf's magic ripped through me, taking hold of every muscle, every instinct. I could not have contained the flood even if I wanted to.

All that magic—that beautiful, painful elixir of pure violence—catapulted toward Asmodeus. The scream ripped through my throat, tore at my lungs, but I kept pushing. My hands burned with the new magic that fueled me, but I didn't stop.

Die.

Die.

Die.

Die for what you've done to us. Die for what you've taken from me. From him.

Pain ripped me apart, but I hardly noticed it. I poured everything I had, everything Wolf had, into Asmodeus.

Something snapped deep inside me, something that ceased my entire body, halted any magic.

I realized instantly what it was—what that void meant.

The bond. It broke.

That archangel-killing power. It was all mine now.

I stood up to make sure Asmodeus was truly dead, standing on wobbling knees and weak legs, but before I could take a step, someone entered from the right, sword raised.

I couldn't have moved to protect myself even if I wanted to.

But the attacker wasn't after me.

No, the attacker aimed directly for Asmodeus. What was left of him, anyway.

It was Luseyar, his white wings now coated in blood, a roar of fury on his lips as he brought the sword down on Asmodeus one final time.

We felt it ripple in the air, like the lifting of a weight that had been holding us down.

Asmodeus was dead.

Finally dead.

A stranger in my own body, I looked down at Wolf. I knew instantly that something was wrong.

I took too much; he gave me too damn much, but I didn't have a choice. I *had* to take it all to kill Asmodeus.

My breath grew shallow.

I fell to my knees, placing both hands on Wolf's chest, feeling for any sign of life.

Someone said my name behind me.

I searched and searched for a heartbeat, begging Wolf to open his eyes.

But Wolf was long gone.

CHAPTER 53
WOLF

Most people die only once. One final death to end it all.

I was not so lucky.

The first time I felt it was the night my father turned me into a vampyre. Vampyres were born creatures, not turned. To accomplish this, my father needed a sacrifice, one worthy of such a transformation.

My life.

It was a swift death. One of his men slipped the dagger into my heart as I lay on the stone table in his study.

I barely felt a pinch, the pain too insignificant to care all these years later.

The darkness that followed, that was what I remembered. I remembered the way I drowned in it, how I fought to climb back up to the surface, to breathe, but there was no air there. There were only more shadows, more black air and void existence, nothingness.

That's when she appeared, her face a beacon in the dark void of my death. She appeared to me first with bright eyes, her power cascading around me and pulling me from that endless pit.

Her eyes were sad.

"Your father has sacrificed you to me, child. He requests that I return you as a vampyre. Are you aware of this?"

Though I wasn't even sure she could see me, I nodded. "He's made his intentions clear to me, yes."

She eyed me carefully, as if deciding whether my life was even worth the trouble. "You'll be useful to me in the future, child. However lost you may seem, however twisted this may all get, I'll need you."

She touched the center of my heart. All the darkness around us spiraled after her finger and followed her touch into my flesh.

"You need me for what?"

The shadows poured into me in waves, though I still couldn't read her face. Her eyes hadn't changed, but the darkness pouring into me became painful. Violent.

"You cannot remain an angel and become a vampyre, child. You are somewhere in between, neither here nor there." More power flowed through my veins. "You will not understand this. You may not even remember it. But when the day comes, you will know."

I could barely speak over the pain that burned like a fire in my chest. "I'll know what? What are you talking about?"

And that was it. I woke up that day as a vampyre, desperate for the taste of blood and flanked by black wings that told everyone what happened.

This time, though, was much different.

There was no darkness swirling around me, no pain, no fear.

No confusion.

"Am I dead?" I gasped. "Is it real this time?"

Era's eyes were not sad as she stood before me, light radiating around her body. "Yes, Wolf. You are dead."

I did not feel afraid of what would happen next. Instead, a tidal wave of peace fell over me.

"You've done everything asked of you," she said, moving closer. "Because of you, because of the sacrifices you've made, there is a fighting chance of saving the ones you love."

"This was your plan all along, wasn't it?" It all came together in my mind. She was behind all of this, behind me becoming a vampyre, behind Huntyr surviving Moira.

"When your father first asked me to turn you, child, I was skeptical. I should have shut it all down before he grew too strong. My abilities in this realm only extend so far in the physical world, but the day I met you, I knew you would be of use to me."

I closed my eyes, reveling in the fact that it was all over. I was done fighting. "You did this? You ended it?"

"It took all your power to end him, yours and the girl's combined. I touched you with enough power that day so you would be able to kill him, but only when met with hers, and only when you were ready."

Fuck, that explained so much. My power had been slowly growing, even more so when I met Huntyr.

My eyes snapped open, my peace halting at the thought of her. "Huntyr—is she alive?"

Era smiled. The calmness within her pulsated toward me. "She is alive, yes."

I let out a long breath. Good. All of this was for her, so she could survive, so she could finally be free.

I would die any day to keep her safe, to let her taste freedom.

"You may feel at peace with your decision to sacrifice yourself, child, but your work is not done."

"What are you talking about?"

"I'm sending you back there. This was not a death of your doing, but one of mine, one I required of you for the bigger plan. I will give you the gift of one more life in this realm, Wolf, but there is something I need from you."

Though I could not feel my body, I lifted my chin. "You're sending me back there?"

She waved her hand and showed me a thousand moving pictures. Huntyr, Jessiah, and Rummy ran through the forest. Huntyr collapsed over my body, sobbing uncontrollably. *Fuck.* She was going to be *so pissed* that I'd gone and gotten myself killed.

Again.

But the next picture was the ruins of Scarlata, hundreds, if not thousands, of vampyre survivors tending to wounds, hugging each other, leaning on one another.

"They need you," she pushed, pictures vanishing. "She needs you. There was a time when all of Vaehatis lived in peace, Scarlata Empire too. There was a time when all my creatures existed together. I have seen your heart, boy, and I have seen hers. She may have a good heart now, but the light fades without you."

My throat tightened. "What are you saying?"

"I am sending you back to your wife, Wolf Jasper. Only this time, you will have everything he took from you."

"Everything he–"

"And once you're there, I need you to give the girl a message."

CHAPTER 54
HUNTYR

I became vaguely aware of Rummy yelling my name, then Jessiah.

I hadn't moved. I wasn't sure I would trust my body to hold me up if I did. Time disappeared entirely, and my vision tunneled around Wolf's unmoving body, around the blood that now poured from his wounds.

The cut on his hand wasn't healing.

Nothing was.

He gave me all his damn magic.

Tears streamed down my face, but all I could think of was the fact that I wanted to undo everything. Asmodeus. The magic. The bond.

Undo all of it and give Wolf back.

"Huntyr!" Rummy yelled. She gripped me by the shoulders and hauled me backward. Jessiah scooped me up from under my arms and forced me to my feet.

His mouth was moving, but I couldn't hear the words. It wasn't until Rummy stepped in front of me and started shaking me that I finally understood.

"They need you to fight!" Rummy yelled. "They won't stop until Scarlata has no survivors. Even with Asmodeus dead, they'll keep trying. You need to stop them. Go, Huntyr! Before everything is gone!"

Before everything is gone.

I knew, deep down, that killing Asmodeus wouldn't end this all. They all wanted power as badly as he did. These fighters lived under his rule for decades, all of them learning to chase the same thing.

Greed and hunger.

They *all* had to die.

For a split second, I debated giving up. Laying down. Taking a damn breath.

But Wolf's voice flashed through my mind. *It has to be you.*

If Wolf was really gone—which was not a fate I could even fathom—at least I could do this. At least I could finish what he started.

As if in response, his magic tickled my veins.

I wasn't sure if it was that last ounce of his magic or the anger that flared deep in my body at the sound of fighting still raging, but my eyes glazed over.

Jessiah crouched next to Wolf, putting pressure on his wound. It wouldn't work.

It was already too late.

Too late to save anything at all.

I couldn't fucking feel it. The bond, that small tickle in the center of my heart that reminded me I would never be alone again. It was gone.

I started walking at first—slow, torturous steps toward the war—but it quickly turned into a slow jog, then an all-out sprint.

Before I knew it, every bit of anger from everything I lost

fueled my body, and I was sprinting toward the fight, dagger in hand, power thrumming under my skin.

The sky cracked above as I screamed in anger, and magic poured from my body without any sign of stopping.

Fuck them. Fuck them all for taking everything from me. Fuck them for wanting this much power, for not being happy with what they'd already ruined.

They were greedy enough to want more. The Golden City wasn't enough.

They wanted to ruin everything.

I wasn't sure what magic was mine and what was Wolf's. All I knew was that I didn't want it anymore. I didn't want any of it.

So, I let it go.

I let my magic kill every single one of our enemies. Angel, fae, vampyre—it didn't matter. Tears and snot and blood smeared across my skin, and I wiped my eyes with the back of my sleeve so I could see who else lived, who else raised a sword against my people.

For Wolf. I would do it all for Wolf.

I killed every single one of them before I finally slowed. I spun in place, making sure the fighting was over.

People screamed and cried, but I became more aware of the sound of my own breathing. It pissed me the fuck off, because I shouldn't be the one still standing.

I didn't want any of this.

It should be him.

I was seconds away from erupting in another burst of magic and anger when the boy from earlier stepped into view. His lips were moving, and I took a deep breath to quiet the blood in my ears before looking him in the eye. "What?" I asked.

"It's over," he said, voice high with hope. "It's over, Huntyr. You did it."

I looked around one more time. The words were too good to be true, too sweet. I didn't want sweet.

I wanted more violence. More fighting. More destruction. It's what they deserved.

But the boy was right. There were no more attacks plaguing the kingdom, no more enemies crawling through the streets.

Just bodies, lying in the streets, dead.

It was over.

It was over.

It was fucking *over*.

My legs gave out before me. A whimper escaped me as I crashed to the ground and ripped open the skin on my knees.

Hands fell to my shoulders, lifted me up. I became a ghost in my own body, barely there.

"Don't you dare lose it now," Voiler's voice cut through my trance. "Hold it together, Huntyr." She knelt in front of me, pulling my face into her hands, forcing me to look at her while she surveyed my injuries.

"He's dead." The words felt foreign. Empty. True. Fuck, every ounce of my soul knew it was true. The bond was gone, broken entirely. Not a single part of Wolf remained.

She stilled, eyes meeting mine. "I know."

"I can't do this without him."

I felt Jessiah's presence behind me. I couldn't look at him. I couldn't look at any of them.

It was all my fault. He was the one who saved them all. He was the one who sacrificed himself, who saved me time and time again. Why the fuck did he have to save me? There wasn't a single piece of me worth saving, not without him.

Why didn't he see that?

Grief didn't come like I expected it to.

"Wolf is dead." Jessiah's words cascaded over the gathering group of survivors.

A few gasps rang through the air, a few screams, cries.

Not from me, though. I was too empty, too hollow to feel a single damn thing.

The sun wasn't far from breaching the horizon. I sat on the blood-soaked ground of Scarlata, surrounded by furious males, wounded females, and crying children.

"You should see the healers," Voiler said, forcing my eyes into focus.

Jessiah's footsteps approached behind me, and Voiler looked up at him with a warning glare, but her features immediately softened.

She moved aside, making room for Jessiah to kneel in front of me. His sunken, tired eyes were rimmed with tears. A deep gash sliced his face, nearly missing his eye. He reached out and grabbed both of my hands. "We're going to get through this, Huntyr."

His voice sounded like he actually believed that, and that was fucking heartbreaking.

"I can't do this without him," I repeated. "He was the one who was supposed to survive this."

Jessiah's jaw tightened, and he took a long breath while his eyes fluttered closed. When he looked at me again, something like determination lingered in his features. "He wanted you to end this fight, and you did. He wanted you to become the blood queen, and you did. Now, he wants you to step up and raise Scarlata Empire from the ashes. You need to do this for him, Huntyr. You have to finish what he started."

No, no, no. This all felt too wrong. This was a nightmare, and I was going to wake up any fucking minute now.

"I have to go see him." I used Jessiah's body as a brace to keep me standing. He stood with me, holding his hands out like I was going to crumble at any second.

Wolf was my everything, but he was Jessiah's brother. I couldn't even look at him, knowing *I* was the reason his brother was dead.

I set my sights on the woods. I needed to see him one more time, needed to touch his lifeless body and confirm in the pits of my soul that he was never coming back.

My feet moved beneath me, though I wasn't sure how. Jessiah flanked my left, and Rummy quickly stepped to my right, tucking her arm around mine in solidarity.

She said nothing. She didn't need to.

We walked through the forest. The others cleared our path like I was going to erupt in flames any second.

Maybe I was.

We walked and walked and walked. I knew exactly where we were headed.

Which was why, when we arrived at the spot where Wolf died, when we arrived at that clearing in the forest surrounded by bodies and blood, we all stopped.

"He was right here," Jessiah said.

Then, the scariest fucking thing of all happened. I felt *hope.*

"Wolf!" Rummy let go of me and spun around.

The numbness faded as hope took over like an infectious disease.

Wolf. Wolf. Wolf.

I turned to Jessiah, eyes wide. Rummy called after Wolf in

the distance, running around like he could have crawled somewhere.

I didn't dare say the words, and neither did Jessiah. We stood there, staring at each other, hearts fucking pounding so hard, I could literally hear his beating with mine.

And then we heard shouts.

Not shouts of fear or of terror. Not cries of pain or grief.

They were shrieks of excitement. Laughter.

Rummy started running first, yelling "Wolf!" over and over again as I sprinted after her.

Jessiah followed directly on my heels as we made our way back to the kingdom.

Everyone gathered on the other side of those crumbling walls, looking up to the sky, watching something, *pointing* at something.

Rummy gasped, and I gripped her arm so hard, I probably drew blood.

It was Wolf. I recognized him immediately, my body flooding with relief the second I laid eyes on his form. I would have recognized those sculpted shoulders and broad chest anywhere, even when he was flying through the sky with massive, glowing, *golden* angel wings.

I nearly dropped to my knees at the sight. Truly golden, they were nothing like his black wings, though those were damn impressive. These were nothing like the white ones the others wore either. No, these were something special, a gift from the goddess to remind everyone what he went through, what he did for us. They were still black at the base, but the fiery tones of the feathers reflected the sun that still crept over the horizon. It looked as if each black, silky feather was plucked by the goddess herself, dipped in a sea of golden magic and molded to Wolf's body with divine precision.

Black—because Wolf would never go back to the innocent angel he once was.

And gold—because he was our savior, the one who sacrificed *everything*.

Wolf used to hate his black wings; they were a reminder of everything he wasn't. But these? These were *everything*. His face beamed as he scanned the crowd, searching for me. Wolf would *never* feel unworthy with wings like these.

I couldn't imagine anything more *perfect*.

CHAPTER 55
WOLF

The second I saw Huntyr in the crowd below, I dove for the ground. *She's alive. Fuck, she's alive.*

Nothing stopped me from catapulting down to Earth, covered in blood, landing on both feet directly in front of her.

She stood with Rummy and Jessiah, the three of them staring at me with open mouths and wide eyes.

I didn't blame them. I had golden fucking wings.

"You're alive," Jessiah stated.

I didn't take my eyes off Huntyr as I answered, "That I am, brother."

"You were dead," Huntyr said. "You were dead. I drained you. I felt your body."

She stiffened as if she couldn't believe it was really me.

"I did die," I explained. "I was dead. It had to be done, Huntyr. I needed to die in order for you to take my magic to kill Asmodeus. It *had* to be you. Our powers combined at their full strength was the only thing that was going to save us all."

"How are you here?" Jessiah asked, taking half a step forward. "How are you alive right now?"

I glanced at him for only a second before returning my eyes to Huntyr. I couldn't look away from her for more than that. "Era brought me back. It was all part of the plan; it was all supposed to happen this way."

The three of them stood motionless, taking in my words.

"Era the goddess?" Rummy asked, finally closing her gaping mouth. "Era brought you back and gave you golden wings?"

"Why?" Jessiah added.

I was still staring at her, still trying to decipher all the emotions running across her face. Without our bond, I couldn't feel it. I had no fucking clue what she was thinking right now, what was going on inside that head.

"The magic I possessed—it was a gift from her the night Asmodeus sacrificed me. She never wanted The Golden City to turn into this. She never anticipated my father's thirst for so much power. I knew she had a plan for me, but she liked to keep me in the dark. Apparently, all of it was for this, so we would get to this moment right here."

Nobody moved. Nobody spoke. The weight of my words fell on everyone, lacing the air with a thick tension. This was all Era's plan. All the pain, all the betrayal, all the suffering— it was all so we could end the corruption and evil that flourished here, so we could become who we were truly meant to be.

I was confused before, but not now. I saw it all so fucking clearly now.

"Huntress. Say something. Please."

Her breath hitched as I reached out and brushed her arm.

397

She looked to where our skin touched then back to my eyes with brows drawn.

"Fuck you," she mumbled under her breath.

"Wha—"

"Fuck you!" She stepped forward and slapped me in the chest, *hard*. When she reeled back to do it again, I caught her wrist and yanked her into me, wrapping my arms around her. Fuck, she looked so tired, covered in blood and sweat and tears.

"Fuck you," she said again, but she relaxed into my body. Her voice broke, tears finally flowing freely down her face to dampen my neck. "Fuck you, Wolf."

"Careful, Huntress," I whispered into her hair while I inhaled the blood and sweat mixed with the perfect scent of cherries. "You're being rude again."

She pulled back enough to look into my face. "Don't you *ever* do that again. Ever. Do you understand me, Wolf? You are never allowed to die again! You are never allowed to scare me like that again!"

I gripped her face with both hands, swiping my thumbs across her wet face. "Yes, my love. I understand."

Her hands fell onto my shoulders. She patted me gently before gripping my shirt in both hands like she never fucking wanted to let go.

And then she laughed.

It was broken at first. Weak. But it was a laugh, filled with fear and exhaustion and relief. Then, the few giggles turned into a complete outburst, and before I knew it, I was laughing too. And Jessiah. And Rummy. All of us stood there amidst bodies and ruins, my golden wings spanned out against a backdrop of the rising sun, laughing.

It took hours to gather the bodies of the fallen, and even longer to dig their graves, to pay respect to their losses, every last one of them.

We worked until every single fighter was buried properly in the forest around us.

Something lingered in the air, something foreign and still.

Huntyr didn't leave my side the entire day. She refused to see a healer, but I was able to heal her with barely even touching her. My magic felt different now, ever since I woke up with those damn golden wings.

It wasn't until the sun set and the survivors gathered around a massive fire in the center of the kingdom that Huntyr and I could finally talk alone.

She sat on a fallen log beside me, face glowing in the flames. I draped an arm around her shoulder and pulled her close.

"Tell me what you're thinking," I whispered against her messy curls.

She relaxed against me, resting her head on my chest. "You're the one who died and broke our bond. You don't get to know what I'm thinking at all times anymore."

I let out a low warning growl I knew she could feel. "Where's the fun in that?"

"It's more fun this way," she teased. "It means you have to guess."

"Fine." I let a finger trail down her back. "You're thinking about how relieved you are that you're free now. You're feeling overwhelmed. You have no idea what to do next. You're exhausted."

She lifted her face to mine and replied, "Damn, you're good. Maybe the bond is still intact after all."

I sighed. "I wish that was true. I miss feeling you all the time. It became second nature."

"Yeah, now you won't know when I'm pissed off at you."

I smiled, gaze flickering to her perfect lips. "I have a feeling you'll let me know."

She giggled, and fuck, I didn't realize how much I'd missed the sound of that. She nuzzled back into me, wrapping her arms around my waist as silence fell over us, the crackling of the fire taking over.

After a few minutes, I said, "He's really gone this time."

Her hand fell onto my thigh and squeezed. "I know."

Another beat passed.

"It's really all over."

"No." She pushed herself up and looked at me again. "The shit is over. The violence is over. The war is over. But the rest? The rest of it is just beginning."

Tears welled in her eyes. I leaned down and gave her a firm kiss, reveling in the feeling of her. We were both alive, both still here, still breathing.

But Huntyr was right. This was just the beginning.

We were interrupted as Jessiah and Rummy joined us on the next log. They handed us both a piece of cooked meat from the fire, and my stomach grumbled from the sight of it. Hells, we really were exhausted.

"Those wings are really something," Jessiah said. "I suppose you'll have a hard time blending in around here."

"What, these old things?" I flexed my wings on either side of me. They were much, much larger than my original wings, but somehow, they were light, weightless. The gold feathers had a silky finish to them, and I let my right wing flutter across Huntyr's shoulder until she shivered. "I think I could get used to them."

"I'm glad you got your wings back." Jessiah's tone turned serious. "If anyone deserves them, it's you. Our father had no right to take them in the first place."

We all focused on our meat, and I swallowed before replying, "Thank you, brother. For everything."

He shook his head. "No thanks required. I would do it all again tomorrow if I had to."

"Still. You didn't ask to be dragged into this mess. You didn't ask to be thrown into a kingdom with vampyres."

He shrugged, taking a bite. "I guess vampyres aren't so bad. Just don't go drinking my blood when you get hungry, okay? Or Rummy's. I have to keep my eye on her now."

Rummy blushed but shared a knowing look with Huntyr.

"I think we'll all be much, much safer here than we ever were in Midgrave," Huntyr said. "This is our home now."

"And you are the blood queen," Rummy said, simmering with pride. "The way they look at you, it's incredible. It's like they know you're going to change the world."

Huntyr shrugged. "I did what any of them would do. I'm sick of powerful people taking advantage of everyone else. I spent my entire life without control, and that changes now. It changes for all of us."

Her words lingered in the air.

"What happens when the others hear about this? What happens when the other fae and angels realize we've killed Asmodeus?" Jessiah asked.

"We'll tell them the truth, and we'll offer refuge to all vampyres who have been living in hiding, afraid to show themselves. We'll meet with the fae and the angels to show them that what they've been taught is a lie. Vampyres are not blood-hungry monsters with no control. We're just like them. We deserve a home. We deserve peace, just like they do."

I placed a kiss on her temple, not giving a fuck that Jessiah and Rummy were here. "I'm so fucking proud of you, Huntress. You have no idea."

She twisted and looked up at me. "Proud of *me*? Hells, look at you, Wolf! You sacrificed yourself to save us all. We wouldn't be here if it wasn't for you. Whatever Era planned, she chose you for a reason."

The memory of Era's voice flooded my memory again. "Ah, that reminds me. She has a message for you."

Huntyr straightened beside me, the others snapping their attention in my direction. "Era has a message for me?"

I nodded. "She wants peace. That's all she has wanted since my father took peace away from these lands. To *expedite* the process, if you will, she's told me how to stop the curse of the hungry ones."

They all stared at me, waiting, but I kept my eyes glued on Huntyr.

"It's me, isn't it?" she breathed. "I'm the one who can cure them?"

My smile could not be contained. "Your blood continues to be the one thing that will deliver peace to these lands. Bleed and live, Huntress. Bleed and *live*."

CHAPTER 56
HUNTYR
FOUR MONTHS LATER

Wolf soared passed me in the air. His golden wings nearly blinded me as he narrowly avoided my face. "You'll have to be faster than that, Huntress!"

This smug bastard. Some things really never changed. I pumped my wings harder, faster, soaring through the air beside him and twisting my body around so we faced each other. "You may have more practice with this," I started, "but those glorious wings of yours do have one major flaw."

He flew closer to me, our wings nearly touching. "Oh yeah? Do tell, my queen."

Hells, I was never going to grow tired of looking at him like this. He beamed with happiness as we hovered in the air above our kingdom. His new wings quickly became a talking point, not just in Scarlata, but in the rest of Vaehatis too.

Wolf was the magnificent, powerful male who saved us all.

Before, he hated attention. He was used to walking

403

around The Golden City with his head down, lingering in his father's shadow.

But not here. Here, children screamed with excitement and ran to him when he walked into a room. Here, his golden wings were a sign of safety, of protection from the goddess herself.

Brought back from death and touched by gold.

"They're too damn big for your own good. Good luck keeping up with those!" I zipped past him, soaring even higher before funneling myself toward the ground and diving —fast.

Wolf's wicked laughter rang out around me as he caught up effortlessly. We both knew the size of his wings was nothing short of perfect. They were the biggest wings anyone had ever seen, and he maneuvered them like he had worn them his entire life.

I stopped myself in the air a few feet over the roof of our building. Rummy stood there waiting, waving her hand in the air to get my attention. Wolf was right behind me. We lowered ourselves to the roof with ease—something I had to practice a few times before I got the hang of.

"Look at you two," she said. "If I didn't know you two were the damn saviors of this place, I would be scared shitless."

Wolf sauntered forward, his wing brushing over mine and sending a chill down my spine. "Maybe we *want* to scare them all shitless," he joked. "It'll keep them all far, far away from here."

"Ignore him." I pushed his shoulder. "You're back early. I wasn't expecting you until tomorrow."

The smile grew on her face with every passing second.

"What?" I asked. "What is it?"

"It worked," was all she said.

"It—" My heart stopped. "It worked? You're sure?"

She could hardly contain her excitement, bouncing up and down like she used to do when we were young. "It worked, Hunt! We traveled miles from this place, and we didn't see a single hungry one. It's been months since the last one was spotted. I know you've been waiting on some big sign or announcement, but this?" She waved her hands to the side of her, motioning to our kingdom. "This place is safer than it ever could have been, all because of you."

Wolf cleared his throat beside me.

"Oh, shove it," she sneered. "Your head isn't big enough with those wings yet?"

Hells, I loved her. Wolf pretended to look shocked, but I was too focused on the words that came out of her mouth.

When Wolf told me my blood was the cure to the hungry ones, I was skeptical. It all seemed too easy after how difficult the rest of our lives were.

But a few drops of my blood spilled into the lands of Scarlata, followed by Wolf chanting in an odd language I was certain only Era spoke, and it was done.

The hungry ones were actually *cured*.

It was a massive relief that our own people wouldn't have to fear the sickness, but it also sent a wave of ease through me at the thought of everyone else changing the way they viewed us. Vampyres weren't blood-hungry, depraved animals who couldn't control their cravings.

We were just like fae, just like angels, only way cooler and with some odd dietary restrictions.

"Come on," Rummy pushed. "They're waiting for you both down there."

"They're—" I glanced at Wolf, who appeared equally as

clueless. "Who's waiting? Rummy!" But she was already leaving, already running down the steps of the tower.

I took a long breath, retracting my wings with my magic. Luckily for me, I could still contract them at will. Wolf, however, had to bend and maneuver his body—permanent wings included—through the window of the roof to get into the stairwell. Still, I knew he wouldn't want it any other way.

I didn't even try to hold my laughter back as I watched him.

"Careful, Huntress," he sneered. "You're being rude."

We descended the stairs together, the anticipation in the air growing heavier and heavier as we approached the bottom. The last four months were a whirlwind. Scarlata was literally being rebuilt from the ashes. It helped that there were so many vampyres willing to assist us, but the memory of what happened that day lived in everyone's minds.

We could live in peace now because of the sacrifices of so many, and nobody wanted to see violence like that ever again.

I made it to the bottom step and paused, waiting for Wolf. His hand slipped into mine, something I grew very accustomed to when it came to facing our kingdom.

And when Wolf pushed open the door, I nearly dropped to my knees.

"Headmistress Katherine," I breathed, taking in her tall figure. "Commander Macanthos." He stood tall, looking much happier than he ever looked back in Moira. "What are you doing here?"

In fact, they *both* smiled, which was already freaky enough.

"Your friends here paid us a visit and explained everything." Commander Macanthos stepped up, pulling my free hand into his as he added, "I knew things weren't right. I should have spoken up sooner. For years, something deep in my gut told me not to send anyone else to that damn city."

So much emotion coming from him. I was used to him being the hard-ass, the strong rock who didn't put up with bullshit. "It's really okay," I replied. "All of this was part of Era's plan. Nobody knew what was really happening beyond those walls—nobody *could* have known."

"Still," Headmistress Katherine added. "We came here to say we are proud of you, Huntyr. You have exceeded all expectations, and you've saved the lives of those not even born yet. You've changed the fate of this entire kingdom."

Don't fucking cry, Huntyr. Not in front of Headmistress and Commander.

"It means a lot that you came here," I replied. "I wish I could have saved more."

Headmistress Katherine bowed her head. "That burden is not only yours."

These two were sending people to their deaths for decades now, not truly knowing anything about The Golden City or what was happening within it. Asmodeus did a very good job at letting the outsiders believe what he wanted them to believe. He did a very good job at controlling people with fear and magic.

Not anymore.

"Are you staying?" Wolf asked from behind. "We have plenty of space. You're more than welcome to—"

"We only came by in passing," Commander Macanthos interrupted. "We're actually headed to The Golden City."

I paused, dumbfounded. "The Golden City?"

Voiler then stepped into view, along with a few others. "It's time we turn that city into a place that actually helps others. We were thinking of transforming it into a sanctuary for anyone who needs a place to stay, for anyone who'd like to come learn magic."

Yeah, I was definitely going to start crying.

Wolf's hand moved to my shoulder and stayed there. "You're all going?" There was a small group of them, maybe eight, but we grew close to everyone here over the last few months.

"If it's alright with you two, of course," Voiler pushed. "It was Headmistress Katherine's idea to teach magic to the others, and with the wall broken and all, I figured that might not be a bad place for it."

I couldn't even speak. These people—my friends—were going to build a haven for those who wanted to learn. Not just for the elites, either, but anyone. Children. Wanderers. Families. Anyone could go and learn the extent of their abilities.

There were no more limits, no more walls keeping us contained.

"That is okay with you, right?" Voiler's eyes widened with panic.

"Yes! Hells, yes." I pushed the others aside to get to her, pulling her into my arms and holding tight. "I'm so damn proud of you, Voiler. You saved my life. I'll never forget that."

Her eyes were glossy when she pulled away. "It was my honor. I would die for the blood queen, even if I don't have a drop of vampyre blood in my body."

I laughed, though it sounded more like an uncontrollable squeak. "Come back soon, okay? I'll miss you too much while you're busy sharing your wisdom with everyone."

"I will," she replied. "I promise."

"Take care of them," I said to Headmistress and Commander. "And try to be a touch nicer to the students. I don't know if either of you are aware, but you come across a bit intimidating."

Neither of them laughed, but Headmistress cracked the faintest bit of a smile. "Will do, Huntyr. You take care of yourself."

The group of them turned, heading down the cobblestone street that led to the forest. We managed to pave a small path, enough to make traveling through the kingdoms much easier.

Which was why now was the perfect time for them to go.

Even if it sucked to watch them leave.

"Hells, if I knew you were this much of a crybaby, I would've told them to leave without saying goodbye." Rummy sauntered back into view. She was wearing a jacket she hadn't been wearing earlier, and my stomach dropped at the sight of it.

"You're not leaving too, are you?"

"No! Hells no, relax!"

I took a long, shaking breath. "Good, because I don't think I could let you go. You're stuck with me forever."

"You know, I quite like being one of the only fae living among vampyres. It makes life exciting."

"Right," Wolf added from behind me. "Because life wasn't exciting at *all* before."

CHAPTER 57
WOLF

I knew the hungry ones were cured long before Rummy said the words to Huntyr. She knew too, deep down. I saw it in the way she slept better at night, in the way she actually grew excited when others finally got their first vampyre cravings. The fear of the curse slowly dissipated, but when Rummy said those words today and Huntyr actually felt it...

I would have gone through the entire damn war again if it meant giving her relief like that.

Huntyr ran off with Rummy, likely to drink cheap liquor off one of the old roofs again. I didn't question their late-night hang sessions, but at least Huntyr had wings to catch herself if she ever fell off one of those damn roofs.

Rummy was just crazy.

I think that's why Jessiah liked her so much.

The sun already set, but I made my way to the large fire that lit up the center of Scarlata. These nightly fires were something that started before the war, but they never really ended. There was something comforting about these people having a home to crawl back to at night, a home of people who cared about them, who had their backs.

Getting together like this was a nice reminder that we weren't alone anymore. *They* weren't alone anymore.

Some of the vampyres were survivors of the original war. They were the ones who spoke the most on nights like this, when the moon was high in the sky and young ears were eager for more.

But those vampyres did not speak of violence, nor did they speak of hate for what the fae and angels did to them all those years ago.

They only spoke of love. Of forgiveness. Of living with your heart and spreading joy across all the kingdoms.

These were survivors of much, much worse than anything we endured, yet they did not hold grudges. They had no desire to seek revenge for what was taken from them.

"You weren't angry at the fae for attacking you?" one of the younger vampyres asked.

The older male held his finger up, quieting the small crowd around him. "At first, yes, I was very angry. But listen to me when I say this, child: the fae did not attack us because they were evil beings. They did not slaughter this place because they held hate in their hearts." I stepped closer to the fire, careful not to make any noise as he continued. "They attacked us because they were afraid. They did what they did because they too had families to protect. If we believed they were evil, if we retaliated and did the same to them, would that make us any better?"

The children were silent.

"Would it?"

"No," the children answered in unison.

"That's right. You love them—not because they deserve it,

but because they're just like us, just trying their best to survive in this world. And we all know how hard that can be sometimes."

Chills erupted down my arms. Damn, I really needed to listen to this man more often.

Something tugged on the arm of my shirt, and I turned to find a small girl standing beside me, gawking up at my wings.

It was Abigail, the young girl we saved from the forest.

"Here," she said, handing me a plate of food. "This is for you."

I knelt and took the food from her. "For me?" I asked. "That is very kind of you, Abigail. Did you get your own dinner already?"

She nodded, her teeth shining behind her big smile. "I did. Two plates, actually."

"Two?" I gasped dramatically. "Don't worry. I won't tell if you won't."

She turned to run away, but I stopped her. "Hey! Where do you think you're going?"

"Bedtime," she answered. "Miss Peggy says if I get plenty of sleep every night, I could have my own vampyre wings when I'm your age!"

"She did? Well, you better listen to Miss Peggy, then. Go on." I watched her run down the street, looking away only when she made it inside Peggy's building. She became one of the caretakers around here. We all worked together, everyone doing their part to rebuild this place.

I glanced around the fire, taking in the smiling faces, and actually let myself relax.

"It's crazy, isn't it?" Jessiah said from behind me, clapping me on the shoulder as he approached.

"What is?"

"The fact that we spent our entire lives in that damn castle and nothing has ever felt more like home than this."

He was right about that. I was always on edge with Asmodeus. I was always being watched, being used, manipulated.

But not here.

"It is nice. Strange, but nice."

Silence fell over us, but it was a peaceful silence. Jessiah and I were closer than ever now. He was my right-hand man, the one I turned to for everything. And the fact that he, too, thought this place felt like home made my chest tighten with happiness.

"You better get home," he said after a while. "I saw Rummy and Huntyr stumbling through the streets about ten minutes ago. Any more late rooftop nights, and I might have to teach Rummy how to summon her own wings."

My heart ticked at the sound of Huntyr's name.

"Yeah," I said, turning toward the tower. "Good luck with that, brother."

I left the fire, left the others to enjoy their dinner and company. *I had a wife to get home to.*

I took my time climbing those stairs to the top of the tower. We rebuilt much of these fallen lands, but Huntyr still insisted that this is where she wanted us to stay. This was home to us, atop this same building that overlooked all of Scarlata.

Though there were much nicer buildings to live in, this place was ours.

Our bond technically broke when I died, when Era brought me back and gave me these wings. It was different from the first time, when both of us died during the Transcendent and the bond stayed untouched. We still needed it back then. Era still needed it.

There was no longer a need for us to connect our magic.

But even so, I could feel Huntyr in the bedroom, our connection growing stronger as I reached the last step and pushed the door open.

It could have been because we shared blood so frequently now. Hells, it could have been pure delusion, but we didn't need a magic bond to bind us anymore. We were fully connected, her soul completely intertwined with mine in a way I never wanted to undo.

She was mine, just as I was hers. Nothing was going to change that.

"I thought you were never coming home," she drawled from the bedroom at the back of our unit.

The room was dark, but the moonlight filtering in from the large glass window across the back of the bedroom lit up the delicate curve of her body wrapped in the sheets.

Her naked body, I might add.

I didn't realize a growl rumbled through my chest until Huntyr sat up, eyes wide. Her wings were gone now, giving me a full view of my wife in the moonlight. I prowled closer, taking my time as I inhaled the sweet, alluring scent of her.

Those damn *cherries*.

"I'll always come home to you," I replied. "If I knew *this* was going to be in my bed waiting for me, I would never fucking leave."

I was only half joking.

She smiled and shifted in the bed as I stepped closer, unbuckling my belt and tossing it to the side. I pulled my shirt over my head next and watched Huntyr's eyes trail down my torso.

"Careful," I purred. "You're staring, Huntress."

She rolled her eyes, but instantly arched toward me as I wrapped an arm around her waist and pulled her closer. "Have I told you that you can be arrogant and annoying?"

"Mhmm," I kissed her neck slowly. "Many, many times. But tell me again, please." I moved my lips against her delicate skin until she gasped. "I love it when you talk dirty to me."

"You are arrogant," she said, breath hitching. "And stubborn." I kissed her harder. "And incredibly annoying."

Goddess above, her body was made for me.

I paused before my kisses reached her lips. "And?"

She sighed, but pressed her bare chest further into mine, reaching for my kiss. "And you are *mine*."

Acknowledgments

Firstly, thank you to all the readers who made it this far in the book! So many of you have been with me from the very beginning, and I continue to be overwhelmed with love and support from you! These books truly wouldn't exist without the readers who read them and encourage me to keep writing, so thank you.

Writing a new book always seems impossible. There are so many things that go into planning, marketing, and plotting a new story. And then there's the actual writing! It's like climbing a mountain you can't see the top of.

This book came very, very close to beating me. I wrote. I re-wrote. I edited. I re-edited. To Lauren, my superhuman PA, just know that this book wouldn't exist without you. I would be curled into a ball somewhere drinking a margarita and forgetting all my responsibilities. I appreciate you caring about these book babies just as much as I do, and for taking the time to talk me off the ledge when I'm nearing a mental breakdown.

Thank you to Jack, who reminded me over and over again that I always hate the book right before it publishes, and that it's not in fact terrible.

Thank you to Hailey and Clarissa for beta reading this story and reminding me that it's actually exciting!

And thank you again for every single one of my readers

who took a chance on Wolf and Huntyr, and who cared enough to keep reading until the end.

I love you so, so much.

You can follow me on Instagram and Tiktok
@authoremilyblackwood

You can also look for signed copies and special editions on my
website, www.authoremilyblackwood.com

And join my reader group to hear about all romantasy
updates!
Join Blackwood Faeries